T0381078

The

Order

The Tale Of The Sabor Guardians

Written and Illustrated By

Casey Parker

Order this book online at www.trafford.com
or email orders@trafford.com

Most Trafford titles are also available at major online book retailers.

Print information available on the last page.

ISBN: 978-1-4120-1336-9 (sc)

Trafford rev. 05/14/2015

 www.trafford.com

North America & international
toll-free: 1 888 232 4444 (USA & Canada)
fax: 812 355 4082

Dedicated to the Loving
memory

Of

My Beautiful, Smart, Funny,
Talented, Loving, Happy
and most of all
MISSED

MOMMA

R amona Jean
P ar k er

I love you mom, and I finally
did it, I made it
I miss you and I always will

Your extended family
Michelle, Peyton and
Caden Parker
Love you too
they wish they had gotten
to know you

Love always
Your son
Casey

Thank You

First and foremost, I would like to thank my Lord and Savior Jesus Christ, for giving me the talents and countless blessings without which I could not have written this book. Then, I would like to thank Michelle Parker, Peyton Parker and Caden Parker: My beautiful Wife, Daughter and Son, for putting up with me for the year and one half it took to write this novel. Next, Phillip Ellett I: Thanks buddy, for all of your hard work editing and bouncing ideas with me. Good luck in Cali, any Hollywood hotshots reading this, look out for Phillip Ellett! Brad Cowell: The same thanks for not strangling me when I would ramble on endlessly about the story, thanks. Long live DOC!! Lance and Jen Shipley: What else can I say, without you guys this wouldn't have gotten done when it did, thanks for the blind faith in my vision. Jason Brooks: For the conceptual art man, thanks a bunch. Jacob Thompson: Thanks for daydreaming with me and keeping me focused. To my family: who has never given up on me, no matter how much my artistic side caused me to flake out, Ha THANKS. Clint Minge: Thanks for the one liner, damn I'm glad you're a redneck. All of the employees at Marathon thanks for letting me share my world with you for awhile. Last, but certainly not Least, My Dad, who has always been there for me, unconditional love rocks, thanks Pop! Kathy Parker, thank you for being the wonderful lady you didn't have to be, I love ya!

!THANKS!

CHAPTERS

Introduction
of
The Order

Before you read the tale that is wrapped in these sheets of lifeless paper, I would ask only one thing of you. Please unlearn all of your facts, the absolutes you have been force fed and accepted, throughout your lifetime. Unlearn your certainties, for they are all but half-truths, partial and inaccurate at best. They have been written by men ignorant to the actuality and certainties of true life.

The yarn living within these sheets, is an absolute. "An absolute what?" You ask. I answer with this; it is an absolute truth. As you take in the meandering rants of an old warrior Gargoyle, know the sacrifices recanted here, are given you, so that you will never know the brutality that is the actuality of life. Living your daily existence's blissfully ignorant to the true horror festering just below the surface of your <u>FACT</u>.

A slight delve into the history, is a necessity now. Life, more importantly your life. Has been guarded selflessly for centuries by a silent force known as The Order of the Sabor Guardians. The Order is composed of a quintet of families chosen by God and evolution to protect the frail balance of black and white on earth, as well as the frailties of the human race, from their own extinction. This extermination will be brought on by the anomaly born of the malice of brothers, fed by the fear and loathing of man, known as Dvanken.

The Order has stood for eons, the sole defense of the peaceful beings of earth, against annihilation. In one form or another, a variation of The Order has stood against the negative as a balance to the overwhelming power and abundance of evil.

The children of the human leg of The Order, known as the Sabor Guardians, are all male and all born in mass births, known as *Replina* in formal conversation. The heirs of The Order go through an amazing metamorphosis, climaxing on their twenty-second birthday. To clarify a bit, the *Replina*, or mass birth, is what we of The Order call the strange occurrence when the women of The Order, wives of brothers, are blessed with children at the exact same time. This miracle helps in keeping the ranks full, even in the unlikely event of a cataclysmic decimation of great numbers. If this terrible fate should befall The Order, the ranks will remain, strong and focused, prepared to fight for life. The *Replina* creates great classes of men to carry on the mission of keeping humanity alive and ignorant to their dire situation.

Oh, excuse me, how rude, I ramble on. Allow me to introduce myself. I am your narrator, Master Cranden Vinglon. I am the last of the mighty Gargoyle tribes; keepers from long ago, in the age just before the rise of science. My people were reaped by the beast, all, save myself and my mother Iruati.

Enough stalling, please allow me to begin. My story commences in the days before we of The Order knew of Master Sabor Lindon's true place. Before the Avenger became more than a mere legend. I will now tell you the intriguing...

Tale of the Sabor Guardians

Enter the Evil

A dark, husky frame stood poised, tense and serious. Pitch black concealed the beast completely, as he hungrily watched the lives scurrying about, ignorant to each ones dire situation. The unyielding blackness of the alley presented the perfect place to hide and he/it was taking great care not to be seen. Suddenly, the beast sniffed a hint of food in the air, and let go of a soft slow gurgle, like the growl of a distant but growing storm. Still the unsuspecting passers by never noticed the death stalking them, a few short feet away. The deep sounds grew louder, and the darkness gave way to a soft greenish glow. The hollow eyes of Dvanken opened slowly to reveal the true hell concealed in the shadows on that dank midnight. The gurgles amplified into hungry snarls and long deep scratches in the red brick walls of the alley. Dvanken sensed something in the air and it delighted him. He smiled, for he would eat and for the first time in days, he would eat well.

The thick, scaly neck, muscular and solid had two thorny rows of spikes on either side with large scarlet tufts of feather like fur on the ridge and at the base of each spike. The shoulders of the gargantuan beast were hunched, compensating for the enormous weight of the life-stealing jaws and head. Solid as any wall, his strength was legendary, within The Order. The beast's hunger was unholy and insatiable. His mandibles were lined with four rows of saber like fangs, saliva drenched and rancid. The roof of his mouth, perforated to allow the monstrous canines to protrude, adding the ability to tear flesh, even if the mouth were closed.

The air moved, tainted with the hopeless consuming grief of the red head by the bus stop. He had spotted the unsuspecting plump woman, waiting there picking her flowered skirt from her large backside. Her pillow-like flowered blouse, three sizes too small, symbolized her unconvincing attempt at fitting into society, as one of the beautiful people. *"Hey look at me, I'm wearing a size twenty,"* which for now, the size twenty gleamed a brilliant white.

In her hand, she carried a brown paper bag of groceries. The woman's thoughts however were not on her cucumbers and ice cream. This day worry consumed her completely. How was she going to tell her husband that she just lost her job at the shoe manufacturing plant? Especially since their rent was three months over due, and the landlord had recently placed an eviction notice on their door, pending the payment. Heaped atop the rest of the mounds of fret crammed into her small life, she may be pregnant. The only thing she had going for her now, was the fact that she had just recently taken out a large life insurance policy on herself and her death would be a welcome end to the worry.

7

She stood wondering if it would just be better for her and the world if she would simply step out in front of the bus, ending it all.

All the while, hanging in the sunken pitch, the soft glow slowly morphed from neon green to a deep electric purple. Evidently, the change was brought on, when the hellish creature had found what he was looking for...UTTER DESPAIR.

"Mmmmmm" Dvanken thought aloud," she would make a fine meal for me, this night,"

The snarling, heartless shadow began to soften the noise around the dense city streets, slowly focusing his mind and silencing the corpulent woman's universe, as she toiled. The only life belonged to the distraught woman standing on the bus stop and the beast now. Ever so quietly at first, but progressively louder the monster began to repeat deep in the woman's subconscious.

"I would take it from you, you know. I would take all of the hurting away. You need nothing but merely to ask it of me," The mantra repeated deeply, over and over in her swirling thoughts.

The words danced between her reality and her dream world. Weaving in and out like a shuttle on a rug maker's loom. The woman, so wrapped up in her troubles, desperately looking for her simple way out, any way out was a welcome and easy target for Dvanken. Besides, the beast would be more than happy to take away her suffering, thus giving her the sweet bliss of rest. And what's more, if the woman was indeed pregnant, this would be but an added bonus for him. The misery it would cause her clueless husband would taste that much sweeter when he reaped it from his useless body.

Again, with a stronger sense of urgency, he pushed the woman. To her mind he said. "Come with me. I will lead you to everlasting calm. No more worries, no more, no more, so come. Say the words, just say the words. The words are your key to a happy life,"

The woman snapping back to her normal consciousness and realized that she was in fact not dreaming. Standing dazzled by the fact that time had halted for her. Not one person moved, everything quiet, everything frozen. Even her watch was stuck at 12:36 A.M. A strange purple and red, miasma (an evil fog, that foretold of the evil Dvanken) seeped up from the ground, crackling with electricity around her. The odd nature of what was happening captivated her even more.

"Who, wh-what words do you need me to say?" She asked of the faceless voice resonating from the silence.

A booming, almost gleeful growl came bellowing from the monstrosity. "I need you to ask me to take it all away. All of your worry, all of your despair, all of the day to day mundane toil in your life the heartache you feel is just a few words from being relieved. All you have to do is say the tiny word please," he said with an evil grin, becoming more visible from the shadows. "Well my lady, do you wish me to grant you this peace? Or would you like to scurry on home to your stack of problems and that sad sack of a man you call husband,"

The woman examined her options. It seemed almost too good to be true, all of her troubles gone. She was so exhausted with worry. She was so tired. She looked down guiltily, and softly said a single word, "please," She looked down as the word, for some reason, burned her throat, leaving a horrible taste.

The enormous shadow lunged forward, revealing himself to her. The sight instantly destroyed the woman's thoughts of a peaceful resolution to her predicament. This new emotion added the delicious flavor, of oozing fear, dripping with regret and despair, to Dvanken's meal. With a very acrobatic back flip, the fiend found himself mounted atop the confused woman. His breath was warm and unholy on her face. The saliva drenched bones poking through his gnarly face, heaved with anticipation. His large paw raised far up behind his head. A swirl of yellow and purple electricity radiated from the raised veins in his massive forearms. His muscles worked precisely, forcing the shards of hardened bone, razor-sharp and countless, through its thick leathery skin. They ascended through the flesh on his hand and pulsated with energy. Dvanken released a thunderous howl of ecstasy into the still air. Then, the enormous abomination shivered and quaked with the bliss of releasing his life revoking barbs. He turned his enjoyment to the woman and forced his hand through the soft tissue and organs of her mid section, grabbing her by the spine, he raised the fleshy woman, high above his head and licked her blood from his cheek. The pain did indeed seem to be gone from her face, as did all other expression. She was now at peace, and the monster had kept his hideous promise to her. She had been released from her debt to this life, and now, she could rest. And with his evil work done, he grimaced at the left over bits and pieces of carcass.

"Thank you, m'lady, sleep in peace," he said in a sarcastic, and surprisingly human tone.

Just then, a knife-like slab of light pierced the forest of shadows created by the towering buildings here in Old Frington. The street lamps, and the unbearable obscurity of the alley, wove a beautiful blanket for this final duel. An old man, well built, stood in a dark leather overcoat. The crest of The Order of the Sabor Guardians was embedded on the right breast pocket of the long coat. His unkempt hair was long and aged. His muscles drew no attention to themselves, but a strange amber glow seeped from every crevice in his attire.

9

With all of the fury of hell, or heaven, he roared.

"DVANKEN! Your tormenting ends tonight, in this alley. We of The Order are done with you! The cycle has been allowed to linger for far too long," The stern, proud voice of the Guardian bellowed. His unyielding eyes and angular face dripping with hate and sweat.

"Take no peace in any of your endeavors here, demon," He said, the melodic words demanding enormous respect. The impressive darkness standing before the Guardian snarled and squared itself then smiled down at the old man. The hollow red smoke seeping from the fiend let the old Guardian know that the trouble he sought was coming and he stood ready for anything.

"Demon, you say, old one? Who is this, this Demon that you speak of? I am Dvanken, divine in nature. These beings you protect, they need me. They need horror. They need loathing. They need hate, revenge. They most of all, need an end," He bellowed in a deep voice growing more human with every word.

"Would you arrogant fools of The Order deny the humans that which they have created that which they have grown to depend upon? Oh you pompous fools. They, these cattle, they desire me! So tonight, my old rival, you will at long last feel the peace, which they, the humans desire,"

As the words tore from his lips, the beast collapsed into a defensive crouch, ready. His back twitched violently, as a hellish pair of scarlet horns grew from his bullish shoulders. His hands morphed into masses of sharp bone, attached to crushing, impressive arms. The street cracked beneath the mass of the mammoth Evil.

The man stood fast, never relenting in his task to rid the world of...IT. The amber glow grew weaving about through the backdrop of unsuspecting humans trapped in the vortex Dvanken had twisted about them. The frozen humans remained ignorant to the rampage about to take place amongst them.

The Knight threw off his cloak, revealing an armor-clad body, with a wonderfully intricate pattern of golden Celtic weaving; the Crest of The Order of the Sabor Guardians stood prominent on the center of the chest plate. His powerful arms sported large pads resting on his forearms. The pads were made of some highly polished metal, a tight golden rope traced around each end of the pad. The protection turned, forming a large trident at the end, by the wrist. A scoop with a golden mouth sat round, midway up the forearm. The glow was intensified there at the opening. The mans muscles twinged all at once, in a readiness, and focus far younger than his appearance. Slowly, from the scoops a large scraggly blade slid its way out, battle scarred and ancient looking, then

10

from the other arm, the same. Just beneath the tridents came two twelve-inch blades on either side of his hands. Slightly curving up towards his elbow.

'Standing there old man, you appear as if you could defeat me. But I want you to know the grief caused by your death will satisfy my appetite for many years!" The beast chuckled, then lunged. The ancient warrior dodged, then sliced with the precision only experience wields. The monster slid tumbling past the refreshed warrior.

"You have underestimated me on this day, Demon,"he whispered smugly to his bleeding adversary.

'Die old one. Die with true fear writhing inside your puny human heart. Please, I ask of you. Do this one thing for me and I will make your death quick," he responded with his own whisper.

The battle raged on, each combatant pushing the other to the edge by slicing, biting, tearing and swiping. The blades of the Guardian sparked on the bone-covered forearms of Dvanken. The colorful lights flashed wildly amidst the swirling onslaught of the old Guardians sabors. The attack took its toll on the both of them, leaving them heaving in exhaustion. The battle raged on for a few hours, neither combatant ever really knowing how long the battle had endured.

The elder fighter stepped in close as the huge beast narrowly missed with a shattering overhand blow and forced both of his glowing weapons on either side of the beast's neck. "Your tale ends here, Dvanken!" He screamed, then pulled both blades as hard as he could inward and down. A shower of purple blood covered him in an instant. The blood soaked Guardian rolled out from beneath the collapsing beast, just inches from being crushed by the load of the falling mass. In a long awaited moment, the brave soldier, sensing that he had given the fatal blow, relaxed letting down his guard and thanked the star filled sky above him. The wound was deep, to the neck of Dvanken, the evil heap of flesh which just seconds before, had been fighting so ferociously. The evil was now lying on the ground bleeding and writhing in a pool of purple goo.

The bruised and aged Guardian rose to one knee and collected his things. Preparing himself to return to the Halls, to tell the other Head Elders that the world had been rid of the evil one at long last. And the time of rejoicing was now at hand. How he wished to see the face of his youngest son. Overjoyed that he would never know the horror of these battles. The amber glow subsided and a white, pure light began shining throughout the alley. His weapons put away firmly, he knelt and began praying. Thanking God for his victory, with an old prayer of the Sabor Guardians.

Behind him, the slow breathing started again inside the beast. The air of

11

the alley, filled with a loud crackling sound. The ground started shaking violently and a deep rumble shook the dust and plaster from its hold on the red brick walls surrounding them. The alley where the battle had concluded turned a deep blood red. The odd electricity started forming large spear-like structures around the praying Elder. The immense purple arms, now with all possible bone shards exposed, appeared very alive and very dangerous. The victorious Elder, immune to his surroundings, was so blinded by the joy and fulfillment of ending the Cycle, at last, that he remained unprepared for what rose behind him. Dvanken stood quickly, presenting himself, broad and powerful.

'I told you, old one, that you appeared as if you could beat me. But that is all that it was, an illusion. It only looked as if you could destroy me. Foolish humans, when will you of The Order realize, I am eternal and your fleeting humanity will be a means to your own pathetic end.

'Now Guardian, I intend to reap my rewards with the blood of your family. As for now, you will be at peace,"

Dvanken pulled both arms back in a large arch giving the massive limbs, the most possible power, catching the Guardian off guard. The monster pulled the colossal, tree-like arms together, passing straight through the ancient warrior. One arm taking the head, as the other separated the torso from the legs, leaving the once dignified member of The Orders council of Elders, lying in three pieces on the slimy alley floor. The mighty one let out another hellish scream, prophetically warning the stars, and anyone looking on them, that he was coming. And they should all be anxious and troubled, for it would make them taste better, much better.

Sabor Lindon, a bright, young man with angular features, a spitting image of his father at his age. He wore a short trimmed goatee with long slender side burns. A muscular build, stalky, and very fit marked the eager young man as an athlete. Hopelessly unaware of his true role in life, uncaring of what great fortune he possessed, and his families status in the world. He was a star tail back in high school and college, and his narcissistic pursuits dominated his personal landscape, for as far back as he could remember. His only true passions in life, aside from his own ascensions, were art and his lovely fiancé Chelle.

An all-together uneventful life was all he could boast at the ripe old age of twenty-one years and it was all that he could have hoped for. His father had accomplished so much, and thus, was never around. Which is the case in most similar situations. So he felt that his life should be devoted more to his friends and family, and of course his own pleasure, rather than to the pursuit of worldly accolades. I guess what I am trying to say is life had given him a selfish lean on things.

His great twenty-second birthday loomed one week away. This event or benchmark seemed to be planned for him as long as he could remember. It was the sole topic for his father, and uncle's fireside chats. Honestly he had no idea how important this day was, just that it was. For after the ceremony, his Discovery was coming, and nothing would ever be the same. But to Sabor it was another day and it would be just another party. Though it did hold an inescapable certainty, that his father would be there and his reason for being there would be his son. That in itself, was reason enough for Sabor to be excited.

This warm August evening found the birds a little louder and the crickets especially hyper. He looked at his lady sitting under a tree, thinking how beautiful she looked consumed in her paperback novel. Pretty, smart, she was more than he could have ever asked for. And the feeling of merely looking at her was overwhelming. Finally was forced to stop reading her book, for the light was subsiding, being chased behind the horizon, by the surging moon. The elongated shadows stretched around the large oak, sitting in the park outside of his family home. A look of frustration broke over her beautiful face.

"Uuggh, I was just getting to the good part. Blasted light," She smiled as her eye caught a silhouette beside her.

"What ya reading, baby?" He calmly asked.

"Oh nothing now silly, you're here," she said, as she flung h erself at him, causing them both to fall to the ground. "Besides, the light has ran away, and I can't see the words," She said slapping him on the chest sharply.

"Tell me again how much fun we'll have once I am a Lindon, and you better spill your guts about where we will be going after for our honeymoon!" She demanded satisfaction with her tone.

A Cheshire grin cracked his surprised face, and he quickly responded. "Fun? What fun you will be at home, raising our sons while I go and have many adventures with wild women. You can forget about afterwards. We will not be having a honeymoon. I cannot afford it!" His tone dripped with sarcasm as usual. A look of dislike steamed from her face as she smacked him with the thick book she had been reading.

"Now give me an answer that I like, or I will pop you a second time," Chelle said as she shook her fist in his face, then a look of compassion came over her face. "Oh my god! What is with your rash sweetie?" The conversation lost all playfulness.

"What are you talking about, I know the rash has been worse lately, but damn you know I'm self conscious about it," The rash was in the shape of the full Crest. The very Crest that was saturating every aspect of his being. The rash, only the night before was a shapeless mass of red bumps. She grabbed his goatee, and forced him to look. In amazement, he examined the irritation that he had come to see as just something to live with. The bumps had lined up, and his skin seemed translucent around them. An odd amber glow showing through pulsed with every beat of his heart.

"Get away from me, I'm a freak!" The distraught young man screamed as he flew from the tree running to somewhere, nowhere, anywhere but where she could see him. He stopped finally in the stable, where a full-length mirror sat by the large open door. He looked, and the more he concentrated on the irritation, the more intense the light flowing through his veins become. "Holy Shit, what is this, why now?" He asked some unseen power. Just then the young mans' mother, Noelle Lindon scampered in and locked eyes with her son, that she had been watching from the front steps of he home.

"Sabor, why did you rush away, like that? Chelle, is worried sick about everything going on honey, she needs you to be normal for her sake. So please, if you would get your butt back out there, and tend to her," She pleaded with her visually upset son.

"No mom, I have to deal with something that neither you or Chelle either one could understand. I have all this crap about my birthday from Dad and this stupid rash, which no doctor can explain to me for some damn reason, just keeps getting worse. And you come in here yelling at me about how much she needs me! I need some compassion too ya know!? I'm sorry Mom; I just need to think. Now could you please, just go and leave me alone for a little while," Announcing his plan to sulk, he hesitated then called to his mother who was grudgingly walking away, with her head down. "MOM!" She turned to him, smiling a bit, that her son wasn't a heartless beast. "Tell her I love her, and I' m sorry. You can take those words for yourself also, Okay," He said, winking and making everything right with the world again.

"Your father wi ll speak with you tonight about your arms honey and I will tell her for you, my little Sabe," She said calming her son for a second.

"Mother how did you know?" He demanded.

"Oh, Chelle told me," his mother said telling a tiny white lie. After all , she had gone through this with her husband some twenty-four years earlier. She slowly walked back to the house, a song in her heart, and humming the same tune. When she came to the main house. Chelle sat on the front stoop, crying uncontrollably.

"What is it child, what is it?" The frazzled soon-to-be mother-in-law asked.

"It, It, It's Zandalar, He, he, um," she proceeded to wail, not knowing what else to do with her grief.

"What, Is it darling? Just calm down and tell me what is wrong with my husband, my dear," no response came back from the small ball of a woman on the floor, crying hysterically. The bewildered Noelle, grabbed Chelle, shaking her violently, frustrated she asked. "Tell me. Please, what has happened to my love? To your loves father, snap out of it and tell me now, everything will be alright child," she said raising her voice, something she hadn' t done in years.

The frightened young lady sobbed and squeaked out. "He has been killed, Captain Linx just called and said he was on a routine case, and he was killed, gunned down in the line of duty. I am so sorry Noelle, I am so sorry,"

The pigment streaked from Noelle's aged, but pretty face. She fell to her knees, as her heart seemed wrenched from her chest. Instant fear, doubt, and pain consumed her almost crushing her pure soul. The anguish sunk in quickly and completely. She had lost her rock, the man that had been there for so long, would never be coming back to her. Her love was gone.

Just a bit later, the newly fatherless son stumbled up to the main house, seeing his mother on all fours pounding the ground cursing and his soon-to-be wife lying beside her weeping as well. His meandering waddle, turned into a world class sprint within one step. When he got there, his mother was wailing,

"Not my Zandy, not Zandy Take anything, anyone but my Zandalar, my love, please,"

Bewildered, and angry, he called for an answer from Chelle, "Tell me. Tell me now; damn the both of you. Someone tell me what has happened to dad! WHAT?!" The urgency did nothing to the women on the ground before him, only making them sink further away from him. "I am so sorry mom, I didn't mean to yell at you again. What is it? Is dad okay? Please, please just tell me everything is okay,"

His mother looking up at him sadly, and tried to talk past the lump wedged in her throat said. "OH, my dear, dear sweet son. Your father, he is well, he's gone Sabe. He has been taken away from us by that stupid job. Taken by that damn Mason Linx," she went back to her feverish cry, releasing the hurt onto the concrete steps.

The words sliced the young man in half, tearing at everything inside of him with a double-edged sword of disbelief and hatred. Suddenly the column of strength that had always been there, fortifying the young man, was instantly and permanently gone. There was nothing that could be done about this horrible truth, nothing Sabor could say or do at all to fill the cavern of unsaid volumes and wasted opportunities that now lived inside his chest. The young mans eyes.

I swear to you, his eyes grew so cold, characterless and hollow, he could have sliced the world in half with their emptiness. He had relinquished a chunk of his humanity, for an extremely tangible reason. He stared into the sky, swearing vengeance upon the one that had taken away from him, the only constant he had always longed for. The closeness that would have been given to him, from the love of his father.

Not one in the group saw the grin that their pain placed upon the face of the evil, watching outside. It waited, hoping to hear one of them to ask for the sweet peace of death, asking for what he was so eager to give. Hidden in the obscurity of shadow, he snarled and hissed, "They will be ready soon, soon I tell you. Patience will lead me to one of my finest meals. So, for now I will wait for you Lindon and savor. But, for now I am hungry, I need to eat. As for you young Guardian, be afraid, full of hate, and most of all keep your promise of revenge," Dvanken slithered off to find himself a new meal. He allowed the family to grieve and wallow in self-pity, marinating themselves for him.

A long black luxury car shuffled its way through the traffic of the day and pulled up to the house, where the grief stricken trio sat and stood.

"Damn, I had sincerely hoped they would not find all of this out until I had arrived. Linx dropped the ball again on this one," the dark figure inside the vehicle thought out loud, then opened his door, the alert chimes ringing because he had left his keys in the ignition. "Hello Lindon's!"

"Uncle Saimus, have you heard, did you hear? Dad is dead, killed while on another case for that damn captain Linx. This...It's all his fault. I swear to you, that I will blame him for this until I die. I always have and always will, that prick. My father was too old to work for him, doing all of his crap jobs, while he sits all safe and lazy behind some desk, answering phones. My Dad should have been behind some desk somewhere. Calling him at all hours of the night, come break up this crack house, come break this drug ring. Why didn't he get a younger man, a man who had less to lose to do it? Zandalar Lindon had a family and his family loved him. DAMN HIM! I swear before you now uncle, I will get my revenge," seeming to run out of hatred for the moment, and he trailed off.

"Young man, chin up. Your Father chose his own path in this life, he chose to stay out. He chose to fight for the good in mankind.

"I understand the swelling of anger inside of you nephew. And I also concede that accepting this role of the hatred you are feeling right now, is completely normal, Sabor. But it necessitates exactly what your father was working against. You must control this hate, never suppress it, but harness it and turn it into all consuming joy," the wise man spoke, trying not to upset his nephew too badly.

"Are you not listening to me? My dad has been killed, your brother, he's gone forever. Have some compassion, I need some answers, help me. I have nothing to go on here, you tell me to control my anger, but I don't know how. I'm lost, here," Sabor said as he wiped a tear from his eye.

"Sabor! You stop that right now! My brother would want it that way. No remorse, no toil over the inevitable theft of his breath. He fought to keep you ignorant of the truths flowing in your veins. But, after your party tomorrow, you will understand more about the hidden world, more than you ever thought possible, or ever wanted to know, I assure you. You will know how to smile at death. You will recognize how to harness negative. Learning your true potential and taking your place among the men of the Lindon line. You are a Lindon, and that is more than just a status, or a name. It is a heritage, a blessing as well as a curse. The name of Lindon is the only thing your father, my brother, had to believe in. So please, do not make his life or death, vain. Calm yourself," hearing these words Sabor felt better, more confused than before but strangely better.

"Uncle, what is so important about tomorrow? Why will it be *only then* that I will understand? Have you guys been hiding something from me?" He asked.

"My precious Sabor, tomorrow is not about hiding things, or prolonging your suffering. It is about life, about all things positive and good. You will make a secret journey tomorrow. A journey that your father, his brothers and countless others in our Order have taken," Added Saimus helping the boy in front of him cope.

"What do you mean *Order*? Why is tomorrow so important? Damn it; answer me NOW," The young man thundered.

"My demanding little man. Know your place and go get some rest. For your *Discovery* awaits, on tomorrow's morning shore and you will need every ounce of your strength,"

Sleepless Nights

Bewildered, Sabor collected his mother telling her the words she needed to hear, to calm herself down and rest at least for this one night. He then turned to Chelle, adding some measure of comfort there, trying hard not to remember his own burden of hurt.

'Honey, I think I need to be alone tonight okay. Please don' t be angry with me. Just give me tonight to be isolated-alone with my thoughts, please," His soon-to-be wife reluctantly agreed, expressed her love, and then grudgingly left.

As the mother and her son entered the house, the television news anchor delivered the headlines of the evening.

"And in tonight' s broadcast, we have the shocking details of a brutal bus stop killing. And in the headlines tonight, the death of a local hero, remains unsolved. Leaving police nearly clueless, as to who the assailants are.
'Detective and soldier in the governmental task force on violence, Lt. Zandalar Lindon was slain last night. Lindon was brought down, our sources say, by a local group of terrorists, who at this point have taken great care in only leaving, a small trademark at the scene. A tell tale sign they have left on all of their victims. This, says our source, is the only lead police have at the present time. If you have any information in regards to this investigation, the Old Frington police ask you to please call the number on the bottom of your screen, now to Bruce with the weather... " Sabor picked up a vase and flung it through the television filling the room with the smell of smoldering electrical parts.

'Damn them. How can they crawl all over this like it can't possibly hu rt anyone? Those bastards need to be shut down! They all need to just go to hell," Sabor muttered, not realizing the effect his words were having on his fragile mother.

'PLEASE Sabor, I have lost a husband and my best friend. Give your anger a rest tonight for me okay son. Help my day to not end with more senseless death, it has had more than its share already. Help your dear old mom to bed, and for my sake, for your fathers' sake, and most of all your sake; please just get some rest. Tomorrow is a big day, and you can't have it clouded with rage or hate. These feelings will kill you and your mother couldn' t take that," she pleaded with her son.

19

'Okay mom, I'm sorry I get it. But I'll tell you, if one more person tells me how important my birthday is, and doesn' t tell me why. I' m gonna go crazy, I swear it,"His mother now had a large smile on her porcelain face, which did Sabors' heart good to see her light.

'Don' t worry buddy. You will know soon enough, stop rushing your life away. Hold it for as long as your fingers still grip,"She replied and off to bed they went.

Realizing he had sent his little darling home without telling her he loved her, he called leaving a message for her to call him when she came in and that he loved her more than breathing.

The rest of the night was sleepless, tossing, turning, rolling and wondering how vengeance would actually solve his problem. It would only hurt his life, not make it complete, but on the other hand, rage does have a way of healing his hurt, at least it had always done so in his past. Sabor lay staring at the ceiling sorting out the feelings racing inside his chest. With his deep thought his arms began itching and his head started to spin. He closed his eyes, trying to override the spinning, only to discover when his eyes closed, the strange glow in his veins transferred to his eyelids, becoming impossible to ignore.

He began wondering about this new life promised after his big day. How would just another day transform his life? What answers would this all-important sunrise bring? Why has his lady not called him yet? His mind raced, every thought he had, had in his short life flew by, revolving around his axis of consciousness. Well, there was nothing he could do about any of the situations in his life today, he thought.

Sabor slowly opened his eyes and glared intently at the ceiling and announced. 'Father, I love you. I always did. Even though we didn' t say it always, I really did. I will need you from time to time so stay close, but please don' t worry. I will do whatever it is you needed me to do tomorrow. I won't let you down. I remember what you always told me, I will keep everyday as if it will be my last. That is what this has taught me, we are never promised anything and life is too beautiful to cut short with pain and sorrow. I guess just one more thing Pop. Thank you for always being you, no matter what,"The tired young man curled into his comforter, drifting off to sleep.

All the while his father sat in the corner, unseen and unheard, smiling. So proud, so relieved to know his son was this strong. His words had proven him sturdy enough to be a great Guardian, sound enough in mind to lead a noble group of men and wise far beyond twenty-one. He stood, floating across the room. Leaning gently over his son kissed his forehead. A single teardrop fell from his eye landing on Sabors' slumbering cheek.

Startled, Sabor flung from his coma-like nap, seeing a soft white mist dissipating above him. From amidst the waif of cloud a faint voice spoke, "Son, I remember watching you sleep like this when you were just a tiny little boy. You never knew I was there, but I watched you sleep every night of your life, so peaceful, so far away in your dreams, your pillow covered in drool,"

The voice continued as it laughed a loving chuckle. "My dear, dear son Sabor, just as I was there when you slept, so will I always be here for you. Simply think my name and I will be there. Never forget that I love you and I thank-you for your love in return. The words you spoke to me on this night keep them above all else in your heart. Do this and they will save you? One day, you will need these emotions. Keep your love and joy at the forefront of all situations,"

As sure as the voice was there, it was gone just as quickly. Dismissing this, as a dream would be too hurtful, so Sabor accepted it as fact, intending to hold fast the words his father gave him, never forgetting. He couldn' t help but doubt it may have been a dream. Whatever it was, he finally slept and it felt good.

"Thanks Dad. I love you too. And I will, don't really know why I will or even how, but I will keep it in my mind. I promise,"Sabor said, snuggling in for a rocky night of slumber.

"Wake up, Sabor. It's time to go, baby," Noelle said, sticking her head in his door, but not too far in case he wasn't decent.

"Just five more minutes, Mom. Please, I'm not ready to move just yet," Sabor said sarcastically, sitting up and wiping his face.

"You listen to me Sabor Lindon, that little game of yours has never worked and today isn't going to start the trend going your way, mister. You get up and get your bag ready. After the funeral, we are going to the farm to get away from the city. Okay?" Noelle said, teasing her son, outlining his schedule for him.

"Okay, Mom! I'm up, I'm up. You know I'm only joking, when I do that anyway. Go on, I'll be right down," Sabor threw off the covers and slipped into his tattered cloth house shoes, then shuffled to his closet, wiping the sleep from his eyes and yawning a foul smelling stretch.

"What to wear, what to wear? It isn't everyday that a twenty-one year old man has to bury his father and has the biggest birthday of his life, all at once" Sabor said, wiping a salty, wet ball of grief from his cheek.

"Sabor honey, the car is out front. Are you ready to go yet, my boy?" Noelle asked sweetly.

"Not yet Momma, I'm still in the shower," Sabor yelled down stairs as he leaned

"Mom has Chelle come yet? She said she would be here early. I don't want to leave without her," Sabor yelled as he flipped his long black tie around, completing the knot. A delightful smell swarmed into the room. A soft, white hand grabbed a bit of lint from his shoulder and smoothed out a wrinkle on his lapel that had formed from months of hanging in a dusty closet.

"Mmmmmm. Lilacs and spring rain. Hey baby, I'm glad you could make it," Sabor said, not even looking to see who was standing behind him.

"You know I wouldn't miss this for anything in the whole world," Chelle said as she kissed her man on the neck, instantly making life better for him. "Come on, the car is waiting for us, honey. You do look sharp though hone, I love you," she said, leaving him to himself.

"Thanks honey," Sabor whispered, giving his all black, tailored suit one last glance before leaving to place his father into the family section of the South Frington Military Cemetery between his great grandfather, Secil Lindon, and his uncle, Victor J. Lindon. Both had died in the line of duty, either in the police force in Victor's case or in the Great War in Secil's. That was the story handed down as truth in the Lindon household. When in all actuality, the real truth stood as this, the South Frington Cemetery was not reserved for veterans or police. It was, in fact, a burial ground for The Order.

"Alright Sabor, be strong," Sabor told himself. "Dad, wherever you are , sorry you won't be around for my important day, but whatever it is, I'll do my best to make you proud,"

"Sabor, the car is outside and the services are going to start at any minute. Please hurry," Noelle called up the staircase to her procrastinating son.

Sabor came down the stairs, seeing his mother in a black three piece dress, accented with a large golden pin shaped like the symbol hanging on the walls all around her, and the Crest on her collar. On her head she wore a velvet hat with a diagonally cut mesh veil covering one side of her face. Chelle wore a long straight-cut dress, with her hair pulled back in a tight ponytail with small tendrils of highlighted hair dangling on either side of her face. Both smiled at the handsome man walking sadly down the stairs.

"There you go sweetheart. I know this won't be easy dear, but somehow your Father will always be with us, at least in spirit. I know that is hardly a consolation, but it is all we have now," Noelle whispered as her son gave her a strong, deep hug. "Remember, us girls need you now. We love you and we are still here,"

"Mom, don't make it sound like I'm gonna kill myself over this. I know I still have loads to live for, okay. I love you ladies too," Sabor said, grabbing the pair and squeezing them both. "Now, if you don't mind, the car isn't going to wait on us forever, sheesh. Besides the services are going to start soon. Just like women, always late," Sabor joked, concealing his deep grief.

The day was warm with a forceful breeze whipping across the cemetery grounds, tussling the trees and tall evergreen shrubs. Row upon row of chairs were placed around the twelve by five hole cut six feet deep into the ground. A circular, woven maroon rug covered the bright green grass. Golden thread lined the rug, creating a square, embroidered pattern around the edges with two large Crests on either side of the hole. A towering canopy stood fifteen feet above the ground, shading the final resting-place of Zandalar Lindon.

A line of black limousines and other luxury cars sat on the shady maze of asphalt arteries, crossing the memorial park. A small marching band assembled in the shade of a poplar tree adjacent to the graveside. A steady flow of mourners ushered themselves from their vehicles to pay their last respects to the great man, who had touched each of their lives in some way, each made better by simply knowing him. Sabor, Chelle and Noelle pulled up to the head of the line and stopped.

"Wow, all of this for Dad, huh?" Sabor asked Noelle, helping her from the backseat.

"Yes Sabe. Your Father was a very respected man in Old Frington. Quite a diverse group of people loved him in life and apparently in his death," Noelle replied, straightening her dress, shoving the tears down with a subtle quiver of her bottom lip.

"I can make it out, sweetie. Why don't you help your mother to her seat? I'll catch up," Chelle said, hoping his answer would not be," *okay, are you sure,*"

"Thanks baby, but I think we all need to go together," Sabor said, staring at his lovely bride-to-be, wishing to be anywhere but where he was at that moment.

The band played continuously looping a soft, deep, pulsing ballad. Suddenly the ensemble stopped playing as Sabor and his party approached their seats. Not one person was sitting down. All waited respectfully for Lady Noelle Lindon, who Zandalar had chosen as his life partner. The elegant and lovely Noelle bowed her head in respect to every soul in attendance, then faced the aperture and cried. Sabor stood behind his mother, paying attention only to her and his beloved. Chelle sat beside Noelle in the chair reserved for Sabor, stroking his hand and patting Noelle on the leg comfortingly. All were misty eyed, each person lost in particular memories of the man they stood to honor.

Suddenly, the trumpets in the band blared out a cutting note. Everyone snapped to attention, turning their focus to the thunderous sound of hooves clomping closer and closer on the pavement. Sabor saw a group of twenty children dressed in long, brown, thick cloth-hooded robes, which hung from their tiny frames, dragging the ground behind them. They walked in a V-like formation, tossing large bunches of white roses high above their heads, creating a drizzle of bleach-white floral dancers, floating to the ground, perfuming the breeze and adding an air of regality to the procession.

A massive, crystal coffin encased the peaceful Guardian for his eternal earthly sleep. The body, brutalized in the assault, was completely covered by a traditional hand-woven silk-cloth death shroud, and adorned with a sheet of white and blue wild flowers. The body lay on large mound of cloud-like satin pillows, trimmed in tiny embroidered crest shaped designs.

A mystical vibe resonated from within the wind as the carriage creaked past the vehicles. Contrasting the polished vehicles, a team of twenty gargantuan Clydesdale horses pulled the thin, ivory cart up the lane. The muscles of each impressive horse rippled with every step, shimmering with the highlights of the drape they wore. A maroon cloth, sticking out from beneath a large breastplate, covered each beast. The cloth was decorated with a strange group of symbols along the hem, which for as massive as the cover was still dangled a few feet from the ground.

Large metallic helmets encased the heads of the massive stallions. Hinged in large sections with woven gold wire, the flared sections of metal, decreased in size as they neared the ears. A long squared piece ran along the snout, covered in a strange type of luminescent metal, forming progressively longer spikes as they got closer to the nostrils.

A Crest, fastened at the center of the equines chest, connected two form-fitting plates, intricately decorated and solid. The metal of these great plates looped up coming to sharp points ending on both sides above the shoulder.

Stringy tufts of hair surrounded the huge feet, braided and separated into three sections, one dangling to the front and the others on opposing sides of the hoof, recoiling with each step. Oversized golden shoes were attached with nails, whose heads matched the strange symbols on the hems of their maroon drapes.

Oddly, no driver sat atop the hearse carrying Zandalar's still body. No reins attached to the horses' faces. Instinct drew the beasts to this peaceful place.

The sight of her lifeless husband overwhelmed Noelle, who began to wail, overflowing with grief. Sabor's knees buckled slightly before catching himself on Chelle's shoulder. The beautiful, young lady smiled a crooked smile at her beloved then hugged the pair of them as hard as she could.

A man dressed in a flowing robe stepped to the head of the graveside. It was Symon Divin, an Elder in The Order of the Sabor Guardians. He cleared his throat, pulling a small scroll out from beneath a layer of his stately rob. Then, with a look at the trio of grief sitting huddled in front of him, he smiled a thoughtful, loving grin.

"My friends, please be seated," Symon began as the casket came to a halt parallel to the burial place. The crowd sat in unison, all but Sabor.

"We have gathered to celebrate the life of a great man. A man who gave more, much more, than he received in this harsh life. A family man, though he was a tireless worker, he loved his adoring wife and son. If... " Symon continued, but Sabor drifted away unappreciative of the words being spoken. Staring into the engraved crystal sarcophagus, holding the remains of the man who "would always be there," with his tiny grasp of what life meant he pondered how he came to be here.

Sabor watched the children clad in the hooded robs step to the sides of the coffin and, as if by magic, the crystal case seemed to float above their hands. Sabor looked around to see if anyone had been disturbed by what he saw, but everyone stood oblivious to the miracle. He shook his head and watched the clear box holding his father slip into the ground, slowly.

Sabor's edges then blurred and he fell away into the blissful memories of a distant childhood. He grasped at any image of his father his sub-conscious would release. Before Sabor knew what had gone on, he stood alone with his thoughts. Not a soul around him, he was standing solitaire, staring into the nothing of a shadow.

"Mom! Where did you go?" He asked, glimpsing her slowly walking up the hill to stand by him.

"I went for a little walk, looking around at row after row of these identically cut, soulless headstones, marking the ends of so many rich lives. Seems a meager reminder for all your father had given to this city. You know?" Noelle said, letting her guard down, ceasing to be a protective mother and becoming only a woman that had lost the most important man in her life.

"I had an idea honey," she added.

"Oh yeah, what's your plan, Momma?" The young man smiled.

"I sent Chelle home and canceled the celebration tonight and was hoping that my son and I could drive out to the country for a little get-away grieving time. Your uncle will pick you up for the big day tomorrow. What do you say does that sound good to my little Sabe?" The matriarch said, grabbing her boy and squeezing. "Sounds perfect Momma. Sounds absolutely perfect. Let's go,"

Lindon Farm

The pair went home and packed for the forty-mile drive, to the red wooden panel farmhouse, that had been passed down through the Lindon family for ages. Sabor pulled the car around, beeping the horn to signal Noelle that he had gotten everything but her into the car, and was ready to leave.

"You know better than that, Sabe. Scoot over. I will be doing the driving. You know I get carsick every time you drive," Noelle scolded. "You drive too fast and it scares me," she added under her breath.

"Okay, okay. I'll let you drive, but if you lolly gag about, I will push the pedal for ya, understand?" His mischievous grin made them both feel better, almost whole again.

The trip had gone on with little conversation or outward expression, save an occasional sigh or shift in the seat. Sabor turned, placing his forehead on the side glass, watching the wiggling white line hovering dangerously close to the grass traveling at nearly light speed beside the blacktop.

The trees along the side of the country road stood regal. Their enormous roots tangled exceedingly close to the asphalt. The leafy canopies, outstretched nearly touching, shaded the winding lane from the blistering noon sun. The sweet hint of honeysuckle and rosebuds danced in the air, rushing through the air conditioning vents, marrying the interior of the vehicle with the expanse of nature speeding past Sabor's window.

Sabor filled his lungs with the nectar-tinged air and let out a saturated sigh.

"Sabor, what is it? What's wro ng, honey?" Noelle asked rhetorically.

"Oh, it's nothing. I just miss him so much, that's all. And do you want to know what the bad thing about all of it is? I don't even know what it is, that makes me miss him as much as I do. It's not like he was even around all that much, even when he was alive. Ya know?"

"My sweet little Sabe. None of us ever know what it is, that means the most to us, at least not while we still have it beside us. It is perfectly natural to take your world and everything in it for granted. Not dwelling on the death or loss of someone or something, until it happens. The questions of "why" and "I could have or should have done this or that" begin to surface in all of our minds. Because now the time that we had to do anything, has gone forever. Yes, had we known about Zandalar's death, we would have tried more. Made him stay home more often. Made him sit with us at dinner. We simply would have made him live with us instead of wasting his years on that silly job;" Noelle stopped herself before she said anything extremely upsetting to her or Sabor.

"I'm sorry I brought it up Mom. Don't worry about me, I'll be okay. I promise," Sabor proposed.

The car rumbled onto the gravel strip, telling the pair of the proximity to Sabor's childhood playground, the old Lindon plantation. Twilight had settled onto the fields of the farm. An invisible army of crickets filled the air with a chirping concerto, playing to a troop of lightning bugs, flickering a brilliant lightshow against the dimming backdrop, that twilight pulled across the world.

Past the lumbering oak fences, down the lane the car jumped and chattered loudly. Finally slowing, coasting to a gentle stop in the large cul-de-sac type drive in front of the modest farm house.

"Hasn't changed much around here. Has it? It's actually the same as it was the last time we were here. The house is in need of some paint, but other than that not much has changed," Sabor said.

Sabor shook his head remembering back to a hot summer day, when his father and he, had painted the house. What a disaster. The ground, as well as the two Rembrandts doing the painting were covered much more evenly than the house. Sabor kept a picture of the aftermath in his wallet, forever preserving the ordeal.

"Nothing much changes out here son. Except maybe the leaves," Noelle said leaning over and kissing her son on the forehead as he looked around.

"What was that for? I'm sorry, I meant to say thank you. But, I really didn't deserve that one mom," Sabor said.

"Yes you did," With that, the pair thumped out of the vehicle.

The night was full of hot cocoa and stories of their shared love. The enormous void his passing had left inside the two was slowly filling with the love they were pouring out to one another. The hours slipped into the mid-night and Noelle excused herself off to bed, under the excuse of age. Sabor sat up a few hours later, staring into the fire and pulling his Father's face out of the flickering flames. If he by chance grasped a flicker that resembled Zandalar, he would close his eyes and hold the yellow silhouette for as long as he could. He then dismissed himself, begging the fire's pardon for his early departure.

With daylight breaking on the farm, the outside bustled with the symphony of sounds flowing from the country. Sabor loved this place, far from the hustling, unfriendly city. He slowly jostled himself from the bed, tugging his pajama bottoms up, and wandered downstairs, scratching himself. The thick, buttery, spicy smell of sausage and eggs cooking on the stove pulled him quickly downstairs.

The woman of the house sat at the table, staring out the dusty window. Sabor had witnessed this scene unfold many times, although he could not deny something was missing.

"Hey Mom, you doing alright?" The concerned son asked, knowing whatever answer he received other than, no, would be a lie to make him feel better. "The sausage smells good. Is it ready yet?" Sabor added to lighten the heavy conversation.

"Thank you. And yes honey, I am as well as can be expected. How are you?" She sounded so unconvincing and hurt.

"Mom, It's okay to feel bad you know. This is something you can't be strong for. You need to cry, Mom; you need to be human. Get it all out. Look, I know Dad is dead. Those are hard words for me too, but the truth is something that will haunt you. The truth does not have to find you if you hide, instead it lays quiet, until you stop, and then it reminds you of why you ran in the first place. So Mom, just cry. You'll let go, and move forward for doing it," Sabor said, hoping not to hurt his mothers' feelings.

"Oh my beautiful boy, you've grown up so fast and so strong. Come here and give me a hug Sabe,"

Sabor did so, without hesitation, squeezing as hard as he could, letting go of another tiny piece of his own grief with the long embrace from his mother. It seemed too easy, almost blasphemous to release the pain so easily. How could forgetting his father's death ever be okay? Why was he needing to remember what happened?

Sorrow of a Beauty

Meanwhile, a few blocks away at the apartment of Chelle Jonson, the beautiful young lady was being watched. Her admirer smiled at her tears, the tears for Mr. Lindon, and the tears for the way her fiancée had dismissed her when she figured he would want her most. The uncertainty she now felt about the feelings of her man and their upcoming wedding manifested themselves as heartache and dismay.

The joy of the wickedness outside her house was disgusting. The smile forming about his fangs was unsettling and smelly. Chelle, too lost in her thoughts to check her messages, paced past the machine, doing this and doing that, never noticing the blinking red light on the machine. If she answered the light, her pain and confusion would split, her only sadness belonging to the man in the farm house miles from her one bedroom. She went about her duties, showering, cleaning, and preparing herself to go to the farmhouse to see her beautiful man. She looked around her apartment. All the pictures, all the happy memories staring her in the face, she couldn' t help but be a bit happy and disappointed about her smile at the same time.

Dvanken swooped in and ripped a truck-sized hole in her wall, destroying the reflective moment Chelle was sharing with the photographs on the wall. The force of this magnificent entrance, flung Chelle across the room. She came to rest in a shower of glass, under the pictures she had been admiring. She screamed a siren-like scream, shattering the remaining glass in the room.

As the sun flooded in, fear swept over her, sending massive chills running up her spine. The smell was sweet smelling to the villain consumed in the sunlight. He stretched his new spear-like growths, quivering because the addition felt good. A thin membrane of skin he hadn' t noticed before, stretched from the tips down to his heels, creating wings of a sort. He smiled to find such a welcome addendum. He extended the new toys and blocked out the sun. The world swirled to a screeching halt. Nothing was allowed to breathe, the world congealed in fear.

"What do you want?!" She shrieked as the red mist began to rise from every crack in the floor.

"Your worry, need to lie more, with what I'm going to take from you, my lovely young lady," He hissed. "Now child, appease me and keep that tongue of yours silent while I make a proposition. You are troubled, are you not? Why has

30

Zandalar been stolen from you? I can sense he was like a father, a caregiver, and a love. Why did your soon to be groom shun you, why did he push you away, doesn' t he love you? Doesn't he know this hurts your feelings, to be cast away like some rag? Your father left your mother, didn't he?" The evil taunted, as Chelle tried to answer he threw a finger over her lips. 'Shhh, I know that he did, I have seen it in your pain. But he only left after you came along. Tell me young Michelle Jonson what is it about you that makes the men in your life push you away, or rather. What makes them run away from you? Maybe, it would just be better if you weren' t around anyone anymore. After all, they will all leave you alone and hurt you, if you stay. Maybe, you need to be taken away from your pain for a while. Maybe, you need to be the one to run away from them this time, show them the hurt that they have always given so freely to you. You need to come, come with me to the peace of solitude. Tell me child, do you still have trouble sleeping? I can give you rest, you know? I can help with all of the pain, all you need to do is ask and nobody will ever run from you again," the slick shadow spoke so eloquently. 'Oh, and please do not forget to be polite about it when you ask. I would ask only one thing of you, before making your world newborn, you must say, please,"

One never knows what goes on in a person's head, when an outrageous situation presents itself. Chelle's mind began to wonder, what **was** wrong with Her, maybe she didn' t deserve a man, maybe she didn' t deserve to be alive at all, maybe.

'I am so scared. I don' t know anything anymore. I need, I need some kind of release, some sort of outlet. I'm too bottled up. I'm all-tight. You say you can ease the pain, I want that so much. I need it. Okay," She parted with the words with such ease that maybe it was the right thing. If she could say it with such clear conscious, then maybe it was right, she reasoned.

'PLEASE!"

The word was like a razor, it stung. Regret tried to grab the word and pull it back, but alas it was too late. The cycle had been accelerated, Dvanken was triggered.

His eager eyes, a deep purple, turned from deep green. His snarl grew deeper somehow. He was set in motion by her permission. And nothing could stop his hunger, nothing.

The deep purple and red electricity snapped and popped around her, stinging her and hinting her existence was in jeopardy. She looked for escape, finding nothing but a brick dislodged by the great evil, when the beast entered the room. She picked it up heaving it as hard as she could. With a thud, it thundered down at his feet.

Looking down at it, he slowly glared up at her not moving his head, but shifting his eyes upward. "You should be happy. You are about to know true peace, pure bliss," he said teasing her.

With no indication of what was coming, he darted through the air. The petrified girl slid out of the way scurrying across the floor, on her backside, narrowly avoiding death. The gargantuan mass slithered right behind her, destroying yet another wall, as he charged forward, pursuing his dinner. He inadvertently hit the button on the answering machine. A loud voice come over the small speaker.

"Hey honey, sorry about tonight. Thanks for being at the funeral, you looked nice in the black dress, Dad would have loved it. Anyway, I love you baby, even more than breathing. I would love to hear from you, I need it so call me when you get in and we'll talk, Okay? Just please remember, I love you always, and can't wait till I hold you again," BEEP, the machine rang out, repeating every heart felt word. As the message played, it rang true in her ears, giving her peace, the peace that only true love can give. She smiled, even in the face of her own death; his love made her smile. The weight of the monster falling full force would have killed her on impact, yet he decided to take care, and save something to identify. Perhaps leaving a small morsel of sweetness to the main course.

Dvanken stretched his right arm, claws at full extension, an odd red spiral cascading up the arm, A fraction later, his spikes plunged down below her breasts, ripping her ribcage wide open, slashing her lungs with a loud pop, and making the soft sacks release the last breath of air. Delicious he thought to himself. The paw came to rest with a thunk on her spine the core of her taste, the center of the pain and suffering.

"Have you ever noticed that when you're scared, you get shive rs up your spine? This is why I am eating it. Your fear lives here; your hate lives here. It is your negative core, delicious. It is my favorite," the disgusting demon whispered in her dying ear.

He chewed her backbone, quickly devouring every bit of her, desperately trying to taste her. He got her half of the way down, before he realized that her meat had been tainted, tainted by the rancidness of love.

"The message! Damn that message," Dvanken realized the short rant of the distraught boyfriend had undone everything he had tried so hard to do. All of the preparations he had gone through to get her taste just right, all for naught now. In a swift heave, he regurgitated the half-digested mass of what once was the love of Sabor Lindon onto the floor of her apartment. Then slurked off into the shadows, certain that this sight would add an abundance of flavor to the pot. And he was going to enjoy this very much. As for Chelle, there would be no glorious ceremony, no crystal coffin. Her body was in such horrible shape, that her remains were cremated. Her mother left the ashes in a marble and gold urn, on the mantle of her home, allowing nobody to visit. She sat grief stricken, with the lights off. For the rest of her days, glaring at the final resting-place of her daughter.

Delay of the Slumber

In a dimly lit penthouse across town, tastefully decorated with art from all countries, sat a large oak desk. Centered in front of a twelve-foot tall oval window, trimmed in carvings of gargoyles. In the center of the pane of the window, held a solid hand crafted iron crest. The crest cast an oblong shadow on the ground, creating channels of illuminated dust cascading to the ground.

The room was still, except three Elders were engaged in deep discussion about the coming "Slumber," a time of peace as it were for the Guardians. The beast Dvanken would kill for twenty long seasons. At the end of these killing seasons, the exhausted beast slept collecting his strength for five seasons. This was known to The Order, as the Slumber. The Slumber did not, however, mark the end of killing in these peaceful times. The seeds that evil plants blossom in the time of the Slumber and humanity becomes it's own evil, devouring itself and insuring that the cycle would continue.

This was a difficult situation for the Elders. A time that would challenge each individuals faith and knowledge of the History. The Guardians too, were beginning to dream, and not the normal kind of day-to-day dreams. These dreams told of an unseen Guardian, one who would rid the world of Dvanken. These dreams could be mistaken and dismissed for child-like hopes for peace. Had the dream not been identical in every facet, for each of the Elders, and Guardians.

Head Elder, and my friend Symon Divin turned to Saimus. "The time for the Slumber is near; all of our dreams are turning to salvation and this mystery savior. Who do you think it is? My instincts point to the young Keni Divin," The wise man inquired, then offered.

"Elder Symon, you know it is not like me to guess, especially in a matter as important as this. But judging by my dream and what I have read of the History, it will be one who enters his Discovery at the same time as Dvanken drifts into his Slumber. As you know my brothers' son is a solitaire. The first one in centuries, and is set to begin his Discovery today. So, if Dvanken is indeed asleep, then the young Lindon may be the one,"

Just then, a young, eager boy ran in, sweating and very out of place standing with the stately gentlemen poised in the center of the room. "Sirs, I am sorry for my intrusion. It, its Dvanken. He struck again, this time leaving her body behind, only taking her spine," The boy collapsed with exhaustion on the floor.

"Come and take him" Symon bellowed. Two small well-dressed men, never looking up hustled in and gathered the young boy. They drug him into the hall one closing the door, the other dousing the boy with water. "This changes it all. He cannot be asleep, if he has killed last night. The Slumber has been delayed. This is not good," a distraught Symon explained to his colleagues.

"I do not believe this signifies a delay in the Slumber, necessarily," said Yorge, a large hungry Elder who had been silent as usual, not wanting to force his opinion on any matters, yet had opinions on everything. Now spoke freely, not holding in his opinion," I believe he has grown greedy, and may have bitten off more than he could chew with this latest victim. Why else would he have left the body? This victim was not a brother of The Order," He concluded his statement as a small voice, squeaked from over a speaker mounted on the wall.

"Excuse me sirs, our messenger has just told us the name of last nights attack. It was brother Sabors' fiancé, Chelle Jonson;" the voice cracked and then went silent.

"We must go and tend to the issues at hand, and a scertain weather or not Dvanken is in fact in Slumber or has he decided to elongate his run this time. We should also check the teachings to see if they tell of any clues to the Guardians identity, who's Discovery coincides with the Slumber. This is our task. Yours Master Saimus is to check in with Cranden and see what he has gathered from his vantage. Make sure the boy hears the news from you, this tragedy could be the end of the Lindon line of The Order. This must not happen. The Lindon line is the oldest, and most stead fast in The Order. You must keep him strong and remain calm throughout. Nothing negative must come of this," Symon spoke with a power that could command the earth to break away from itself with a mere word. "Good luck, and lets bring these dreams to life brothers for we are too old not to see an end to the suffering. Let us also remember, Sabor could be the savior we need,"

The three men stepped back in unison; all six eyes attached to the shadow on the floor. Their blood began to flow faster as they stared at the crest being projected by the light.

"For The Order, and for hope," Saimus proudly bowed and left, saying nothing else but those six sincere words.

Sabor decided the two of them should leave a bit early and gather his things for his big day. He had left a pair of photo albums on his dresser. To save his uncle a long trip, he would meet him in the city. The trip back home, was as in most cases, a great deal faster than the trip to the farm. Sabor pulled into the garage and entered the side door of the family home. Simply soaking in the entirety of the rooms. Every cobweb, every creaky floorboard had a story. He accepted a simple fact as he looked around; this was to be one of the last times he would be here for awhile.

Sabor smiled, plopping himself in his father's old dusty chair and turned on the television. The news was blaring yet again and his favorite anchorwoman was delivering headlines.

"The late story this evening is a bleak one, ladies and gentlemen. The crime rate in the city has skyrocketed, throughout the past six months. A recent poll put the murder rate at an all time high. Never before has a plague of premature death descended upon our fair city in such a way. I am standing here at another crime scene on a fifth night in a row. Excuse me. Serena Valiant with eyewitness news. Could you tell me, Chief Lindstrom, who was this young lady? And do you have any leads in the recent string of murders?" The young brunette woman finished, shoving the microphone into the visually upset policeman' s face.

"No! You know I have no comment on the cases over the past few weeks. I have told you that, on and off the record many times Ms. Valiant. As for who the young lady is, all we know for sure is, it was a woman and I stress the word, was,"

Sabor looked at the screen, having recognized a street light, which flickered like a strobe light, in the background. "Wait just a damn minute, that's just outside Chelle's place. She hasn't called, or anything,"

A horrific thing then happened, as I watched as well. The paramedics, removing the body, tripped on the wet pavement, dropping the revolting remains out into the streets, on a live broadcast. Unmistakably Chelle's blood soaked face lay in the trickling black water of the gutter. The angry policeman grabbed the cameraman by the lens, flinging him to the ground, but not before he focused on the young ladies face.

Sabor rested, seated on the floor, silently in the dark. All of the pictures that once created a mosaic of memories on the wall towered in a pile on the floor behind him. He sat holding one particular frame, rocking back and forth, sobbing. He heard of the murder, and was first filled with rage. It grew into fear of what he would do without the woman to whom he had pledged his life. Then it tapered off, turning from fear into an unsatisfying void. The hole left from his Fathers passing grew three-fold and swiftly filled with hatred.

Sabor stared into his hands, concentrating on the new pulsing lights surging in time with his heartbeat. The veins of his forearms felt alive with light. The small contours of his hands seemed to glow as well. This was odd to him, no doubt, but it paled to the other happenings in his life. Why was his family being targeted by some mad man? Rage filled his body, knowing that someone had the blood of his father, his girlfriend, and who knew whom else, on their hands. Maybe he could track him down and kill him. Maybe his revenge could be slow and painful, making the bastard pay for taking his world.

As the hate built in him, his face grew red, a look of untainted malice broke his normally happy features and he began to lose control. He sprang to his feet, the glow billowing from him. He flipped onto the wall, shifting himself to the side and darting through the air rolling to a sudden halt. He saw himself in the full-length mirror on the opposite wall. He looked magnificent. His eyes shot out spirals of amber and white magic. The soft light gave his sharp features an even more angular appearance. His muscles seemed to grow before his very eyes. He felt as if all of his movements were not his own, as if he was outside himself watching.

A strange pulling inside his forearms forced his attention to the tendons and bone. The fibers in the arm appeared to move instinctively. Sabor's mouth dropped open as "Shkkt," Sabor's weapon slithered out for the first time. A jagged, highly polished blade pierced the skin just above his wrist. He also noticed the rash had formed into a solid line, almost a neon orange tint painted the skin around it. The design was no longer sporadic and unkempt. It was a smooth polished line, and indeed was the crest.

"What is this?" He pondered as the blade pushed itself out inch by inch, revealing the intricate designs and deadly ridges. It was the most beautiful thing he had ever seen. The strangest, but it seemed so familiar, as if it had always been there. This he seemed to know without being aware of it. This marked his first step to his own *Discovery*. The blade stopped growing at three and one half feet long. The blade, dripping with magical spirals and flashes of multi-colored lights, seemed to breathe. The room was dancing, alive with these phantom-like lights.

Sabor marveled at the new appendage. The light hurting his eyes if he looked directly into the luminescent sabor. "Oh my God!" Sabor said as he rubbed his hand along the length of the blade and shaking his head in disbelief at his condition. "Well, they were right, my birthday is certainly something special,"He said as the monstrous blade retracted, concealing itself inside his forearm, then back out again.

Outside, Saimus had appeared on my balcony. "Has he heard? Tell me Cranden, am I too late?" He urgently pushed me for to answer.

"He has heard old friend, and he for now, has accepted it. You don't give him enough credit. He is after all, always under my eye, telling me everything. And I am pleased to rely that he has also begun the *Discovery*, he is changing. And his progress is very impressive. I have never seen anyone so in touch, so fluid, on his inaugural day. The boy has his sword out, playing with it now,"

I had to laugh at the look I received, but I had done my job, keeping an eye on our star pupil. Even if he didn' t know I could talk, he always knew I would listen.

"So the Solitaire is ready. He has harnessed h is hate, and overcame it? I am relieved, what a welcome turn of events in the halls. Maybe he will indeed vanquish the hate, and bring an end to the death. I am hopeful, but... " His tone seemed uncertain.

"Saimus, if I may be so bold, shouldn't you go in and properly begin his *Discovery*?" If I hadn't interjected, the man would have stayed out there all night.

"Yes, oh, yes I am sorry; you are right as always my dear Cranden. First though, I have a question for your all-seeing eyes,"Saimus said, as he paused, and placed a hand on my shoulder.

"Yes, of course ask me anything friend,"I answered.

"Is the Slumber upon us this night, or is the time of death to continue?"

I had no choice but to give him my honest opinion.

"Old friend, I know the dreams of the Elders, for I have had them too. I also know what the teachings say. They both go hand in hand. The salvation will come to us with the *Discovery* of a solitaire, coinciding with the Slumber. And the solitaire has begun. I don't see the beast anywhere, but he is a shifty character and his shadows consume all. I cannot see him, but he is still there.

What' s more, I think he knows that young Sabor is a special boy, maybe even the one who will bring about his end. That is why he is focusing on the

38

young one's family, and why he is stretching the time between Slumbers. For this Master Elder, I think he will be weak. This gives us time to train for this time of the Slumber begins tonight. Whether the beast wants it or not. I have seen these things in the faces on the street, they are unconsciously relaxing, and somehow they know the Slumber is near. Now go. Sabor needs you. Do not worry, I will keep a watchful eye on things down here,"

He agreed and pushed open the balcony doors. The flowing silk curtains engulfed him rippling, around, blown by the wind, allowing the noise of the city to saturate the room.

"Young nephew, I see your *Discovery* has found you alone. You are not meant to deal with all of this, not in this manner, but circumstances have made it so that you needed some time alone. Our situation has become grave and the time for your full Discovery is upon us. So in the morning you will come with me. But first, put your sword away, please you scare me. Get some sleep, I will be back for you as soon as I can in the morning," and He smiled a gentle smile, and motioned him to get some sleep.

The killing wasn' t ging to end. I was right; Dvanken was trying to prolong his stay this time. He wished to keep the attention of The Order, so they could not teach Sabor, at least the way he needed to be taught. The stench of death was thick this night, and Dvanken hungered, in fact the longer he delayed his Slumber the hungrier he became. Deep in a crevice he scanned the street. He knew the preacher would be by in a few minutes. Billton Coliffson, that was his name.

A hypocritical saint and a power hungry businessman, he juggled them both the best a man of his intelligence could. His egocentric, chauvinistic ways were only be overshadowed by his bull shit. He walked with an air of pseudo-confidence, pseudo because deep down he knew his soul was impure. He felt destined to go to the place he condemned so many in his congregation to in every sermon. Hell would be a welcome end for him. He would not give up his ways on this earth just to get into a heaven, especially since in his mind this heaven he was striving for wasn't promised. His life was a prime example of duplicity. On one hand he played the part of holy man and on the other a sinner extraordinaire.

The reasons loomed large. He had been caught having sex with an employee in the parking lot of his workplace. In return for keeping his job, he satisfied the plant manager, orally. The feelings of that day haunted him. You see, he had been molested as a young child. His nights filled with visions of the man's face, which had stolen his innocence. He lived with so many demons. He lived with so much fear and pain, never knowing if his employees' would find out and make him relive the hurt. Or worse, someone might report him to the company men and CEO's, who would most certainly take away the tiny measure of power he had. After all, having his masculinity taken from him in other ways, his job as a supervisor remained the only thing that made him feel like a man. Taking it from him would be a fate worse than death, in his skewn mind.

Dvanken loved the taste of a true hypocrite. Hypocrisy was the sweetest tasting negative of them all, but finding a pure hypocrite proved almost impossible. People often carry two faces; some lie looking straight-faced, and never blink. Coliffson could stand and lie to himself, as well as a congregation of people, and knowingly lie to his God. Then he could go out and screw a co-ed and never think twice. He stood tall, embodying the truest form of hypocrisy and a welcome meal for Dvanken. The only thing missing from the meal, was blood boiling fear? The kind of fear that turns men white. Dvanken would enjoy this, and he would do it slow to savor the nearly unique taste.

The preacher scurried along on his small legs, almost a shell; his hair was done perfectly. His chipper mood masked his true fear, always looking over his shoulder. He handled his business dealings with the delicacy of a bull, and so made many enemies. Many promises of death always hung inches from his head. This day found him doing errands and whistling. His pace quickened, and he didn't know why. He feverishly looked around, as he felt the pressure of eyes on his back. Panic boiled over.

Dvanken scurried along the wall, masking himself like a chameleon, changing pigment to perfectly suit the partition he had clung to. This power had never been inside him before. Perplexed and ecstatic about his new capability, he vaulted down upon the street, licking his lips. He crept along slowly, following close behind his target.

"Hello preacher mans. Nice day to die, isn't it? I think your insides will be the sweetest I have consumed in a lifetime," He softly imprinted his words in the mind of the reverend. Coliffson's pace quickened, but for no reason because his pursuer had frozen everyone, the birds, the cars, even the watch on his arm was stopped, everything but him.

"What is this? What the hell has gotten hold of me? Why have you chosen me?" The coward spoke quickly. "I am a man of God and I alone control his armies. Leave me or I will call upon them, sending you to your death!" The pompous holy man yelled running past the various scattered still life' s on the street. Knocking their belongings to the ground as he pushed by, he fled from whatever unknown followed him. With every step, he plunged deeper and deeper in the sorrow of his impending death. He was uncertain after all his words of condemnation towards others; he realized how much they should have meant to him inside the confines of his own existence. How easy it is to see your faults, when death arrives at your door, ready to collect your debt.

"Surely gospel man, or should I call you an ally for evil, in your teachings, I am certain you have taught you reap what you sow. I have been there when you proclaim you are a preacher on Sunday, and a business man the rest of the week. Well Hypocrite, today is Thursday, and your judgment is here. Do you wish to rethink your devotions? If so, I do know he is forgiving," the hellish creature told him this, not knowing why but with the words, he slowly revealed himself, coming out of his new toy.

Billton, seeing the aberration for the first time, stumbled and pissed himself. Looking up at the huge creature poised above him, he asked. "Kill me, for I am ready. I have my house in order, and I will be in the house of the Lord when you are done, peaceful and happy in my oasis. PLEASE, PLEASE!"

Dvanken roared back that moment saying. "Ssssshhhhhh, say not another word. That is all I need to hear to take away your pain and hypocrisy, and I am afraid if your mouth keeps moving, I will let your God handle your sorry ass. Believe me maggot, you want me to do this instead. The oasis that you seek is a place only for the truly holy and your two-faced nature is not welcome there. Besides, your imperfections will taste perfect to me,"

The entire conversation saw the greenish-purple haze grow, flooding the scene. A red hat of miasma sealed off the sky. The electric pulses screamed past their heads, popping the ground. The deep tan and always strong demeanor of Billton faded, leaving a pale hump of sniveling man.

Dvanken's jaws opened, releasing the stink of rotting flesh and a musky hint of sulfur. He raised his face to the sky, then snapping his head down, slammed the chest of the preacher hard to the ground. Then, seizing Billton's shoulders, Dvanken shook the man until the drool and blood poured from his face.

He slammed Coliffson's head down saying to him,"And another thing, you little worm, and I am *NOT* a demon. I am a creation like you, and I really loathe the comparison, which will make this even more enchanting,"The force of the blow crushed the back of his skull, exposing brain and hollowing half the bowl of bone onto the ground.

The man was alive, and remained conscious. His wounds forced his head to point towards his feet. He watched the gigantic razors Dvanken had for teeth slice through his stomach, exposing the foul odor inside. As the stink billowed out, the hungry beast reached in, piercing the intestines. Dvanken pulled them out, and lay them on Coliffson's chest. The sight of the reddish-yellow fat and pale pink tubes proved too much for the small-minded fool on the ground. He cried out to any that would listen:

"Oh my God, why would you do this to me, after everything I have done for you?" The words teemed with hate and resentment.

"I guess you weren' t listening to me earlier. I said, that I wanted to do this, so SHUT-UP!"Dvanken said, amazed that even after all he had told him, Coliffson still wouldn't change. He snarled, and growled, dripping with the insides of the fallen man, At that moment, he crushed the skull with his enormous right forearm.

With the last breath oozing from the body, Dvanken smiled. He knew the man would taste magnificent, and he may not get such a chance for some time. He savored every bite, ripping off small pieces of internal organs. Finally he came to the spine. Reaping it from the body, he popped the vertebrae off one by one, sucking out the nectar from each. His eyes rolled back in ecstasy. With a shudder, he clutched the rest of the body, and carried it off.

Dvanken arrived at the office where Coliffson worked. He now took the man's dignity as the desert. He hung the body over the canopy where his co-workers and colleagues would see him. Dvanken crouched in a shadow, watching as the people filed out. With an eerie appeal that made him love these humans even more, they collapsed in small piles weeping. Some were doing it because they didn't know Coliffson's lies, others did for they knew them all and felt no remorse, and still others wept to fit in with the crowd, but all were astonished by the sight. Dvanken slithered off, feeling satisfied with the pain he had caused.

Blaring, the news came on interrupting the regularly scheduled program. The well kept woman sitting behind the well-lit desk proclaimed the respected minister, and business man Billton Coliffson was slain in a brutal slaying, then his body was hung outside his place of business. The news anchor then suggested that in perhaps some form of bizarre Satan worshiping ritual.

The Order sat in their respective homes watching the news and shaking their heads in disbelief. Sabor and Saimus sat together watching the breaking news in disgust as well.

"We must start the training. We must. This delay in the Slumber is very troubling indeed. Why is he prolonging the inevitable, why? We must hurry," Saimus was obviously upset, so Sabor sat back shaking his head at the news he heard.

"Uncle, I know this is off the subject, but should I still be mourning the death of my Dad," the young Guardian inquired.

"My boy, I am so sorry. This is a tremendous burden on a man, losing one of the constants in his life. Of course you should mourn, but you should not let it rule your decisions, or any other aspect of your day. Don't worry though my nephew, sometime in the near future, I will teach you how to deal with your feelings of rage, sadness. And all the other emotions swarming in your head. But for now, know I am here for you, and keep revenge far away from your train of thought. Do this for me and for your dead loved ones," He wanted to ease the pain, not add to it by force feeding the young man all of life's harsh truths at once.

"Okay sir, I will," he agreed, but did not understand why he couldn't just show him right then. The loss hurt so much. He knew he had to go on though, because no amount of wishing or tears would bring either his father or his love back. He would strive to remember, remember the way she laughed, the way she smelt, the way she would scrunch her mouth when he would do something crazy to impress her. And his father would be easy to remember. He was dad.

"Uncle, I have spoken with Dad. He came to me last night. Well at least I think it was him. I had just drifted off to sleep, when I felt something wet hit my cheek. It was salty, like a tear. Above me was a strange white cloud. My Dads' voice, I heard him say to keep my words in my heart, remember he would always be there, and he told me that he loved me. Then he thanked me. Why would I have that dream when I was awake?"

"My dear boy, the mind is a wonderful thing. Not only does it give us the abilities we have, but it also allows us to control them. It does have its drawbacks sometimes, like bad memories. But it gives us hope too, in the ability

44

to remember. Maybe your mind gave you a gift. Or maybe he was there,"Not anxious to give everything up, Saimus felt amazed that Sabor could talk to the dead members of The Order, on only his second day as a Guardian. This act was astonishing. He hadn't even started the Discovery yet. This was truly a great man sitting on his floor.

"We will talk about this later. Now I have to get your things ready for your journey. Relax and remember what I have said, and what your father has said. I love you Sabor, and I hope you know how important you are,"His wise uncle had never spoken to him like this, and Sabor was a little uncomfortable.

"Thank you unc, I will,"He went back to being consumed by the glowing television, totally oblivious to everything that had just happened, as his uncle raced off to the Halls of The Order.

The day flew by as Sabor watched TV and Saimus prepared everything. Saimus called The Order to a full meeting with every member to attend. The discussion needed everyone present.

He snuck to the meeting hall. It was an impressive structure, shooting almost straight up with hard wood railings and intricate carvings spiraling around each one. Large wood chairs, covered in purple leather, featured a golden crest inset each headrest. A golden cup sat in front of each one. A large painting of the first battle between the Sabor Guardians and Dvanken was elegantly lighted on the ceiling.

An enormous flat section of floor was set aside for the speaker. Any brother of The Order could speak freely there. On this particular night, the platform belongs to Saimus Lindon, a head Elder and a respected man in all walks of his life. The four halls leading into the massive room bustled, with rumors, and gossip, none knowing exactly why the meeting was called.

Saimus broke through the door, and all talking stopped, as all eyes turned to him. He smiled, looked at each member with love, and spoke.

"Everyone, this is a grave time this fact cannot be mistaken, but come with me and I will help put some fears to rest,"He proceeded into the meeting hall of The Order, assuming his place at the podium. A strange bell controlled by the speaker chimed, signaling the time had come for everyone to sit. The halls slowly emptied, and each chair was soon occupied by a great man. Three hundred and fifty was the number of The Order, and they were all there, save Elder Zandalar. His chair remained vacant, staring each one of them, in the face.

"Guardians, we are a proud group, an ancient group. We fought and trained together from as far back as I can remember. Now our common bond,

Dvanken pushes us closer to extinction. We cannot allow this to happen. My brother has been slain. I do not want another to perish. We all know how the cycle goes. For twenty years, the beast kills. And for five years he sleeps. We are upon the Slumber now, but our foe does not seem to be content, to just go to sleep.

"I fear Dvanken has grown powerful enough to avoid his Slumber, and will continue killing. This is my theory. Other members of The Order believe he is merely putting the Slumber off, trying to draw conflict. Trying to push us into doing something obtuse. Either way, death is still coming, and we have not been able to kill the beast, or force it to sleep.

"The news spoke of a preacher dying in the way of Dvanken tonight. But it told much more to those who know how to listen. It spoke of a new more dangerous enemy, one who risks being seen in the daylight, or one who cannot be seen. He has become bold, becoming everything we have hoped he would not. He is getting greedy. The most recent killings trouble us in other ways. He clearly shows emotion, He is starting to think about the repercussions to The Order, and not just the added pain each death will causes Man. He grows, and after this Slumber I fear he will be too strong even for us the human Guardians to handle. The horror he inflicted may be over my brothers.

"The teachings of the History are very unclear on who exactly The Avenger will be. With the passages concerning the parents of the One, hanging as the only opposition, the Lindon line seems to have a very fine candidate. The young solitaire, Sabor Lindon began his Discovery, and is starting to learn on his own. I remind you of this, because another class is not beginning at this time, he is alone. He has the knowledge to manipulate his sabor; he has also spoken of the Plane of The Order and his contacts with it. These things came much sooner to him than any Knight of The Order I have trained and would wager the same to you all. His Discovery has begun and the twentieth season since the fall of Caden Divin has ended. The Slumber should be upon us, yet the killings persist.

"I need the help of The Order to create a net of sorts. We need to know everything even more than normal. We need our senses at full boar we need complete intelligence vision. We must know when the time of the stillness begins. The Slumber must be watched intently and brought to our attention immediately. EXTINCTION, this is what we are up against. The total loss of mankind, so please do not take me lightly, we cannot afford to let Dvanken get an advantage, and he will use it against us.

"Now if there are no questions, or if no one else wants the floor, I will dismiss this meeting, and send us to our assignments,"His grand, deep voice echoed throughout the hall, sending the incoherent whispering into a storm of excitement. Every Guardian, Knight, and Elder seemed stunned by his almost definite proclamation of Sabor Lindon as the Avenger. The Solitaire from the teachings of The History. Although the evidence was overwhelming, the statement still rang bold, taking all of them by surprise, even Master Saimus.

"I must go and oversee the Discovery of my brothers' son. I beg each of you to keep your eyes open. Thank you, my brothers,"His large frame stepped down and strode through the huge castle-style oak double doors behind him. Having said his peace in the hall, he stormed off, not angrily, but deliberately saying nothing to anyone. He was fixed on getting back to Sabor, to begin the Education of Sabor Lindon.

The Education of Sabor Lindon

Saimus arrived at the house of Zandalar Lindon and started up the decorative steps of the four-story brownstone crammed between the endless tunnel of apartment buildings along the street.

The house was a magnificent piece of architecture. Perched in the front, a large marble set of six steps, with golden rails running on each side, lead to the entrance. The enormous glass door accented with a large iron rod crest stood majestically atop the stairs. A mosaic of beautiful round tiles displayed another crest of The Order on the porch area. A large balcony graced each of the windows on every floor. Each terrace guarded by a pair of large sculptures depicting the Knights of The Order from the Lindon line.

Saimus barged in and announced his arrival. "Lady Noelle, are you in here? It is your brother-in-law Saimus Lindon. I have come to bring you a great bit of news,"

The lovely older woman dressed in very nice clothes, especially for just sitting about the house, wandered into the room were he stood. "You! You're going to take him away from me aren't you? You bastards in that damn club always take the one's I love away. Can't you just leave me my baby? Sabor is special. He doesn't need your brainwashing! He will be just fine here. You just leave him here for me. I am alone with Zandy already gone and Chelle taken away. Just leave my boy alone!" The hysterical woman was beating him on the chest crying uncontrollably.

Saimus, consumed with emotion, wanted to leave the boy for this woman who had given so much and never asked anything in return. But he knew the boy she spoke of could make all of the pain bleed from the world. And this was something he would risk everything for.

"Noelle, my sweet sister, you have always been the loving one. The one we all have ran to for our daily dose of sanity. You are my strength, just as you were my brothers. I will never forgive myself for what has happened, or for my never being here as much as was needed. And even though I will be taking your son for a while, I assure you of that, with all of my heart, it is only temporary. He has a path before him and no choices where to go. He needs your support most of all. He was born for this, you know that, and you must accept it. His journey will not be an easy one," The woman's face went from heartbreaking and tear soaked to understanding.

48

"You see Noelle, you are right. He is special, very special. And he will make you and his father proud. No matter what happens, he will live a long life. You can take that on my word as a Lindon. Say your good-byes, and keep them just that, good," The words made her calm and his appearance made her believe.

"You take care of him then. Help him with life; help him more so with death. Saimus, you promise me now, promise me he...will love again. Promise me he will see a young blonde haired boy running in these halls screaming and shooting unseen enemies with a plastic gun, dressed in nothing but superhero underpants. Promise me this or I cannot give you my son, she said smiling, reassuring Saimus she would help no matter what, the words heavy with a serious edge.

"You are promised m'lady. Above that, I swear to you, you will see your grandchildren,"

With that she stepped aside, crossed her arms, and rubbed them vigorously up and down, erasing the cold shiver the conversation gave her. She was being forced for the third time in as many days to give up her love, and she was being asked to do it with a smile. Something only a mother could do, and she would do it with the grace and power of the Lindon name.

Saimus walked past and took the lift up to Sabors' room. He entered reflecting on the heartache he would cause the widow downstairs with his actions, but no matter, he had to do it.

"My boy, have you slept well this night?" He asked. He gazed around the room, seeing no shadow, no form. He saw no one. He frantically threw open the closet. All of the clothes were gone. He turned around briskly to see that all of Sabors' things were gone. The room had been cleaned out.

"CRANDEN! Where is the," he yelled before he had gotten out of the room onto the balcony,"...boy ?!" He finished, sounding very upset.

I glared back at him with a mischievous grin. "He is there,"

I pointed to the smiling youngster perched on the shoulder of his fathers' favorite statue, a likeness of Sabor's Grandfather. Sabor smiled, pointing to several suitcases and trinkets scattered about on the balcony.

"All this fuss over little o' me unc? I am truly flattered,"

The boy was having as much fun as I was with Saimus. Let's face it, all of the brothers in The Order could use a little fun in their diet, especially with

49

Dvanken's recent scare tactics.

'Sabor, this is not funny. You are much too important to be playing games like this. Now come and bring one suitcase with nothing but hygiene products. That is all you will need, The Order will supply everything else you will need,"he scolded the young student, trying to make him see his place. Sabor obeyed as he was told, preparing his things.

The two men had a rapport that suggested they had lived together everyday for years. In fact The Order had kept Saimus away, but the bond was there. Sabor and Saimus came down to the first floor into a grand entryway. The room split a game room on one side and a living room on the other. Noelle crouched on the large woven area rug. It held embroidered with the design of The Order. Much like everything in the house, the crest was everywhere.

Noelle stared at the large painting above the huge marble fireplace. The painting depicted the whole family. Young Sabor looked so mad. On the morning they had the painting made, his father told him he would have to wait to learn how to drive until he was older. The memory broke through the sadness and left a hint of a smile on the aging woman's face.

The two men entered the room, standing one on each side, placed a hand on each of her shoulders, and looked up at the portrait she was admiring.

'I was so mad at him. I think it took me about three months to forgive him totally for not letting me get behind the wheel. I thought if he could do it, then I should be able to. What a brat. Glad to see a smile on your face, Mom even if it's only a half hearted one. Mom come up here, I need a hug,"Sabor said reaching out to his smiling Mom. Noelle looked up into his big eyes and began to cry. 'Please don't cry. I'll be back soon, and we'll get another picture done. Okay? This time I promise I won't ruin it with my attitude,"He instantly felt warm, and so did Noelle. Saimus was amazed at how much his nephew had grown.

'Besides Noe, I already promised you. This journey, it's not forever. It will be over when he learns to control that attitude of his,"

They shared a good chuckle, and then Noelle smiled at them both, kissed them gently on the cheek, and whispered,"My boys. Thank you so much for trying to make me feel better. It worked, I have almost forgotten that you are going to steal my son and that my one and only baby is leaving me,"Noelle said with a tiny hint of humor.

'But, Mom that's not what's going on. Uncle Saimus isn't stealing anything;"Sabor said then was interrupted by his mother.

50

"I am only playing, my boy. I knew you wouldn't stay here forever. It's just this is too soon. But I guess it wouldn' t matter if you were one hundred years old. You will always be my little Sabe. Don't worry about me, I will be okay and so will you, my son just go,"She pulled him close, and kissed him on the ear.

"Take care. Always remember I love you and anything you want, you can achieve. You are a Lindon and that means a lot. I love you and will keep your room ready for you. Bye,"The words stung Sabor, but he somehow knew he had to leave. Not tomorrow, or even in a few hours. He had to go then and it made him sad.

"Come Sabor, It is time for us to go,"Saimus grabbed Sabor's bag as the young man squeezed his Mom one last time before his new journey.

Then the pair headed outside to the curb below. Sabor stepped into Saimus' long black car. With one last longing look, he stared at his childhood home. How he loved it. A single salty teardrop trickled down his right cheek.

"Sabor, stop looking at this place as if it were the last time you will ever see it. You will be here again. You will raise children here, just as you were. I made a promise, and you will come back, even if I have to drag you here myself,"the old man chuckled at his joke and squeaked the vehicle from the curb.

They proceeded down streets Sabor had been down millions of times, but for some reason he felt as if he was seeing them for the first time. He took in every red brick building, every painted window, all of the children playing in the fire hydrant, the squirrels playing tag in the tree's, and every sprig of grass in the cracks of the gray concrete sidewalk. Everything moved in slow motion, everything fuzzy and surreal.

Blasting the unadulterated confusion of the moment, Saimus said,"You are on your journey now. No more distractions, young Lindon. Take the pain you are feeling and turn it into joy. Harness it and you will learn the true bliss of being a Guardian.

"The 'Order"is a society. It protects the knowledge of an evil no man possesses. It is the sole heir to the power of the sabor. The power these blades give us, is unmatched. But this is not without a huge cost to us all. You are immortal, now and forever, but with your immortality you must and will fight. And with each slice of your new dagger you will age, dying a little each time you spill the blood of your enemy.

"For the peace it will bring, we will all gladly give this, freely. We pay to purge the world of this evil, to bring the end to unnatural death. Do you understand your destiny? Do you think you can fight, for your kind? Your father was one of us, Sabor. We kept this from your mother and you, to shield you from the harshness of being a Guardian. Your mother wouldn't have let her Zandalar out of the house, if she knew it was to go off and fight. You, you were pretty young and destined to be a Guardian, so you had to remain happy, free of pain or suffering. For this deceit, I am sorry Sabor, but as you will see it was all necessary,"The old man babbled on, Sabor only catching bits and pieces.

"Uncle, what are you talking about? What evil are we fighting? Is it the guy who killed my Dad cause if it is I swear to you, I'm gonna kill him,"Sabor snapped without thinking.

"Good, now put a leash on that and we'll have our savior,"

They pulled up to the perimeter of The Halls, a large white brick fence with bronze accents stood dividing Sabor from his destiny. The large gate was formed from sculpted metal tweaked into the crest with the names of The Order formed onto the top. Legendary names like, Lindon, Vettin, Linx, Danglin, Divin stood proud. Beyond this gate lay a sprawling field of tall fescue. Sprinkled about on the plains were, remnants of large statues the constant wind had weathered each into rounded stubs, each standing six to eight feet above the dancing green grass. A narrow road lay before them, littered with the names of what appeared to be fallen warriors carved into the earth. The lane weaved in and out of the weeds, connecting the outside world with the interior of the Guardians world.

"The entrance to the Caverns of the Teachings and The Halls of The Order," Saimus said pointing to the distant horizon, a quarter of a mile away. They crept towards the site, barely letting the car more than idle down the road.

"This is it. This is how it all begins, huh? This mysterious thing I've been waiting my whole life to do, but never knew about any of it," Wondered Sabor aloud.

The entrance was guarded by two magnificent granite Gargoyles standing thirteen feet above the tall grass. A long, winding road went far into the earth beyond the two immense rock figures. The car slammed to an unexpected halt. The young man glared at his uncle, his eyes asking. 'What the hell was that all about?' Saimus glanced back, nodded his head, and smiled. He then reached for the door handle and stepped out of the car. Eager to get this experience started, Sabor quickly followed stumbling and forgetting his bag.

"Young Greenling, you will not get far with just the clothes on your back. Get your bag please," Saimus shook his head and started walking into the cavern.

"Wait u p! I'm coming Saimus. Please wait," Sabor sprinted, trying his best to catch the wise Elder who was now many yards in front of him.

Inside the shadowy depths that lay just behind the hooded door, an unforgiving walkway waited with shear drop offs on each side and with nothing but a dark abyss welcoming whomever fell. Torches marked every ten yards along the path. With no walls to see, the torches seemed to float by some enchantment, that also swirled about them in the dark spaces not lit by the torches. The air was wet and an unmistakable electricity emanated from everything.

The two spiraled down into the blackness on a brown stone staircase. The path widened a little as they walked. Sabor quickly searched his surroundings, since they had slowed down, and around them walls began to creep out of the shadows. A white mist escalated from the floor. A tremendous round materialized in front of the Guardians. The ceiling drew to a high point at the top. A long spiral of light swirled from the summit, creeping down to the floor. The dim light illuminated carvings lining the walls.

"The busts of all whom have been brothers of The Order," Saimus solemnly explained. A place of great importance hung above the door. A hollow depression with a haunting scripture below it read, The *Avenger will appear, the Solitaire will control our destiny. This man belongs here. The peace will follow him.*

"You will be there, if you believe," a booming voice echoed from around them. Saimus seemed to not hear the deafening sound, however. Sabor covered his ears and fell to the ground.

Saimus looked down at the boy and said sternly, "This hallowed place has no room for your childish games. Stand and step through. *Discovery* awaits,"

The voice was everywhere, but nowhere. It was strange. And it sounded familiar. It was Zandalar. He was encouraging Sabor. It made Sabor feel wonderful, like he could do anything.

"Uncle, can you not hear him? Can you not hear dad?" Sabor asked looking so happy.

"My boy, you shouldn't be hearing him yet you haven't even stepped into the *Discovery*," Saimus was surprised and barely willing to believe the boy, since he hadn't heard it himself. But Sabor had no reason to fake this, or even the knowledge that it would at some point be possible for him to accomplish such things. It left no choice, but blind faith and a watchful eye form the Elder. What wonders would Sabor surprise him with next?

"Uncle; I want you to know I will give whatever is beyond this room everything I have. So please relax, for I will need your help, that much I am sure of,"

The reassuring words gave serenity to Saimus, as he reached for the huge door handle. The door clunked with a sudden jerk. Dust that had collected for some months was whisked around by a strong swirling wind. The wind nearly knocked the two men down. The room on the opposite side was well lit and in the center was a huge statue of a four armed man clothed in long robes. Beneath was the armor of the Knights of The Order. At his feet were two women and a small baby. The detail was awe-inspiring, almost looking at the two, begging them to come inside. The room seemed to consume Sabor. The various paintings depicting the different chapters in the Guardians history burned themselves into Sabor's memory. The paintings were elegant, but some were beginning to look frayed and weather-beaten. The floor was uneven rock with small iron pyramids lacing the grout between the stones. The walls appeared to be hand carved from the limestone, and granite of the original cave walls. It formed a large oval room with three immense oak doors. Again torches floated around the door jams. A soft white and amber glow springing from the molecules of the air flowed everywhere. Each door bore a description on a decorative plaque.

"These are the chambers of *Discovery,* my boy. We are in the Great Hall of the Brotherhood. The spirits here all noble, they give this place its beautiful glow. Beyond these halls lay the challenges and the lessons that will shape your life from this point on. The things you need will come from the people and experiences of this place. Watch all you can. Be a sponge. Soak in the experience.

"I will return, for I too have my part to play in your Discovery, but for now, I have to check our intelligence, to see how much activity has been. I must find if the evil is sleeping, or if his trap is widening. You must go to a man called Ellett Vettin. He waits for you in one of these chambers. He is wise, listen intently to his every word. You will learn the bulk from him,"

Saimus exited, leaving Sabor wondering still. What was he doing, Sabor he asked himself, fighting his urges to follow the great man walking away from him? Sabor turned slowly and started towards the door marked with the plaque that read. *"The road to knowledge begins with the first step behind this door,"*

Sabor took a deep breath and choked down his feelings of fear and uncertainty. He shoved the door, pushing very hard because it appeared to be a huge solid oak door. The door slammed against the wall behind with a loud thump. The corridor behind the massive door was long and at first very dark. At the end of the hall a dim light called the confused learner. He tread lightly down the hall into the darkness. He took thirteen steps into the blackness, before the large aperture slammed tightly behind him.

Startled Sabor yelled out "Damn it, what the hell is going on?" He dove back from where he had just come, grasping in vain at the darkness where the door had just been. "DAMN IT," he stood up, dusting himself off. He had gashed his elbow on the floor, and it was bleeding pretty badly.

Laughter started to echo softly, throughout the hall. A man, and for that matter a very large man with a peculiar glow about him, illuminated the tunnel. He laughed louder, clapping his hands sarcastically, then strolled up to Sabor, extending a hand.

"Hello Sabor. My name is Ellett, Ellett Vettin; " the man in front of Sabor was a large square framed man. His arms exposed, his sleeves apparently cut from his garments. A beautiful dragon tattoo encircled his left arm, originating below his elbow and ending breathing a large flame across his basketball-sized deltoid. He stood around six foot five inches tall. His eyes, sunken and intense, but with a definite gentleness, pierced Sabor to the core. His face was square, and defined. A thin line of a beard lined his face, accenting the square jaw line, then bushing out into a bushy goatee. His massive build made Sabor stare in disbelief. This enormous man was the most intelligent Elder, in the entire order. Sabor knew there had to have been a mistake. Ellett seemed more suited to be the weight lifting champion or something along those lines.

"You're Ellett? The man who is gonna teach me everything about my destiny? How do you suppose you can do that? You don't look any older than me. What makes you so wise?" Sabor said, convinced this was some sort of joke. Yeah sure this fellow was large, but he had a youthfulness to his face. How could this be the person, who would guide his future? How could he tell Sabor more about himself than his own Uncle, Saimus?

"Young Guardian, you must stop knowing what you know, or this experience will end very badly for you. The enemy we fight century after century, eon after eon will prey on everything you bring to battle, your fear, your disbelief, and your pain. Therefore, you must forget them, if you cannot forget, then you must change. Switch your pain for happiness, your sorrow for joy, this is the essence of the Guardian and the strange new blades you posses They are your personal essence, keep them happy,"

The instructor went straight to his task of filling Sabor with the knowledge of the past as they walked down the hall. Large buttresses raised the huge ceilings, bracing the tons of rock from falling. The hall floor was a polished, almost glass-like, stone. A light, flowing through the cracks revealed the path. The light, the strange amber and white illumination, seemed surround Sabor since this whole *Discovery* started.

"Why is everything around me glowing? This white and orange glow is starting to worry me," Sabor asked.

"The glow is much like your weapon; it contains the essence of The Order. Mysterious and wonderful isn't it? Not I or any other Elder will be able to answer all of your questions for some of the questions in life have no answers, the events and mysteries just happen. A rather fun truth don't you think? As for the lights, they are goodness, they are happiness and they are pure positive energy. Like I said before, they are the essence of The Order," The explanation felt a little longwinded, but was good enough for Sabor.

The statements had taken them to the threshold of the *Library of the Teachings.* Ellett held out his arm as if to tell Sabor to go first. The world on the other side of the door was a night and day comparison to what Sabor had seen so far. The ceilings rose eighty-five feet high. Huge four armed men, with full battle gear and the cloaks of the ancient order, stretched their arms high above their heads keeping each corner of the enormous room from falling in upon itself. The floor gleamed a brilliant version of the entryway in the hall, gloriously radiant. At the other end of the long room, stood a large double-door oval with great iron hinges. The hinges had large gargoyle profiles etched by hand. The light shade of the wood accented every crack in the ancient timber. The door appeared small from were Sabor stood, but the distance did not fooling Sabor. This room was a grand sight, and the distant doors were massive.

Two rows of polished, deeply stained wood cubicles, accented by frosted glass rectangles inserted near the top of each cubicle wall. In each was a smooth glass etching of the crest and a small torch lighting each small box. The cubicles were designed for reading the millions of texts collected by The Order. Behind the cubicles, which stood three deep, were countless rows with countless volumes of dusty script.

The room felt alive with the bustling of the brothers hurrying to learn all they could. In complete silence they went about their tasks, not paying a bit of attention to each other completely engrossed in study and thought. It was an exhausting sight.

"These are the teachings, The volumes of the History and various other texts. The other volumes here contain useful information used to educate us on styles of fighting, weaponry, Dvanken, the history of The Order, everything we here have any knowledge of. " Ellett tried to make the whole thing sound exiting, but one word stood out from the rest.

"Dvanken, what is that Ellett?" Sabor was very intrigued by this word, and he didn't quite know why.

"He is the evil we all speak of. He is death. He is finality. Our enemy in this life and your destiny to defeat. He is the reason we are all Guardians. Our blessings come from the necessity he has brought into the world. Our job has been, and will always be, to bring an end to his reign" The statement was confusing, yet filled in a lot of blanks at the same time.

"So you're saying that I am going to fight the devil?" He asked naively.

"Not at all. Dvanken is a creation. A creation of human nature, a being who sustains himself with our fear or pain. These emotions are his sustenance they live in our spines, which he targets with his ferocity. He will not eat the rest of the body of a Guardian, sort of a sign that he kills us for sport, not for a large meal to keep him alive. Every day, run of the mill people however, these poor souls, he devours completely. His victims in some sort of disgusting power trip are pushed and shown all of the degradation in life, until they give up. He forces them to say "please" He will do nothing until they do so,"

The words began to fill in a puzzle for Sabor. Saimus said his father was a Guardian and he died. Now his life was forced down this road. This path of the Guardian and then, Chelle dies. Actually they were both killed! They didn't die of old age they were stolen from him. And the thief was being forced into the light with this conversation. A hate-filled look painted itself on Sabor's face. The anger pouring forth again, now with a target.

"This Dvanken son-of-a-bitch, where can I find him? He killed Dad didn't he? He slaughtered my Chelle!" A tear cascaded down his red-hot face, pulling a lump into his throat as it fell. The pain, the rage, all became too much. Sabor's soul sucked the darkness he felt deep into the center of his chest. He felt the contraction of all his muscles at once. His breath came strong and hot. His heart felt like an anvil. The agony began to consume him and a faint chuckle resonated from deep inside him. He shook uncontrollably, trying to fight his malice. He collapsed at the waste, hands clasped around his head, crying with rage.

A bright light seeped from the front of his stomach. Suddenly, his body lunged backwards, releasing a shockwave of rage. The etched glass shattered from the circle of percussion bursting from the young man. The room trembled, every Guardian readying themselves to fight, their sabor weapons extended and glowing. Ellett, blown down the hall came to a squeaking halt by the feet of one of the statues holding the ceiling in place.

"My boy, my boy," The amazed teacher shook the concussion off and stared in amazement at what he saw, and felt. The other knights realized what happened and the chatter of gossip echoed throughout the library.

Sabor stood in amazement at what he had done in the middle of the isle; his torn shirt left only strands of cloth hanging from his shoulders. His glow pulsed from amber to a bright white keeping time with his heavy breathing. Both of his massive sabor weapons were fully extended, as if by reflex. He looked down at each of them, watching as they slowly shrank back into his forearms.

"I; I; I'm sorry everyone," stammered the young man embarrassed by his actions. He never knew his anger was so powerful. Ellett walked back to the young learner.

"Sabor, that is amazing. You're anger and rage must be harnessed though, or you or those around you, will be destroyed," Ellett said smirking and laughing a bit. "Dvanken has been around, as long as The Order has. Changing with every kill, growing with every Slumber. He is very intelligent, and he knows how to use your anger against you. That is why you and I and the rest of The Order are here. We will learn what other wonders you posses and teach you how to control those new wonders," The Elder felt out his conversation. He did not want Sabor to know this explosion was something new and very impressive to say the least; for pride was dangerous to a Guardian.

Ellett led Sabor to a cubicle that had not been destroyed by the waves of power the young man had projected. "Sit here, and read everything I bring before you" With that Ellett slowly turned and walked to a fallen, seventy-five foot tall book case and lifted it as if it were a feather. He reached into the dark cherry shelves and grabbed a dusty leather bound, gold and silver-laced book. The cover and spine of the novel were also leather with bright glowing metal rings.

Ellett was standing with a book that almost overshadowed the man holding it. Sabor slowly looked up at the oak of a man standing over him. With a thud and cloud of dust, the book found itself in front of Sabor. The title on the book was simply "HISTORY".

In astonishment and disbelief Sabor announced. "What the... That is thicker than you are sir," For the first time, Sabor showed respect to the Elder. Either because of the awesome size of the man or his position in The Order, Sabor felt a growing respect for him as his time passed in this place.

The book began with an encouraging passage:

"The distinguished eye beholding these words is blessed. For only a true Knight of The Order may look upon the HISTORY. So be at peace, for your Journey is at hand, and your destiny is near, no longer on the horizon. Learn the words they will save you they will guide you. Good Journey, and the best of luck, Guardians.

The background in the library fell dark and silent. All of Sabor's energy went into soaking in what the book had to offer.

The history begins, shortly after man fell out of the good graces of God. The garden, Eden, was a memory to the couple, faded and distant. They lived the best they could, having their world ripped away from them for their sin against God. They conceived two sons, their names being Cain and Abel.

A great deal of jealousy festered and swelled inside Cain. His brother was loved by the Lord and Cain's offerings were dismissed by the Lord as a feeble attempt at a sacrifice. Cain's anger boiled, and the jealousy churned into an uncontrollable force, as a result of the loss of favor in his Lord. Cain was tempted and pushed to rise up against his brother and destroy him.

The Lord God found a void in his perfection, then asked of Cain "Where is Abel, thy brother, Cain?"

He then lied to his God saying," I know not: Am I my brothers' keeper?"

This act pleased Dvanken, who was born from this sibling rivalry. The punishment handed down from God to Cain became too much for any human to bear. And the repercussions of the punishment merely added to the pain, the jealousy, and rage Dvanken desired.

This child of hate, DVANKEN, the ugly aberration, ran rampant over the land. His destiny had been placed in front of him because of jealousy, and his destiny pleased him. He sought to cause as much pain as one could. Talking to the minds of the humans, he preyed on the newly found treats. No human ever knew the predator, only the death he inflicted upon him or her.

The words were troubling. How could this, a holy story taught to him his whole life, be the beginning of the world's death? He was drawn into the pages, trapped by their knowledge. He flowed through the text learning of Dvanken's role in the problems of the world. The History told of the origin of war. It, by it I mean War, begins in the mind, with the pride and hatred of men in power. Dvanken enjoyed toying with the thoughts of generals and dictators to feed on the terror of battle and the hardships of the rebuilding process. Sabor read of another example of this, Hitler's hatred, was feathered, and cared for closely by Sabor's enemy. For Dvanken saw how the outrageously charismatic man would supply him a full belly for generations.

And through Sabor's history, that had until now, always been so cut and dry his entire life, bullet holes of actuality pierced his veil of comfort and let the truth shine through. He realized what hundreds and hundreds of Guardians before him had realized. It was all Dvanken's fault, all of the death, all of the heartache. He did it and he would continue doing it until one of the Guardians stopped him. The harsh realization overcame the boy and he tried to prevent the connection from forming.

"Chelle and Dad they died for nothing. They died,"He glared up into the high ceilings, trying to glimpse his loved ones, straining his eyes for just a single smile from Chelle, or a furled brow from Zandalar. Suddenly, like drawn into a black hole, his face slammed back into the HISTORY needing to find some passage or verse that would make everything coherent.

Time passed, and Sabor grew wise in the HISTORY. A month and a day passed and Sabor had read many volumes, eating when it was time to eat and sleeping when the evening came. Ellett pleased with the progress of the student made many reports to that effect to the other Elder' s. Time accelerated. It seemed as if Dvanken had indeed fallen into his Slumber and Sabor, the Solitaire, had begun his *Discovery*. Could it be as the teachings had written?

The Wrong Way

Elsewhere, familiar woman felt overwhelmed herself. Noelle, so down for lack of a better word, despaired deeply. The pain of losing her precious Zandy, a life long partner, and a young lady, who felt like a daughter to her, being savagely mutilated tore at her heart. She didn' t even have a suitable corpse to mourn. With the flowers not yet even beginning to wilt on the graves, Noelle had to say a premature farewell to her only son, Sabor. For the past month or so she couldn't even remember when her son had left her. She tried to drown the pain with alcohol. The vastness of the house and the echoes of time and memories haunted her with every turn. She had nothing.

Sabor was alive and that made her glad, but she couldn't see him. She couldn't hear his music or his laughter. She wanted to hug his neck, tell him how badly she had missed him, and shower him with the love that her husband could no longer have. The huge house they built with their love now seemed to tear her down with pain. Nothing helped; singing, watching television, inviting friends over, nothing erased the hurt. Zandy was gone. The cancerous grief chewed at her mind causing her chest to collapse on itself.

In a fit of tears she thrashed her clothes to ribbons. She ravaged her face with her neatly manicured fingernails. Noelle frantically scoured the room for some solace, anything that would bring her back to the safety of happiness. Her clouded eyes found no life preserver, the room filled with only obscurity. The aching in her body choked her. She gave in to her bickering thoughts.

"Should I end it all and go to my Zandy?" She asked as she grappled with her will to live. Oh, how she longed to see him. "Or should I stay for my Sabor?"

Staying would mean constant anguish and loneliness. But leaving would bring peace, rest, and her love. These won over the rest. She gave into the pain, letting go, and lost the fight. Her bottom lip quivered She searched to get a handle and whispered,"Please,"She sat in the center of the entrance to the house, dead center. She sat in the middle of the crest.

Staring down at the amber bottle, she swallowed the lump of fear and uncertainty, and opened it slowly. Noelle quickly emptied the entire bottle of sleeping pills she had carried since the departure of her son. Then she finished the bottle of high-dollar vodka she had been drinking. The world let her slip away and this began to frighten her. She laid back, her legs crossed in a rather uncomfortable fashion, her arms outstretched, and her eyes weaving in and out of clarity.

Just as her grasp on life was weakening she glanced up at the picture of Sabor and Zandy on the mantle, the scrapbook she created on her den walls of the happy times now in perfect focus, and she longed for the world she was leaving. Slipping into the black unknown, Noelle cried a single tear. In vain, she desperately tried to grip the life rapidly flowing up and around her, but alas her life was reduced to shards of blackness, as she drifted away from the only reality she had known. She fell hard into the abyss, faster and faster downward. She could see only Sabor, and it made her happy. She was gone, at peace and now resting with her Zandy.

Sabor looked around, searching for Ellett. Not seeing the head Elder, he decided to do some exploring. He wandered down a small corridor created by the bookshelves tumbling into each other. He felt drawn into the small crevice by some unseen voice. The tome he found was a petite book with a plain jacket, the only writing faded, and obscure. He dusted the volume, squinting to read the words,

"The unknown origins," He sat down in the exact place he stood and began to read.

"Reader, You will now find the true origin of the Chosen, and the Avenger who will lay this terrible death to rest. The Order was formed, as you know, with the solitary purpose to defeat Dvanken, an all-consuming creation threatening to one day make the world void, and desolate with his hunger. The natural checks and balances took over, after the day of the birth. For on this day evil was dealt a trump card. Dvanken was a creation unlike any other, Solitaire in nature. So goodness needed a catalyst against the massive

imbalance. Guardians became this catalyst. From this Order of Guardians a Solitaire would arise. A single man, born of two Guardians, who will grow to change everything.

They are the next step in evolution in a way. The goodness emanating from them is the only weapon capable of harming the creation of evil. The sabor weapons were born from this positive energy, herein lies their strength. Evil in its own right, is just as powerful, maybe more so for it is so much more abundant and much easier to sustain with our nature, as humans.

Dvanken grows with every meal; he adapts much quicker than Man does. For this reason it seems we can never win. Many tribes have tried to destroy him, and all are lost.

The Gargoyles, or Granlin leg of The Order, were the first Order of the Balance, they fought valiantly but in the end, only man-made replicas remain to ward off the evil.

The Quatrine, or Quadin leg of The Order, were the second form that goodness took in its evolution. The four armed warriors, drew closest to the glorious day when Dvanken would sleep eternal. But alas their numbers dwindled as the dark one grew stronger.

The human leg has proven a very worthy adversary, but for their greatness, the Solitaire has yet to present himself. The balances require this appearance, or Dvanken will reign supreme over them all as well. The humans are harboring the ultimate weapon however, the Avenger. The Avenger will be born of two Guardians. He will be born a

Solitaire. A single baby born with a single purpose. The Discov. "

The text ended there for as Sabor read, the remnants of the following pages burst to ash and dust in his hands. Leaving only crumbled paper and wavy edges for the end of the book. Leaving so many of Sabor's questions unanswered and leaving the end of the true beginning a mystery yet again.

Sabor decided, with the discovery of the book and its mysterious spontaneous combustion, he would ask Ellett or his Uncle Saimus about the book and what it had said and done. He was extremely confused about the last passage, how could he be the Avenger? How could anyone be the Avenger? There were no women here in The Order, at least not as far as he could see.

"The young Lindon sports a magnificent talent. He leveled the library with some type of energy burst and he has already read the History volumes one through seventeen. His progress is unprecedented. He is leaps and bounds above my other students who have completed the *Discovery*," the other Elders looked at each other, amazed that Ellett was this impressed.

"Does young Sabor have the ability to actually be our Avenger? Or do we have to wait longer to destroy the beast?" Symon asked with sincerity.

"I believe that he is gifted beyond this level of The Order. In fact I am leaning towards the belief he may be the one to save us. He is, after all a Solitaire; " Ellett's answer reflected the sincerity of the question.

From the deep shadow behind the Elders convened in the chamber, came a disapproving groan. Keni Divin stepped out into the light, shaking his head. The Elders turned and gave the young man their attention, as he cleared his throat. Keni demanded their attention with his presence. After all he was the nephew of Elder Symon.

"If you ask me, he is just another punk, not worthy of so much attention. Who cares if he was born a Solitaire, his parents were not both Guardians and that fact is just as important as his solitude. Train him and get him out fighting. I mean, come on, his profile doesn't fit the one that will kill Dvanken. We need to stop looking for the "ONE" and start fighting," Keni's words oozed with green jealousy.

"Young nephew, you must control your jealousy and strive to be positive. Your life outside these halls depends upon it," Symon snapped at his student/nephew.

"Forgive me uncle. I will try and I will achieve," Keni replied dripping with sarcasm. With that an expression of surprise broke Keni's face. And he left in a hurry shouting. "Oh please excuse me, I almost forgot, I am due in the arena for sabor practice. Thank you for your time Elders!"

As he bolted out of the office, his shoulder slammed into an equally eager man running into the room sending them both into a staggering spin, coming to rest facing each other on opposite sides of the hall. It was Sabor, and each young buck wore a stare of dominance on his face.

"Why don't you watch where the hell you're going Greenling, before something painful happens to you? Before I happen to you!" Keni glared hard at Sabor, with his sabor weapon gleaming ready to pounce on the Greenling.

"You had better put your Swiss Army knives away and erase that hate from your eyes, before you force me to finish this little misunderstanding. Just back down, there is no shame in being fearful of what you don't know," Sabor said giving no ground to the Guardian in front of him. The pissing contest lingered in the air, until Keni realized he was still late for sabor practice. Keni presented a last look of disapproval, and darted off.

"Hey Swiss Army, just remember where I am. I'll finish this whenever," Sabor got in the last word, proud of himself and remembering what his mission was before he was so rudely interrupted. He looked down, and the book was on the ground. He grabbed it up, and pushed his way into the head Elders chamber.

"Excuse me sirs, but I have found something in the library I think you would like to see," Sabor sheepishly announced as he slowly entered the room, his head bowed in respect. The Elders, Ellett, Symon, Mason Linx and Saimus all turned and looked upon Sabor in astonishment.

"Why are you here boy? This is a private meeting and you were not invited. Besides every volume in the library has been cataloged and read thoroughly thousands of times. So I'm sure your Discovery can wait until our meeting is over," Mason Linx barked at Sabor in a tone saying he didn't believe this Greenling could possibly be their Avenger.

"Sir I am not trying to interrupt, but this book called to me. I think if you don't wish to see it, then with all due respect, Master Ellett would be more than interested in what it would have to say. Sabor's tone reflected the distaste he had for Mason. Mason stood, erect at attention, being taken back by the strong words of a mere Greenling. He squared his shoulders, and his amber aura swirling about him intensely.

"BOY, you should hold your tongue in these halls. Do you know who I am?" With that he started at the young man.

"Yeah, I know who you are. You were the man up until I came here, that I held responsible for my fathers' death. So please forgive me if I don't buckle and kneel in your presence!" Sabor retorted sarcastically. Sabor took two steps in Mason Linx direction, before he ran head long into a barrier of a man named Ellett.

"You should understand your place here Sabor, Mason is an Elder and demands some respect," Ellett scolded.

"You see my boy we Elders stick together, we demand. " Mason began with a scolding of his own, but was sharply interrupted.

"You too should know your place Elder, and not let the statement of a Greenling entice you into a confrontation. You, above all, must control your anger for you are a Guardian;" Symon chided from his spot.

"I am sorry brother. I lost my focus. It will not happen again,"Mason walked back, returning to his chair.

"Come Sabor. Show us the text,"Symon urged the young man to come forward. Sabor brought the book placing it on the desk before Symon. The book seemed different from the other writings in the library. It had a luminescence about it. It was special.

"Ellett, have you ever seen this volume before?" Symon said, implying he hadn't.

"No brother I don't believe that I have. ' *The unknown origins*.' This is a title I do not recall ever seeing, and a book such as this, I would remember," Ellett turned the book and read from the text, finishing in a few seconds.

He then slid the book back around to Symon, who in turn read a section of the manuscript. His jaw dropped, and he placed the text on the desk. Saimus Lindon stepped in reaching for the book.

"Let me see what the book says,"Saimus said. As the words soaked into his mind, he looked up at Sabor and gave a reassuring, proud smile to the anxious boy. Mason was the last to read the book. Convinced, as he was that Sabor was not the Avenger, it disappointed him to read this. All of the brothers knew there were no women in The Order, so to have a Guardian with both parents as members of The Order would be impossible.

"This is indeed a problem, and most disheartening. Our prodigy, is indeed a Solitaire, but he is not born of a pair of Guardians. Furthermore, we cannot make assumptions on what the remainder of the book would say; yet the words are clear. And this is a terrible blow to our hope. So close to the end, yet so far from the true solution. We must discuss the interpretations we have; " Symon was clear on that. He motioned for the young Sabor to leave their presence. Not wanting to anger the older members of The Order, Sabor left not saying anything.

"My brothers, we must call to the other head Elders and discuss what we have learned," Mason and Saimus left the room to go in search of the other brothers, leaving Symon and Ellett to mull over what was just heard. Young Sabor returned to the Library to continue his studies, trying to learn why the Elders had reacted in such a way. He returned to the cubicle he had been in, opened the book wide, and began to read.

Keni was busy in the center of the *Bleeding Grounds* battle arena, slicing through granite boulders and acrobatically flipping over the huge space. Other Guardians and Greenlings were they're practicing their techniques. Mastering the movements of the ancient style. The sound of sabor weapons piercing metal and crushing rock was deafening. Some of the more experienced Guardians sparred with each other in violent exchanges of technique. Greenlings were not allowed, because they were still very dangerous, since they lacked control.

The more experienced warriors wouldn' t dare challeng Keni Divin. For this day, his demeanor alone would slay the majority of them. He teemed with rage, yet his sabor was a beautiful sight. The blade measured four feet long a samurai type of blade. Sleek and sharp. The fierce weapon possessed large ovals throughout to allow him to swing much harder than most. It had a strange glow about it, a reddish tint running through the center in only a thin line, the color was that of hate. The others stopped and watched as the young Master swordsman sliced some unseen enemy in a tantrum of hate. The stink of malice and anger thickened and it was never to be this way, here.

With a mighty scream Yorge Danglin, who had been watching the sessions that day, threw his large body nimbly behind the pissed off fighter. "STOP THIS! KENI STOP IT!"

The booming voice threw all other Guardians into a cower, but not Keni who proceeded to pummel some unseen enemy screaming," You are nothing. I am just as devoted as you are. I have the ability. I am the one, not you!" His babbling became more and more hateful and loud.

Yorge deployed his sabor weapons, coming out as two large cylinders. When they reached two and a half feet from his large bear-like hands, they achieved their full extension with two razor sharp wings unfolding and hardening instantly to form two large battle axes. In a pure white glow, powerfully precise, the large man swung one arm then the other, slamming the out of control Keni to the ground, burying his axe heads six inches into the earth and trapping Keni's weapons beneath the enormous axe. Yorge glared at Keni then slammed his foot into his spine, knocking the warrior to one knee.

"You will learn control young man or y ou will suffer a far worse fate at the hands of Dvanken. You must never, ever let anger taint your blade. The hate is weak and will cause your sabors to weaken and break. This will do nothing to help you in your battles. Control this or you will be confined or worse. Do you understand?" The teacher was always watchful and willing to help when the time was right. A commotion in the hall grabbed their attention.

"All head Elders are to report immediately to Symon's office," the voice of an unknown messenger rang out calling in a dead sprint as it passed every room. Yorge looked at Keni removed his foot from his back, and his weapons from the ground releasing him.

"Class is dismissed Master Keni. Let's not have a need for the same lesson again. Okay?" He turned and left Keni to dust the shame and embarrassment off with the dirt.

"Sir I am sorry and thank you for my lesson. It was taken to heart," Keni replied before Yorge disappeared.

"Head Elders, we have learned that either our numbers are much greater than we have imagined or the teachings of the Avenger are false. Either way, I must admit I am confused," As Symon spoke Mason came in the back door and nodded as if to say all were present.

Symon sent the book around the room saying," I beg each of you to read this. It would seem that women, a sex until now having no place our Order never showing the ability to produce sabor or being in tune with the Plane of The Order. But it seems now we have a stronger link to our counterparts than first expected. In an optimistic mind set, they are or soon will display these characteristics, thus making our teachings valid.

"However to play the devils advocate, this may mean the teachings, which have never let us down, have done just that. I plead with each of you, stay optimistic and never doubt our heritage. The concrete answer is, in my opinion blowing in the remains of this first passage. Fear is still a dangerous thing, but doubt in these times when we are so close to victory, it can be venomous,"

As Elder after Elder read the text a large wave of exactly what Symon warned against crashed over the group. One of the small men came running in and whispered to Symon.

"Master Symon, the widow Lindon has done away with herself this day. Here is the report from the coroner. As with all members of the brotherhood, we had to send her to our coroner sir. Sorry to interrupt," The strange little man sounded even stranger saying that. With a bewildered look upon his face, Symon dismissed the tiny man.

"My brothers, I must read this," Symon sat and read, as the rest of the room filled with gossip and the passing of different ideas. Each Elder tried to get a handle on what was going on around him. Symon's face lost all expression, and he slumped in his chair.

Astounded, he began to speak. "My brothers," he said with a smile. "Today is a glorious day, at least at first glance of these papers. Noelle Lindon has committed suicide. Now this in itself, is a tragedy that can never be fully overcome, but my brothers, her body was taken, either by mistake or by some divine intervention, to our coroner. The results conclude she indeed possessed the power. No weapons were in the body, but he found a thick concentration of glowing liquid around her heart and brain. She was a Guardian, an unknown member of The Order.

Let me make this clear, we may have found the Avenger. Though we have found an even stronger link the Lindon line produced the Avenger, no one should tell young Sabor what has transpired. The happenings will cloud his judgment. He will not devote all of his attention to the training and that will benefit no one. Does everyone understand and agree?" Symon' s word was taken as if law in the Halls of The Order.

"We understand Symon and agree!" In unison yelled the group. And with that, Symon dismissed the gathering and continued reading.

70

The Bleeding Grounds of the Sabor

Ellett decided to return to the library to begin training Sabor with his sabor weapons. He proceeded down the long corridor, glancing at the many statues along the hall. He turned into the library and saw Sabor pacing the floor as if he were done and had decided to go somewhere, only not knowing where.

"Hello my young learner. This is no place to learn anything. Let us proceed to the next level of your journey, SABOR TRAINING," The old one could barely hold his excitement for he knew Sabor was indeed the Avenger. And was anxious to see what he could do with his new armaments.

"Well its about time Master. I have needed some excitement, to get my mind off of everything; " the impetuous little man could not wait to get a hold of some fighting.

"Follow me. We go now to the *Bleeding Grounds of the Sabor*, Where generation after generation of Guardian has learned the deadly arts of the mighty weapons they possess in their forearms. Master Symon Divin will be your instructor. Watch intently and focus on your task and you will do fine,"

The pair exited through the large hardwood door in the West End of the library, Sabor behind Ellett. The hallway following, was a vaporous green. The floor of the hall was a wavy uneven mess. Sabor glanced down, the fog so thick he couldn't see his feet.

The mist settled after a few steps revealing the path and it's horror. They were walking on severed arms, legs, and heads, glazed over with a shiny resin. The faces were frozen hauntingly gazing, mouths open as well as the eyes. The arms and legs were waving a morbid rug down the hallway. The path did not extend to the walls. Large ropes, around three feet in diameter, suspended it instead. The haunting green glow of the hall seemed to be emanating from beneath the walkway.

"This is very freaky M aster; I've never seen anything even remotely like this. Tell me, for a place that is supposed to be so beautiful and in such a continuous peaceful frame of mind, why is everything here so gloomy and Goth? I thought this place was going to be full of life and good vibes," Sabor inquired.

"My boy, harmony of light and dark. These are the truest principals of life and so, the ways of our Order have been shaped to mimic the harmony. It is the nature of good, to possess some measure of darkness. You must get used to strange things; this will not be the last odd occurrence you see here. The balance surrounds us at all times, dictating a great deal of what happens in our small existence. Good and evil, evil and good in a constant struggle for dominance, but neither ever gaining a decisive edge simply coexisting despising one another," the Elder replied trying to squeeze a great deal of true wisdom into the short reply. "Acclimating to the fact that life is not cut and dry is essential to a Guardians existence. White and black, there are answers in this life, that simply pose more questions to you, rather than giving resolutions to the issue," the tunnel seemed endless giving Sabor time to ask many questions. Queries that had been burning in his brain since his arrival.

"Elder Vettin, I read in the HISTORY about the Gargoyles, how they were once Guardians...like us. I was always led to believe that they were nothing but fancy rain gutters. Also, I read they were outrageously large and fierce on the battlefield. How extraordinary were they?" Sabor asked then began again before he could get an answer. "Oh, and who, or what were the Quatrine? I have always heard they were nothing but a fairy tale legend, too. Are they real?" Sabor's mind was obviously swimming with questions, after filling his mind with the abundance of information in the library.

"Greenling, there is nothing but truth in the teachings. The Gargoyles were revered fighters, ferocious and agile... " Sabor interrupted the speech.

"Hold on, do you mean that Cranden-my Cranden is alive, and is-was a Guardian at one time?" Ellett reached over and closed the young man's mouth.

"Yes, he was once a Guardian, but not like you or I. He was too young to actually fight Dvanken. He is also very much real. He was assigned to you by the brotherhood, to keep an eye on your progression. Your father was very busy, since Master Linx called him to the latest sightings, all upon his request, mind you. You were vulnerable and alone much of the time. You needed someone to talk to about your changing body and the torrent of other struggle present in your life. Cranden began to enjoy his post as your overseer, enjoying your youthful company and friendship. He has always spoken very fondly of you, young Sabor.

"To answer your question, the one pertaining to the mysterious Quatrine, I will get to the Gargoyle, in a moment. The Quatrine were a very large, but shy race. Their likeness has been all around you here in these halls. They are represented in the pillars in the library and in the main hall entranceway.

"They had four arms and large squared jaws. Their serious, deep eyes sunk just enough to become engulfed inside quadrilateral shadows. The only accent in the eyes were small white circles, reflections from deep inside their souls. The bottom jaw had two large fangs protruding and leaving two small wounds on the face at all times. The teeth were razor-sharp and always in the way, but very dangerous. They were tattooed at the time of Discovery, a right of passage, with two tribal black lines jutting up, vivid and precise. The lines met in a sharp point midway back on the head. In the center of the two jet-black triangles was a bright amber curl, very apparent and bold. The curl accented the dark marks perfectly.

'The Quatrine were the first step. Created as a counter measure to evil, much as the human leg of The Order (The Guardians). The natural progression of things demanded they be powerful, but it also commanded they were to rely more on brains than brawn. Their massive arms could easily crush a boulder, yet they were very respectful of the Arts. Music, life and renaissance compelled them, not conflict. They completely submerged themselves in culture, instead of focusing on the fight they had been given by natural selection. In doing so they made themselves **soft** and for all the reasoning power they possessed, and the unbelievable strength and physical prowess, they couldn't defeat the wicked. Their dependence on emotions and lack of focus proved their undoing. In a huge battle, Dvanken eliminated the bulk of their society in one horrible day. The battle was known as 'The battle of Vindon Sound,"

'Now for your question on the Gargoyles, young Sabor. They stood around eight feet tall at the shoulders, no two looking exactly alike, they were a diverse, sprawling culture. Their strength became legendary as their numbers grew in the magical times, before science overtook the landscape of the world. They were twice as strong as an elephant, blindingly fast as well. Some say as fast, if not faster, than a cheetah. They wore skin as that of a rhino but much, much thicker. They were a **hard** race, known for their sheer numbers and relentless determination.

"Their downfall was their trusting nature, and the lack of reasoning ability, focusing on full on blitzkriegs of brute strength. Not to say they were stupid, oh to the contrary, they were very smart. They simply lacked the foresight to form a plan, or to foresee a plan forming. This made the emerging ability of Dvanken to manipulate the mind, that much more important to his progression. It made easy targets of the gallant race of the Gargoyle. Eventually one by one they fell to Dvanken's ever changing evil. Around this time, a few humans took notice of unusual whispers of the Gargoyles' glory and power. So to protect themselves from their false evils, the humans created statues in the likeness of the violent race and attaching them to buildings and ledges. Thus turning the once proud and noble warriors into the glorified rain gutters that you referred to. Your trusty confidant on the balcony, Cranden, is the last. He is forever immortal and will never fade, but doomed to be the last,"

'This brings us to our step in the evolution of good. It is finally mans turn to fight their battle, and we will prevail. We have the one thing none of the other tribes did. The Avenger,"The Elder was winded, so he stopped to rest. The door, that was so distant before, was now in plain sight. The bright light from the oak door stung their unadjusted eyes.

A silhouette broke the glare, giving some relief. It was a medium built man standing legs shoulder width apart, hands clasped behind his back, staring at the floor. It was head Elder Symon Divin, his concentration unyielding.

"Symon, I have brought the young Lindon, he is ready to begin his training," Ellett whispered quietly.

Symon looked up at the pair, and put his index finger by his lips and said. "Sssshhhhhh. I will be the judge of whether or not the Greenling is suitably ready or just another headstrong victim for Dvanken. Your assumptions will not help him in this journey Ellett, they will only add to an already swollen ego," Stepping close to Sabor, never breaking contact with the young mans eyes; Symon stopped just inches from his face. The gray-headed elder smirked, then slowly turned his head to peer at Ellett. With tension building, the head Elder spoke looking the other Elder up and down.

"You, my old friend, are dismissed. Leave me with this boy. It is time he became a man,"

His glow was an odd, light orange, sort of a dance of yellowish-brown and white lights. The illumination was very intense though, very intense.

Ellett looked back at Symon and replied. "Treat him with the same intensity you showed his us all. No holding back master,"

"I understand Ellett, do not think for one second that he will eek through this training," The Elders, in a good-hearted battle of words, each smiling at the others last comment.

"Excuse me sirs, but can I get to learning what these things in my forearms are for?" Sabor spoke out of turn interrupting the two.

At that moment, a flash of light, and a sonic boom rang out as Symon's sabor flew from its flesh sheath. The blade hummed much like a tuning fork, coming to rest on the bridge of Sabor's nose. A small trickle of blood flowed from the small wound.

"Your first lesson Greenling, is respect. Never, in your lifetime, disrespect an Elder. For that matter, a brother in The Order should be respected as you would respect your father. If you ever interrupt me again, I will take your nose. UNDERSTAND?!" The words were not loud or angry, but calm and controlled, as was everything about Symon.

"And for your second lesson, I want you to think of the best memory you have. Dig deep and retrieve the purest sense of joy you have ever had. Close your eyes and picture it. Can you see it? Can you see the joy and feel the warmth of that day?"

Sabor closed his eyes, thinking back as instructed. His mind wandered to a time not long ago, a beautiful afternoon and a beauty reading silently below a tree. He could smell the fresh cut grass. The breeze was warm. The sounds were the chorus of summer. An enormous, uncontrollable smile broke on his face. He felt the glow, and it interrupted his playback of the memory.

Sensing the disruption Symon said "Concentrate, boy, concentrate," He urged the memory in Sabors mind.

Sabor settled back into the bliss. The gorgeous white glow swirled about him, zigging back and forth around his face.

"What is that Master Divin? Talk to me please. Why is it so bright? Why is that cut getting hot?" Sabor was uneasy and the Elder standing before him tried to calm him once more.

"Sabor you must concentrate. You will learn much if you just listen," Symon said slapping Sabor on the back.

Sabor gave into the words, enjoying the memory. His small wound began to close. The blood on his cheek retreated back into the graze from where it came. The wound healed completely in a matter of seconds. All pain, all redness gone. Sabor was confused.

"You see, Greenling, the power of joy and the memories you possess can be a very welcome ally. Take care of the thoughts you have, they may save your life," The Elder smiled at the confusion his answers gave.

"Are you telling me that I can heal myself with good thoughts, with happiness? That is the coolest thing I have ever heard," Sabors enthusiasm shot immediately through the ceiling.

"My boy, your healing is only the beginning of what being positive can do for you. Those sabor weapons you possess are pure bliss, pure positive energy. And from what I have heard, your body is creating other talents I look forward to seeing; " The Elder then led the greenling into the bleeding grounds, pulling Sabor by the arm.

The Beginning

The Bleeding Grounds. The Guardians grand arena was worthy of comparison to the Coliseum of Rome. The ceilings loomed upward in a large dome with a majestic sculpture of Guardians in battle with dozens of dragons. The sculpture teemed with life, a mass of entangling arms, jaws and sabors. On either side of the floor waited over fifteen hundred seats arranged in a half moon shape. The seats had six sections each divided in two levels. They began eight feet up from the dirty marble floor. The smooth face of the bleachers bore the statues of the small men who scurried about the Halls of The Order.

These tiny men are the Myndgen, the devoted servants and friends of the Guardians. They had been so since the time of the Gargoyle tribes. They ask no questions of their Masters and expect even fewer rewards from them. Their race is programmed to serve, and they are proud of their programming. The Myndgen take care of the vast halls. They are the messengers for the entire Order also.

Other statues, carved into a wall of solid rock, held the seats up from the floor. Always lending an audience to whatever training occurred. The figures depicted Gargoyle high Masters in full battle attire. The intricate statues held above their heads a solid granite banister and in their posture they held the history of an entire race. The expressions of intensity and focus were inspiring.

Behind the rows of comfortable leather seats stood a series of five tremendous stained glass cathedral-style windows. The stained glass was broken up by rods of steel in the shape of the Crest of The Order. A seemingly source less light emanated from behind the great windows, casting the colorful reflections on the center of the floor, so the warriors trained on the crest. No, not on the crest, but inside it.

The atmosphere rang thick with the clanks, and chinking of metal striking metal. The grunts and screams of the Guardians and Greenlings added to the symphony of battle. The room seemed electric, almost breathing with the rich emotions of the warriors.

As Sabor and Symon entered the Bleeding Grounds, the huge presence of the Elder was felt immediately. Out of respect for the Master, each brother retracted his weapon and turned to face the pair. In unison, they bowed their heads and in low voices sang an ancient song of reverence and respect. The sound reverberating through each one, Symon smiled. With a gesture he accepted their adulation, then applauded each of the men around him.

They suspended the song, and again as one, they barked. "Good morning Master Symon, what do you have for us this day?" The crispness of the group was impressive.

"My pupils please continue in a moment, but first this is Sabor Lindon, Master Zandalar's only son. He begins his training and *Discovery* today. Please help him with the knowledge I have given you Greenlings and Knights alike. I would like to thank you all in advance, for honoring this request,"

A cheer escaped the brothers. They gathered close to the newest addition to The Order, and showered him with questions about the unbelievable events in the library and welcomed him to The Order. The pupils had gathered in the center, all excited all but one.

Keni Divin stood by himself still and diligent. He shook his head at the excitement then continued working one of the room's stone bags with his left hand. The bag, was a four hundred-pound slab of marble suspended by four large golden chains. In the center of the stone, a six-inch strip of steel had been inserted for strength. Keni slammed the stone quite impressively, shredding pieces of the solid block off with every blow. His pace quickened the longer everyone stayed swooning over his newly discovered rival.

"I mean come on, what the hell is so damn important about Sabor Lindon? Who gives a damn who his dad was? Yeah, Zandalar Lindon he was a great Guardian, but what has Sabor done? Let him prove his greatness. A man should not be judged by how strong his father was, but what he himself accomplishes," He paused between words letting out a grunt as he struck the stone. With every word he became more and more angry, his jealousy growing leaps and bounds. As Keni chipped away at the mighty stone, Symon Divin noticed what was going on with his headstrong nephew. Keni's normally beautiful orange glow shifted to a tainted green. The color indicated jealously, but even more disturbing was the reddish tint beginning to form at the heart of his blade.

"Nephew calm yourself. I can see your jealously and hate building. I tell you now; your fate will be death if you continue this path. Dvanken will use your feelings against you and you will die.
"Oh how you remind me of your father, so passionate, so impetuous. It took him two hundred years to Master the sabor without tainting his blade, even just a little, with anger. I warn you, it creates weak points in your weapon. Trust me, you will need all of the power of The Order to defeat Dvanken," the caring uncle explained.

You see Uncle Symon that is exactly what I am talking about. I AM NOT CADEN DIVIN! I am Keni. I should not be judged as Caden, not as a Master

Divin like my father. What I want to know is, if that prick is to be our Avenger, the one who destroys Dvanken, then why am I judged at all? Can you tell me that Uncle? Why do I push to be the one, why?" The words boiled with hate as he pointed at Sabor. "Is it simply because he is the son of a Lindon? Or is it his accord that warrants such instant respect? I say let him prove himself. Prove himself to me by fighting...I mean sparring with me," His misdirected anger was flowing red.

"Calm down, or you will face me young knight! He is special just as you are, because he is a Guardian, at least one day he will be. For that he deserves your instant respect And besides, one day he will be your equal, so make peace and leave the negative out of your training and battles. You are a Guardian, a member of the sacred Order of the Sabor. You must act in a manner accordingly. Do you understand?" The words stung Keni, but he understood and agreed to curb his anger, for the moment.

Still clinging to jealousy, he grudgingly added," Uncle, it is only for your benefit that I calm myself, if he crosses me again, I will settle my dispute," Keni swallowed the lump of thick pride in his throat and started toward Sabor.

"Greenling," he said in a condescending tone," we'll soon see what you are made of. Welcome to the Bleeding Ground, school is in session, Greenling," Keni said with a sneer on his face.

Symon cut between Sabor and his headstrong nephew. Symon looked around at his students, and said," all of you, come forward and greet our newest addition. Usually we do this in ceremony, but Sabor Lindon, was born a Solitaire," Symon ordered.

Keni Divin stepped to him first extending his hand and pulling him close.

"We don't want you here Lindon!" Keni whispered.

"What a coincidence. I didn't want to come, but guess we will both have to deal with my being here anyway, alright?" Sabor returned squeezing him a bit tighter with every word.

The upstaged Divin wriggled away and with a huff, shoved himself free of the embrace.

"You just remember what I said. We don't need you here and we definitely don't want you here," Keni's personality shining, he was, as always going to get in the last word.

Sabor shook his head as Keni walked away, then the Greenling continued on greeting the remainder of the men; he was to learn with.

"Oh, pay him no mind Sabor, he's been pissy since he found out you were coming to the halls," A young plump Greenling said, as he shook Sabor's arm nearly off with an overzealous hand shake.

"Thank you, I think. But I don't believe I'll do any good here with only one arm. What do you think?" Sabor said with an only half sarcastic smile on his face.

"Oh forgive me, my Mum says that I get a bit eager when I get excited. Please forgive me, Sabor. But wait, I haven't rightly told you my name have I. It's Seth, Seth Danglin. I was named after my great great grandfather Sethe Valen Danglin. He was the greatest sabor instructor these halls have ever seen. He and your father were great friends, I believe. In fact, Zandalar Lindon was Sethe's Guide, if memories serve. But I ramble so, my Mum says I get a bit long winded when I get nervous too," Seth jabbered on.

"Not a problem Seth, I haven't gotten much of an update on the background here. In fact, I really didn't know any of this existed until recently," Sabor returned allowing Seth to rest his jaws.

"Tell me, what was it like to have him as a father?" Seth asked bright eyed and excited.

"Who Zandy?" Sabor replied, not quite knowing how to take his exuberance.

"Of course, you are the son. The Solitaire son of Zandalar Lindon. You must have so many stories to tell and so much respect for him," Seth said echoing the feelings of the growing group of men pulling in towards the conversation.

"I do have great respect for Dad, but as far as stories go. Nope, like I told you, I have no knowledge of this place. You ask me how it was to be the son of Zandalar Lindon. Well, I'd have to say that it was pretty lonely," Sabor turned hiding the tear tracing his cheek and nearly choking on the grief of the discussion. As if it wasn't enough to lose his father, but to have never really gotten the chance to know him in the first place stung ten fold.

"Now it's my turn to apologize Seth. I didn't mean to unload all of this on you. I mean, all you did was ask a question or two. But, it just that it has only been two days since I lost him," Sabor said returning to face Seth, as the understanding Greenling stepped out of Sabors way bowing his head in reverence.

Sabor stepped past Seth nodding to each man and hugging him tightly with each introduction and line of questioning about his father. Then Symon stepped in sternly.

"Enough! I want all of you to continue sparring and striking the stone bags for an additional hour, then you are dismissed for the day," The students were excited; Symon wasn't usually this lenient, especially in front of a fresh Greenling. He motioned for Sabor to follow him.

The Art of the Sabor Weapons
The Strike

Symon lead the young man through the center arena to a small corner of the massive chamber. A door stood in front of the pair. The crest was etched into the facing door. A large golden plaque was situated on the opposite side. It read," *Greenlings are the first of many steps to* **Discovery***, the challenge of the bliss is the key to the next step," It* was a very confusing plaque.

"What the hell does that mean?" Sabor asked, a look of distaste on his face.

"Your key will not be presented to you without using your mind Greenling," with this Symon turned his back and looked over the varying styles his students were using. He ignored the perplexed man behind him and went about his business quietly.

Sabor searched his mind, going over and over the words. He shook his head nearly giving up, when a lightning bolt hit.

"I got it!" Sabor exclaimed, happy he had figured it out at last. His mind drifted back to an evening underneath a large tree, bringing a large smile to his face. With the smile, the air filled with a thick electricity. The air swirled about him. His sabor slowly slipped from his right arm.

Sabor noticed a small slot placed just beneath the Crest. He took the next step, inserting the exposed part of his sabor. The young Greenling felt his sabor extend fully inside the slot, suddenly the blade stopped with a loud click. Sabor looked down at the lock and turned his arm clockwise. With a shudder and a cloud of dust, the door opened revealing a soft strange black glow. This sounds absurd, but it was a black glow.

To the other side they strode, Sabor looking around saw row upon row of armor, shields and sabers. Sabor turned to Symon asking," If we have built in weapons, why do we need all of this?"

"This is no place for questions, you must choose quickly and quietly," Symon said to him.

Sabor's eye caught a brilliant shield and forearm guard. He turned back to Symon and again asked. "So, you mean I can choose any one of these weapons?"

"Yes Sabor, you can choose any one, but choose with care for only one pair is set aside for each Guardian. It is predestined to be yours, and anything else will reject you. Consider this your first test; be careful," Symon placed his hand over the lower hemisphere of his face concealing his devilish smile. He knew the joke he was playing was cruel, but it had it's purpose.

"Oh, shit what if I choose wrong? I really have my mind set on these two, but what if I'm wrong? I cannot fail my first test as a Greenling. I am going to succeed at this. I have too. For myself and for Symon and Dad, hell everyone I know," Sabor's thoughts rambled on. The conflict of picking taxed him, but he was determined to make his choice, the only one he could make.

"Pick Greenling!" Impatiently Symon barked again. Sabor picked up the shield and forearm guard he had been admiring.

"Master, I want these and I am sure they want me, Well, I think they do," Sabor had never been so unsure of anything in his life, but tried not to show the insecurity in his answer. Symon paused until the silence finished bathing the moment, causing a terrible feeling deep in Sabor's stomach. 'Sir... " Symon interrupted Sabor before he could say anything else.

"Greenling, how well did you think your decision through? Take cares to answer honestly, for I already know the truth," Sabor thought for a moment.

"Well Master Divin, honestly I just went with my gut instinct," Sabor slowly admitted. A smirk of approval came over Symon's face, turning into a burst of laughter.

"My young student, you have passed with flying colors. You picked well. The truth, no matter which you picked, you would have been correct. This test teaches the lesson of reacting, not over thinking any given situation, just flow with the natural stream of life and emotion.
'Furthermore you must realize time is a luxury that we as Guardians do not possess. Your instincts are the key to the finality of the predicament mankind has found itself in. You must rely on your sense of the moment and flow with your feelings. They may be your only way out.
'Dvanken is a horrible foe, attacking from shadow. In an instant, he retreats as quickly as inserting himself into a situation. He kills in seconds, plays with time, and reacts within the confines of his own world, not ours. His ferocity is unparalleled. Your reaction to your surroundings can, and will save you.
'Please take these words to heart and carry them always. You have obtained much wisdom from us, the weapons of the warriors of The Order. Now you must gain the disciplines of The Order. Do you understand?
'Your sabors, are the links to the demise of Dvanken. They draw their

strength from deep inside of your joy and happiness. The bliss you feel is drawn inward; this emotion is then thrust out through the forearms of the Guardians. For each of us Guardians, our emotion manifests differently in our weapons, much like fingerprints no two are identical,"

Sabor interrupted with a question. "So, no other Guardians have the same sabor weapon as I do right?"

"That is exactly wha t I am saying,"Symon continued. "Now for your next lesson, Greenling. Suit up, let us begin,"

Sabor did as told and hurried as much as possible. The two men stepped back into the arena, approaching a stone bag. Symon stepped to the massive chunks of stone. He removed his large leather cloak, having Sabor hold the heavy garment. Symon turned his head. He looked Sabor up and down, as if saying when you can do this you will have arrived as a Guardian.

"Watch what the discipline of The Order can accomplish,"With a deep breath, he drew his arms into an X his wrists crossing, and the small slits on each arm opening his back bulged, and he popped his neck in a circular motion.

Sabor watched the wave of concentration consume the teacher, the orange glow rolling from the slits. The glow flowed from within until it was a pale white light.

Symon's sabors flew from their sheath, his right arm bearing a sword the shape of a slender, but raging flame, and emerging from his left forearm a large blade, split down the center into two distinct blades joined at the bottom by one larger razor. He slowly turned; showing Sabor the beautiful oil slick colored blades.

"My Greenling, your next lesson is STRIKING. The art form has been passed down through The Order from time unmemorable. It is an ancient art maximizing the power within. Watch closely.

Symon turned one more time and lunged violently, yet completely under control. His right arm sliced the air downward, pulling the stones bottom layer apart from the main body of the bag. The large piece fell, crumbling. In swift recoil his right arm pulled back to his side. His left hand in turn surged forward pulling the rest to the ground, severing the connection to the huge golden chains. The stone, cut in half, now lay in ruins. His sabors retracted with a wet, fleshy sound. He turned and said

"Now Greenling, your turn. Concentrate,"Symon said motioning for

Sabor to take his place by the stone. "Take your positive emotions, and feel them push through your arm. Take the pressure from the emotions, and explode with their power. Remember speed is strength," Symon taught.

Sabor took the queue and approached the slab of marble and granite. His nerves ate a hole in his stomach, the butterflies fluttering in his belly almost visible. All he wanted in the world was to impress Symon at this moment. He squared himself to the stone and pushed his feet firmly into the floor shoulder width apart. This time, the swords that had displayed themselves with such ease earlier in his Discovery, seemed as if they were cemented inside. He struggled, grunting hard to exhibit his blades. They eventually slurked out, with an adolescent strain of Sabor's mind.

They were jagged sharp, like shattered bone, uneven and unpredictable. The blades were razor-sharp, the prongs doubling back on themselves forming small holes. The deadly metallic scimitars resembled gnarly tree branches with tightly sharpened edges.

Sabor, so tired from the struggle with his inner blades, could barely breathe. He tried duplicating what his instructor had done, but so far, failed miserably. Sabor's blades glanced of the stone with a shower of multi-colored sparks. Sabor threw his blades around with reckless abandon, striking the stone over and over, barely even scratching the solid marble chunk before him. By the time he finished his fit, he had struck twenty to thirty times, and barely left a pile of shavings from the stone bag.

Chuckling at the young man, Symon quizzed the confused boy. "Okay stop Greenling. Tell me why you have failed,"

"I guess my blades aren't hard enough or something," The answer tasted a bit nasty to Sabor, he had never failed at anything in his life.

"No not at all Sabor. Your blade is as rigid, if not more so, than even mine. Let me explain. When you STRIKE, you must above all else, concentrate. This discipline is not far from the healing exercise I gave to you a bit earlier. In fact, you could probably use the same thought as you did before. Hold that moment, channeling each ounce of the feeling into that one explosive second. Unleash your bliss upon the target, for the desired power. Remember, that after concentration, comes control.

"You must control the blade, as if you w ere manipulating your own fist. When your arm speeds toward the target, retract the blade just a bit. Concentrating on the moment at hand, as well as your moment of bliss. Then, as you come close to contact, thrust the blade out fully. This gives you more depth, and the extra concentration it requires, will improve your accuracy and power. This rule of the STRIKE also applies to the bare fist. As it flows, keep it relaxed until the last possible moment, then contract hard. This creates a much more solid fist and inflicts twice the damage of a normal punch. Do you understand this technique?" The wise instructor asked, as Sabor prematurely nodded his head.

"Next comes release. Coming away, you must turn your sabor, thus inflicting more damage and also allowing for the blade to exit the wound quickly and cleanly. This keeps your attacks coming with fluidity and always on the offensive. All the while, you must keep your mind on the positive energy of your memory. Emotional content in any situation lends weight to that moment. Keep your emotions pure and they will make you strong and best of all, they will keep you alive.

"These are the disciplines of the STRIKE. Learn them. Practice them. Commit them to your instincts and you will thank me one day. Now, Greenling try. When you try, remain disciplined. Concentrate on your bliss and remain strong.

"OH, and one more thing, take care to never taint your blade with hate. You must always keep it pure. Hate, jealousy, vengeance these are the forces that weaken all they touch. Sucking the soul out and allowing evil to replace it.

"To counteract this, you must suck the darkness you feel deep into the center of your chest. You will feel the contraction of all your muscles then. Your heart, extremely heavy, will feel as if it will stop beating at any second. A Guardian will harness this blackness, reaching a point of change. This black hole in your chest is the anger you have boiling inside of you. The anger by it's own nature becomes unstable, reaching the point that your fury causes you to chuckle. Feeling a laugh rise through resentment is a gift, your threshold to the change. The change is the point when you control your malice and begin to manipulate it to make you stronger. When you learn to harness your essence of joy, your strike will be more intense than you can imagine, almost unstoppable.

"Take heed of these words. Never forget them. They will make you strong. Now STRIKE!"

Sabor nodded in agreement, and spun to face the stone again. "You won't beat me again rock," said Sabor. His minds eye drifted off capturing the picture of his beautiful Chelle and how her smile could melt his heart. His sabors flew out, shimmering as they fully extended. Taking heed of what he had just learned, Sabor pulled back with the bliss of her face burning in his heart. The beautiful bluish glow around his sabor was far different than Symon had ever seen. It was breath taking.

Sabor shifted his weight, swirling the blade in a half-moon arc, and sliced cleanly through the air. His body relaxed his mind laser-like. His blade, just inches away from the slab, changed shape just a bit, so little in fact that nobody, not even Sabor noticed. The color morphed into a brilliant shade of purple.

He did as his Master instructed, and focused. His first blow ripped the enormous boulder, a hot knife passing through butter. With a deafening sound. Immediately, as his right hand cleared the stone, his left seemed to act on its own. In a jumping spin, it sliced the Golden Chains in half, leaving the two pieces resting on top of one another.

Sabor stood hunkered over, legs bent and exhausted. His sabors' rested motionless, the tips dragging the ground. His chest heaved, but through all the exercise he smiled, an unmovable gripping smile.

"Master, I did it, sir. I focused then I struck. Damn that was great! Thank-you so much, I have never felt so alive. Did you see how hard I hit that rock man!? I mean Sir,"Sabor said as he wiped the sweat from his forehead and slapped his instructor on the shoulder.

"Yes my boy, I saw. You did it. No thank you is necessary, for this is these are the disciplines that I have been assigned to show you,"Symon's statement let some of the wind out of Sabor's sails, but not enough to make a difference, he still smiled. With a new sense of life, Sabor was ready to learn more.

"What's next Symon? What new thing are you gonna show me now?" Sabor asked with an unmistakable excitement.

"I believe that is all for me today. I will retire for the evening. You though, stay as long as you like and practice striking; " Symon gathered his things and turned to leave.

"Symon... " Sabor stopped the man needing to say this,"... thank you just the same. I really appreciate what you have done for me,"His words touched Symon.

"You are very welcome Lindon. You are very welcome, Good job today," And with that, he disappeared from the large room.

Sabor barely noticed he was alone. Left alone in the room Sabor continued to practice. He took full advantage of the practice time as the minutes turned into hours.

All the while, Master Symon convened with the other Elders, and trading stories of the unbelievable young Sabor.

"I am excited. For the first time since I became a Guardian gentlemen, I am truly excited. The cycle of despair Dvanken has enthralled the world in for thousands of lifetimes is coming to an end. The time of relaxation and retirement for us is at hand, and this Lindon will present it to us. In my opinion, he is the Avenger. I suggest all in The Order began treating him as such,"The faces around the large oak table ranged from strong approval of the statements, to looking down at the table in disbelief that an Elder had uttered the words. "My brothers, you appear divided on the subject. Please let your feelings be known, we are all friends here,"Symon continued.

A large figure stood and in a booming voice, proclaimed. "You are a foolhardy old man Symon, just like Ellett. This Lindon is no different from the rest of us. Yes, he may be a fast learner, but any man can be, if he asserts himself headlong into a task,"Yorge Danglin stood and defying any reaction. He slammed his large hand on the table, almost buckling the ancient furniture. "Besides the Slumber has just begun and the Greenlings are in mid training. We must push them and get them ready to battle. Dvanken is growing. I fear a New World will be unleashed when the Awakening arrives,"with this Yorge yielded the floor and sat down. Symon stood again and shook his head from side to side.

"Do you see this brothers? This is why we lose. Our faith has been all but destroyed and our foolish pride seems to rule our actions. Do you think you are the Avenger Yorge? Or do you Master Ellett or you Mason Linx?" A look of embarrassment broke over each face in the room for Symon knew that they all believed, at least in some part, that they were. "This is the trouble with mankind. We all want to be the hero, and in our own vanity and pride most times, we miss the true hero in front of us. Yorge to believe you must come and watch the boy. Mason, I see your opinion differs from my own, so you come too. The proof is overwhelming. Besides, look at his father. Many believed he would be the one, yet his charisma was the only thing that set him apart from us. His son is so much more than that. He is talent and evolution personified. He **WILL** defeat Dvanken, and he will avenge the loss of so many lives and so many dreams," The conviction pierced them all and a loud roar of applause billowed from the congregation.

"Now let us all rest. We will meet again tomorrow, same time gentlemen; " Symon shook their hands and left the room.

"He is a gi fted speaker, but I still have my doubts about the young Sabor. I will watch him tomorrow none the less,"Yorge said to Mason. Mason seemed to have been moved greatly by the speech.

"Not me, at least not to defraud the boy. I believe, he will be our Avenger, He will save us all,"Mason smiled and gave the big man a large hug. "Goodnight and sleep well friend,"Mason decided to leave before he was drug, head long into a debate with the gargantuan man.

"Yes Goodnight my friend," Yorge said recogni zing Mason's tone.

"Master Saimus, you sat rather quietly during this meeting. That's not like you. What's wrong?" Yorge asked of the Elder sitting quietly in the corner.

"I know who and what my nephew will become. And I didn't wan t my feelings or the feelings of others to draw me into a conflict, with one of you, understand?" Saimus asked.

"Yes I understand brother. I am sorry for my doubt, it's just I have reservations about everything," Yorge said chuckling a bit. "Goodnight Saimus, sleep well," Yorge ended.

Meanwhile Sabor still chugged away in the pit, smashing rock and spinning his blades trying desperately to master the weapons. When the physical work became too much, he would sit, concentrating on the good points in life trying to maintain his focus. He sat for hours, repeatedly working his blade in and out until it felt smooth, almost instinct. His body began to give out with exhaustion.

Sabor looked around at the vast emptiness of the bleeding grounds. Sabor wanted nothing more than to lay down and sleep for a while. Sabor looked down at his arms; they were throbbing and dripping with sweat. He glanced at the watch on his arm; he had managed to smuggle it in, without Ellett finding out.

"Oh, man I have been doing this for six hours," Sabor said as he let out a deep sigh. "I have got to get some shuteye,"

Ellett had shown Sabor where the dormitory was, but had neglected to show him, exactly which room would be his. "Well, I guess I'll just go and take a look around, maybe I'll find a bed somewhere, and just crash, and hope nobody kicks, or throws a bucket of water me for sleeping in their bunk. Sabor stumbled through the labyrinth of tunnels, searching for the dormitory. Finally, he found a tunnel with a large cloth wall hanging, with the words "Dormitory of the Greenling" written in gold thread. "Found it, cool, now I'll just have to find a place to crash," Sabor searched the halls for quite some time, but found only locked doors and plaques with other people's names on them. "Damn I'm tired, I need to get some sleep," Sabor redundantly spouted to himself. Bracing himself against a door jam to rest, he saw a plaque with his name etched into it. "Finally! Home sweet home," Sabor exclaimed.

Pushing the door, he walked in to familiarize himself with his new room. The room left much to be desired, but for as tired as Sabor was it looked like a room at the Ritz. The walls were a pale gray, with a slight touch of green mold. The floor was a porous rock, with tiny plants growing from the cracks. The tiny room only measured around eight feet by six feet cramped to say the least. A quaint desk was situated in the far corner. A small twin bed was pressed tightly against the opposite wall. The mattress was a comfortable goose down old and worn. Sitting folded neatly on the end of the naked mattress were a set of musty greenish brown blankets and sheets. A set of two drawers were fashioned underneath the bed frame as a sort of make shift chest-of-drawers. A small glass dish hung from the ceiling putting forth a strange glow. It was damp and a bit cold in the tiny room, but Sabor didn't care.

He was worn out from the hours in the bleeding grounds. Sabor grabbed one of the dusty blankets, and wrapped himself up tightly. Then with another sigh of relief, he relaxed and drifted off into dreamland. Where a very beautiful dream awaited him.

It was his wedding day. His father was his best man. The ceremony was perfect. All their family and friends were there, he could see the smiles on each face. Sabor was glowing with joy and anticipation. Turning to see Zandalar standing there smiling. His father gave him a quick wink, letting him know how proud he was and it helped Sabor relax a bit. Sabor turned spotting his mother on the first pew shining like a diamond. Noelle gave a small wave and blew him a kiss. Just then the organ began to play the bridal march.

Sabor glanced down at his hands. In the center was the crest. It appeared to be burnt into his skin. In the center of the crest was the ring he planned to give his bride. Seeing it made him smile. He slowly looked up seeing all the faces of the audience at once. They were all now just blank flesh-colored spheres, no expression, no life. He looked down, realizing the only three faces he could make out belonged to Noelle, Chelle and Zandalar. A strange red hue began filling the room, swirling and darting everywhere. No one panicked except Sabor. He franticly tried to do something, but his weapons wouldn't move and neither could he.

Suddenly, the back wall of the church was torn from the rest of the structure. The building collapsed in a cloud of lumber, glass and plaster, in upon itself. The dust settled seemingly in seconds. At the rear of the building stood a menacing shadow.

"Dvanken is that you? How dare you defile this place with your presence, prepare to die," Zandalar bravely proclaimed as he pushed past Sabor.

"Dad wait. Don't go I need you!" Sabor pleaded to no avail. Zandalar sprinted to the shadow and was gone. The form moved a few feet closer, placing itself behind Sabor's lovely bride.

"Sabor, honey please help me. I'm scared. What is going on?" Chelle sounded miles from him now.

"Hold on baby. I'm coming for you. Just don't die. Please don't die. I can't take it; again," Sabor looked at his feet. They appeared stuck to the floor in a cartoonish fashion. The feet stretched, never letting go. Never giving him the chance to stop the death of his love.

Sabor watched in horror as a large hand reached toward the sky and quickly came swooping back toward the ground, slicing his true love, into two pieces. "NO! You son of a bitch! How the hell could you do this? What has she ever done to you, damn it? DIE, die you piece of shit!" Sabor screamed, by the end of those words his voice was horse, nearly gone.

The shadow sprouted a brilliant white smile, antagonizing the man even more. He moved a few feet closer. Sabors mother sat with her hands covering her face. Noelle was heartbroken. She had seen her husband die, and her soon-to-be daughter-in-law killed.

"Son, I need some rest baby. Please hel p me. Come to me and hug me, please," Noelle cried obviously tired of her world of pain and loss.

"Mom, I can't move. Please don't give up. You have to fight. Please Mom, fight. You have to fight damn it woman! You fight mom. Please just get up,"Sabor tried his hardest to break free, almost ripping his own legs off to get to her, but it was no use. The large shadow sneered, grasping Noelle by the neck, he smiled an evil smile.

"NOOOOO!" Sabor screamed his voice wavering from the strain as his conscious mind ripped him from the dream. He was sweating and could barely speak. Sabor shuffled to his feet feeling confused and anxious. "What in the hell was that? Did something happen to Mom?"

He wondered what the reverie could mean. He replayed the dream over in his head, scrutinizing everything he could remember. After fifteen minutes, he decided to find answers with the Elders, seeing if they knew anything about the climax of his dream and what truths it held.

He rushed out to find anyone he could speak with about the dream. He ran past a dimly lit office where a faint shadow perched behind a desk, sat humming a chorus to a song Sabor had never heard, and smoking a stuffy old pipe. The smell was a familiar one. It was the pipe of Yorge Danglin.

Sabor poked his head in, quickly asking. "Elder Yorge, do you have any clue why I would be dreaming of what I can only explain as Dvanken, and why it appeared as if he were going after my mother just before I woke up?" The visually shaken young man barely effected the calloused Elder. "SIR, please, I need to know anything you can tell me,"His plea broke through the shell around the man. Mason, shuffled in the chair, clearing his throat.

"My young Sabor, you are nearing an e normously crucial point in your *Discovery*. You see the evil. This is a special step. Your next progression is to confront. Deal with what the evil has done, not only to you, but also to the world. And hopefully **IF**, and I do mean **IF** you are what they say you are, your final evolution will be to defeat the evil, and enjoy the peaceful aftermath it will bring. Now, that is all I know of your silly dream Greenling, so leave me with my thoughts!" He immediately went back to humming.

The encounter being of absolutely no help, Sabor bowed his head and left. He searched in quite a hurry, for anyone that could help him, tell him anything of substance. He sprinted around a corner; he slammed head long into Ellett. They both shook off the fall and glanced at each other. They picked themselves up and dusted themselves off.

"Why the hurry Greenling?" Ellett asked.

"Actually, I am looking for you. I had a dream last night. I think something horrible may have happened to my mom,"Sabor explained.

"Okay. Well, why don't you tell me about this dream?"

Sabor agreed. After laying the dream out with much enthusiasm, he stood hoping to hear words of encouragement and tales of Ellett's recent conversations with Noelle. The words he heard instead did not taste sweet.

"Sabor, you will never know how much you mean to me, and for that I cannot lie to you. But you cannot, no; you must not let your rage or pain undo what you have done these past days. You have progressed faster than any student I have ever had. I'm sorry my boy, I am rambling. Your mother was found, I mean she was, I can't... " Ellett begun but couldn't force the words.

"TELL ME PLEASE. If I mean so much to you, just tell me," Sabor begged impatiently.

"Okay my boy, you are least entitled to that. She was found dead. She apparently committed suicide. She is gone my boy, and no amount of grief will pull her back from the clutches of the grave. Your mother is at peace. I am sure she would wish nothing more than for you to be, as well. It is selfish for you to want to bring her back from that peace. Human, but it's selfish," Ellett said as softly as he could, not beating around the bush.

"Look Ellett, I know all of that stuff, but I want to be selfish right now. I want my mom. I miss her so much. Can you or anyone else tell me why? Why is all of this happening to me? No, none of you. So leave me alone, and let me grieve," Sabor said, collapsing and pounded the ground repeatedly.

"Get up now, and come with me boy, now!"

Ellett took Sabor to a room where the only light was supplied by four candelabras mounted in each corner. Two large leather upholstered chairs and a single oak table with a carving of the crest in the center, watched the two men. The table rested in the midst of the two chairs. Beautiful drapes hung from the walls. A deep purple, they overlapped on the floor, in a coagulation of heavy fabric.

"Have a seat Sabor. I must speak with you about this. The finale, your end, death. These words are extremely unsettling to humans. Do you know why this is? Because these are the ultimate uncertainties. Our small minds, in all of their glory, cannot grasp the end. Yet in it's infallible majesty, still insists we all have an end. Failing to grasp a world without a definite beginning and end. It is a paradox that will never be undone.

"Our instinctive fear of death springs from our lack of knowledge on the subject. When you die, nothing is promised. It is something new. This change is terribly raw and terrifying for man. Much like starting a new school, or a new

92

job. You have no clue what to expect, and that is unsettling, scary even.

"But unlike those examples, in death, there is no authority. No one person to give you examples, or tips for what is to come. The only way to find out what is on the other side is to go. With that journey, you must leave your comfort and the knowledge of where you are, and where you come from. And to leave the certain, and venture into the abyss of uncertainty, is a huge step. Whose consequences cannot be reversed? They are eternal and whatever they are, nothing can change their reality.

"You asked me the question, "Why all of this was happening to you," and I will tell you. It is because the evil that is Dvanken wants you to be just another victim, a testament to his greatness, a tasty meal as proof to us, the Guardians of the sabor, that no Avenger, no champion will ever be bold enough to present him his death. To him, the end will never come. In his prideful mind, he is infinite. In his vanity, he believes he can never die, and that my boy is "WHY,"

"As far as why your family and loved ones you have are being taken, he is preparing you. Basting you with your own pities and blame. The pain you cling to, your crutch, to explain all of this is what he feeds upon. He tries to make your taste please him. He wants to find the perfect meal. You, we are a game to him, an example of his power.

"That is why you must focus. That and only that will defeat Dvanken, not the revenge you are seeking, not the rage from the words I have spoken about your dear mother. I know this is no consolation, but it is nevertheless the truth. You must accept it. The harshness of this life, the stress of the day-to-day grind, can be overwhelming. Our fear of death merely adds to his theory of his own superiority and dominance, while adding to his growth and evolution. His assumption has been upheld, only because he has evolved and we, as a species, have become stagnant suspending our own evolution.

"You, young Sabor, have begun the flow again. You are the next step, the Avenger. It is because of this, your death will not and cannot happen. You were predestined to save us all from the evil of Dvanken. We of The Order, as well as the unsuspecting human race, are behind you one hundred percent. So put your fears of death away and focus. Put your thoughts of revenge away and focus. You have no worries save one, your training. And remember, I am here always for you," Ellett said his peace and stood awaiting a response. The one he received, however may not have been exactly what he would have wanted.

"You have the balls to stand here; preaching to me of focus, when out of the same mouth you just told me my mother killed herself. How in the hell can you sleep at night? You can take your Order and shove it firmly up your ass! I'm leaving and if you try and stop me, I guarantee you will not make it through to see this Awakening," Ellett stood shocked as the young man brushed passed him, vanishing into the hall. Ellett settled back in his chair and gave a long sigh.

"How am I going to tell the others Sabor is gone? How?" Ellett sat pondering this for some time. At last he realized the only way to go about this was to dive in, and call a meeting.

He proceeded to the great hall signaling for the brothers to assemble and listen. Pulling the rope Ellett stood slumping over. His mind racing with plausible solutions to his dilemma.

After fifteen minutes, the room was full but silent. It seemed to Ellett, as if all The Order knew something was terribly wrong.

"Gentlemen, I have come before you tonight, asking for your help," Ellett scanned the crowd hoping to see Sabor, but found only confused Guardians. The other Elders stared hard, waiting for the point to his speech. "I need your help in finding our Avenger. Young Sabor Lindon has run away," A roar of confusion welled up in the crowd.

"This morning, he came to me in di scussion of a dream he had. In this dream, Dvanken attacked his mother. He asked me what his dream meant, and what had happened. His plea was sincere, and his emotions, I feared, would push him to do something irrational. So, in a moment of misjudgment, I informed the young man of his mother's untimely death. I then, told him of the importance of focus in this time. Looking back I should have told him nothing, but it cannot be changed now. He must be found. I propose we form search parties, and scour the grounds above and below. I beg of you brothers, help me find him," Ellett stepped down, and as he walked out shouted. "I leave now; I am going to check outside first,"

Yorge turned to Symon and said, "He came to me also, asking of this dream. I believe he may be in trouble. We must find him" Symon agreed and stood.

"Guardians, our task is to find Sabor Lindon. I will take everyone on the left side; the other Elders will please take a section of men, and take a section of the Halls. Search until we find him. Understand?" Symon said gesturing to each of the men beside him, showing them, which group to take.

Sabor stood in a shadow crying.

"Why in the hell should I? What the hell has The Order ever done for me? Except, rip everything and everyone I have ever given a shit about away from me," Sabor said, trying to convince himself.

Sabor sunk into the shadow, grabbing his knees and rocking back and forth. His hands began to grow numb from the cold of the shadow. Shivering, he blew into them, but it was no use. As a final resort, he shoved his hands deep into his pockets, finding a small piece of folded paper.

"What is this?" He asked wiping the tears from his face and sucking in a large breath of air.

Dearest Sabor,
 My Boy, you are reading this, because you are off on your big Discovery and I cannot be there with you. I know where you are so rest easy, but knowing where you are doesn't help my heart. I miss you already, and you're not even gone yet. You are sleeping in your room down the hall, just like when you were little. I long for those sweet days my lovely boy. Honey you will undoubtedly be faced with a number of situations, were you will not want to go on, or just won't understand why. When that happens, just take this out, and read it. Be confident in yourself and never be afraid to try new things. You are a great person and I know you can be whatever you want. I am very proud of you. Remember to go for your dreams and never forget what those dreams are no matter how hard it is to get them. One day you'll be so glad you worked hard to get them. I love you more than you know and always remember whenever you feel like you're all alone. I am always there!! And I love you, I love you, I love you!

Your Mom
Noelle.

The words burned Sabor, and he pulled the letter hard to his chest, and cried very hard.

"Mom, I will go. I will avenge what has happened. I will make it all right again. I love you too, and I am ready," Sabor said , drying his eyes.

Sabor stood, while his feelings of self-pity, and mourning melted away. He was renewed, vibrant and ready for his Discovery. And so without knowing what was next, he went.

Life for The Order turned hectic. Many people did not believe in Sabor anymore. How could he be the Avenger if he ran from his destiny so easily? Why was it taking so long to find him? How would he save them all, if he weren't there in the months to come? Sabor became secondary. After searching the entire compound with no sign of him, the search was called off and preparations continued. The Guardians prepared for the Awakening, its time drawing close. The Greenlings were still a year from being fully trained and ready to be paired with a Guide. *(I guess that at this point I should explain. A Guide is the next step after becoming a Guardian. The responsibility of a Guide is to take a Greenling out and give them hands-on experience with Dvanken. Showing them how to fight the beast and sparring with them to tighten and sharpen their skills.)*

Ellett, looking for Symon, stepped into the room, knocking on the already open door. "Symon may I speak with you?" Ellett asked firmly.

"By all means, please c ome in and sit," replied Symon quickly. Ellett stepped in and took a seat in front of Symon's desk.

"I have never had a family, no children, no wife, nothing, only The Order," Ellett sat and stared down at his feet.

"I have no time for family, I am an Elder. I am a Guardian, and hold that title dear," Ellett said.

"I have a feeling we are talking not about just your dedication, or mine. This conversation is about Master Sabor Lindon. Am I right?" Symon asked in a tone suggesting he already knew the answer.

"I am sorry for going against our decision. I just believed so much in the boy and thought he could handle the news. I miss him, I felt as if he was my own. It made me long for a family of my own. Now in his absence it makes me want it even more. Do you understand?" The large man let go of his feelings.

"Yes of course I do. I am just as human as you are. But until I or someone else rids this world of Dvanken. Could you ever feel comfortable pouring your love and time into something as needy as a family? Not to say you shouldn't want one. But, I think to do so now would only cheat your loved ones out of full attention. That is not how I would want it. Besides, look at what has happened to young Sabor. You saw how Dvanken targeted his entire family, picking them off. He lasted much longer than I would have,"

Symon had rarely ever talked this freely around anyone, and it made Ellett feel much better. It made him feel like he wasn' t the only elder with a heart or true feelings.

"I understand. You are not wrong for feeling this way, brother, but you need not worry about that. I still think Sabor will return and help us. He is the Avenger, I just know it," and Ellett said erasing his doubt.

"I share your conviction, but I think we should not count on him for this go around. He is young and bull-headed. He will mature, and I too believe he will save us. But until the day he grows up and takes his place, we must try to stave off Dvanken' s onslaught, saving as many as we can. That is our job. It has been for lifetimes, and we must continue to do this until he is dead. Do you understand Ellett? We must focus on the task at hand, not be distracted by some wild goose hunt, for the Avenger," Symon scolded the Elder without making him feel inferior.

"Of course Symon. You and I both know what has to be done, but I wanted my feelings known," Ellett replied.

"Point taken friend. Let us go watch the Greenlings spar. Shall we?" With that the two walked away. The words left unspoken and the words spilled between the two echoed the buzz in the Halls of The Order. The brothers were scared, the Avenger had abandoned them.

The edges of time gave way, seeming to let the world slip by, The time melted away, the Greenlings became good, the best crop in ages actually. Eight months slipped away from The Order, with no sign of Sabor.

The Order pushed past the fact that the Avenger had left. The whole cycle was firmly back in their control. Ellett and Saimus still swept the halls every night searching for the lost boy, hoping to find the young Lindon not just for the power he possessed, but for the friend they had lost. But alas, never finding anything.

Keni grew into a very respected sabor master; even the Elders were impressed with his ferocity and control. His power focused laser-like on whatever enemy he faced and ultimately defeated. The precision he commanded was legendary, even in life. All Greenlings tried emulating his style, all taking his words and examples as gospel. He had assumed a leadership role, in the absence of a focal point of The Order for so long now. A leader was exactly what The Order needed, to step forward; bridging the gap until the Avenger surfaced.

"Your nephew has been gone for some time Saimus, Why do you think he

97

flaked out and ran away like a pussy? Too much pressure for him or what?" The impetuous Keni asked the now angry Elder. Saimus instinctively threw his sabors out to fight, and slammed Keni down on the table.

"You may be the best Greenling I have taught in many years, but you still are not good enough to talk down about one of your brothers, especially one that shares the same lineage as your Master. Give him the respect you would give you or me will feel not only my wrath, but also when he returns; I will allow him to unleash on you as well. Do you understand?" Saimus said as he let Keni regain his footing.

"Please forgive me Saimus. I am young. However, I do not think, with all due respect, that Sabor has what it takes to kill Dvanken. I mean, shit! You, yourself, Master Yorge, Master Zandalar, and even Master Ellett have failed. You taught us everything we know. How can we be expected to defeat him, much less someone who has skipped almost two years worth of wisdom," Keni asked with conviction.

"Yes. I understand your view young Divin, but you must realize, he has shown us all things never seen and done things that even you are just now beginning to do. Even without your advantageous lifetime of training. He will return, when he finds whatever it is he is looking for. Until then, you will find Dvanken and fight Dvanken. Hopefully, Sabor will not be needed. If however, he is necessary, you will undoubtedly, be a valued ally for our champion. Please, take a degree of solace in the fact, that we live in the time of the one, and that has been half the fight for many generations. We are almost ready to take the world back. Which young one, when that happens that day will be a glorious one. Go, train hard, and keep the jealousy out of your heart. You are just as important as Sabor. In his absence, your are even more, so. We all need your strength, especially the Greenlings. Please go and teach, becoming better yourself in the process," Saimus' words made Keni swell with pride.

With a great smile even a hurricane couldn't blow away, he said. "Thank you so much sirs. I will do just that. In fact, I'll go right now," The dust flew up behind Keni as he left the room.

"He will be a tough adversary for Sabor. Perhaps his tag should be Guide to the prodigal son, should he return," Saimus plotted.

Meanwhile, deep In the remote maze of tunnels known as the Proving Grounds, our hero rested. The Proving Grounds stand as a vast tangle of interweaving, tunnels and chambers, varying by some ancient enchantment with each mans entry. Thus hiding every man in his own personal prison sentenced to wander its mess until at last finding his path to Discovery. The enchantment, stagnated time leaving the rambler inside to no longer need food, or water. The exertion however, caused the need for sleep. That is one theory of why sleep is necessity. I believe the need for slumber, comes from the clarity of dreams. The mind is purest, without the onslaught of information, coming from being conscious. So, when desperately trying to find something, one needs to be focused and what better time to be focused except when devoid of all distraction. But this is a different matter entirely, my theory is not the topic at hand, please dear readers excuse me.

Sabor lay sleeping, exhausted from running for what seemed to be weeks without stopping. He began to stir a little as the wind in the tunnel picked up. Sabor tossed about, and sat up. A familiar voice rolled on the wind, as a strange fog surrounded him.

"Wake up, my boy. Wake up. Your journey is still new and you have much to learn," the voice trailed off at the end, making Sabor wonder if he had heard it or if it were a dream.

"Who is there? Is it you dad?" Sabor said.

"Yes son. Gather up your things. Let us continue your training.... "

Sabor did as the voice instructed, as he always did when his father said something.

"...You must journey through this tunnel and face the terrors inside. My death must not be in vain. You are the Avenger. Your mother's death was not your fault. She dealt with her own demons, my boy. As hard as it may be, put her death behind you, but keep her beside you forever. This will give you strength and help to keep your focus. I love you. Now, go,"The voice whipping around him for moments left, as the wind carrying it.

Sabor without further hesitation started down the tunnel. It was large and dark. The opening was scattered with the shields and helmets of many warriors. The floor was not marble as in the rest of the Halls of The Order, but soft mud-like. There was a stink about the place now, the stink of death. It was so thick Sabor could almost see the maggots chewing tunnels in the air. This was the first time this smell had ever taken shape in this place and it overwhelmed him. He wiped chunks of vomit off his face and spit getting the last remnants of taste from his mouth.

As the wind breezed past him, carrying his fathers' voice, it tugged on Sabor, pulling him down the dark expansion of tunnel. Sabor followed slowly and carefully inside. Staring into the abyss, the darkness penetrated his stomach and seized his spine. It was a different type of hollow darkness than any seen by the man ever before. No light seemed to get past the steely grip of the void. Sabors eyes began to adjust to the consuming black. He searched his surroundings, spotting a torch floating free on the opposite wall. Sabor wandered over, picked it up, and illuminated the hole.

The door was a huge thirteen foot half oval. Perched at the crest of the door, was a large skull. Not the skull of a human, but a huge dragon-like gargoyle. Various skulls of men and beast alike trimmed the rest down to the floor. The torch illuminated a large fire pot in the middle of the room, which filled the room with a dancing orange light.

The glow revealed a wall of horror. A horrific collection of skulls and bones weaving a gruesome tapestry around the entire room. A majority of the bones had been picked clean by flesh eating bugs. The rest were still half rotting with maggots dancing on the red and pale hunks of gangrenous flesh. A continuous flow of blood and maroon chunks cascaded down the walls forming scabby pools on the floor. Sabor stared, disgusted by the sight, a quiver of nausea rose in his gut. He swallowed hard, blinked, looked around. The swelling upheaval of his most recent meal doubled him over. He wiped the excess vomit from his face.

Sabor composed himself and stood at the mouth of the cave peering down into the darkness. He leaned his torch over, stirring up gravel and kicking it over the side. The tiny pebbles never made a sound. The silence the tiny rocks made unnerved Sabor.

"Why in the hell haven't they hit yet? How far down is this place?" Sabor asked out loud. He glanced about his eyes catching a path leading down into the crevice.

It was a narrow spiral, twisting and turning ever downward into the pitch. There was no glow, no light, just obscurity. Sabor felt that he must push forward into the shroud of shadows. He felt a presence, and saw a lightly lit vapor encircle his head, and heard his fathers' voice.

100

'Sabor, you must go. Face all of your fears. Face all the pain and hate. The silence will bring them all to you. The Silence will force you to choose your hate, as well as your joy. You must control them both, or your journey will end within the consuming emptiness of the Silence," The voice and vapor were gone, and Sabor's quest was again laid before him, renewed and refreshed.

Sabor took the first step into the long trudge down toward the Silence. The steep grade of the path proved almost unbearable. His mind drifted slightly to a place where he was happy, a place he was safe. The visions in his mind became more life-like the more he concentrated on them. But the more he concentrated on the visions, the less he concentrated on the path.

Step by step, he moved closer to the edge of the winding path. The sheer drop called to his feet, begging for them to bring Sabor to an early death. Sabor euphorically stared into the nothingness, seeing his childhood with his mind's eye. When his right foot shoved the loose gravel near the edge, gravity took the rest of him. As his adrenaline pushed his heart to jump a gust of wind and a bolt of light grabbed him, slamming Sabor on his back on the gravel path.

'Boy! I told you to focus. Your death here will do us no good. Do you understand? Do you see how important your focus is here? Well, do you?" Zandalar' s voice rang from the void.

"Oh shit!" Sabor said, scooting back on his bu tt. "Yes Dad, I understand. Thank you very much. I was pretty close there, wasn't I?" Sabor asked trying to release some of the tension from the reality of the situation.

"Yes, son, you were pretty close. Now please, focus," Zandalar said.

Sabor shook his body, flinging dust everywhere and began again. Sabor reached the third turn then began to feel that the farther he went down the path, the further from himself he became.

Then, from the darkness, the memories of his life began to spiral in toward him at phenomenal speeds. Instead of in his thoughts, they were broadcast on translucent clouds of smoke streaking ever closer to his face. With each cloud burst, vivid recollections and perfect recreations of the feelings he had on each corresponding day rushed into his heart and mind. Every time his mother scolded him, every kiss and fight with Chelle, the times his Father was **too** busy to teach Sabor the perfect spiral on a pass, everything he had been through was being paraded in front of him on the speeding vapors. The unrelenting memories rushed in, overwhelming Sabor. He fell to his knees and cried, pounding the ground.

'Son, you know now why I was too busy, don't you know? Dvanken had

101

to be stopped. I loved you then, and I love you now. Please understand and stop harboring the pain from those days," Zandalar's voice boomed in, interrupting the young mans self-pity.

"Dad I know, I swear I am not holding on to any of that. My past is just that, my past. I promise you!" Sabor insisted.

"Dearest son, you may believe that you have forgiven, but you cannot lie here, not even to yourself. These visions, are plucked form your own subconscious by the magic of this place, tell the truth. Now, let go of the pain. It is the only way. If you can't control your own emotions here, then how will you do it in a battle with Dvanken? He will use your feelings against you. He knows that your mind can be a powerful ally for him. He also knows it can be his undoing.
Push your pain down and find the good in each situation. Only then, can you truly Discover and become a Guardian,"

Sabor trudged on, walking down into the uncertain darkness. The visions still swirling about his head forced him to chew on the pain he had inflicted with his own grudges and unwillingness to release the negativity he felt. (I guess it is just human nature to seize these things and not let go.) The sound of his fathers' voice had calmed him. He focused on the wisdom of his dear father's words.

"You know what? I need to stop holding on to all the bad shit that has happened to me," he said out loud, revealing his feelings to himself. "My life has been great. I have had a loving family and all the privileges anyone could ask for. I need to stop whining. I am loved and healthy,"

With this statement the memories about him began to swirl faster and faster with more energy and intensity. The visions on them showed the great times he had shared with Chelle, his mom, and dad. The weight and constriction around his heart began to melt away.

The feeling of calm was ripped from Sabor as terror splashed him in the face. A huge, thorny vine shot up from beneath the path and instantly enveloped his ankle. The vine flung Sabor to the ground with a painful thud. Instinctively and with lightning fast precision, his sabors chinked out to full extension. His mind wandered to a time when his heart was happy, a Christmas with his entire family together and blissful. This recollection made his blade glow a brilliant, powerful white. His aura was blinding; his blade hummed like a tuning fork as it sliced true, tearing the vine into pieces.

As soon as he had done this, felt quite good about his control. An army of mixed vines rose from the dark, crashing down violently around Sabor. The razor-like thorns ripped uneven hunks of flesh from Sabor's body. Sabor struggled, cutting and slicing furiously, but the creeping plant was unrelenting and engulfed him in a net-like shell that would not let go. More and more vines followed as he cut them away layer by layer. The weight and strength of the mammoth greenery began to cut Sabor's air, strangling him.

Slowly, Sabor felt fear boil inside him, as he struggled. The fear swelling in his throat nearly gagged him. Suddenly, a consuming peace fell over him. A blinding light to emanated from under him again. A deafening scream escaped from his tired face. A percussion, much like the one that leveled the library, blasted out from underneath his body. Disintegrating the plants imprisoning him.

"That is it my son. Control your fear and use it to your advantage. Push and focus," His father spoke to him again, but still did not show himself.

Sabor rose and gathered himself, breathing heavily. His sabors glowed strongly, dripping with bits of plant. He had harnessed his power, and it had made him strong, nearly invincible it seemed.

"You must push further. You are not yet done with your Discovery," Zandalars voice chimed again.

"I need m ore?" Sabor asked the air around him. "What else can I learn? How much more do I need to do?" Sabor searched his mind for the answer so he would not need to continue this journey. Again his fathers wisdom streamed from the air.

"Your sabor ski lls are not what they need to be, but they will sharpen with time. Your grip on the plane of The Order has grown strong, but it too needs time to flourish as well. All of this will come in time. The time you spend in your discovery is crucial. You are talented my son, but beware your rage. Your rage is your Achilles heel. As you control the run of other negative emotions, the rage seems to overpower you at times. I fear one day it will taint your blade so completely, you will lose it forever. This you must strive to prevent, you must strive to release the fury inside. Push it, far away. When you do this one thing, your mind will be forced to focus. This will keep emotion from clouding your judgment during battle;" Zandalars voice trailed off and vanished from the wind again.

Sabor walking and listening reached the bottom of the long spiral and entered a vast open area. The smell of death grew more ripe in this chamber. Forty or so torches burned at varying locations in the room. An eerie fog crept along the floor; Sabor heard water splashing as if on a dock. The light from the torches illuminated four large fifteen-foot tall cones with huge lengths of rope bound around the bases. They stretched tightly into the water. At the bottom, half lying and half-sitting were skeletal remains, rotting and silent. In his lifeless arms rested a driftwood sign. The single word on the sign simply read "*SILENCE*," Sabor puzzled over what the meaning of the sign could be.

Giving up on the riddle, he decided to survey his surroundings. His eyes followed the rocky ground, until it blended gently into the oil slick covered water. Acclimating himself to the dim light, he saw out into the water, where sat more statues. Both human and non-human sandstone limbs reaching up from the black water to the ceiling. He stared up to see what they were reaching for. On the ceiling was a haunting glimpse of the next leg of his Discovery. On the ceiling were matching statues almost touching, but still inches away form one another, frozen out of each other's reach for perpetuity. Sabor understood the visual; at least he thought he did.

"Reaching everywhere, and being out of reach always. This place is going to suck!" Sabor paused for a moment, searching for his father's voice to guide him, to tell him some kind of encouraging words.

Finding not even a whisper, but with a deep breath, Sabor took his first of many steps into the water. Instantly he was up to his nipples in the quagmire. The water was warm, and swimming with tiny currents, flowing along no certain paths. From that moment he knew that this was no ordinary liquid. Dismissing the feeling, he trudged on realizing this mysterious chamber was separating him from his thoughts and memories. All emotion began to flee from his body. The feeling was unsettling, but he had come so far and experienced so many things. His mind raced with the new knowledge he possessed and couldn't just leave it all, going back to his normal life. He realized his life was gone, taken from him by the evil he was training to kill. A justified smile broke his lips and he continued. Sabor pulled his arms up, grabbing his wrists above his head. The wake he left behind turned blood red, then rippled out, morphing into a deep purple. He proceeded with diligence however, trying to draw the reasoning for these trials.

"What in the hell am I supposed to learn from strutting around in nipple high water, and having my thoughts stolen form me?" He asked, in a desperate search to make any memory or thought stay. The still water stole even those thoughts, as soon as he asked the question. The room took whatever answer he was about to give, sucking it down into the murky depths surrounding him. Nothing stuck in his mind, reasoning was impossible. An eerie consuming silence surrounded him. No breathing, no noise from the water, only stillness and silence. His many demons tried infiltrating the silence to induce the malice and heartache from his life, but as quickly as his mind would bring one of the small terrors back, the void on either side sucked it from his conscience.

"That's what this is. This place wants my thoughts, all my bad memories, everything negative about my history. I've gotta let go of all the negative, offer it to this place, and leave it. If not, this oil, will rip my sanity from me, and leave me like on of those lamppost talker guys, crazy as hell," This thought seemed to stay with Sabor.

"Take i t damn-it. I don't want it anymore," Sabor yelled into the silence and the chest-high liquid around him. The thick liquid began to boil and as the bubbles burst at the surface they formed small dark hands that grasped at Sabor. The words of surrender escaped his lips, sending countless emotions flying from within his body. The feeling was orgasmic. He had let go, and it felt overwhelming. The weight of experiences had been lifted in that instant. He felt incredibly light, the empty numbness scared him a tiny bit, but as he let go, the floodgate inside him burst, liberating a fury of emotion that poured from his constricted heart. The water began to rise with the grand release. The liquid rose form chest-high to just below his ears. Sabor was letting go, for the first time in his life, just letting it all go, not caring about consequence, or image. The freedom it offered made him feel as if he could fly. The pace of the memories quickened until they were but an indistinguishable blur, only color and light surging from his head.

In a moment of clarity, of discovery, Sabor said," Wait, I can't just let my entire personality be lost to this place! My pain, my jealousy, heartache, joy, exhilaration, for better or worse, they are mine, they are I. And I want it back!" Sabor grasped at the visions flying by his head. The loss began to slow, as he grabbed the sprite-like flow of memories.

"These are mine damn you. Give them back," He frantically splashed and ripped the water, trying to grab his being. "I need them; they are me, my whole life. I don't need to allow my memories to rule my actions, but I need my past to remain human.

"Wait a damn minute. That's what this is really about, not giving my emotion to this place, but realizing how much they mean to me. The good and the bad, and I would miss them if they were to be gone. I don't want to forget Mom, or Chelle, or Dad as easy as it would make losing them, they are my life and I love knowing them," The feelings reversed and began spiraling back, piling on him, and forcing his knee's to buckle.

He glanced down. In the black spectrum of the water, he saw his mothers' reflection. She smiled. Dressed in a luminescent gown, her face void of pain and worry, she knew in life. She was beautiful. The sight filled Sabor with joy and longing, reaffirming his opinion of what the room had been telling him. Noelle reached up, her hand protruding from the surface of the water. In her hand, a goblet dripped with the dark liquid. Sabor hesitated, then took the cup and drank the harsh, bitter liquid. The world swirled clockwise at the edges, the center darkening and slipping away from him quickly.

"I should b e the Avenger. I will defeat Dvanken, not Sabor. I am Keni Nathaniel Divin, twelfth son of Caden Divin and a master sabor warrior. I am powerful, and I have the knowledge to defeat him," Keni thought, defying the attitude he displayed earlier during his confrontation with Master Yorge. This he did in silence, in his head, while demonstrating the best technique for decapitating an enemy and still protecting the vulnerable underside.

"Okay Greenlings," Keni said, a little winded. "You guys practice t hat for a few minutes. I'm gonna go get some water," Keni stepped over where Yorge stood and asked sarcastically. "Has our hero shown his face yet?"

Yorge looked sternly at him and said, "No. I think the council of Elders is going to proclaim you as his guide upon his return, which is why I came here to see your sessions today,"

Keni suddenly looked astounded.

"Thank you. I will accept the honor of being his guide, but I will not allow him to make me a joke. My first order of business will be to run him through the wringer, sparring with him. To see what he is truly made of. And to show him what a Divin can do. See what it is that makes him so damn special," Keni proclaimed.

"Do what you wish with your new student, but the Elders are on his side in this. They are still convinced of his superior ability. So tread lightly young Divin, he is a Lindon and that word attached to him alone, does demand your respect. Okay," Yorge was not totally convinced, but very amazed by Sabor's progress, but his absence lent weight to his theory of the Avenger being someone else.

Yorge's words made Keni's eyes boil, a red glow lined Keni's pupils as he stared angrily at the massive Elder.

"You will take care not to stare at me with hate in your eyes boy. For I am a Danglin, and I am certain that name demands your respect. If you continue to stare at me, I will pluck your hate-filled eyes from your skull and feed them to my raven. Understand?" This threat snapped Keni back into the student mind set. He apologized and excused himself, going back to his students, where it was safe.

"Yes by all means, go and teach Master Divin, Go and teach," Yorge smiled as he teased the headstrong Divin. Keni proceeded; his teaching taking on a new found humble attitude.

"That young man is good, but his attitude is going to get him killed," Yorge said, almost prophetically.

Rip Van Lindon
The Long Silence Continued

"Unngggh! When-where am I?" Sabor thought as he began to wake up, the light searing bright, the edges of the world fuzzy. His eyes slowly adjusted from the drink he received from his mother. He peered around with new eyes. He saw the same skeleton holding the same sign, the same oily water. Everything was there, perfectly where he left it.

"Was it a dream? Did I ever even leave this spot? Oh man, damn this place. I'm going crazy anyway, gets weirder with every step I take,"

What actually happened is still today a mystery. How long he had been gone was an even larger unknown. His short beard, usually kept perfectly maintained, had grown out, now lay, tickling, upon his chest. His body was covered in a thick layer of gray dust and sticky cobwebs.

He also found, that he knew things. Things he could not possibly know things he did not know before his taste test in the middle of the Silence. He knew exactly how to communicate with the plane of The Order. His weapons felt comfortable and natural. Coming with only a thought. His knowledge of The Order had tripled. His body was tighter, more muscular.

The oddest new addition though, he could feel Dvanken. Sabor could even faintly see him sleeping in a large slimy greenish brown cocoon. The disgusting cocoon undulated, changing shape, size, and color. If he concentrated hard enough, he felt Dvanken's thoughts. It felt wonderful.

"Hell yeah. I think I'll sleep like that more often," Sabor joked, then sat up realizing that he was alone. Still a little disoriented, with sleep and the location he woke up in, he searched to regain his bearings.

Since so much of him had changed, he decided to tryout his weapons a little. With a hint of thought about his blade, his right arm projected a magnificent blade. It's shell was clear as the purest diamond, and the transparency revealed a deep heart of cerulean and a brilliant white light dancing in and around one another. As Sabor twisted the blade around, checking it from every angle he noticed that the shell had begun to change, and move with his thoughts.

He jumped back a few feet, copying a sword style he had seen in an old Samurai movie. Throwing his left hand above his head in an arc, and holding his right arm stiff in front of him. Pulling back, he let out a yell, as he quickly sliced the imaginary evil in front of him, grunting and screaming as he sliced the air.

The blade morphed as he sent it sliding back and forth through the air. Ending, when he resumed his Samurai posture, a small trident with a sword like spike under the main treble lay on his forearm panting with exhaustion. The spike had two small rows of holes that oozed the cerulean magic that danced inside.

To say that Sabor was surprised, would be a gross understatement. He was awe struck, and could not wait to show Master Ellett. Then, Sabor realized he was alone and wanting to share all of his newly found knowledge, as well as his new mastery of his toys. As the realization hit hardest, the chamber filled with a high pitched cackle, a haunting laugh.

Sabor instantly took a defensive posture with a pair of breathtaking Samurai swords out, fully extended and glowing white. A deep purple fog rolled in, like a humid morning on the San Francisco bay. He saw a set of ginger eyes beginning to break through the haze. A second laugh roared through the fog, seeming to multiply, reverberating from all around. Then, a second set of pumpkin shaded eyes broke the darkness. Sitting slightly higher in the pitch. A long, rickety, wooden flat-bottom boat slurked up to the shore, thunking to a halt.

Along the sides were fifteen, Ding Tups. (These are one-foot tall human-like creatures with large ears, with small holes in the lobes. They were naked and chained together with a glowing chain of light. They each held small wooden paddles, which they had apparently carved themselves, and used to propel the vessel.)

A huge skeletal warrior, a decaying torso of muscle, rotting and disgusting. It's arms were missing flesh from the bicep, leaving masses of red fiber to showing through. The bones dotting his frame were brown with age. His stench was thick and vile. He was draped with tattered red cloth and rusted armor. A small impish creature sat perched firmly on his left shoulder. The two of them sat on a large twisted chair of bone at the rear of the watercraft.

The imp's eyes glowed more intense the closer he came to the shore, closer to the young fare waiting confused by the sign, on the shore. The cackling little imp stood hunkered over, pointing his long lumpy finger at Sabor.

"Hey, you there! My name, is Mink Tong, the keeper of the Silence. This large being beside me, is Zin. He is the keeper of the vessels of the Stillness;" the small lizard- skinned imp laughed as he spoke. "Tell me traveler, do you wish to cross my Silence, he- he- eh?"

The small creature bounced from one shoulder to the other. The huge shoulders and head never moving. Zin only stood, staring intensely at the same spot. Not moving, or making a sound, except for groaning every once in a while.

"Well yes. That is the next step in my Discovery, right?" Sabor asked, confused by the question.

"Discovery, I know nothing of you or your Discovery, but if you wish to cross my Silence it will cost you..." the imp paused stroking his chin, like a used car salesman thinking of a way to con a potential buyer. "It will cost one of your fondest memories, and being I am in a good mood journeyman, I will let you pick the memory you will give!" He smiled an evil grin, looked at his silent perch, patting him on the head. Mink's head writhed on his shoulders stopping; he clasped his hands and rubbed them together briefly, then held one of them out as if asking for something.

"Why do you wait so long to answer? Do you wish not to pay, because if so, then Zin will have fun grinding you to dust? I am sorry, but the rules are clear. You either gives me a memory, or you will die. No other ways. He, hea, ha!" Mink spouted.

"I will not give you my memories. I have fought to keep them, and they are mine. Now please, let me pass in peace," Sabor said loudly.

"Well then, if you will not pay, we must kill you, traveler. That is truly a shame, you are so young little man. There are so many more memories to take.
"Make this easy on yourself, give me a memory. Any old memory. I don't care if it is a fond one," he cackled for a few moments, peering at Sabor with one eye closed.

Sabor raised his right eyebrow, glaring back at the little creature. A slight grin tore his face. The tiny imp's eyes searched for some weakness, or a quick exit, as a strange blue illumination rose from Sabor's forearms. In an instant Sabors blades chinked out, fully extended, battle ready. Rocking the earth with a loud boom, his blades, slicing through the sound barrier, cracking like a thousand whips. The quivering, gnarly hand of Mink Tong lay bleeding on the ground. Sabor stood at ready to take the other.

"Now let me pass you little shit, or I will take your neck next," Sabor said.

His hand lay bouncing on the ground, like a fish out of water. Mink tucked his nub under his other arm, glaring hatefully at Sabor. In an instant, a long frog-like tongue sprung from his crooked mouth and then sucked it back to him with a loud slurp. He pulled the severed limb back to the bloody stump. The skin of both stretched out to one another, like two long distance lovers reuniting after months apart. The flesh joined in porous masses, healing instantly. The tendons and muscle mending themselves. The color slowly faded back into the limb, as the blood trickled back into the lifeless appendage.

"Uhhhnn, you will pay. Hee, heee, ha. You will pay dearly for that stinky man. You will pay, pay with your blood," Mink Tong said with an evil sneer.

The tiny figure slid down the broad shoulders of his horse-sized companion. On his way to the ground, Mink grasped two blades resting in small leather holsters on Zin's back. One a blunt sword, the other was a scythe-type blade. He pounced from behind the pillar of a beast, clanking the rusty weapons together.

"You should have paid our toll, 'cause now, we kill you and steal them all,"

His small, scaly body sprung forward, tumbling wildly. His blades sparking on the floor as he spun along the ground. The tiny whirlwind sliced a huge gash in Sabor's leg, then bounced off, landing a few inches away. He hunched in front of Sabor, arms to his side, smiling at the blood rushing from the wound.

"That crimson is mine now, stranger. You have left it in my silence and we claim it!" Mink twirled along the floor, forming tiny circles, in the dust. Ending staring up Sabor's leg again. He ran one of his fingers and ran it up the wound. Then licked the blood from his finger and smiled. The swiftness and precision of the small imp was phenomenal.

Sabor drew his weapons to fight, and calmly said," you my little friend are one sick little bastard. I didn't leave anything for you or bones over there. All I wanted to do was pass, but you two, whatever the hell you guys are, won't let me. So I guess that means it's time for you to feel the wrath of a Guardian,"

A thunderous right hand nearly took Sabors head. The ringing blow sent him flying a few feet back crashing to the ground. He shook the haziness from his eyes, noticing Zin had taken Mink onto his shoulder again, and was now charging him. Sabor could only assume the blow he had received came from the mountain now running head long at him.

Sabor kicked his legs, sending a cloud of dust into Zin's eyes. Sabor rolled backwards rising to his feet. His arms bleeding and his sabor's humming. The blades rumbled in some strange way, he had never heard. Sabor dismissed the noise, realizing that the dust did absolutely nothing to Zin, since his eyes had rotted out eons ago. Sabor had to do something.

He stood straight up and pointed his right sabor squarely at their two faces saying. "You little son of a bitch. Call off your bull now, before you really piss me off. I have tried to be patient with you. I really don't want to have to kill you both, but believe me, I will. Mink, please all I want to do is get past you okay. No one has to die today. Just let me go," Sabor remained as calm as he could, in the given situation he. Sabor stood strong, and faced them still.

"You think you can beat us? Many better men have tried and many better men have failed, those men now hold our signs, and their bones decorate our walls!" Mink Tong laughed.

Sabor shook his head, coming to the realization that there was no happy ending to this encounter. He jumped landing on his right shoulder, rolling through and knocking the legs from beneath the creature. Zin tumbled and rolled, stirring up a massive cloud of dust.

Sabor's blades hummed strongly as he drove one into the ground halting his tumble. He lunged back in the opposite direction, reaching into the dense fog, grabbing the tiny imp by the throat. Covering his tiny mouth and pulling him out of sight and reach of Zin. Sabor could hear the beast grunting and thrashing, desperately trying to find Mink.

Mink Tong desperately tried warning his partner of the danger, but to no avail. He could muster only slight grunts and wheezes. Sabor had placed the imp's head firmly under his armpit, and was squeezing the life from his body.

"Shut the hell up, I may still let you live, monkey," Sabor whispered to the squirming imp under his arm. Mink heard the cockiness oozing from Sabors tone. Sensing the lax in his attackers demeanor, Mink giggled to himself. The overconfidence gave Mink a tiny ray of hope the millisecond he needed to escape. Mink slowly reached up with his right hand and thrust his retractable fingernails deeply into Sabors side. The piercing relentless pain forced Sabor to throw Mink to the ground, with a thud. Wincing in pain, Sabor grasped his side and lost sight of the little creature and as quickly as Mink had fallen, the little monster vanished into the mist.

Sabor decided to direct his focus on the large powerful foe instead of dwelling on the sprite-like Mink Tong. Surprise was still on his side, since the tumbling cloud of dust had not yet settled. So a hard-hitting surprise attack would be very effective, Sabor reasoned. Sabor steadied himself, took a deep breath then stared into the settling cloud, searching for a glimpse of his adversary. Mustering the courage to fight this half rotted foe. Rolling into the veil of dust, Sabor felt the huge presence standing right beside him. The huge skeleton reached down, grabbing Sabor by the larynx, and squeezing.

113

"Gggggunnnnnnh,"The huge being was glad to have caught Sabor. "Mink will like this. I like it if Mink like it,"

Zin turned trying to find Mink Tong, to show him how good he had done. Sabor dangled, being thrown this way and that. Helpless under the power of Zin, then slowly Sabor began to black out. As he was losing consciousness, he heard the laughter of Mink Tong. Sensing the odds swinging ever more in the favor of the two, Sabor fought desperately trying to stay awake. A sharp pain flooded over Sabors entire body, starting deep in his back. Mink exploded from the concealing mist, jabbing Sabor's exposed spine with his talons. Sabor shook his head suppressing the pain and feeling the rage deep inside him swell.

"Unn, you little son of a,"Sabor could hardly move. "...I'm gonna kill you both,"his strength seemed to be rushing back into his weakened body, for some reason.

His left sabor shot from its slot. Taking Zin's arm just below the shoulder, leaving a dripping bloody stump jutting from the body and a writhing, quivering appendage sputtering about in the dirt. The air rushed back into Sabor's lungs, revitalizing him instantly. A strange sensation of power danced inside him as he deployed his other blade. Sabor pulled his legs up quickly to his chest and kicked straight through. Splitting Zin' s ribs, finding fresh air on the other side. Sabor's right leg had stuck completely through his torso. Instantly filling the air with a thick musk and a foul cloud of reddish green mist. Sabor looked up at the gaping wound. Seeing a writhing mass of greenish white maggots' cascade down Zin's stomach.

"Oh shit, I'm sorry stinky. Did that hurt? I hope so. And by the by, I didn't ask you to spill your guts. ,"Sabor said to Zin.

Zin stared, in disbelief at what had just happened to him, then turned his glare hatefully into the face of Sabor and thundered a punch into the Greenlings nose. The force of the blow, dislodged Sabor's foot, and sent him flying across the floor.

Sabor sprung back to his feet, darting back at the abomination, and with one swipe, he slid past Zin. Smiling, each of the warriors thought nothing had happened. Sabor tuned and kicked the Skeleton, with all the strength he could muster. His foot made solid contact with Zin' s chest. With a tremendous thud, the torso fell. Both warriors stared in disbelief. The Greenling turned, thrusting his sabor instinctively into the neck of Mink Tong. Who had been sneaking up behind, as the two titans had been fighting. Sabor pulled him to eye level, peering deeply into the frightened eyes of Mink.

"Don't be afraid of thi s death Mink. It is peace I go to, my worry is forever gone, lost to the life I had. I come for you sleep. Sleep. No more memory, no time. You will come Avenger, what does that mean journeyman, WH?" Mink trailed as his life crept up Sabor's blade.

"Ooo! This is my end; " Minks arms reached out trying to grasp some unseen essence, slipping from his body. "Why you not just pay the toll. You the first to not pay, the fir," Then the tiny lizard-like body went limp. The body slid off Sabors blade with a high pitched squeak.

Sabor fell to his knee's, doubting his ability to follow through on this destiny. The murder tasted so disgusting in his belly, and the moment was lost on his thoughts of why he had to do what was done. He stood, shaking the remnants of Mink off his blade, and retracting it.

"My Discovery! I will not allow this is to be a waste of my time. I will finish and I will kill Dvanken," Sabor said to the slain warriors now lying at his feet. Feeling a bit nostalgic and full of respect for the pair, he propped the pieces of Zin up, against the sign holder and placed Mink Tong's lifeless body, gingerly on his shoulder.

The tiny Ding Tups jumped off the ship, surrounding Sabor cheering, and celebrating.

"Were do w e goes now master?" We know nothing but to row these wakes, crossing the dreams of the long ones. We not member the ways of before. What do we do know?" The group asked with one voice staring around this dark world with new eyes, free eyes. A pregnant silence hung for a moment, then the newly appointed leader (Not actually newly appointed, it was as if he had been always)

"Home!" He replied, looking each one in the eye. The grayish creatures' eyes drifted off with a smile, drifting off to fond memories of family, and of love, and of children. Life in general without the constraints of the dark and damp caverns echoing around them. The freedom tasted sweet, and the swirls of brightness inside their chests could be seen on their cheeks. 'Home, to the memories that maintained our prayers, and our pleas for him," The tiny hand stretched out pointing at a confused Sabor. "You have given our people the freedom that no other could. You have vanquished the Masters, we thank you. We are free from the slavery; we have endured for so many generations. I have been on that vessel for four hundred years. And I was very tired. Our gratitude will never be enough thanks for what your actions have given us this day. I am Eck and I wish to thank you. We all wish to take you across the Silence. Will you allow us to do this? As just a small token of our thanks,"

The small man motioned for every one to take their places at an oar.

"Thank you all so much. You have no idea how much this means to me. Thank you,"

Sabor stepped lightly into the rickety boat. "Good job my son; you are nearing your full Discovery, Gods speed," Sabor looked around, stopping as he saw Zandalar sitting on the bow of the small boat.

At the same time Eck commanded, "Off Ding Tups, off," and the boat chunked, then pushed forward.

"Dad, oh dad thank you, for all of your help. Can you tell me what do I do next? How much further do I have to go?"

Zandalar smiled, and shook his head. "This is your Discovery son. Only you can tell me what is next, or how much further your ending is. My only advice is to just follow your heart. You can never go wrong with that. When you find your ending, find your true destiny your journey will be over. Discovering who you are, that is what this is about. " Zandalar smiled and was gone, leaving only a familiar smelling mist.

"Damn, just like when he was alive. Great advice, but when I needed him, he turned to vapor and left," Sabor said out loud, but now knew why his father was always gone. He understood.

Sabor looked down at the confused Ding Tups, and said. "Sorry, just a little family trouble. Let's go," The tiny creatures in perfect unison looked up at the massive man and smiled.

"Nipt tonkel!" Eck screamed at the rows of Ding Tups, then sat down in his spot. With great precision the tiny men put their paddles into the liquid and pulled back. The strokes propelled the tiny vessel quickly across the murky water. Weaving in and out of the granite spires and statues. Sabor soaked in the environment taking nothing for granted. Sabor's mind drifted here, to warm thoughts of his mother, and Chelle. As he sat staring into the water, he saw those loving memories he had fought so valiantly for, and it made his chest tingle with joy. He laid back, drifting to sleep. Hypnotized by the melodic chanting of the oarsmen and the rhythm of the water slamming against the wood of the boat, then crashing back onto itself.

"Wake up sir. We are here. We have crossed the Silence. Please wake up," Eck said trying to wake Sabor the traditional way, but gaining no results, had to resort to water on the face. Sabor jumped up clawing and scraping as if the world were ending.

116

"Oh my God! Don't ever do that, please," Sa bor pleaded, wiping the water from his eyes and seeing the smiling Tup, Sinmon standing with an empty pale of water.

"Sorry, but our journey together is over. We thank you, again, for our freedom. Good bye," Eck said.

Sabor stepped out of the boat onto a gravel shore. He watched the boat slowly move away into the darkness. The little men chanting and singing as they rowed off into the mist rising from the water. Sabor heard their song long after he couldn't see their boat. Sabor turned smiling at the memory of the friends he had just made.

"That was a little different, but, oh well," Sabor searched around, seeing that there was a polished gold rail encompassing the landing pad. An air of quiet sophistication and elegance flowed through the room. Fine art hung around the walls. A large oak door separated the Silence from whatever waited on the other side. "I guess the only thing to do, is just go,"

Inspired by the trip he had just endured, Sabor could not wait to see what else he could do. Stepping close to the door, Sabor heard the sound of rain and the rumble of a distant storm. He looked the door over and saw there was no handle, no knob, and no way to open the obese hardwood door. He stood puzzling over the dead end. There were towering rock structures forcing themselves up through the shadowy ceiling of the Silence.

A misty green cascade ran down the face of the tan rocks, pooling on the floor, lending a concerto of bubbling liquid to the expanse. The ever familiar torches stretched upward, increasing in number the higher they got, giving off a cascading glow, as to not overwhelm the eyes as they adjusted back to luminance, after the consuming dark of the Silence. The room had a very pleasant feel, and the air held the faint taste of muffins and Polk salad. Such a familiar and easing place, Sabor was of a mind to sit and just soak this dim room in for a while.

"Wow, man this place sure is cozy. I don't want to leave," Sabor said out loud.

Then all at once, an overwhelming feeling to pull at the door overcame him. To pull at the door, but not with his hands, but instead with his mind.

"Well, Okay I wanted to see what I could do. Here goes nothing,"

The Greenling concentrated on opening the door, making long circular motions with his hands, and urgently trying to open it. He grunted, struggling with himself, trying to gain entrance to the mystery beyond. To continue his Discovery to find his place in the world.

"Come on, open, damn it," He squinted, curled his mouth, and began to sweat. But the door did not budge. Suddenly, the door flung open, revealing a small man dressed in a red tuxedo, well kept and put together. He rolled on the ground laughing as if about to pee in his pants.

"Oh, God please, please stop. You're killing me," he laughed. "Open, open says this guy," The little man said mockingly, imitating every move Sabor made, laughing all the while.

"Hey, cut me some slack. How was I supposed to know there was a doorman?" Sabor defended himself.

"Well, my boy it is a door. You could have just knocked instead of trying to use your dazzling mind powers, to impress it open," The little guy said. "I am the doorkeeper, my name is. Well, you know, I don't rightly remember what my name is. No one has been here in so long, that I can't remember. Odd huh? Oh well, I guess, I'll make one up sometime. But for now, you can enter if you would like, some company would be nice," The little man continued, gesturing for Sabor to enter.

"Thank you, but what exactly is on the other side?" Sabor inquired.

"The Climb. That is what is through my door. Just the Climb. But come, enough talk about business, you look tired. Come and eat, rest and visit. My house is just on the other side as well,"

Sabor followed the little man who ran ahead of him. The red suited man ran fast, then stopped sharply turning to motion Sabor to follow him faster. He passed through the door, finding a one hundred and fifty-foot diameter circular room.

On the right side of the room, was a large pond with a small wooden bridge arching over it. A huge waterfall crashed constantly behind the makeshift bridge. The water, clean and blue, flowed out through a prison-bar guard in the direction of the Silence. A small water wheel turned under the force of the waterfall. On the left, a short hand-carved staircase, leading to a plateau front yard. There wedged in the crack of two rocks stood a small crooked sign reading *"the climb, Dornman's domain,"* The sign was painted a pale green and the writing a deep red, it hadn't been straightened in years, and the wood had begun to rot, form the moisture of the tunnel.

A makeshift clothesline holding tiny garments blowing in the constant vortex caused by the architecture of the room. In large pots throughout the chamber, grew various plants. Tomato plants, corn, peas, watermelon a rainbow of fruit and vegetables. It was a garden that would make most farmers feel inadequate. But not so large that any was wasted.

Nearby was a small cottage-style house carved, apparently by hand in the side of the sheer cliff. The cottage was cut into three cascading parts. Obviously for the ease the design afforded due to the unforgiving rock. A small three-plank oak door sat cradled just under a small rough cut window, bearing a wrought iron hourglass. A miniature rectangular window sat quietly to the left of the door. A jigsaw type chimney sat atop this first room, puffing small rings of delightfully smelling smoke. The second layer of the house gave the home it's cottage appeal, with a rounded pitched roof, with a larger window chattered into the center just under the wavy overhang. A small family of bats hung upside down, swaying in the shadows just above the crossed window. A dark window gave entrance to the kitchen showed a tiny wisp of movement inside. This square window was the only one trimmed in wood, rotting, buckled and bowed against the rocks.

The third tier was barely distinguishable as a part of the house, were it not for the tiny hemp roped railings, and plank door, it would appear as only a rock. Massive carvings had been started in varying locations throughout the hall. Greatly detailed at least the pieces that had been finished. The faces were haunting. Elongated with sorrowful expressions. A dark trace in direct contrast with the joy resonating throughout the room.

The walls proceeding up from behind the tiny house, for what seemed miles. The tan rocks rolled and cracked in upon themselves. Huge vines climbed the length of the sheer. A pleasant aroma billowed in the air, originating from the chimney. Sabor saw the tiny wisp of movement in the kitchen window had turned to a small, portly woman busying herself inside.

"Come on in. I will introduce you to my wife. She ain't much to look at, but she sure can cook a mean pot of stew. What's more, she keeps me groomed. See? My toes aren't never dirty. I can't complain, I guess," The excited little man proclaimed, simply happy to have conversation with a new face.

"Hey!" Sabor yelled, stopping the man and staring. "It would be really great if you could introduce yourself first, there old timer. I don't necessarily make it a habit to follow strange men into large doors in caves ya know. Or do you still have amnesia about what it could be?" Sabor laughed and held out his hand for him to shake it.

"Oh my stars. I didn't tell you my name, did I? Well, I am s o sorry. Just couldn't tell ya. Not 'til I knew if you were worth it. Understand don't ya?" He dusted off his hands and shook Sabor's vigorously.

"My name is Milton Dornman. And this is my home. It is a peaceful chunk of the world, and it's paid for. Can't ask for more than that, ey? " He said as he hit Sabor in the ribs with his elbow, bouncing his eyebrows up and down repeatedly.

"Actually, I carved it all myself. Well, in reality my father and I did. But he's gone now, died around eighty or so years back. Just went out into the muck of the Silence and never came back, he was sickly for sometime before-but enough bout that tale. Besidendat tale is depressin and depressin stories are for Wednesday's, and special occasions, not for introductions. So, come on in and meet my wife, Avril. She's the reason I been keeping meself out here carving these long faces. I call 'em my "keep out of the house, busy work, and faces,"

They keep me out here, so I ain't gotta listen to the old bag," and Milton said waddling into the house

The man stomped his feet and kicked of his polished, black and maroon shoes. A beautiful smell rolling from the entrance of the rock cottage. The moist, flowing air was easy to breathe. The entire room glowed with a homey, peaceful feeling.

"Come on young man. Kick off your shoes, rest awhile," Milton said, stretching backward popping his back standing on the threshold of the half open door.

Sabor hadn't felt this happy and accepted in a long time. The feeling he got here reminded him of Noelle and her lovely glow.

"Thank you so much, thank you. I appreciate this," Sabor said as he kicked his shoes off and followed him into the house.

A short, but pretty in her own way old lady stood on an oak foot stool, washing dishes in a beautiful hand-carved ornate sink. There were small statues and carvings of all sorts of animals, and other creatures that Sabor had never seen covered the sink and countertops.

"These carvings are amazing," Sabor complime nted.

"Well thank you, my dear boy. More of that work I was telling ya about outside," Milton said then whispered so his loving wife wouldn't hear. "I have spent a lot of hours on them, over the years. And it does my heart well to know they are appreciated. It wouldn't hurt some other people around here, that shall remain nameless to say if they liked them once in a while," Milton said in a sarcastic tone shaking his head at the lady slaving away in the other room.

"Hey Milton, I heard that. I tell you plenty, how much I love this house. Will you stop blaming me, you little twit," Avril snapped, never looking up from her duties. "Now, I need you to clean the living room from your little wrestling match last night," Avril added laughing after she was done.

"Now Ave honey. That is no way to act in front of the company!" Milton said as if to regain the pants from the lively woman in the kitchen.

"Oh Milty, I didn't know you had company dear. I am so sorry. Sweetie, come in and sits rest yourself. You look very tired; I am cooking a very nice stew, and an oven full of biscuits. I sure hope you're hungry.
"Milty honey, could you set the table and turn on the radio for our handsome, young guest," Avril said, as she smiled, then winked, smacking Sabor

121

on the butt.

"I tell you Sabor; she get's hornier than a rose bush in spring down here. With just me and the wind to, well you know what a husband does to his wife," Milton said, turning beat red with the realization of what he was saying.

Sabor sat back in a large down-filled easy chair, and propped his feet up. He rolled his eyes back in his head and drifted off to sleep.

The sounds of forties style music filled the cave, echoing thorough out the house. Milton came in dancing swinging his index finger and spinning in tight circles.

"Now, that my boy, is music," He stopped mid-sentence and hurried back to turn the music off so as not to disturb Sabor.

"Ain't he cute ma? Makes me wish we had some little babies around here. How bout you, huh? You wanna go practice a little? If you know what I mean?" Milton said with the twinkle of a twenty-year-old in his eye.

Avril kicked him in the shin and snapped him with her dishrag. Her eyes bulged as she went to check the dinner, cooking in the kitchen.

"You lost the lead in your pencil years ago honey, besides you have to get that table ready," She smiled without letting him see. Just a game the little woman played from time to time. Teasing the child-like old man.

"Fine! I'll go set the table. It ain't like I need it or anything. I just thought I might help out an old woman with her mood," Milton said softly, as he grudgingly went about his chore.

"I heard that, Milton Dornman. You had better watch y our attitude with company here," Avril snapped. Displaying the radar ears, most women develop with age.

The two busily set the table and prepared the spread for their guest.

"Wake up honey, wake up. It's time to eat. You have been sleeping for about an hour now my boy. The dinner is pretty warm still, so come on," Sabor stirred, blinking the fuzz from his vision.

"Oh, I'm sorry. I did not mean to doze off. I apologize," Sabor said as he rose to his feet and straightened himself up.

"Oh nonsense, my boy," The pair said in unison. "That is why we let you sleep. You needed it, especially since you have the Climb ahead of you,"

The beautiful, hand-made table and table cloth were inset with the crest of The Order. Various wild flowers sat still in a clay vase in the center of the table; helping to build the depth of smells floating in the room. A grand feast had been prepared without the knowledge of any company. Laid out with brown buttered rolls, vegetables with some sort of a brilliant orange sauce and a plethora of other tastes, the table was awe inspiring and welcome to the hungry Guardian. The enticing aroma bubbling from the stew pot at the head of the table, made Sabors stomach roll with even stronger hunger. A large pumpkin pie sat cooling on the windowsill, topped with a sprig of mint. The spread made Sabor smile, with recollections of past family gatherings.

They all sat together having great conversation and delicious food. The evening was as relaxing as Sabor had ever had.

Sabor looked at the couple, realizing for all of their eccentricities and odd little quibbles; they were very much in love. This made him remember back to he and his beloved Chelle, making plans for their own eternity together. The minutes melted into hours, the topics never running dry. There were reflective pauses once in a while, but no searching for places to begin again, no searching for laughter; it simply found them happily. The trio sat, lost in time and family. Not caring about the world, just the friends each one had found and the fresh stories they had so much in common with.

"Well mom, we haven't stayed up like this in decades. I think we had better turn in. I'm super tired,"Milton turned and said to his wife. He stood and stretched, placing his hand on Sabor's shoulder; he tapped him approvingly, then proceeded past to his bedroom, slowly.

"Thank you again Avril. It was a great meal. In fact, I don't think I have had a meal that good in years. And I think a little shuteye would be great," Sabor added with a smile.

Sabor lay restless, tossing and turning on the sofa. 'Son, you sleep too much lately! Arise and continue your pilgrimage, continue your Discovery. Your time grows shorter with every breath,"Zandalar's voice echoed in the open room. Sabor rose to a sitting position and looked around, clumsily trying to find his father's face hidden in the unfamiliar obscurity of the Dornman's front room.

"Dad, I can't help it. I'm tired. I need my sle ep. I miss you so much Pop. How have you been?" Sabor asked, barely making out the broken outline of his father standing at the end of the couch.

'I am fine my son. Your mother sends her love. She loves listening to you think at night. She says it is one of her new favorite pastimes," the shapeless cloud replied.

"M-mom is there, with you?" Sabor asked, through the large lump in his throat. "Well yes, of course she is. She has passed on my son," Zandalar said with a chuckle.

"Is she o kay? Was it a bad death?" Sabors eye's welled up with tears, his words breaking with hurt.

"She is very well now, son. She misses you a great deal, but her worldly troubles are gone," Zandalar began, but was interrupted mid sentence.

"Would yo u two quit acting like I'm not even here!? I can hear the both of you, and I can surely speak for myself," Noelle's voice was like honey to Sabors ears, sweet and pure. "My loving boy, you know now, as I do now, that I am a Guardian also. The Plane of The Order is beautiful. And I am truly happy here. I can spend the rest of my days in the solitude of this green, lush plane, and enjoy your father's company without any quilt or regret.

"Often, I sit and watch you as well. I lay listening to your brea thing, and collecting your dreams as they escape while you sleep. I am here honey. Stop troubling yourself with my well being and get through this. The world doesn't know it, but they need you. They need the hope, and rest you will bring them with your talents. Forgive me, my little Sabor I ramble. All I really wanted to say is I love you, and good-bye for now, my son," Noelle evaporated back to shadow, leaving small dancing rings of smoke dwindling in the air.

Zandalar stared at Sabor. "My litt le man, I am so proud of you, I can't begin tell you how much it means to me, that you are following the path. Take some comfort that your forefathers are watching over you. Keep it in your thoughts as well that, I love you too," Zandalar placed his vaporous right hand on the back of Sabors head and rustled his hair, then was gone.

"Damn. I wish they would just stay and talk," Sabor said with an air of disgust. Reaffirmed by the words of his parents though Sabor wrote a note, and ventured out into the swirling winds, to the next leg of his journey,

The Climb

Early next morning, Milton woke to the sound of his pet rooster tied to the headboard of his bed. The bird was clucking, and pecking frantically at the oak headboard.

"Okay, okay I'm up!" Milton said as he slapping the fowl sharply in the neck and sending the poor bird hurling to the end of its hemp leash. Then with a snap and a thud, the bird flopped and bucked on the floor, clucking a bit slowly, and out of rhythm.

"Milty, you are so rough on poor little Chester. Just get up. You know that is all he wants," Avril scolded.

"Sorry Hun, but I just love to watch him snap back like that. Sorry," Milton responded sarcastically. Milton pulled himself slowly from beneath the down filled comforter, slipped on his fuzzy red house shoes, and strolled into the living room whistling a song from his youth.

"Hey Sabor, you awake yet? How bout I whip you up some world famous flapjacks, Avril's specialty, ya know?"

The silence of the reply confused Milton.

"Boy, are you in there?" Milton asked louder. Scared, he rushed to the couch to find the blankets neatly folded, and a fresh flower laid upon a note sitting on top of them.

"Well I'll be, hey honey, Sabor has left, and to beat all, the boy cleaned up after himself, and left a note and a flower for you.

Dear Dornman's
 I am Very sorry to leave in such a hurry. So very sorry, but my journey is not only with myself, but by myself. I will be by here again I hope, as to repay your unwavering kindness and generosity. I will always be indebted to you. Here is a flower for the lovely Mrs. Dornman, Avril I will never forget you. Milton, you keep up the good work with the entrance. And take pride in what you have accomplished, your sculptures are great. I will love to return someday to see the finished product, but until that day I must thank the both of you and continue my journey.

Once again, I am indebted

Much thanks,

Sabor Lindon

P.S. Take Avril out dancing. She is going insane down here.

"That boy is a saint I'm telling ya, honey," Avril said, wiping a private tear from her cheek.

"You are very right, my dear. What say you to a little romp around the ol' living room, my darling?" Milton said as he spun, moving all of the furniture back, turning on the old dust-covered radio in the corner, and then holding his hand out beckoning his lovely wife to join him in the recommended waltz.

Meanwhile, out in the deafening winds of the Climb, Sabor surveyed the daunting task he was to embark on. Staring straight up the vertical face, he judged it around fifty to sixty stories tall. Huge vines climbed the sheer rock, anchoring themselves with webs of razor sharp roots, that dug themselves into the stone, causing the rock to bleed water. Sabor took a deep breath, then with a grunt; he grasped a hunk of greenery and pulled himself up, quickly ascending the cliff face.

"This is going to be tough. I have never climbed any thing remotely like this before. Guess there is always a first time for everything," Sabor said to himself. But he had been spurred on by his mother's words, and would not give up his Discovery, not simply because it had become a little more difficult than he was accustomed to.

He grasped at every hold, his knuckles white with blood red rings, quivering from the strain. He kicked and pulled until every muscle in his frame cried for him to stop. A paralyzing tightness began to set in, gripping his muscles about two hundred yards from the ground. Shaking off the sting of the cramps in his hamstrings, Sabor pushed further and further up the Climb.

The whole time thinking to himself. "What is this damn thing trying to teach me? What am I supposed to Discover, by falling off a huge cliff,"

The answer was not in the rock he was climbing or the tornado force wind that was trying it's hardest to rip Sabor from his footholds, but the answer lay inside him, yet again. The rock face represented fighting the inner demon's trying to stop us from achieving greatness. It proved to Sabor, in a tangible way, anything worth having comes with sacrifice and toil, most of all a lot of hard work. That is what the climb was about.

Sabor glared up at the blue sky and paused his ascension for a moment and just stared. The beauty of the robins egg sky dotted with silver-gray lined cotton balls of clouds dancing across it was awesome indeed. Sabor momentarily lost his breath and his grip as he stared heavenward. He slipped back, his feet the only part of his body touching solid ground. Just as gravity was about to grab Sabor and hurl him at the ground to his death, a small, but beautiful, flower bent and seemed to stare at him. A net of root and vine shot from the base of the flower, ensnaring him.

"Oh, Shit! Thank-you so much, little flower. You saved my life; "Sabor said as the vines pulled him back to his solid stance. He shook the vertigo from his head and looked up at the rest of his climb.

"Damn that was close," he thought, as he shook the gravel dust from his eyes.

As Sabor tried to pull himself free of the tangle of vines, the grip from the creeper cut the circulation to his ankles. He struggled, slamming his fists into the green prison, and found he could not deploy his sabor's. Trepidation gripped him, negative emotion paralyzing him and his defenses.

The vines began to tighten and tiny thorns sprouted along the entire length of the green rope-like plants. The main flower opened its beautiful burgundy petals, almost smiling at Sabor. The life force driving Sabor to make this climb was drawn from him by this parasitic plant, leaving him clinging to his strength with the tips of his fingers.

Sabor inhaled deeply and began to spin a memory of his mother. The calming effect was immediate. Instinctively, a huge wakizashi style sword shot out above his elbow jutting up past his shoulder, nearly taking off his own ear. A broadsword sabor sliced the skin on his forearm and a pair of long tendon-like whips cracked from the slot as well.

"Ha, you little bastards, just don't know when to leave a man to his climbing. Do ya!?" Sabor yelled as his left arm turned into a whirling, clanking whirlwind.

The green vines that had enjoyed such a tight grip now laid on the tiny ledge in shreds. A large petal swooshed away in the vortex spiraling upward. Sabor smiled, happy with his new rapier. He shook his head in disbelief, and then his confidence gave way, as did the ledge. Sabor fell faster and faster, dissolving all of the progress he had made and plunged to the front steps below.

The Order prepared for the Awakening. Two years and a few month's had crept by since Sabor had disappeared, and The Order had changed. It focused on preparation rather than on the recovery of their prodigal son. The halls were alive with impressive once new Greenlings that had now become guides.

Keni had mastered all the techniques, of the blade, quickly becoming a great leader and example in the Halls of The Order. Much as he had hated to admit it, he looked forward to tutoring Sabor, showing him what Dvanken could do, and learning a bit from the awesome things Sabor brought to the table. He sat many hours reading the stories of the History and the tale of the Avenger.

"Master Ellett, I cannot tell you again how sorry I am for how I treated Sabor. I fear it was my fault he left. Maybe not entirely my fault, but I did not make it easy for him to stay. I've cost him a lot of training and time with the brothers. Will you please forgive me?" Keni said with his eyes fixated on the floor.

"Master Keni, you are most certainly forgiven. You did nothing wrong, save being human and as much as we wish we did not have such a flaw, we bare the inconvenience of our own natures. You and young Master Lindon are a pair cut from the same cloth. Smart, strong, dangerous and above all of these arrogantly pig headed. But that is just youth mixed with ultimate power. And all of these perfectly understandable and forgivable," Ellett replied. Ellett's words not only helped Keni, but took him by surprise for Ellett; a man he respected very much had called him a Master. This was something Keni desired since his first day as a Greenling.

"Besides, I have a suspicion our young Avenger has not been left out in the dark. He will return, and if I know Zandalar, he has been watching and assisting our rogue these two years past. I have tried to contact him on the plane, but I cannot find him. So, in my assumption, he must be entirely too busy for us, thank God," Ellett added with a grin.

"Well thank you, Master," Keni added returning the respect he had been given. "I feel a great deal better," Keni graciously said, trying to remove himself gently from the conversation that had begun to become too serious.

"Do you feel the air in the world, brothers?" A deep voice bellowed an interruption the voice belonged to Elder Symon, who found himself strolling into the conversation. "It is evil and the breeze unsettling. I have not felt this measure of anticipation and amassing of evil, since the season of the Vettin campaigns. You remember those dark days Master Ellett, don't you?" Symon said with a disturbed tone and expression.

"Of course I remember, that was when I lost my place, but what does that have to do with the present? If I may ask Master," Ellett came back with his own expression and tone. Keni stood, wanting to step back into the intriguing discussion now, but recognized his place and remained silently spongeful of the history being exchanged.

"I fear the Awakening may be upon us. We must set apart the pairings and send The Order back into the world until the Slumber comes upon us again. The cycle of despair is never-ending... " Master Symon said.

"That is exactly the kind of thinking that has perpetuated the cycle these thousand years. That is exactly it. We as the protectors must change," Ellett briefly interrupted him.

"...That is why I am urging the quick insertion back into the world," Symon finished.

"Sir's, excuse me, but what do you think Dvanken will be when he awakens?" Keni asked no longer keeping his restraint, overcome with youthful curiosity.

"In my experiences, he is much faster, harder hitting, and hungry. This is your first Awakening, isn't it young Divin?" Ellett replied, then asked. Keni stared weak-kneed at the Elder and replied.

"Why, yes it is. I could not be more excited about the experience. I will be facing the newest, fastest Dvanken yet, and I will have the Avenger as my learner. Who could ask for more?" Keni answered with an air of excitement melting away his fears.

"Your enthusias m is an asset, but make certain your ambition does not cloud your judgment. Keep your eyes ever watchful, Dvanken is a wily foe. He will cloud you in new ways after his Slumber, taking new approaches with his evolution. For Sabor has not seen Dvanken, it will be new and intimidating surely," Symon said placing his two cents on the table, figuratively speaking of course.

The halls were full now and a portly bubbly Greenling named Mcgwire passed by and heard the talk of Sabor. Awkwardly striding and a bit clumsy without his sabor engaged. Mcgwire was known as a very fierce fighter, very focused on defeating or helping in anyway to end Dvanken' s cycle as were most in The Order.

"Excuse me, I could not help but hear you talking about the Avenger. I was there, I watched in the library when Sabor did the weird thing with the light. I must admit, I have been trying ever since then to do it. Can you help me Master Symon?" The plump Greenling asked quite innocently.

Symon looked down at the ground and excused himself from the discussion with the others. Then shook his head, a little put out at the rude nature of the interruption. His sabor skimmed from his forearm.

"You have interrupted yet again Greenling! You must learn patience," Symon yelled, becoming more enraged the more he thought about the insolence. He drew his arm back, slamming the eager young man to the ground with the broad side of his blade. The clumsy Greenling looked up from the floor with a look of panic.

"Sir, I am so sorry. Please, don't do that again. I am so sorry!" Mcgwire said thrusting his hands in front of him, shaking them, and trying to distract the angry Elder from his intent of hurting him again. He sprung to his feet, dusted himself, and bowed waiting for any type of response. He waited in total silence.

"I am sorry to be so harsh, but you have been warned before. The amazing feat you saw in the library was unbelievably isolated. I have never seen it's equal, and certainly I could never recreate the feat. So, therefore I do not possess the knowledge to teach a technique such as that. Perhaps you should ask Master Sabor. Now please, leave us to our discussion," Symon turned without another word to him.

Mcgwire stood and shook his head, at the fact that a Greenling knew of a technique that a high Elder did not. He slowly excused himself and left with no response, only a nod to each of the men.

"The Greenlings are all becoming very restless, Symon. I need to see Sabor, badly. I admit that his absence has been troubling, not only to the Greenlings, but to myself too. I do believe and I have always believed he will be back, but faith is fragile even for an Elder," Ellett said, an air of shame in his voice.

"We have all shared these thoughts. Don't be penitent. It is human nature to miss people;" Symon calmed Ellett, placing a hand on each of his brother's shoulders. The trio left the hall, discussing the steps until the prodigal son's return.

The fall disoriented Sabor. He fell for what seemed to be minutes. The strange, but familiar, orange glow surrounded him, morphing colors radically. The descent slowed, an odd solidification of the glow began to take place.

Sabor glanced down in the midst of the plummet and spotted the glow wrapping itself and around him tightly forming an armor of some sorts. The armor, glistened a brilliant rainbow of colors at first, it then hardened into a solid grayish gold, formfitting shell. The light formed a chain mail mesh over the entirety of his body. The mesh colored a deep gray with shimmers of amber light dancing about it. The forearms were smooth except for the row of studs trimming the outline of his forearm and the two small knife blades on either side and a rigid spire jutting up toward his shoulder, uneven and razor sharp. The knees of the armor were festooned with a single large claw-like spike curving downward toward his feet. The shin guards had a row of raised pellets; the center of the row was raised just a bit, giving symmetry. A long leathery patch of the chain mail dangled from the belt line. It bore a wonderful translucent crest, which danced with light. The breastplate was a sight to see as well, with intricate Celtic markings encircling the chest and curving around over his shoulders. His head was encased in a gargoyle-type helmet. The sight was truly awesome to see in the armors maiden appearance, I'd wager, and the first emergence of the sabor armor of the Avenger.

He fell ever closer to the ground, until he crashed to an instant halt, bouncing on the ground and finally coming to a rest by the pond near Milton' s house, with quite a noise. Sabor looked around, counting his limbs and checking for broken bones. He peered up, catching the spot where he had fallen from. It was a broken cliff about one third of the way up the tremendous incline. Astounded that he was still breathing, and even more bewildered that nothing was broken or severed, he stood and looked for the first time at his armor in the reflection on the pond surface. He wondered how in the hell the armor saved him from certain death?

In a rush, Milton ran out onto the porch for his modest home, and stood bow legged and wide eyed at the sight. He had a tablecloth tucked into his collar, and a trail of food and dishes followed him outside.

"Milton Dornman, you get your behind back in here and clean up this mess. I will not clean up after you forever you know... " Avril yelled, running out the door behind her husband. She slammed into Milton's back as he had stopped dead in his tracks at the sight of Sabor's armor.

"...Who is that?" Avril said as she tapped Milton on the shoulder, then ducked behind him for protection.

"Sabor is that you my boy? Is that you?" Milton asked, wiping his supper from his face.

"Yes my little friend it's me. I don't really know how I am able to talk to you right now, but I am. It looks like I have a long climb ahead of me again. But it is still me," Sabor said with a sigh as his armor changed back into a subtle glow, as he relaxed. "Look's like I have found a new toy, huh?" Sabor asked the awe struck pair. Avril darted out behind Milton.

"I think that is a very nice toy m y boy. Especially if you fell as far as I think you did," Milton added shaking his head and walking closer to Sabor.

"Are you sure you're okay, honey?" Avril's mothering instinct kicked in. She spit on the tablecloth and began to wipe the dirt from Sabor's face. Sabor turned his head attempting to get away from the spit rag. "Okay, okay. Thank you Avril, I'm fine. I guess I had better start up again," Sabor turned and waved, then jogged back to the wall.

"Oh but honey, you have had a terribl e fall. Why don't you come in, have a bite to eat, and rest a little while?" Avril asked, grabbing his arm and pulling towards the house.

"I really appreciate that, but I need to go. I have bothered you both entirely too much, and besides I have a really important appointment. Good bye," Sabor smiled lovingly at the tiny woman, reassuring her with his demeanor, then sauntered off.

"He is going to do well, don't you think?" Milton asked his loving wife.

"Yes I think he is. I really think he is," She replied, grabbing her husband by the arm and pinching him. "You could have spoken up a bit more. Then maybe he would have come in and seen me, I mean us, for a while longer. You old fart," Avril, then turned and walked back into the house, slamming the door sternly.

"Now you listen to me woman. Don't you walk away from me before giving me a chance to answer your remarks. Avril, you let me in there now. You hear me? Let me in that house right now, or so help me," Milton screamed, his words overpowering even the torrent of wind, whistling about him.

132

The Journey, within the journey

The sound of the argument put a smile on Sabor's face, and a tiny sprig of home into his determination. Sabor took to his climbing, grasped and dug into the cliff with every bit of strength in him. After a few slips, and near falls, he approached the summit. The lessons of the climb were of perseverance and reflection, on who and what had pushed him to it. The questions dotting his mind slowly faded, finding the answers with every grip. Could he really make this climb? Did he have the will power to make it all the way out? What did this leg of his Discovery mean to him and his destiny? All the of these questions were answered, as he reached the last grip and pulled himself onto the solid secure plateau at the end of The Climb.

Sabor gazed out onto a lush green valley, stretching out until it met the deep blue sky. Far away in the hazy green distance, past the grasslands and forests. Just beyond the farm houses dotting the fields, Sabor could faintly make out, where the stone Gargoyles stood vigil over the entrance to the Halls of The Order.

The vivid brownish-orange tinge of the rocks at his feet melted down into the rich greens of the valley. The plain was speckled with clumps of deep green underbrush. In the distance, the small clumps of trees blended softly into a bluish-green forest. The haze brought about by the distance caused the colors to fade, and melt into one another. The horizon oozed from forest green to a soft white and sky blue. The scene nearly stole Sabor's life with its beauty.

On the horizon, just above the entrance to the Halls of The Order, which now seemed so far away and so long ago, a small, but brilliant, light hovered swaying slightly. Sabor's attention was intently directed at the ball of dancing light, so much so, that he failed to notice the soft rain falling on his weary head. He watched as the field began to sway and dance in the swirling wind generated by the impending storm.

The drizzle rapidly gave way to a pounding storm. The tempest began to tear the sky with its fury, never relenting. Sabor stood enchanted by the light in the distance. It was beautiful and for some reason the orb, would not release his attention. The rain softened, and a large bolt of lightning slammed the ground in the distance, shattering the melodic rhythm of the rain with a boisterous clap of thunder. Within the sound of the rolling bass, Sabor heard a faint whisper.

"You have made it my son. We of the Plane are proud of you, our Avenger. We look upon you with fond hearts and youthful enthusiasm. You stand as our revenge; you are the savior of the ones we have left behind, through our own incompetence. We all love you. Most importantly, my son, I love you and I am so proud to be known here, as the father of Sabor Lindon, the father of the Avenger," The words were merely a whisper, so quiet Sabor wondered again if he was only imagining the sweet words.

"Dad?! Where are you?" Sabor asked, frantically searching the horizon for some sign of his father. A solid hand grasped his left shoulder and gave a loving squeeze. A look of relief broke over Sabor's face as he felt his father's hand. He turned to see him.

"Oh Dad, am I so glad to see... " Sabor's expression turned from relief, to confusion. The plateau was void of any other life. The pressure on his shoulder was gone.

"Dad?" Sabor searched the moment and the ground. Lying on a rock, neatly folded, was a leather jacket. The coat was folded so the brilliant crest shown brightly against the dirty brown leather.

"This my son, I would like for you to have. Wear it and bring the family name dignity, more dignity than I did. I know you can do this, I have seen it in your eyes. I have no problem asking it of you. Good-bye for now my beautiful son," Zandalar's voice echoed on the storm.

Sabor wiped a tear from his eye and knelt down. He grasped the cloak, hugged it tightly, and murmured under his breath," I will kill Dvanken. I will avenge your deaths. I am a Lindon. I am the Avenger. Don't worry Dad, I will make you proud. The hunter is now the hunted. Enjoy your reign for now, Dvanken, I'm coming," And with that Sabor started to the light and the entrance to his destiny.

As the drizzle subsided completely, Sabor glanced reflectively back over his shoulder at the opening of The Climb. He caught a hint of a new argument raging below him, deep inside the earth. The bickering made him chuckle.

"That's a crazy pair. Gotta love 'em," he said to himself. The soaking wet Guardian turned to accept his next 'Journey". The treacherous gradient beckoned and Sabor answered with his first step.

The rocks resting on the nearly vertical slope were jagged and loose. Sprigs of six-inch grass gripped the soil, breaking up the monotone landscape of the rock. Sabor slid down the first few feet of the decline. After finally hitting a patch of soft dirt, he steadied himself on a root cluster from some unseen tree.

Sabor dusted himself off, looking up from were he fell. "Well, that sucked,"

Gingerly, Sabor made his way down the remainder of the steep rock, at last coming to the unkept grass living at the bottom. The confused Guardian searched for something familiar to point him in the right direction. He found nothing, until spotting something that resembled a head stone peaking out of the tall grass surrounding a large oak tree. Brushing the grass and dust off the stone he read the markings.

"Weary traveler. The lengths of The Journey cover miles. The lessons of the lengths cover a lifetime. The lifetimes spent in The Journey become weary. Welcome traveler to The Journey," The words of the plaque confused Sabor even more, but one thing was clear, he had yet another Journey to undertake.

The expanse of the great plain began to play tricks on Sabor's eyes. The grass, in places, did not dance with the wind, instead appearing to blow around some invisible entity. The eerie feeling of eyes watching from the empty places in the grass sent shivers up his spine too. But, he continued on, taking in the beautiful, fragrant air and the awesome serenity of the animals simply living life. They did not care about Dvanken. They had no worry of anything and he envied their bliss.

A long stretch of green symmetry lulled Sabor into a trance as he rambled ahead. Sabor trudged along, noticing little more than a cloud morphing shape, forming a turtle, when out of nowhere, he slipped through waist-high white flowers. He had fallen into a murky pond, overgrown with vegetation that perfectly matched its surroundings. Thrashing about under the water, he felt his arms and legs tangling tightly within the long reeds.

His air running thin, Sabor felt reality slip away from him. Then, he relaxed, giving in to the situation, accepting his end. Sabor felt something break the surface of the water, then thrash around searching for what he assumed could only be him. Desperately he pulled. Then, as if someone had turned on a light, he slammed his sabor out, freeing his arm to grab his savior. A massive paw grabbed his wrist, wringing him up from the water in a tremendous arc. Sabor landed on his bottom, concealed in the tall grass. He winced and turned quickly to find what it was that ripped him from the water, friend or foe.

"Thank you, I think," Sabor said. "Hello! Is anyone there? I know somebody pulled me from that damn deathtrap. Don't be afraid, I ain't gonna hurt you," Sabor spoke to the wind again.

Sabor looked around confused. Nothing was around. Not a single bird or anything.

"Humph!" An unseen voice drifted with the breeze. Then, an invisible shoulder nearly slammed Sabor to the ground.

"I am never gonna get used to this crap!" Sabor screamed into the solitude of the grass. "Here I go again," The wet Guardian walked an exaggerated circle around the camouflaged pond.

Sabor waded through the tall grass, pondering the long walk and the journey he had been on. He watched, as the horizon grew gradually thicker with leafy giants. The scattered thickets began to coagulate, forming small, yet tall, sanctuaries for the shadows following him, keeping their watchful eye fixed upon his progress. The translucent creatures had been following Sabor closely, since one of the small sanctuaries, or watchtowers, had reported of a man coming toward the dark forest.

Sabor caught a whiff of a familiar smell, swirling on a warm breeze. It smelled like the farm in the summer, when Noelle would bake pies...apple pies! A renewed vigor swelled Sabor's lungs full of life as he followed his nose to the origin of the odor. Cresting a small hill, he found, nestled in the valley below, a bountiful and fragrant orchard. A tiny path led down the middle of the picturesque coppice. Small buckets and ladders were scattered along the beaten walkway. The middle of the orchard opened up, forming a large empty circle. The expanse was empty except for a hardwood preparation table sitting stretched out in the center. The weathered table measured easily twenty feet by fifteen feet.

Sabor decided to camp here for the night. He was exhausted, and the opening seemed so inviting. The feeling of being watched was gone here, and the perfume of the apple blossoms added to the cozy atmosphere of the space.

Twilight crept along the valley, shrouding the world in darkness inch by inch.

"I need something to eat and somewhere to stay tonight," Sabor looked around, somehow blind to the fact that all around him were crisp, ripe apples.

"Duh! I guess I am in an 'Apple orchard'. What a dork," Sabor thought, extremely happy nobody was around to see his stupidity. He walked over to the rows of trees, selecting the best fruit from the closest tree he could find.

"I can't quite reach it...almost there, uh-mm," Sabor strained, standing on the tips of his feet, his bounty dangling three feet away even for all of his efforts.

"Hey!" Sabor said, suddenly struck with an ep iphany. "I could use this;" Sabor looked at his arm as the long blade slid out, skewering a group of four apples.

"That should do it," he thought, full of confidence. The use of his blade for usual, everyday things had never occurred to him. But, an entire New World of possibilities opened wide to him now.

Sabor had his food for the evening, so he set out to get a roof over his head. He walked to the table and steadied himself against the wood. A strange glow spiraled out of his eyes and crawled down his arms, finally melting and seeping into the pores of the wood. Grabbing it with both hands, Sabor fell back, pulling the four hundred-pound table, hurling it high over his head. With a tremendous thud, the table glanced off the ground, throwing a cloud of dust, then twisted and flipped, coming to rest against three sturdy trees. From the impact, a few of the iron nails had tumbled out, loosening some of the boards. But the rain and wind would be kept off of him and that would do for the night.

A few feet away from the hut, Sabor again released his blade, digging a small fire pit and lining it with a group of stones he found strewn about the expanse. After the arduous task was complete, he stood, arching his back, leaning and popping all over his body.

"Man, all of this, just to get a roof and some grub," the words came along with the realization of needing some sort of fire to burn in his new contraption.

The floor beneath the trees was scattered with dry leaves and dead twigs, perfect for building a warm fire. Gathering up the debris, Sabor spotted a shadow glaring at him without eyes. A double take revealed his dementia for there was, in fact, nothing there. Shaking off the eerie feeling, he saw a half-dead tree that would be great for keeping a roaring fire alive through the night. He sliced his way through the wood, gathering it up and placing it in a pile beside the pit.

Before long, Sabor enjoyed a roaring flame, roasting his apples on the end of his sabor and staring up at the stars.

"Haven't seen a sky like that since I was staying on the farm. Man, that sure seems like a long time ago. I wish I was still there, it was all so damn simple... " Flowing again into the river of memories, Sabor bit into the crunchy, sweet apple and smiled. "But I wouldn't change how things are going now for anything. I was such a little, stuck-up jerk back then. Who in the hell was I? What made me so special? It wasn't me, it was you guys," Sabor said, focusing on a pair of brilliant stars and speaking to them with passion in his voice.

Sabor leaned back, picking his teeth with his left sabor. His stomach full, he was finished for the day. Nightfall had blanketed him hours ago, and he had stocked the fire with an abundance of fuel. The night sounds of the crickets and other nocturnal animals began to sooth Sabor. Crawling under the wooden shelter, he wore down a comfortable spot in the dirt and fell asleep.

A soft light woke Sabor from a terrific dream. "Crap, always just b efore I get the girl," Sabor joked, rubbing his eyes and stretching his legs.

A split second after the sleep dripped out of his eyes, Sabor came to the realization that it was cold, damn cold. The dew rested silently on the leaves and fruit in the branches above him. A thick, white fog had kissed the ground and began to sway around everything, leaving drops of moisture to quench the worlds thirst. Sabor's large, billowing exhale hung in the air, swirling and then freezing in mid-flight. A long icicle dangled from his nose, making it numb.

"Why is it so cold?" Sabor asked himself as he vigorously rubbed his shoulders and rose to his feet.

The friction radiated and manifested in an independent blue glow. Swirls of power around him began to heat his body up. Sabor was so cold and that was all he could focus on. The luminescent swirls of turquoise light bolted through the trees, vaporizing the dew and simultaneously scorching the thick fog into oblivion. A cocoon of heat churned around the Guardian, who had stopped rubbing himself, and enjoyed the wonderful light show he had seemingly created. A bolt of the blue luminance slammed into the charred hole lighting a blaze that overflowed the small recess, warming whatever the darts had not touched.

"That's better," Sabor said, an air of 'What was that'? Permeating the statement.

"Do not dawdle traveler," a very understated voice said quickly. The voice though extremely soft seemed to come from everywhere all at once.

The awkwardness this voice would have presented only a few days earlier, now seemed common place to Sabor. He assessed the situation, seeing if there were any threats, then went on about his business of gathering himself to continue on his Journey.

"I guess, I should put this table back but screw it, its just too heavy," His thoughts poured outside again.

Stretching the stiffness from his back, Sabor pushed on through the orchard, plucking a few apples from the trees for the road and humming an old song that just found its way inside him. Happily, he trudged on humming the rogue song and jumping every few yards, slapping at the dew soaked branches.

Outside the orchard, the piercing stare of Sabor's unseen admirer shot through him again. The distance to the large forest was now much closer. The farther Sabor walked the taller and more sinister the trees became. The smaller groups of brush and saplings dotting the grassy valley coagulated into larger and larger groups of very tall, very dense trees. The horizon seemed to march towards Sabor just as much as he marched towards the horizon.

Topping a hill, Sabor found an old, ran-down shack, small and made of rotting wood. A small, rusty, black stovepipe stood up from the back of the house, puffing out small dark gray rings of smoke. A rickety outhouse sat a few yards away, sinking into the ground a bit. A small bearded man, draped in a decorated smock, crouched under a large cauldron, cursing and slapping the huge cast iron pot.

"Whooo-hoo!" A shriek filled the air, taking Sabor by surprise and off guard.

"Ohhh shut up you! I see 'im, I see 'im," the old man screamed in a thick Scottish accent, at an old but very large owl, as he got slowly up dusting himself. The human sized owl sat perched on a huge cross-made of driftwood and decorated with large dreamcatchers dangling below the majestic bird.

"We've been a waitin' for you, young human. We have. Ever since Blanchard recessed back into the woods there, because of ya,"

"Waiting for me? How could you be waiting for me? I didn't even know I was coming here," Sabor demanded, finding it a bit peculiar that the old man could have been watching him. "Are you the one that saved me from drowning in that pool, the one that's been following me?" Sabor asked again as he and the man came closer to one another.

"Gracious no, my boy. These legs will barely carry me around this tiny plot of ground. They...told me," The eccentric old man said, pointing behind him.

"Who? Who told you I was coming?" Sabor asked.

"A little thick, aren't we there, my boy? I already told you. It was them, the watchmen of the scattered sentinel towers of the Agramin. Besides, you don't have to see to be seen. Ha, ha, hum! They line this valley, telling us of humans, **like you**. Humanity wishing to push us deeper into the hard-to-reach places of our world with their *science*. Tricky bunch those humans. If I had my way, we would have taken 'em a century of centuries ago."

The gruff old man sat down on a dusty log, resembling a large easy chair and pulled up his smock, grabbing a long saxophone shaped pipe that had been hidden, resting in a holster on his thigh. He lit the yellowish weeds sticking out from the end of the wooden pipe with a flame that rested on the tip of his right index finger. Then, with a tremendous wheeze and barrage of lung-rattling coughs, the old man settled back into his log, glassy eyed and looking a bit confused.

"The Agramin? Could you tell me who, they are?" Sabor asked again, trying to find out as much as he could about this strange world. "But wait how rude of me, before we get into all of that sir, could you tell me what your name might be? Mine sir, is Guardian Sabor Lindon, of The Order of Sabor Guardians. I am on my Discovery, the third leg of it, as best I can tell," Sabor said remembering his manners.

"No, excuse me Sabor Lindon, Guardian of The Order. I have heard tales of you Guardians, magic-humans. Such a queer marriage of terms, that is if you ask me, but you are at least a bit worthy of my company. So, dear sir, you wish to know my name, do you? The name hallowed throughout the ages, the name that by its very make up demands respect. That the very syllables that once choked the wicked chicken of Nettle. Well, I will tell you my name. Some call me...Tim," he said with an awkward smile on his lips and his accent growing thicker, as he rose up from his perch and slapped the owl, who was making a terrible racket beside him. Tim went about dusting off an old boulder and covering it with a large red cloth.

"I do apologize about my bird. Persiea can get rather agitated at the slightest little thing;" Tim quickly motioned for Sabor to sit. "But, please come, come and have a seat and prepare yourself, my boy. I have a few things to get fixed up, but tonight, tonight you, Sabor of the Guardians, will dine like a king,"

Tim scurried about, mixing things, throwing strange powders and pieces of animals into the large cast-iron cauldron. Pulling a small, rickety table from behind a tree, he placed a large, crystal ball with a long bouquet of black and purple candles burning atop the centerpiece. From out of the shadows, a pair of place settings flew from within the tiny shack and landed softly on the table. A self-satisfied look and a confident wink flew over the old man's shoulder as he readied the focal point of the meal, some sort of thorny meat, resembling a hog, turning on a spit.

"Amazing! Tell me...Tim, are you an enchanter or a magician of some kind?" Sabor asked, astounded by the display.

"No, my boy! And I take offense to being called one. Humph, an enchanter is little more than a normal human conjuring parlor tricks. I, my young Guardian, am a Mae. An ancient magic flows through my kind. Wizards, as some of you humans refer to of us, are the most magical of all beings. So, no, I am not Tim the enchanter, I am simply Tim. None the less, no harm done with a question. There you are my boy, a feast that would make any royal gala an instant classic," he said, his back turned to the cooking feast and his arms stretched out wide.

"Um, excuse me, but isn't the meal going to need some sort of flame or heat to cook on?" Sabor asked, barely containing his sarcastic laughter.

"Well of course, a great Mae such as myself would never prepare a meal without first getting the flame ready, humph," so convinced of his method, Tim refused to turn and check his results. Sabor grinned and pointed to the lack of fuel under his food. "Well, wouldn't you know it, a no good human shows up and my magic doesn't work anymore,"

With the tension of his own blunder in his voice, Tim began to cant and recant ancient sounding spells, flailing his arms in large semi and full circles. Frustrated with the lack of flame and the continued lack of pity from his guest, he crouched down on all fours under the heavy cauldron. Mustering little more than a single, small, spiraling spark of magic. He turned, propping himself against the pot and wiped a bead of sweat from his brow.

"Hmmmmm, don't know. It usually works. Maybe, yes maybe if you were to close your eyes, perhaps,"

That suggestion flopped as well, not a complete failure however, Tim did manage to set a floppy eared rabbit ablaze, which scurried out of the bush and began tearing around in tight circles around the shack.

"Oh my dear gracious!" Tim shouted, waving his arms and spouting a short limerick. A tiny bucket of water flew from the old stone well, dowsing the small creature, which, in turn, grudgingly smoldered off into the brush again, giving one final angry glance back towards Tim before disappearing. "My goodness, that sure was a close call for 'im, now wasn't it?" Tim sat back trying to get the fire started, under the thorny meat.

"Would you like some help there, friend?" Sabor asked, walking over to him.

"No, no, now, you are my guest. You sit there and rest, my boy. I must not be reciting something correctly," With that Tim turned, focusing again on the meat. Tiny sparks flew everywhere, but none found the kindling under the meal. With Tim's undivided attention leering upon the spit, Sabor reached his sabor down into the dry wood and grass, instantly igniting it.

"I think one of your sparks caught over here, Tim,"

"Yes, that was it. The timing in my tones must have been off. You see my dear lad, it is, as in most things, 'tis the timing that counts, you see. You humans are so smart, with your science. But very close minded about your knowledge. Always second guessing what you see. 'Oh, no one could start a fire without flint, or matches'. So, therefore no being could have that ability, if I do not possess it. No, that would be impossible..." Tim rambled on and on about things that did not interest Sabor, but Sabor sat listening intently and politely to the old man, nodding and never disagreeing with a word. The concoction of frog, snake, lizard, and beetles began to churn as it softly boiled in the brown liquid. Bits of mushroom, rolling in the broth, filled the air with the aroma of fungus.

"What kind of meat is that over there anyway, Tim?" Sabor asked.

"Oh, this? It is spiked boar, a rare delicacy for certain. But, I don't usually get to entertain many humans.

"And that cauldron, is that some magic potion or ancient remedy bubbling around in there? It surely can't be our food. Can it?"

"No twit, this is our lunch. A Mae's magic flows from within him. Not some putrid concoction boiling in a pot," Tim said, not thinking about the fact that the concoction was actually their meal, so calling it a putrid concoction may not have been the best thing to do.

"Okay, well, I'm sorry then. I didn't mean any disrespect. On another subject though, you said that, 'They/Them' had told you I was coming," The words barely got from Sabor's mouth before Tim responded.

"Yes, Them. The trees, there my boy. They have and always will know. The problem is, they always have and always will hide at the sight of a human. Took me eighty years to get them to talk to me, I resemble you humans so much. They are a stubborn and untrusting bunch," the old man whispered, hoping not to disturb his wooden friends. "I knew you were coming because my oldest friend of the Agramin is Blanchard. He is the keeper of the peace inside the middle forest, second in command if you will, here in the Forest of the Agramin..."

"Second to who?" Sabor asked interrupting.

"...Second to the Patriarch of the wood, Vanth Pinn Goth. A remnant of the once great Quatrine. I believe his enemy is the same as your own, at least it was, until he came to live here. But, that is a story for someone else to tell. For

142

now Lindon, let us eat,"Tim said.

"Okay. Thank you. This should be quite an experience?" Unconvinced, Sabor moved to the small table and sat by his place setting.

The meal marched behind Tim in a whimsical dance. The proud Mae walked to his place and sat down, smiling at Sabor the whole time, as the ladles of soup and the meat fell onto their plates and into their bowls. Persiea, swooped in circling the feast, then sat on the end of the table, stretching his wings and staring at Sabor.

"Please, don't mind Persiea. He is always rude to company, a snooty sort, but kind enough once he knows you. Now, I have only one rule during mealtime. Please, no talking while we eat. The practice leads to all sorts of disgusting situations you understand,"Tim asked politely.

The group sat eating. Sabor was a bit uncomfortable with a huge bird perched on the table, but he dare not risk upsetting his new friend. The meal didn't last very long; Sabor choked down his food rather quickly. The surprisingly good taste impressed Sabor and when he was done, he complimented.

"That was delicious. You are quite a great cook, Tim,"

"I told you Guardian, no in fact, I warned you! No talking while we eat. I even went so far as to say please,"Tim stood, slamming down his spoon, whipping back his robe, and grabbing a softball-sized silver ball. He held the reflective sphere high above his head. The ground rumbled and the sky swirled with dark clouds. Persiea flapped his wings, leaving feathers dwindling behind, and swooped off into the safety of the shack. A brilliant bolt of lightning slammed the ball hard, bending Tim's elbow and electrifying the orb.

"Hey Tim! I meant no disrespect, I thought you were finished. I'm sorry, I'm sorry!" Sabor screamed, holding out his hands trying to relax the enraged sorcerer.

The plan worked, Tim lowered the ball and settled back into his seat. The clouds rolled back and the ground returned to nothingness.

"You are forgiven Sabor. But, you no doubt have better things to do, than sitting around with an old man and his bird. So, I will ask you to take your leave from us, and let me finish my meal. Find an open place in the wall of trees just behind us, and then follow the path to the other side. There, you should be able to conclude your Journey and go home. Good day Sabor Lindon, Guardian of The Order of Sabor Guardians, farewell,"Tim looked down angrily into his soup bowl and stirred it quickly.

"I truly am sorry, Tim. But I will remember you fondly, my friend," Sabor gathered himself up and left after patting the Wizard on his shoulder.

"Yes, yes, I know Persiea. He will do great things, I have seen. I am sorry he had to leave, but he would have dawdled here, wasting our time for another week if I hadn't made him go," Tim said to his feathered friend, who flew out, landing on his shoulder as Sabor trudged off out of sight.

The Dark Forest of the Agramin

Sabor searched the tree line for a break, but found nothing. The trunks of the massive trees squeezed tightly together, barely letting sunlight through. A seemingly large gap in the bark appeared a few yards ahead. Sabor grinned, then looked down as he ran. When he looked up, relieved to have found a way in, he shook his head in disbelief as the gap (that was so plainly there before) was now gone completely. Sabor lumbered forward, the tiny shack and eccentric old man, now nothing but a recent memory.

The forest, loomed extremely dark, more so since dusk was only now beginning to settle down upon the land. The long shadows falling across his path created a peculiar strobe effect as Sabor tried desperately to find entrance to the wood. A strange rustling paralleled Sabors gait on the opposite side of the tree line as he searched.

"Hello?! Is someone over there? I am on my way back to the Halls of The Order of the Sabor Guardians. I was told to come this way by Tim, the old man at the mouth of this forest. May I please come through these woods?" Sabor paused, glaring deeply into a small crack in the trunks.

As he approached the opening, night grabbed the world, holding it captive for another slumber. The trees collapsed, imploding into the thick of the forest, opening a large road, trimmed with mighty trees. The shady lane was dark and cool. A slight breeze flew through the tunnel of foliage, rippling Sabors cloak behind him.

The tired Guardian tentatively strolled into the shadows of the row between the imposing vegetation. Bodies of the dark forest, appearing alive, moved slightly, dancing within the stolen light of the full moon. Cautiously, Sabor threw off the fear of the presence he could not explain. Thoughts screamed through his mind, recollections of the odd things he had encountered, of his family, of life in general. He thought of the terrors that may await him on this latest journey and on the eyes watching from a plane hidden deeply behind the shadows cast by the towering timber.

The deep gray walls of wood on either side pulsed, almost breathing with a subtle blue light. A dance of illumination, backlighting the leaves, threw prismatic silhouettes all around. Closing in, the path slowly swayed, as the trees pressed in closer and closer. Once Sabor's eyes acclimated to the dim light, he saw large flowing tapestries, shields, swords, spears, and a veritable arsenal that seemed to grow out from the bark of the towering trees.

A quick shadow slithered in and out of the trees, unnoticed by the alien human. Only one at first, but gradually the number grew to twenty strong. A strong sense of community permeated the atmosphere here. Even the trees focused on Sabor, who noticed a swift, dark outline tuck itself behind a tree. Immediately, Sabor slid his weapon out, illuminating the dark place between the two trees. He caught only the quick glimpses of the stubborn shadows. The formless shadows did not flee at the presentation of his light.

"That's odd," Sabor thought.

Ahead, a large circle opened in the forest. The walls of trees, forming an arch over the entrance and a row of slightly smaller saplings and thorny brush, grew into a rustic gate. The beauty and grandness of the sight caused Sabor to stare at the growth for what seemed hours.

"Who goes there?" A voice boomed from behind the tangle of a gate.

"Sabor Lindon, of The Order of Sabor Guardians," he said, wondering who he was talking with.

"Your business could easily take you around our forest. Why do you choose our wood as a bridge to your Order, human?" The booming voice inquired.

The brilliance of the blue lights converged on the perimeter of the opening. "I don't really know what brought me here. But, I am here now and have come too far to turn back," Sabor said

"We do not know of your purpose, nor do we care. Your Journey could and must take you away from this place, human. Your kind is not welcome here," the voice bellowed.

"Okay, I really would love to stand here, answering the questions of some unseen smart ass, but I have a destiny and a piece of crap Evil to destroy, so anything you could do to speed me on my way would be greatly appreciated," Sabor said, realizing he was wasting his time here and remembering that Dvanken would be waking soon.

"MOVE Kaylein!" The thunderous voice bellowed from behind the gate. "Young Sabor, enter the realm of the Agramin. I do apologize for our stealth; our situation necessitates our invisibility,"

"Your situation?" Sabor asked the faceless voice.

146

"Yes, our situation,"

The gate pulled back, the large trees creaking and snapping as they rose, filling the air with cascading leaves. In the center of the opening, stood an enormous oak tree. Its gnarly roots spider-webbed across the expanse, touching every side of the area. The branches hung so full of leaves, they nearly scraped the ground. The air was thick with the sprite-like lights darting back and forth, creating a glow around the place of blue highlights. A large face sat a few feet from the base of the tree. An enormous mouth rested below two large wood grain eyes. A tuft of moss rested above the raised brow, forming a quaff-like hairdo. The huge voice originated from this jolly face on the tree.

"Our situation is one of dire consequence. If you humans were to find us, we would be little more than fairy-tales. Locked inside cages, or worse. That is why we hide, safely here amongst the mighty forest, the last of it's kind, I think," the tree laughed a melancholy chuckle, then stared at Sabor, who was doing the same.

"May I ask what you are staring at Boy !?" He asked.

"I was going to ask you that same question. I'm sorry, that was rude of me. It's just I don't talk to trees everyday, ya know? I have been followed by some damn thing, don't know what it is because, I can't see it, been saved by the same invisible man, I was kicked out of a Wizard's house, for talking, and to top it all off, now I'm talking to a tree that talks back," Sabor rattled.

"Oh yes, Tim. He is a little temperamental every once in a while. Pay him no mind. I have a bit of an apology to make myself, but I don't know how to tell you why," the tree replied.

"Blurt it out. Just tell me, it's always been the best way for me to get something off of my chest. If you want, you can start by telling me your name," Sabor said, trying to help him.

"Yes, yes my name. Could have bought a bit of time with that tad-bit of information, huh? My name is Blanchard, Blanchard Linstin. Come closer, so I can shake your hand," Sabor did so cautiously not taking his eyes off of the massive tree, with his sabor blades still glowing and outstretched. "No need for your knives here, Guardian. We are now a peaceful people, not having any conflict in ages," the tree said.

"We?" Sabor asked.

"The Agramin," Blanchard replied, pulling down a branch for Sabor to shake. "Come closer, come. I am not what you think I am, and neither is this

147

forest," the face said, as it crept forward.

The edges of the bark around the face began to give way, pulling away from themselves, like a snake shedding its skin. The moss smoothed itself out, folding inside revealing a smooth forehead. Two large scaly arms pulled out from behind the trunk, reaching around and shivered violently, throwing bark soaring through the air in every direction. Soon followed the rest of the eerie camouflage, leaving a man-like lizard standing with his scaly hand outstretched in friendship. Sabor jumped back, taken by surprise to see that the talking tree was in fact a chameleon/human creature. "I can only guess at what you are thinking, but believe me, we are just as frightened of you, traveler," Blanchard said in a soothing tone and reaffirmed his act of trying to shake Sabor's hand.

"Yeah, I guess you are right. So, what do we do now?" Sabor asked and shook Blanchard's hand firmly.

"Well, I could introduce you to some of the others, then send you to Springs Willow Bend and Vanth Pinn Goth. I am certain he will want to see you, before you leave. Crazy, but he enjoys the company of humans. Sorry," Blanchard said, grabbing Sabor and turning him back toward the entrance. "These are my brothers," the large Agramin slapped Sabor sharply on the back then stretched his arm out, pointing to the trees that lined the grove.

Then he said," Ungai, ya ungo, injanijna o vinto nee. Gaaa!"

With those words, the trees began to fragment, breaking into faint silhouettes of upright beings stacked one on top of the other. The weapons and cloth that dangled in the branches began moving each tree then stepped forward. There standing on one another' s shoulders, the Agramin towered like a huge circus family practicing their act. The large males on the bottom were huge and thick. Progressively the creatures began to thin a bit, the higher up the formation they sat. In turn, each one dismounted, flipping to the ground until the wide open space was full of battle ready Agramin, displaying swords and spears and brilliant shields. Slowly the ranks changed colors from the realistic tree bark pattern to their original green and faded red hues. The rich brilliance of the color in their weapons and flags was matched only by the amazing transfers of their skins.

Blanchard introduced Sabor to the mass of creatures huddled in the center. They were a magnificent looking lot, huge barrel chested beings with tremendous forearms. They had practically no necks whatsoever, their heads melting into their shoulders and chests. The legs were crooked and muscular with large but very human feet. Then he proceeded outward with the smaller more agile looking warriors. The mass of readiness, stared at Sabor as if he, were the odd one in the group, as if he were the ugly one and this made him very

148

uncomfortable.

"Okay, it has been terrific meeting you all. But, I really do need to get going. It's late and I need to get to my Order. Once again, thank you for your welcome, but I must go," Sabor said, then turned to Blanchard. "You said something about getting me to a Vanth Pinn?"

"Yes, Haben here will take you as far as the outer rim of Springs Willow Bend. But, we do not venture too far into his land. He gets grumpy at times," Blanchard said, motioning to an anxious Haben Linstin, then whispering into the Agramins ear. Then looking up at Sabor said, "he will take you as far as the bridge but, be careful he likes to talk alot," Sabor nodded, then followed the Agramin east.

The woods were electric with excitement, the word of a human, a Guardian, spreading like fire from odd creature to odd creature. The pass was watched with anticipation by all, scurrying about trying to glimpse the human that had been allowed entrance. A few of the odd creatures, bravely ventured out behind Sabor, forming a small impromptu parade. The rustling behind Sabor, gave him a strange feeling, but somehow among this diverse group of beings he felt safe, as if he belonged with the magical people of this forest.

The lumber stretching up on each side of Sabor and Haben began to swell the deeper they ventured into the wood. It swelled with the strange blue lights that had been dotting the air all around him since he came into the forest.

"Wow! A real human. I cannot tell you what an honor it is to meet you. I mean, do you realize what you are?" Haben said, shaking his head left to right.

"I guess," Sabor said feeling a bit uncomfortable, by his guides kind words.

"The others, they don't understand, but I am infatuated with your kind. I have read bits of your history inside the books at Springs Willow Bend. Vanth Pinn doesn't want us to learn of your ways, but I can't help it, I mean your knowledge and lust for living it pulls me in every direction all at once on the inside. Wow, what it must be like inside your head," Haben rambled?

"It really isn't that special in here, Haben. I don't really have a lot in there, except questions," Sabor said, as he watched a small wood imp burrow for termites in a dead log.

"Yes, yes I can imagine. You are a Guardian right, so you fight the Evil, don't you?" Haben asked quietly, so none of the others behind could hear.

149

"Yes, don't really know how I'm going to do it, but. I'm supposed to be something special, the Ave. " Haben jumped in front of Sabor stopping him dead in his tracks, a small flying creature slamming into the back of his suddenly stationary head.

"Avenger? Are you the Avenger? Because if you are, I mean extra Wow, this is a great time. Maybe you could help get us back into the real world. That would be so great. Imagine humans and magic folk walking together again, happy and peaceful. That would be a dream come true," Haben said as he began walking again.

Sabor gave up on replies and simply listened to the constant babble coming from Haben, and smiling at the company.

The forest was now growing a bit darker, long strands of moss and web caught the soft lights, glowing eerily. Sabor glanced down still listening to Haben. Scattered around on the ground, large skulls and bones bleached by time and warning of the terror ahead.

"Haben, the bones. Where are you leading me anyway?" Sabor asked

"Oh, don't worry Sabor, those are just wooden carvings, bleached and scattered about to scare humans away. No need to worry," Haben said reassuringly, then continued his ramble.

The distinctive sound of rushing water filled the air. Smells of fresh springs and ripe fruit seeped through the shadowy world. A strange glow, like that of daylight, overtook the pale moon shining down from the sky. Birds sang and a wonderful watery mist swept over Sabors tired face.

"This is where I leave you, Sabor Lindon, Avenger of the Sabor Guardians. Take the Labinah Bridge just as the light of Quatrine turns our dark forest to the Springs Willow Bend. There, you will find Vanth Pinn Goth. Remember that he can get grouchy, so mind your manners. Good bye, and fare well on your Journey, Sabor," Haben said, then immediately scurried off, trying not to look too eager to leave, but not wanting to dawdle.

Vanth Pinn of
Springs Willow Bend

Sabor looked back at Haben, then into the unknown of Springs Willow Bend. The dark sinister woods gave way to a peaceful grove, brimming with life and joy. Most of the trees were now only bushes. Grass and small plants were the dominant foliage here. Sabor walked towards the sound of the rushing water, sure that is where he would find Vanth Pinn and through him, a way out of the forest.

A long, wooden rope bridge stretched from a center support carved from solid rock. The huge ropes twisted down, braided with colorful strands of dyed cloth and ribbon. A huge flag with a strange design blew in the constant zephyr living in this place.

A large statue stood watch at the head of the bridge. The statue resembled the column supports of the library, the enormous four-armed men, only this was a smaller version. The two large hands attached to the lower arms rested on the grip of a mammoth sword, the other set of smaller hands grasping a sign bearing words

"Welcome to Springs Willow Bend"b urned into the rock sign.

Sabor crossed the bridge, but as he reached the midpoint he looked down. The massive bridge towered only six feet off of the ground, rendering the structure worthless and somewhat an overkill for such a tiny indentation. Then, Sabor remembered he had read the Quatrine, were an artful race, a peaceful race and it all made sense. All of this was for decoration.

On the other side of the bridge, Sabor noticed scattered statues and deteriorating works of art, laying about. A walkway formed out of rocks. A beautiful green lawn stretched out, eventually marrying the trees in the distance. The rock walk curved around a massive limestone bluff, the sound of the spring originating from behind the bluff, in some unseen pool. The richness and beauty of the landscape and the craftsmanship of the art amazed Sabor. Little did he know, the beauty was nothing compared to what lay ahead.

He turned the corner, and there it stood. The largest tree he had ever seen. The roots stood ten to twelve feet tall. Enormous house-sized branches jutted out from the body of the tree. Millions upon millions of large multi-shaded green leaves covered the tree; each lit by some kind of interior light.

Between two of the huge roots, a door frame had been carved, and a plank door filled the fifteen foot tall with an elaborate, far too elaborate for the setting door knob and lock. A fire pit lay a few feet from the house, circled in brilliant glowing rocks. A large balcony sat under a carved window with a lattice wood gate closing it.

A landscaped path wound around, leading up to the spring. Small faces had started to be carved into the soft limestone. A beautiful bench sat beside the cascading spring. A turquoise fountain rested in the middle of a pool that collected from the spring water raging from above the hill. Then the crystal clean water, overflowed into a larger pool below, cradled in the roots of the tree.

Sabor knocked on the large door. A resounding thump echoed throughout the tree, but no answer. Again, he knocked.

"Hello! Vanth Pinn Goth. I am Sabor," Sabor said, then a deep voice came from behind the tree, finishing his sentence. "Lindon. Yes, I know who you are. I have been waiting for you for some time. Please young Lindon; do not call me Vanth, but simply Pinn. My Agramin Sentinels told me some two days ago of your ascension from the Climb. They followed you here, letting me know how far you were from me,"

A long, dark cloak hooded the large frame of the Quatrine, stepped from behind a large root on the left of the tree. The overcoat was old and had been mended and repaired with hundreds of make shift patches over the years.

"I am pleased to finally meet with the son of Zandalar. You favor him a great deal. I was saddened to learn of his passing, you have my condolences. He was indeed a great Guardian and friend," the eight foot tall Quatrine said, grabbing Sabor with a large pair of wrinkled hands. "I am descended from Guardians, as you are, young master. The mighty Quatrine. I am the last, setting up here on the dawn of the human leg. I have waited for eighteen hundred years for your arrival. The one, who will avenge our losses," Pinn led Sabor up the winding path. He sat down on the carved bench and began throwing stones into the waterfall in front of them.

"How do you know who I am? And how did you know my father's name?" Sabor asked.

"Your father was a dear friend of mine. The only human to enter this wood, for centuries. He ventured through on his Discovery and returned from that day on, to exchange stories of the outside, for tales of when the world was a much grander and magical place," Pinn began "He never fell into his role as a head Elder. He was more contented to fight, rather than direct the action from behind the scenes, trapped in his Halls, helpless," Pinn continued, looking deeply into Sabor's face.

"Excuse me. Centuries? How did no one find this beautiful forest for centuries, Pinn?" Sabor asked politely

"That answer, is a simple one, Guardian. Our forest does not wish to be found. Therefore, it is not found. Much like your Halls of The Order remain secret from your world of science," Pinn finished.

"Well, how then did I and my Father find it, when the other Guardians did not?" Sabor asked genuinely.

"Yes, so you both did. No matter, any blind fool could find a forest here," Pinn Goth said with indifference.

"But, you just said... " Sabor said

"I know my own voice, Lindon! Do not anger me with your presumption. I am but joking young Sabor. I told you, I knew your father, and I told you, I had been expecting you. This wood is my domain. I have kept its inhabitants safe, with the help of Tim and the Agramin for years. We all wanted you to come, Avenger," Pinn said, grabbing Sabor by the shoulder with his two right arms, and shaking him.

"Avenger? How do you know all of this stuff about me?" Sabor asked disturbed.

"The volumes of the History tell of your unique situation, does it not? A Solitaire, on his Discovery as the Evil sleeps. And as I told you, your father was a dear friend of mine, so I have spent many hours sitting in this very spot with him listening to stories about you. In fact it was your Father which brought me the volumes of the History again and reeducated me on the subject. We loved to tell each other, that we were wise, due to our age, you know," Pinn said, reaching out his hand, taking a drink of the falling water.

"Vanth Pinn, that is what the Agramin called you, Vanth Pinn Goth. Why do you only want for me to call you Pinn?" Sabor asked again amazed by the Quatrines use of his arms and voice in unison.

"Vanth is a title my boy, a title that I can no longer keep. When I came here I was a warrior, and I commanded warriors. Vanth was my title, much like your 'Greenling, Knight, Elder and Guide'. It is nothing more than a rank. Since I have deteriorated so much now, I cannot fight, so I am no longer worthy of my title," Pinn said, disappointed with his age.

Even with the centuries of deterioration, he stood eight feet tall with arms much larger than Sabor's. His skin, no longer tight and sleek, now hung from his body in places under the strain of gravity. He was losing his vigor as well. Still, the enormous Quatrine stood ominous and strong looking.

"Tell me, what you know about The volumes of our History? Do you know where it came from? Do you know if it is truth or are we investing our efforts in an illustrious story?" Sabor asked the elderly Quatrine as he poured two large glasses of crystal clear spring water.

"Of course I do, Sabor, of course. After all, I am older than your entire family. Eighteen hundred years old, not bad eh?" Pinn laughed, then handed Sabor a refreshing glass of water.

"Actually, I give myself a bit too much credit. I will be that age, this next season. But enough with the talk of age. Sit, get comfortable, and I shall give you your answers. Your query is a definite mystery to most. As I told you, your Father brought me the History again, allowing me to refresh my memory with it. I asked him to bring me the volumes, since it had been centuries since I had seen them. And when he brought them, it reminded me of just how long I had been away from it. I only learned the text through an old acquaintance, almost purely by accident. The lost messenger stumbled into my forest on his way to delivering it to your Halls. But enough on how I learned of the text let me tell you how the world received them.

"Minonoly, that is their name. A noble, reclusive, peaceful tribe, who resided high on the barren, volcanic cliffs of the Hennesil Mountains, the northern mountains of the free tribes. A black, marble range crested in limestone and volcanic ash, dotted with gargantuan peaks, towering out of sight, high above the thick, poisonous clouds. The clouds puffed from within caverns that cut deeply into the crust of the earth. A faint, white ring hovers above the sulfuric smoke rings, hiding the Zanoni, the immature, unchanged Minonoly, nestled deep inside the center of the largest crater of the Hennesil, living in peace. Some would argue that their location lent itself to their peaceful existence, rather than a choice to live that way. But that is a different story all together.

"The spires of the Zanoni, rose high above the crater, delicately carved, spiraling upward to the sky. Sharply cut windows lined the huge limestone towers. Each window bustled with candlelight, thriving with life. In the crater, huge farms flourished in the rich volcanic ash. Growing beautiful floral decorations and wonderful vegetables, the deep craters mimicking your tropical islands.

"The people of the Zanoni stood a comfortable five and one half feet tall. An extraordinarily, large man would measure five-nine. They were a husky race, most thick through the shoulders and thighs, and strong, but soft through the middle. Large tufts of course hair grew up and around their necks, a small amount creeping up their scalp, slightly resembling the mane of a lion. Most had round, plump faces with large, yellow eyes. That, of course before their change.

"Their maturing into the wise Minonoly was referred to as their Becoming. After this Becoming, they lose the thick hair around the neck and head, and their eyes glaze over, hiding the torrent of information frothing inside their minds, assaulting their conscious with visions of past, present, and future. None knowing which visions they would receive. They simply scribbled the visions, until they would eventually passing quietly away, leaving their history and little else behind,"

"You mean, they just changed, wrote what they saw in a dream, then died?" Sabor inquired.

"No one ever said that being a historian was easy, or glamorous. But, no in fact, it wasn't just a single dream, but a miniature lifetime played back from different angles and through different eyes.

"The men of the Zanoni were the only to receive the 'Gift of the Becoming' It came to them late in their lives. No matter their age, they began to see the visions five years before their death.

"The gift of omnipresent thought was a blessing and even more so, a curse. It was a common fate that the men of the Zanoni had grown to accept and, in some cases, long for. On the one hand they knew all, everything from corner to corner of the world, your world. And on the other, they were doomed to spend their remaining days recounting the feverish visions playing in their minds' eye.

"In the beginning, before the time they knew of what was being given, many men did not know to record their visions, thus with the recounting would release the mass of information, preserving their sanity. Those unfortunate few set an example with their violent insanity that led to the culture accepting their fate as a means of sheer survival. Not to mention the knowledge of one's own death plaguing whatever shred of personal thought they had left. They never slept, eating only when the young Zanoni would bring food, and would pause only long enough to receive another empty volume of parchment to continue their tiring work, also given by the Zanoni. And so were their golden years until death, each settled into the vision spiraling inside their own thoughts and minds.

"Until...a single man e scaped this sadistic fate. A man called Sampoan Minonoly **awoke** after his fifth year of chronicling his vision. He started, slowly getting used to his almost lifeless legs, and began reading over the shoulders of the twenty-two Minonoly absorbed in their death work. He found a miracle, a tremendous happening that even they, the Minonoly, could not have foreseen; " The old Quatrine paused, adding tension to the moment.

"What? What did he find? Quit smiling and tell me!" Sabor said, teetering on the edge of his seat.

"They matched! The entire body of work was precisely the same,

155

recounting the exact same events, groups, and choices of the exact same time period. The Guardians 'History' was born.

"Sampoan sent for his ward, the Zanoni assigned to take care of him, and gave him a large trunk full of what they had written. He instructed the ward, on where to take the large case and to return for the rest after the delivery had been made. The ward accepted, and the trunks for The Order were sent to the home of the first human Guardian. Who in turn found the names, locations, and duties for the entire Order of the Sabor Guardians. The History recanted boundless information, it told of their weapons, techniques, and even their mystical origins. Sampoan censored the work sent to your brothers long ago however, for the hope that maybe the heinous visions could all be changed. That the future they locked away, keeping it safe could hopefully be nothing but a false vision, fed to them by a pattern of violence," Pinn said, being interrupted, politely

"Excuse me, but you said the home of the first Guardian, right?" Sabor politely asked.

"Yes,"

"Could you tell me who he was, maybe?" Sabor asked as polite as before.

"His name, I believe wa s...Elijah Lindon, first born son of Leod Lindon,"

"My family was first? Then, maybe I... " Sabor said drifting back into the words of Pinn Goth

"Though very detailed, the Chronicles of Sampoan Minonoly were still vague and incomplete to your Order. Yes, the volumes were extremely special, but the horrific future they predicted had to remain incomplete, and therefore, so did the end to the horror.

"You Sabor Lindon, may in fact be our Avenger. Or you may simply choose to believe that there is in fact no Avenger, that no single being could rid the world of Dvanken unaided. But in choosing to believe **that,** you will not live in a future that needs an Avenger and hopefully you of The Order, will finish the fight.

"Your choices make you what you are. Be proud of them. Leave nothing to want. That at least, is my romantic view of things young Guardian,"

Sabor looked at Pinn with compassion and true understanding of what the four-armed man had said. The silence between the two warriors was thick and unpleasant, as was the obvious next step in the conversation. So, Sabor changed the subject, not quite ready to assume the role as the savior of the earth and his race.

"In the Library, I found a volume, 'The Unknown Origins'. It called to me

156

by name and pulled me to where it lay, dusty and covered with dark ash. As I read, it told of the origins of the Avenger. As I neared the middle pages, just before the ending began, the pages erupted with ash and burnt away, due to no fault of my own, hopefully. But, the other Guardians, even the Elder's had never seen this book. But, they all seemed to know remotely about what it said concerning the Avenger, being born of two Guardians and the tales of war and all of the words, but not the book itself. Do you know where it could have come from? And how The Order had knowledge of the words and not of the book?" Sabor asked

"I would probably say that the volume, may have been the embodiment of whispers. The lost censored word of Sampoan Minonoly, somehow smuggled into your keep, accidentally. The text dissolved, because of the enchantment upon it. You, or no other Guardian for that matter, were meant to know the entire truth of your future, or, the Minonoly reasoned, that you would all simply stop fighting entirely. But, their future, your future is not set into granite, it can be changed. This is one reason I would say that, Sampoan found it necessary to censor his work. Do you understand?" Vanth Pinn offered.

"I understand, it's just a bit o dd, that they could all know about it. Especially if it is supposed to be such a big secret," Sabor said.

"The words in that book have a life of their own, Guardian. And like my forest, and your Halls, that do not wish to be found. The vital words of the 'Unknown Origins' long for the day that they will be discovered," Vanth said, visibly uncomfortable with the conversation.

"I know this is off of the subject a bit Pinn, but would you mind telling me what this is?" Sabor pointed to the brilliant blue light hovering millimeters from his nose.

"That my dear boy, is a spirit of the Quatrine, and a nosy one at that. Ms. Adena Linston, meet our guest, Sabor Lindon," Pinn said, reaching up and letting the spirit rest on his finger, just in front of Sabor and himself.

"They are the keepers of the verges and pruning of Springs Willow Bend and for that matter, the forest as a whole. As in life, so are they in death. They remain dedicated to the tender beauty in all things around them. It is our way, and has been since the time of... " Pinn stopped mid-sentence, a look of distaste on his face. "The tale behind the loss is deep with hatred.

"The battle of Vanth Merick Losir raged for two years, and left the Quatrine nearly extinct. Dvanken had decimated our noble race, leaving almost none alive. Leaving him to rule the world yet again, or so he thought.

"A hidden force lay in man and the river of blood cascading down the mountain from the Gates of Yinne hid a secret of its own. The souls of the fallen rolled with the blood, pooling in the green meadow below.

"Within weeks, a mighty forest rose, a lasting sanctuary for the Quatrines' lost souls and a legacy they could pass to their single heir, me. The spirits you see are the souls of my people keeping the beauty of this place as they once did in days of yore. They light my tree, and give the trees their haunting glow at night," Vanth Pinn, drifted off into a thoughtful stare.

The sad tale reminded Sabor of his complete loss, the two connected in a brief, eternal moment. Sabor picked up some stones, tossing them high into the air, then watched as they came splashing down into the rippling pond. The sprites began to slow and the world awoke to a new dawn, casting shadows west and scorching the blanket of dew from the ground.

"We have rattled away the midnight, young Lindon. Haven't done that in quite sometime. I rather enjoyed it," Pinn said, stretching and sipping again from the spring.

"Yeah, I haven't rattled on since before al l of this happened. It all seems so long ago, my birthday, the Discovery, burying Dad. I've been through a lot," Sabor said, nervously, popping his sabor in and out, creating small holes in the limestone path.

"You know what you must do, Do you not, Sabor Lindon of The Order," Pinn Goth said as he stood and looked down at the boy hesitating to grab his destiny.

"What? What must I do now, Pinn?" Sabor asked very child-like.

"What my people and the Gargoyle before could not. What your father and many, many great men could not do. You must WIN! Kill Dvanken, bring a halt to his destruction," Pinn took Sabor's hand, shaking it gently, he turned and walked away, over the hill.

"Pinn! Pinn!" Sabor screamed, with no reply from his target. "Ho w can I do it? How can I do it, when so many great men have all failed!"

The Journey was a downhill battle from there, only a short five-mile hike from the end of the forest of the Agramin. A downhill battle, Sabor fought with the demons stalking him inside. The rage and pain festered inside him. But, deep down, he knew something was different about him and about this new dawn.

The Halls of The Order were a bustle with activity. The brother's were communing into the Assembly hall for a meeting. Ellett called the session to announce the pairings, as well as to rally the troops with the traditional Awakening speech. I sat in the balcony and looked down upon the assembly, as Ellett began.

"Brothers! We are upon the shore of another Awakening. The Evil awaiting you is unexplainable. I have not seen it's equal in my tenure as a Guardian, and I feel as if I speak for the other Elders, when I say that neither has any of them. The carnage and death you will see may take you, making your knees weak with disgust. But if you take a measure of faith onto the battlefield with you, as well as a great deal of the training you have received here, you-you will endure. The people, outside these walls, there in the world beyond The Order, are ignorant of Dvanken's evil. This is just as well, I think. The knowledge of this evil is our responsibility alone, for we are the only who have the ability to deal with the consequences of such knowledge. We are Guardians, and our God given duty is to save the ignorant from an untimely death. Every cycle the evil increases as he harvests the seeds he has sewn in the past, and as he prepares more for the next season. The evil grows, always.

"We do however, have a trump card for his growth. Whether you choose to believe, or simply wish to continue the cycle of despair, Sabor Lindon could be a means to the end. I know many of you have heard the halls echoing with the rumors that he is gone and he has turned his back on us all, but I have faith, as should all of you. He will come back! He must come back;" Ellett was very animated as he spoke. Staring deeply into every soul in the auditorium, as he lectured. Searching to find the lines of allegiance breaking away from one another within the brothers.

"The lists of pairings will be posted outside. Please, check it as you leave," Ellett added.

After Ellett finished, he stepped down. Returning to his chair, the large oak door on the opposite side of the huge room smashed open, crashing into a million splintery pieces that bounced on the floor. A brilliant bluish glow swam over the audience, putting each back at ease. A shadow stepped through the smoke and light.

"Zandy is that you?" Symon asked himself quietly. "No, it couldn't be, it just couldn't," and He answered himself.

"Who are you?! What do you want here?! Answer!" Ellett screamed, assuming his place back at the podium. The figure stood motionless five feet from the once magnificent door. It wore Zandalars cloak with the hood overshadowing his face, intimidating many of the Greenlings.

Two of the more headstrong students, Bryant and Blaine, looked at each other and spotted an opportunity to make names for themselves. They nodded to one another, then rushed the intruder, sabors drawn and ready for battle.

They made it only a few feet when the shrouded man raised his right arm and extended his fingers as far as they would go. Simultaneously, he shuddered and nodded the other direction. A single strand of illumination jutted from his hand sending Blaine tumbling backwards through the air suspending him a few inches above the on looking crowd, mouths agape. The nod took Bryant, flooring him instantly, as well as clearing the first few rows of all occupants. The percussion was nearly invisible, only a faint blue shimmer indicated what had thrown the men around. With his hand, he lowered Blaine softly and laid him on the ground next to his counterpart.

With a courteous nod he walked confidently past the pair, never looking directly at either of them and proceeded to the front of the room, to the waiting podium. He stepped upon the stage, shook Symon's hand, then turned to Ellett. The cloaked figure grabbed him by both shoulders and gave a reassuring jiggle. Then he turned to the astounded crowd. Ellett nudged the stranger out of the way, approaching the podium.

"Brother Guardians, I am extremely proud to introduce to you, the Solitaire of Lady Noelle, our Avenger, Sabor Lindon," Ellett proclaimed like a short-winded boxing announcer.

A wave of surprise and joy swept The Order, and not one person remained seated. Even Bryant and Blaine stood, dusting themselves off, to applaud his long awaited homecoming. Sabor took the hood down and shook the rain from his hair. No eyes drifted from him. The focus of the crowd nearly sliced Sabor in half, but he cleared his throat and proceeded.

"Brothers we gather here together on the threshold of a new tomorrow. The seeds of peace and joy have been planted, and it is now our season to reap those as rewards for our dedication. We have to plow through the old ways of hunting Dvanken for sport, in teams of two, like the fox hunting clubs of old, rich southern gentlemen together to plump their ego's with a kill. Dvanken will fall to us, not because of some "Avenger," but because we will take him with overwhelming force and numbers. For as good as we have been, we have not been a unit and we have lost.

"I am coming into a situation where the mind set is three and punt, give up and wait until the next Awakening. THAT STOPS NOW. The time to wait for the Avenger to do it is bygone. I, the Avenger am here, and I have a plan. We will all see a time of peace. We in our days will see the end of the Cycle.

"Brothers, pride is the thorn in our side, the sole reason we have failed at our duties. You are not, nor am I, going to be able to defeat Dvanken alone, one on one. We have tried this for centuries, either out of blind habit or the need to be the hero. I cannot determine which. But I know that we must all swallow this lump of pride, every member of The Order, from the head Elders behind me, down to the freshest Greenlings. We must all step out of the shadows of tradition and prepare to fight in unison as one unstoppable team! We have no choice but to challenge conventional styles, they have failed for so long. We cannot afford to delay our progression any longer. Dvanken has eclipsed us for ages. He has morphed, evolving leaving us stagnant. Falling furthers and further away from an even stance with him. In my opinion, it is because we have stopped trying to better ourselves in some damn fairy-tale hope of some Solitaire, or Avenger. This one who will single handedly present you with easy victory. Well I stand here as this Avenger, and I am telling you my Discovery has shown me that even the Avenger cannot do this alone. I as one person am weak and vulnerable, but we as an Order are the most powerful forces ever known! Together we are the force to rid the world of Dvanken, forever and our time is now,"

The words pierced the heart of every man there inspiring a huge eruption of applause and adulation. All but one stood and praised the initiative taken by this Guardian. Keni Divin sat glaring hatefully at the returned hero. The sight turned his earlier acceptance of Sabor as the Avenger into a boiling jealousy that instantly overtook him and incensed him with rage. Keni sat quietly as one by one the other brothers walked up and shook hands with Sabor, then filed out to check the lists out of sheer habit.

Ellett and Symon were the last to go. Each hugged the young man and chuckled in amazement. Keni, seeing that no one was left in the auditorium, took his chance at alpha male and approached the Avenger.

"You are not what they all think you are!" Keni said, pointing behind him at the other members of The Order. "I am just as dangerous as you will ever be, and don't you think that you can run away for years, then come back and take what I have worked so hard for. I, alone, will defeat Dvanken. I will go down as the legend, I will! Not some quitter that got the title because of his father," Keni said as he stepped closer and slammed his finger into Sabor's chest.

"Good... " Sabor said swatting Keni's hand down, then clapping. "...That is exactly the kind of talk I want to hear. The old way has been getting us killed, one by one for far too long. I checked the list in the hall; you are to be my guide aren't you? I guess that will keep us side by side a lot huh?" Sabor said with a certain peace in his voice.

"I will show you first hand why I am going to be the Avenger. And why your myth Master Lindon, will die with him!" Keni said as he spun and walked up to the large door.

"Master Divin, your services will not be needed as Guide, that ancient practice is over as well," Sabor said, getting no answer from the man he was speaking to. Sabor stood and watched in amazement at what the Divin had said, then his lack of respect. Never one to back down from a challenge, Sabor stretched his hand out and grunted, trying to control the red boil inside his chest. A thin blue bolt slammed Keni in the small of the back. Not enough to hurt him, but it grabbed his attention none the less.

"KENI, do you wish to prove your superiority to me in the arena or do you wish to show me some other reason why you should take the Avenger's place?" Sabor asked after getting the headstrong mans attention. Keni stared, his pride throbbing more than his back. He pointed and nodded approvingly.

"I will prove my superiority to you and to myself. You meet me in the Battle Grounds;" Keni backed out, keeping close watch on Sabor. Sabor glared at him with a childish grin.

"You will have me, I will be there," and Sabor sat down and stared at his feet. He shook off the disbelief again, then stood to proceed to the Battle Grounds.

The Battle Grounds were desolate and strangely cold. The usually beautiful light cascading from behind the stained glass was absent, and only the glow of a few torches lingered. Sabor entered, finding Keni with his shirt off, wearing a pair of baggy pants. He busily struck at a stone in the center of the floor.

"So, at least I know you're not a coward Avenger," Keni spouted after spotting Sabor.

"Your mouth has gotten us both into something neither of us wants. But, I'll tell you one thing my old friend. This is something I do not take lightly," Sabor retorted. Sabor stepped out of his father's cloak, and tossed it lightly over a rail on the side of the auditorium.

"Are you ready for a lesson?" Keni asked, his sabor springing to full extension.

Sabor nodded approvingly, crossed his arms, and deployed two jagged

162

scimitars, each glowing a beautiful powder blue with veins of navy blue. "I am more than ready, Guardian. Let's roll!"

Keni lunged and rolled along the floor, springing up just in front of Sabor, swinging wildly with both arms attempting to take Sabor's head. Feeling the pressure of his own rage, Sabor stepped back and slapped Keni on the face sharply with the broad side of his weapon, sending Keni tumbling to the ground in a cloud of dust.

"Get up, Keni," Sabor pushed.

With a scream, Keni bolted to his feet, slamming Sabor backwards into a wall. Sabor's head bounced off the solid wall with a sickening thud. Jumping back, Keni flipped to a safe distance, then thrust his sword headlong towards Sabors prone face. The Solitaire shook the impact off just in time to see the blade speeding toward his nose. With one swift motion Sabor moved, grabbed his attacker by the back of the neck, and slammed him face first into the granite. Keni's arm caught a bit of a lucky break as it were, for it found itself broadside, the back of Sabors head, splitting it wide open and throbbing.

"Well buddy, it looks like you have drawn first blood, but it ain't over, till it's over," Sabor said as he rubbed the back of his pulsing cranium, feeling the crimson life flowing from a six inch cut.

"Agreed Avenger. This isn't over, you will pay for my nose, bastard," Keni said, resetting his broken snout. As if a light switch had been turned on, Keni's expression changed into rage. His very mannerisms changed, he was angry and out of control.

"Calm yourself Keni. You must keep control!" Sabor instructed.

"DDDIIIIIEEEEE !!!" Keni shouted. As he came to his feet, swinging his blades with deadly precision. He slashed and ripped small wounds on Sabor's extremities.

Sabor did well to keep his head on his neck during the viciously, fast onslaught. The Avenger found himself retreating from Keni, and then a loose foothold found him flat on his back.

"You are mine Lindon, and all will know that I am the true Avenger!" Keni said, raising his right sabor high in the air. The blade shook, and tiny capillaries of blood red hate, filled the core. The hints of hate began to circulate inside the sabor, weakening the blade. Keni let out a howl, and charged with all his strength straight down for a kill shot.

Sabor rolled up to one knee and held both of his sabors above his head to block the blow. Sabor's scimitars were deep blue, untainted by negative emotion, pure. When Keni's blade collided with Sabor's, a huge flash of light saturated the air, nearly blinding the two warriors, each questioning whether the blow had flown true.

The brilliance faded, and each man found himself almost intact. The hate in Keni's blade caused the tip to disintegrate. He lost short of six inches off his mystical blade. Both stared in disbelief at Keni's right hand, where the blade hung limp.

"Are you okay?" Sabor asked, retracting his weapons.

"I think so. Where my blade was stings pretty bad, but I am okay, for the most part," Keni said, astounded he had tried to kill Sabor, but Sabor only worried if he was okay.

"Thank you for asking though, Avenger," Keni said quietly, as he stared at the ground, held out his left hand, and gestured for Sabor to shake.

"I have no intent on disrespecting you Master Divin, but you have to earn that. Respect is not earned with an apology, but with actions," Sabor said turning his back and walking away. "But keep your head up, Master guide. You had me!" Sabor smiled, shaking his head in disbelief and pain.

"Maybe we should go get this thing looked at, what do ya say?" Sabor asked as he stopped, and motioned for Keni to follow.

The Awakening

The dark cavern sustained a foul smell, an unearthly smell, vile and putrid. The stout musk of Death hung stagnant in the echoing cave. The odor had festered here for five long years, the malodor was overwhelming. The entangling mist, hovering about pulsated brilliant purple and the earth a slimy green dotted with brown rocks. In the center of the cave rested a heap. The large ball of seething, webbish material emitted a soft purplish light. The mass swelled with breath and a sound rumbled from deep within. The unholy Dvanken' s Slumber gave way to the Awakening, meaning Dvanken's time had come, and his hell was to be unleashed upon the world, as it had for centuries.

Dvanken's eyes broke open, the pain of a lone warrior piercing his Slumber. His massive body began to shift and move. Slowly, he freed his massive arms and brushed his eyes. They glimmered an unholy red with deep swirls of blue and a slight purple danced along the edges.

A long, gnarly finger broke the shell. A hiss erupted, a cloud of purple vapor billowing up and expanding on the ceiling. The long finger gave way to an enormous scaly hand. Next, came the massive forearm approximately twenty inches in circumference and covered with luminescent spikes two to six inches long. A second hand pierced the shell, arced down, making contact with the ground, and pulled the mammoth shoulders and head from the cocoon.

His head and face had changed. It no longer stretched forward to accommodate row upon row of razor fangs; rather it had become blunt, like that of a lion. His mouth was no less deadly though. Four fangs protruded, two extremely long, jutting down from the roof, and two smaller ones at each corner curling up below his eyes.

Starting at the back from his crown, a long bony red horn ran down the entire length of his back, forking at the tip. Dvanken's arms and shoulders remained very massive, but their lack of sustenance had drained some of the bulk and strength. This was a drawback his hunger would soon remedy.

His body seemed more erect, less dog-like in stance. The skin on his body had grown from a reptilian texture to a more refined human-like skin. It had a blackish purple tint to it with brilliant red and green highlights streaking all around him ending at precise points like knives on his back. His lower limbs were covered in bony shards angled and barbed. They were extremely weak from the growth and the lack of movement.

He pulled himself up and stood, for the first time, like a man! His evolution moved him ever closer to what he hated, what he needed, what he ate. His ultimate form, and the ultimate evil, was progressing naturally to become human. His posture was that of a human, but he still possessed a distinctive bestial hunch. His very stance warned that this being was not to be trusted. He was death.

He folded his large black wings back behind him, fashioning what appeared to be a flowing cape. His forearms ached with a newness; the veins alive and illuminated like spider webs. His fingers had grown long. Knife-like bones jutted from every knuckle and joint on his body. Each dripped with blood and a luminescent purple ooze. Dvanken's entire body itched and ached from the new additions the Slumber had brought about.

His mind raced with the thoughts of food and the thousands of meals he prepared during the last Awakening. His stomach churned at these propositions, and he grinned.

"Ooooohhhh, how good they taste. I will enjoy this body very much," the evil beast proclaimed as he retracted, then forced the bone shards in and out one by one.

"Avenger, I have seasoned you with loss, and your pain is mine to reap. You have pathetically mulled over the dead long enough. I have hungered for five seasons, hungered for your death!" Hate laced the words. Malice radiated from his eyes, spewing his feelings outward. "And in time Avenger, I will come for you. For now though, I will fill my belly,"

Dvanken cracked his joints to relieve the pressure, and to regain some of his mobility. As he loosened, he focused on the world, searching for a close meal. His mind slammed across the miles; pulled by the pain he had caused Sabor. His soul felt pulled to a field where the Avenger rested between two towering, weather-beaten and crumbling Gargoyle statues. The Avenger sat, legs crossed, sobbing, dwelling on his loss. A disgusting smile broke over Dvanken.

"Well Avenger, if y ou wish to die now, then so be it. At last, I will rid The Order of hope and fill my hunger with the anguish of the all-powerful Avenger,"

Dvanken leaned out of his shadow, crying a blood-curdling howl. Ripping the shadow in two, he lunged, sprinting and tearing his way across the void. Digging and pulling at the earth, desperately trying to get where his mind had seen. Sabor sat still, just staring at the ground and intermittently slamming it with his sabor.

Dvanken ran through the fields, his knuckles tearing at the grass every few steps trying to gain a boost of speed. He so badly wanted to taste flesh and savor the pain of complete loss mixed with consuming hopelessness. And this was exactly what Dvanken was sure he had reduced Sabor to.

The unholy beast found himself charging past the bus stop, where he had devoured the cucumber lady. The smell was familiar and welcome. Then, he spotted Sabor walking with his hands in his pockets, staring at the ground wondering what might have been, headlong towards him on the sidewalk. Dvanken slammed his claws deep into the concrete and stopped dead.

"Pssst...." Dvanken said as he hunched up and grinned,"...Avenger, so at last we meet. I must say, I am not as impressed as I should be,"a purple mist wrapped around the pair, the world outside the miasma froze.

"You will be, I promise. You took my world, you piece of shit. Dvanken, your time to die is now. I am the end of your reign of terror! DVANKEN, it ends tonight. We are now done with you!" Sabor screamed, his sabors dropping into sight from inside the sleeves of Zandalar's jacket.

"Young Guardian, how ironic, those were the words your father spoke to me. Just before his own arrogance gave me the door to gut him like a pig and feast on his spine," Dvanken paused, laughing, and raised his jagged finger pointing down the alley where he had slain Zandalar. "It was there, where your father squealed like a girl, as I ripped him into pieces," again, a sinister smirk broke over his face, taunting Sabor's rage. Sabor slowly raised his right arm and looked over his shoulder as if signaling something, but nothing happened.

"What's wrong, Avenger? Your friends desert you, like your mother and girlfriend did, huh? Oh, poor baby, that bodes well for me. Surely this will add some flavor, loneliness tastes so lovely with a pinch of rage," and Dvanken grinned, slithering around Sabor quickly.

"I ..I don't understand, they were supposed to be here,"Sabor stood tall in the face of death and isolation. He brought his other arm up, readying himself to fight. "Get away from me you evil bastard. You've already taken everything away from me. Just let me die in peace!" Sabor said, a single tear running down his face.

"Good, you said the magic word, boy. Thank you. Shhh, no need to cry little Lindon because now, I will purloin the last shred of the your family line. And from what I see the weakest shred. Now you die, and my hunger dies with you!" Dvanken said as he traced the shape of Sabor's face, following the trail of the tear.

"NO!" Sabor yelled, a look of determination and clarity taking over his face. He stood renewed, ready. "I am your end Dvanken, and I know it scares you. I have come to kill you, with or without The Order.

"Your beautiful wife-to-be would have made a suitable meal, had your love, not spoiled her perfect pain," Dvanken added with disgust, hoping to destroy the young mans resolve. The tactic seemed to work as Sabor retracted his blade a bit, and lowered his guard.

"Impetuous boy, this fight is quite pointless. Your struggle between Good and Evil, your fight to stay alive, even you must realize it is pointless to fight for life. You are human, and you will die, your kind always dies. You must know that there will always be good, and for you to appreciate this good, this precious gift you have been given, then, there must be a measurable amount of evil. Why will you not realize you have nothing left to fight for? All of your struggle has already been resolved for you. I have taken all the reasons you have to stay in this fight," Dvanken said, as he rubbed his stomach. "Do you know how many humans would love to have that situation? DO YOU!?

"Your precious Order has abandoned you when you needed them the most. Your parents are gone, oh excuse me, I mean dead. I took them both for you and your fiancé Chelle. Damn it, that taste still disgusts me! Your struggle, your fight is for nothing. You have no tomorrow to fight for. So, just give up the pointless and accept the inevitable. DAMN IT! Just give up. Give up and let me eat!"

With those piercing words, Sabor darted forward, catching Dvanken in mid-sentence, and off guard. Sabor's left blade ran true and sank deep into Dvanken's chest. Dvanken writhed in pain, slamming the ground with his right arm. An earth-shaking shriek shattered the air around the two. With his free hand Dvanken instantly, without thought, grasped the glowing blade and ripped the rigid razor out inch by painful inch. A purple stream of luminescent liquid poured from the wound.

"Hunngh, the pain makes it feel good, Avenger. I thrive on it," Dvanken said quivering with satisfaction. A web of flesh weaved itself across the gash, healing the wound completely in an instant.

Dvanken pulled his hand from the ground, clutched Sabor's face forcefully, and shoved him with every ounce of reserve he could muster, ripping large gashes deep into Sabor's head and face. Sabor tumbled backwards, flipping and twirling thirty feet away, crashing through a newspaper stand finally coming to rest on his back. Sabor pulled himself to one knee, and glared at a smiling Dvanken and prepared to charge. Dvanken stared at Sabor, running his blood-soaked finger through his lips, slurping the life from the red liquid.

"Indeed, you will be worth my wait, Avenger!" Dvanken said as he stoop over, then sprang, twirling and spinning through the air, landing in front of the crouched Guardian. Sabor deployed his weapon on his right arm.

"Not today Dvanken. Not here and not now. I have you,"

Sabor lunged forward aiming dead center, at the hollow heart of Evil. Dvanken, sensing the move, stepped back and then forward, grabbing Sabor by the wrist and ripping him from the ground, and held him dangling a few feet from the earth.

"You do, indeed, have me human. You have me as the last vision your eyes will ever see,"

Dvanken's mouth opened wide, preparing to rip the sustenance from Sabor's bones. Pulling the young man closer and sinking his long fangs deep into the soft belly, Dvanken reached the spine with ease. With a quick jerk of his massive head, Sabor's entrails streamed through the air, leaving a mass of red and yellow tissue stringing along the ground.

The taste was lovely and satisfying, but the experience would be fleeting. Dvanken's eyes ripped open from the deep Slumber. The intense dream filled him with ecstasy and joy.

"Damn it. The taste was mine, the victory at hand. The whole time, it was only a lie. Where is the Avenger? Where am I? This is my resting-place. My hunger still lives. What kind of... " Dvanken's mind ran with questions and came to rest on what he had exploited and used for eons, the isolated ability of humans to dream. Dvanken had never experienced this phenomenon, and it was very disorienting for him.

"...This dreaming thing, I hate it. But, I did enjoy the thrill of tasting Sabor,"Dvanken mused. He rubbed his stomach, realizing that he had broken free of his cocoon. He saw the vision in his dream had held true. His body had changed just the way he had seen. And he was pleased, pleased and hungry.

"I must eat. I will enjoy my future confrontation with the mighty Solitaire, but now, I will fill my belly with many sheep,"and so began the Awakening and Dvanken's hunt.

169

Eldon Seymore had been married to his lovely blue-haired wife, Unis, for fifty-one years. Well, at least it would have been in mid April. The cancer stole her precious life, some three days ago on a bitter December evening. This not so warm night found him driving down a country road, one that he and Unis had traveled everyday of their fifty years together. The road was very difficult to see the soft tears of loneliness had fogged over his eyes.

"Why, why did she need to die? Why, God, please tell me why? She was a good lady. She went to services every Sunday, even made apple pie for the bake sales there," The gray headed old man in denim overalls and his best flannel shirt sobbed, and with one motion wiped the snot and tears from his leathery face.

"Look, all I know is Lord, I am lonely. I'm hurting, and I miss my Unis. Please, give her back to me. Please," With that said, the old man began to get lost in the vast scrapbook in his mind. As his mind gripped a pleasant memory, a salty tear rolled down his cheek, and a brilliant bolt of lightning struck the ground, foretelling of the immanent rain.

Dvanken had heard the words, and he was pleased to feel the loss. A Cheshire grin broke across his hellish new face.

The road was a time warp for Mr. Seymore. He pictured himself in his old 56' Chevy cruising, listening to the radio, and checking to see if he had remembered to bring flowers and candy for his new girlfriend, Unis. She was so angelic he remembered red hair always pulled back in a perfect ponytail, and her eyes, so deep and twinkling. His mind swam in the pool of memories.

From the corner of his eye, Eldon spotted a shadow, a deep consuming blackness that flickered, and was gone just as fast as it had appeared. The old man shook his head, blinked very hard, and did a double take at the point where the void had been. Seeing nothing, he let out a sigh of relief and continued down the road. As he got a little further, his headlights illuminated a large mailbox, with large reflecting tape that read "JONSON". He laughed, as the glowing red word, gave him an old familiar feeling. He reached over into the passenger seat and rubbed the material lovingly back and forth.

"Hey, honey look. It's the ole' Jonson place. I heard a story in the barbershop the other day about old Tony's great-granddaughter. Heard that she went off to the city, and got murdered. Barely had enough of the pretty little

170

thing to identify. Damn shame. If you ask me, I'd say it was a damn shame,"

After a minute of ranting, the old man realized that he was talking to the air and holding not her leg, but a pretty bouquet of wild flowers meant for her final resting-place. In defiance of his discovery, he asked. "Anyway, do you remember skinny dippin' in his old cat tail pond, then romping around in his hayloft? I do. Those sure were the days, huh?" The desperate old man clung to the memory, and began to cry just a little harder.

"I love you ma, and I miss you Uni. I sure do miss you an awful lot;" He wiped his face clean again.

Eldon noticed on the opposite side of the road, unmistakably, was the same shadow from before. His car swooshed by, and Eldon hoped with all of his heart that he wouldn't see the figure again. The hurt of losing his lifelong partner added to the fear of seeing this void.

The fear smelled like a gourmet meal to Dvanken. Mr. Seymore's heart beat furiously, and he became short of breath. In fear, he frantically searched, straining to see the evil stalking him. His eyes found the night hollow and formless.

It was eerie how still the world had turned. Eldon' s foot became heavy, saturated with pain and new found fear. The speedometer pushed clockwise, faster and faster. The old man felt uneasy over the stillness of the night. Eldon's eyes glanced down at the orange dash lights, which told Eldon he was traveling at eighty-five miles per hour. Being much faster than he was used to, he tried to slow down. But his sense of fear and self-preservation pushed him to go faster.

Almost without thought, Eldon peered out the passenger window. In the darkness, he spotted his end. Death had come to his window, and he could see it's evil face. Dvanken ran stride for stride with the speeding Chrysler. An evil smile streamed across Dvanken' s face. The terror outside, cocked its head from side to side, then vanished.

"What in the hell?" Eldon asked himself out loud.

A greenish-red miasma seeped in through the air conditioning vents. In a strange sort of twist, the miasma did not freeze the world around Eldon. Instead, it drew his memories from the recesses of his mind and broadcast them, like a movie, projecting all around him. At first the scenes were joyous and happy, visions of Unis and the years they spent loving one another. The ghost Unis spun around, suspended at sixteen years old, full of life and happiness. The memories seemed so real.

Unis broke from her spin and locked eyes with Eldon. She smiled the smile that embodied the whole of their relationship. She leaned in to give Eldon a kiss. The butterflies of the first time fluttered in his stomach all over again. The moment broke when her warm lips pressed against his. He opened his eyes and saw his beautiful wife's face. He began to sob just a little.

The vivid picture perfect visions drew him in, and he seemed to relax a bit. The memories soon turned to visions of pain. Unis's face turned to a skinless, fleshless bone. The skull laughed at him. A wind from nowhere blew the skull to dust, carrying the particles away.

"Why? Why is this happening to me? Damn it! Why!" Eldon screamed into his hands. "God make this all stop. I can't handle anymore of this," Eldon closed his eyes tightly, but the miasma penetrated his eyelids. Gruesome visions of Vietnam, flashbacks of his two tours, shone brightly, vividly inside the darkness. He endured the depictions of his best friend ripped in half by a nine-year-old with an AK-47. Heartache and confusion streamed from every orifice on his face. The tears on his cheeks stung, his chest began to constrict.

"What the hell do you want to accomplish with this DEVIL? I done been through all this. I live it everyday, so if you want to scare me just come out and do it," The defiance was fresh and unexpected to Dvanken.

"You will know my reasoning soon enough, old man," the unholy howled as he leaned in and knocked on the window.

His sleek new look was even more intimidating than before. The elderly man, seeing his death, released the steering wheel and his stern attitude. He cowered in the seat, putting his knees up to his chest and shoving his hands in front of him. His back against the door, his eyes searched the darkness outside for Dvanken who dropped in and out of sight as the two tore through the night.

"Your fear is ready old man, and I am hungry!" Dvanken slammed the speeding vehicle with his massive head and jaws. His long teeth ripped the sheet metal as if it were rice paper. His head smashed the glass, spraying shards of razor-sharp glass into Eldon's face and chest.

"Look, you Devil, I will never give you my soul. I know all about what you are and what you do. I have read the good book, and I watch movies. I want my soul, so you just leave me be! Get thee behind me Satan,"

"Ha, ah ha ah ha, my stupid little old man I am not Satan. He is weak, and, in turn, I cannot be the Devil. I am Dvanken, and your pain smells good to me. I wish only to consume it all, my dear boy. I need only one thing from you, the permission to take the pain. I can and will give you back your Unis. I promise you. I will give you her life back, and your love will last forever. All you have to do is ask me. Say the word and your world will be restored,"

The old man wrought with agony and confusion, looked around the car for some sort of answer. The car felt as if it continued speeding down the highway, yet no tree, cloud, or star moved. The outside world was stagnant; the monster weaved in and out of sight.

Eldon searched for a hold on the moment. *"Is this real, or have I been awake too long? Oh, Unis, please tell me if this is real or am I dreaming some sick dream, PLEASE,"*

Eldon sobbed harder, questioning everything in his mind. *"Why would this thing do this for me? Is it my reward for my good life, has God heard my prayers and answered them with this thing. Well, he does work in mysterious ways, don't he?"*

Eldon reasoned with himself for a few moments, then asked the beast," What word would you like for me to say?"

"Please, just be polite when you ask me. Do as your mother has taught you and say please,"Dvanken said to the man.

"Well, I guess I will have to ask you then. I miss my lady so much. Please mister, please give me my Unis back. She means everything to me. Please, oh please give her back to me!" The words stung. The realization of what was happening broke over him when he saw the hate and pain well up and glow in the eyes of Dvanken.

A snarl rolled on the lips of Dvanken. He brandished his large teeth at the man in the car and laughed. "You will rest with her this night, old man. Please, enjoy her company,"the unholy voice thundered.

"But wait, you said I would have my Unis back. You said all I needed to do was ask!" Mr. Seymore proclaimed, scared and even more angry. The damage had been done. Like millions of times before, Dvanken had been set in motion with one little word and he could not be hindered.

Dvanken opened his huge mouth, the rows of teeth glowing a faint purple. A deep red spiral accented his throat. His right fist clinched and his wrist burst with a bouquet of fifteen inch bone shards. His arm arced forward with the force of a jackhammer, slamming the grill, pulling the car to a complete halt. The blow crushed the radiator and ripped through the engine, shoving them both in to the passenger seat. The left arm pierced the roof, peeling the sheet metal back like a sardine lid and exposing the frightened little man in the car.

Dvanken howled in hunger, staring at the moon. "You will die this night, the first of my Awakening. I thank you," shaking his fist at the sky and all around him, perched astride the roof of the car, he screamed, "Guardians prepare your Avenger. Make him strong, proud, and silent. For I have prepared him well myself, saturated with loss. His body will be a testament to my superiority. Dvanken slumbers no more, and the Awakening has come to pass. *Death is here among you all. I will make your hopes disappear, just as I have with all other incarnations of your precious Order.* Prepare now!"

With this, Dvanken's left hand reached down and clutched the man by the head, his palm muffling the pleading screams. Dvanken slowly squeezed, crushing the mans skull, until his fingers touched. Gray fragments and blood red matter sprayed out, coating the remaining windows with a maroon tint.

The enormous beast shuddered with excitement. Killing felt good, and eating would be even more enjoyable. With the butt of Eldon's skull attached to the spine he desired so much, he pulled up and over his head, separating the chain of bone from the lifeless old man. The links of sharp bone pulled chunks of brown liver and large portions of intestine, and various organs out behind them. Dvanken choked down the spine and its tag-along goodies, furiously savoring nothing.

After disposing of the rest of treat, Dvanken stood straddling the remains of Eldon. Small fires from gasoline dotted the road and the body of the car. He again shouted at the moon. "You be at peace with your lovely wife, old one. I have granted your request; " He smiled and picked his blood stained canines. The beast then warned the wind crying into the night air, "Guardians, when I fill my belly, I will then come for your savior. Present him to me, and I will spare the rest,"

The Halls of the Order bustled with excitement. The Avenger had returned and he was taking charge. The mindset had changed; all training was now done in large groups, instead of one on one sparring and bag work.

Sabor stood holding a large metal plate, adjacent to Mason Linx, who was doing the same. The pair was bracing themselves as Keni Divin slammed away, targeting whichever shield moved first with his broken blade. An evaluation to note the strength of the blade.

"So Captain Linx, do you think Keni will be okay to fight or does he need to sit the battle out?" Sabor asked with concern.

"Hey, I am not going to have anyone tell me whether or not I can fight. I have one whole sabor left, and besides my damaged one isn't that bad. I'll just file it or something," Keni snapped, showing his lack of control yet again.

"I just wanted to see if there were any ways to fix the damn thing!" Sabor replied defending his comments.

"You will do as the Head Elders and I decide. Exactly as the rest of the brothers do. You, however talented, are not above the rules, do you understand? The laws have been passed down through the ages for a reason. To supply an order to chaos and a guideline for headstrong warriors like yourself. Do you understand?" Captain Linx offered sternly.

"I understand that you are no longer in any position to tell me what I can, or cannot do. I am an exceptional warrior. Sabor's plan calls for us all to band together to win. Surely you, a Head Elder won't voice an opinion opposing the Avenger. The Solitaire sent here by the heavens to save us all, would you?" Keni retorted sarcastically.

"Be that as it may, your blade is in fact broken. You may become a hindrance, since your blade broke as a result of your blatant lack of composure," Mason said, letting down his large metal shield and slamming a strong block with his right sabor.

"Keni, come on, man. You will do well to not to question the Elders. However old fashioned they are, they do have our best interest at heart," Sabor replied trying to calm the tension. "Look man, you'll be fine. I will try to pull some strings to get you some time on the field, just kidding. You know I wouldn't want anyone else out there next to me other than you. For now though, get better and try to rest up. The time for us to claim our victory is just around the corner," Sabor grabbed Keni, slapped him on the back, and motioned for him to leave.

"Thanks, well I guess that's my cue to leave. I'm gonna go and soak my arm. Try to get some sleep. After that, if you need me, I'll be in the battlegrounds seeing if I can learn something new for our next little scuffle," Keni said dripping with sarcasm. He then smiled a cocky smile and punched Sabor on the shoulder.

"I'll see ya out there, okay. Hurry up though, we don't have much time before Dvanken picks a fight with all of us. Gotta get ready," Sabor said hopeful. With those words, Keni left holding his wounded blade, shaking it slowly and mumbling profanities at it.

"Avenger, for your sake, I hope this plan of yours will work. We have done things for tradition and for a reason. To stray from these ways will be almost impossible for us older ones. But, we all believe in you, so we will follow you. So, do not let us down," Mason reached messing Sabor's hair and laughed reassuringly.

"Okay Captain, listen to me. You don't have to worry about the plan. You do however, need to prepare for battle. I believe our time is running out and all must fight this time, no exceptions. You should show a little more understanding to all of us. We all have been thrust into this, and it is new to each of us, not just the Elders. Surely, you remember when you were a Greenling and these halls were just polished rock mazes. You haven't forgotten your roots have you?" Sabor asked sarcastically, then without giving time for an answer, pressed on. "I am sorry. I should show you a little more respect than that. For so long now, I have blamed you. Blamed you for everything wrong in my life. My father always being gone, never sharing his life with me, never looking at me, and saying, *come on outside, and lets play catch buddy.* I always knew he loved me, but your escapades kept him from showing it. This was always your fault. My mom staying up late, crying into her pillow, missing her husband, and not wanting to upset her son. The times in my life where my Dad was supposed to be there were filled instead with a shadow, a hope that maybe next time he won't be out chasing some bad guy or saving the world. You were the son-of-a-bitch that sent him away. Away from Mom and me. I blamed YOU, for my father's death. I blamed you that my kids would never know how awesome Zandalar Lindon was. Hell, I blame you that I never knew how awesome he was. I have hated you my whole life for this,"

Mason defended himself, interrupting Sabor, "Sabor; it truly was never my fault. Your father was a Guard... "

"Let me finish!" Sabor thundered, backing the older man down. "As I was saying, with my Discovery, and the volumes it has shown and taught me about The Order and about life, I realize that you were just doing your job, the work of The Order. He too had some responsibility in staying gone. He tried to make death come slowly for all of us, to give us all a chance to see old age and experience each other forever, to be able to see his son and his son's kids grow old.

"So, I would like to apologize, and thank you. You gave my life a chance. Your enemy and mine are the one that will reap the loss of my father.

"Don't worry, the new ways will work and Dvanken will die. I promise you this, as a Lindon, and that is enough," With that, Sabor knelt down at Mason Linx's feet and said," Please, forgive me for my words and thoughts of hate. I am sorry,"

"Of course Sabor. I knew you and your mother thought ill of me, about all of us. For what we were doing though, I could stand to take a little dislike from the both of you. You are forgiven. You were forgiven the moment you thought them. But, enough talk about this. You are alive. You are strong. You make your father, and the rest of us, extremely proud. Along those lines my boy, I would like to congratulate you on your progress and commend you on your entrance earlier, could have been a little flashier though," Mason said, adding a shimmer of humor to the heavy conversation.

"My God, Sabor, you really had us all worried. Please, in the future, if you decide to run off again, at least tell one of us where you will be going, okay? Will you promise me that much?" Mason said, putting his hand under Sabors chin, raising his line of sight, to looking the elder in the eye.

"Your father will watch your adventures and smile. He will see your children, and you will see him in them. I promise you. Always remember, I, as well as all of the other Elders, see you as our son you belong to The Order. We all love you very much," he said, a single tear containing his sorrow for Zandalar, his pride, and hopefulness concerning the young Avenger, cascaded down his left cheek.

"I will see you later young Lindon. Right now, I have so many things to tend to. You have asked much of all of us. And apparently, I need to hit the battlegrounds for a refresher, got a battle to win for you," Mason taunted Sabor, smiling, and tapping him on the stomach.

"Me too. Me too," Sabor whispered and stared at the wall.

"Hey there old friend. It is good to see you. Excuse me Sabor Lindon, but an old friend would like to talk with you," I approached snapping Sabor from his

177

dagger like stare.

"Cranden! Hey man how are you? I have missed you so much,"

"And I you. Tell me what has happened and leave nothing out. It will be as old times. Simpler times weren't they, everything cut and dry. I was but a confidant on your balcony, an inanimate object for you to spill to. No talk of Dvanken, no looming battles, no hardship but how to hold the ones you love, and what the weekend will hold,"

"Yeah, that was a great time. Why only NOW is it a great time? When I was there in the moment, the weekend was so far and the endless droning of my pointless little world consumed me, churning all of the unnecessary b.s. To the surface for me to reflect on. I never focused on the greater aspects of my life," Sabor said as his words and mine turned his stomach, bringing back visions of Noelle, Chelle, and his father.

"I mean, why the hell are we like this? Why do people have to look at their situations, seeing nothing but the crap, and looking back on the unchangeable? They only focus on the troubled. You know? I mean shit!

"I didn't take time to just love 'em. I could have done so much more. Why did I blow up at Mom? She just wanted to make me feel better. I did the same thing with Chelle and Dad too. All they wanted to do was love me. And, and now their all gone, all of them! I would give my whole life, everything just to be able to rub my mom's feet or tussle with my baby again.

"I'm just saying, why do we all have to think that life is forever when we all know that it's not? We all suck! We take everything and run around playing like our lives will never end. Closing our eyes and pushing the truth down to where we can be comfortable with it and control it. Bull Shit! Now, my life is full of these thoughts of why and poor me. Its all bull shit, too.

"But, I have a chance to end it all, I can be the one that puts life back in the hands of the living, and take away the premature endings to so many good lives, and maybe hindsight will change to foresight. No longer dwelling on an unchangeable past and focusing on a brilliant tomorrow. Maybe, just maybe, with no end in sight, we can change, look at everything like we will see it after the sun rises, not take anything for granted, instead fill the new dawn with greater things than the day before. Maybe the changes I make today will work for tomorrow. Do you understand?" Sabor cried and clung to me. It was the first time I could actually hold him and console him. I believe I needed it this moment as much as he did. He sunk deep into my chest, thrashing and sobbing harder and harder.

I reached down rubbing his head. "You are right, my boy. You have a chance to make life worth savoring instead of merely trying to cram as much living as one can into such a small amount of time. You wish to give us all the gift of full lives, long lives. I understand Sabor, truly I do. You remind me of someone, someone from my clan. He would have changed it all, but the changes became too much. We could not keep up with the evolution of evil. My race was eradicated by the trust in our hearts and our eagerness to live and fight, regardless of the consequences," I offered, squeezing a little harder and dwelling on my own unchangeable past. "Your mother understood, and so did Chelle and Zandy. I know this because they were young once too. They took their world for granted just as all of us have and still do. So, don't be so hard on yourself, they never stopped loving you, ever. After all else, they still clung to the "Love" inside of them, you see. You must believe me. You do, don't you?"

"Yes. Thank you, old friend. I knew that you could help. I'm sorry about the outburst though. That has been building up in me for a long time, since I read my mother's letter and left. Sorry buddy. I'm just having a hard time with you actually helping me, not just sitting there like a statue. Instead of my own mind figuring itself out after spilling my guts to you. But thank you none the less," Sabor hugged me, then continued and laid out his entire adventure up to this point. I sat and listened to Sabor as I had done for as long as I could remember. I sincerely enjoyed every minute of it.

Faulty plan
Dissension via embarrassment

Deep in a corner of the battlegrounds, the two valiant Greenlings that had endeavored to save The Order by heading off the big bad intruder (a.k.a. Sabor), Bryant and Blaine sat discussing the mind-boggling events of the past few days.

"Man, I don't think I can just sit around waiting, especially for some crazy plan to unfold. I need to go out and fight now!" Blaine said shaking his head.

"Yeah I know what you mean. That son of a bitch made us look ridiculous. I mean he's cool and all, but I think we have come far enough we could beat Dvanken by ourselves," the young Bryant said flirting with blasphemy.

"Man, you need to watch what you say. We could have to go in front of council for words like that," Blaine scolded, slamming Bryant in the arm.

"Okay, okay, I realize that this is taboo for me to say, but damn, we are ready. I say we should do it," A look of agreement washed over Blaine as Bryant' s words flowed with ambition and a strange logic. "Alright Blaine, tonight we go on a Dvanken hunt," Bryant said slapping his friends chest.

"Agreed brother," Blaine retorted, shoving the other Guardian returning the favor, a bit harder than he had received. With childish intentions, they snuck off to the city in search of death.

Back at his family house, Sabor sat staring out the window. He smiled, and bathed in the feeling that was home. He relaxed about the time Bryant and Blaine set out, in turn defying him. Sabor felt the two energies pulling away from the others and worried. He decided he must follow the pair of overzealous men, just to watch and insure their safety.

The world teemed with people, scurrying inside each one's own personal hell. The streets overflowed with food for Dvanken. The two Greenlings knew that hunting would be great, it was the dawn of the Awakening. They searched for cold spots distraught downtrodden souls. The cold spots were a dead giveaway that Dvanken was feeding in that spot. A "cold spot" served as a figurative door to the alternate world Dvanken took his victims into, to perform his terrible acts. A safe zone if you will, a place where no Guardian could stop his meal.

The two sported regular street clothes. Blaine, a large oafish looking fellow with thick, dirty blonde, short- cropped hair, would fit in perfectly with a southern Missouri back road bon-fire party. His counterpart, however, was the exact opposite. A thin, tall bald man with a pointed jaw trimmed in a small line of course blonde hair and a rock star air about him. Bryant moved down the street eyes glaring, both stood focused and determined. Each sabor weapon, sticking just outside the skin, suspended and ready.

"Man, I don't see a damn thing out here," Blaine said.

"Yeah me either. Just a bunch of stinking hobo's and ignorant people walking around like nothing in their puny lives could ever go wrong. Huh?" Bryant replied.

Suddenly an icy chill gripped the spines of the green warriors at the mouth of a particularly smelly and dark alley. The electric feel of the cold spot froze their hearts. The small hairs on their neck stood erect. Instinctively their sabors sprung into action. The pair slammed back to back, searching the area above and all around for signs of a rip. They found nothing but stink and mist and a filthy, brown cloaked man. A hobo sat at the entrance to the alley talking to his right hand and petting the appendage as if it were his favorite pet.

"The, a... um, Master, he sits eating. Sits juts there, mmhhnun. He blesses me. He chose my alley. Mmnn hha," the deranged tramp rambled, stroking his hand faster. "You, you are not welcome in my alley, mmnn hha. You are stinkin' an we don like your smells. My master love your taste, though," the mans words took on a different tone. He never looked up.

"You would be wise to move along old man. If what you say is true, then this place is about to get rowdy, and we wouldn't want you to get hurt," Blaine said being extra careful to not get too close.

"Who are you talking about? Who is your Master?" Bryant asked, pushing Blaine to one side, and kneeling down on one knee.

"You know him. He has told us to watch for you and your brothers. Told us to warn him, told us to, uh no, no, no. Sssshhhhhh! Get out of there that is my business, young man. You should go. My Master is coming, and he won't like you being here," the old man looked up, his eyes hollow and black. His face, covered in filth, had been ripped down each side. It looked as if he had clawed at it until the flesh had tore away from itself. Maggots climbed and writhed in his facial hair, weaving in and out of the massive rips in his cheeks. He leaned in licked his lips, grabbing one of the off-white flesh eaters, and said, "You, you were unwise to stay as well. He heee he," He laughed, bit the maggots in half, sucked the thick puss filled insides out, and spit them in Blaine' s face, chuckling

181

heartily as he licked his fingers.

"You stupid son-of-a-bitch. I should gut you for that," Blaine said, slamming his foot into the old man's throat.

The old man, choking, grasped at the boot, then stopped and smiled. He pointed his disgusting finger slowly over his shoulder.

"What the hell is it, old man? You actually think I'm going to see something back there?" Blaine turned out of curiosity and self-preservation in the slim chance that something was back there.

Ten feet tall behind him, stood Dvanken. He muffled Bryant's face in his right hand with two large scarlet horns protruding from each forearm, one in front of his victim and one behind. Dvanken arched his shoulders and tilted his head back and forth in confusion at the actions of Blaine. He stared straight into his soul, feeling his fear grow.

Watching his blade turn from a light blue to a deep green, Blaine stood frozen, shaking in that spot, his mouth agape from the sheer size and evil of Dvanken. He slowly brought both sabors up to his chest crossing his heart.

"You should release my clansman, before you anger me, BOY," Dvanken shouted, leaning in just inches from the young Guardian's face.

"You first," Blaine said weakly, but as bold as he could at that moment.

"Who are you, Guardian, to ask of me anything? I owe you nothing and I will give you less. Your friend here will be my example to you, the example of my power, and my first Guardian of the Awakening. My clansman will enjoy watching this," Dvanken said, an evil grin shattering his serious face.

The hobo sat up and bounced happily on his knees ready for the blood rain after the Guardians death. Dvanken looked deeply into the tramp, warning him to step back. Dvanken, arched his arm, bringing Bryant up, separating him from the ground a few feet, and twisted his hand back, popping the air from between the Guardian's vertebrae. Blaine tried to move, but he was frozen, unable to move. Frustrated, he tried to yell, but nothing came out. He was doomed to watch, and then suffer the same fate. Hindsight told him he should have stayed and listened to Sabor. But that was all for not, he was going to die, nothing would stop that.

Dvanken howled and tossed Bryant up into the air. Bolting around the Greenling, Dvanken shoved his claw-laden hand through the armor that had formed on Bryant's chest. His massive hand slipped past the spine, ripping muscle and tearing flesh until it leaped out the backside of the Knight of The Order. It looped up grasping Bryant's forehead with his hellish fingers. Smiling, he pressed his palm firmly against Bryant's scalp and pierced the defenseless man's eyes, probing his sockets with his ghastly digits. Slowly, he turned, grasping the skull firmly, exposing the horrifying sight to Blaine.

"Do you see? Do you see why you and your pitiful human brothers could never defeat me? I am Dvanken. You, you are nothing, disgusting humans bound together by weakness and tied down with your own self-absorbance. I will make examples of you all. I will rid the world, my world, of you disgusting parasites," Dvanken said complacently, grasping the remaining Guardian by the throat.

"Now watch, as I rip your friend's core from his body, digesting his fear and loathing," Dvanken said stroking Blaine's jaw slowly.

The Evil one then shuddered and summoned in the rolling, tumbling purple and red fog, playing the most heinous moments of each of their lives over and over. Then, gaining momentum by lunging forward, Dvanken slammed Bryant broadside into the slimy wall of the alley. With a twist and a pull, he ripped the life, as well as the head and spine, straight up and over, slinging red and yellow matter painting the alleyway. A stream of amber-colored light flooded the alley like a searchlight. Leaving only a lump of flesh lying heaped on the ground. Dvanken stepped back. He kicked his feet back, slinging gutter slime and stagnant water over the once proud body. With a devilish laugh, he picked the body from the ground and rubbed the spine and face of the fallen warrior across the body and head of Blaine.

"Taste your friend. Delicious aren't you? You, the humans, I have enjoyed killing the most much more than the Gargoyle or Quatrine. Throughout the years, you have given me the most joy. You have found new ways to make my job so much easier. War, this is one of my favorites. Cater to the ego of a maniacal and he would follow with a minimal pull. The holocaust, was one of my favorite periods in your recent history. So much senseless destruction for nothing, so much suffering and hate bread from one mans charisma and quirks. Adolph was quite the ally in that respect. Always hell bent on ruling all of you pathetic humans. And so willing to be lead down many different roads. Why? Your kind is nothing, insignificant and stupid. But enough! I do not want to waste my time telling you of my joy," Dvanken said, then choked down the skeletal core of Bryant. Licking his face and smiling a crimson smirk. Then started toward the Guardian standing frozen with fear and pain.

Just then, a knife-like Slab of light pierced the forest of shadows created by the towering buildings here in the alleyway. It was Sabor. He had come to set the situation right again. He stood sabor weapons out, brilliantly glowing blue and white. The long slender blades were barbed near the hilt and a harshly contrasting amber pulse surged throughout the blade. He slowly shoved out two small tridents above the awesome blades.

"DVANKEN!" Sabor screamed, stopping the impending death of Blaine. "I am here to stop you, devil! And I do not intend to fail," Sabor threw his father's cloak, whirling to the ground.

"Oh, this is indeed a great day for me. I will feed upon the blood of the Avenger, and destroy the soul of The Order with one foul act. How lovely," Dvanken hissed, shivering all over his putrid body.

"You, you're a pretty cocky lump of crap, aren't you Dvanken. My brothers had told me you were arrogant, but I didn't expect it could be even close to this bad. But, trust me demon, I **will** not die tonight. I have a score to settle with you but I think tonight is too soon. I want to let you brood on your demise for a little while. However, I will take my friend here, and place another slice to your debt for my fallen brother over there. Do you understand? Oh, I'm sorry of course you don't. Allow me to give you a visual example," Sabor asked displaying his two broadsword-style sabors. One brashly pointed directly at Dvankens forehead, while the other wrapped around resting on his fallen brother's chest.

"Demon? Your attitude seems to be hereditary Guardian. A dismal trace of your lingering bloodline shows," Dvanken said sulking over his lost meal.

"Do not stand in my presence flattering yourself, with ranting of your capability to defeat me, an immortal. Or your idle threats and declarations of supremacy. Your hollow words and insults mean nothing to me.
"Though, I cannot resist my urges to rid the world of it's hope, your looming death consumes my every thought. I will strive, unrelenting until you are but another victim of The Relinquish, and the world is mine for the harvesting. It makes me quite angry, human," Dvanken proclaimed, excited by the lack of respect coming from a puny human.

Sabor faced Dvanken squarely preparing for an assault on the evil. In the mass of confusion, the transient sitting at the mouth of the alley somehow went overlooked. Slowly, he lowered his filthy, brownish-green overcoat and pulled up his sleeves, revealing an arm void of muscle and skin leaving only bone. The entire length of the bone that remained had been sharpened, ending in a razor-sharp point. It formed a kind of hinged sword, bleached a brilliant white with hints of blood surging throughout. He wiped his mouth, and smiled an unholy, maggot filled smile.

"You will have no such victory this night, Guardian! I am Otin Gange and standing there is my Master, and I will defend his honor to the death! If need be," The old hobo screamed as he charged and leapt on Sabor's back, pulling his arm/sword back to deal a lethal blow to the neck.

Instinctively, Sabor's gargoyle shaped helmet, and neck protector swirled around his head, as he spun around, trying to shake his attacker. Otin crashed down, his bone blade slamming against the helmet with a blow much stronger than Sabor expected, simply by looking at him. Sabor stumbled and went to one knee.

"What the hell? Where did you come from, you stinky old bastard? And where do you get off jumping on my back?" Sabor angrily inquired.

Repeatedly, Otin unleashed his fury on Sabor. He screamed, chuckling with every strike.

"You will never hurt my Master. You are but a nothing. A Pig!" Otin screamed in Sabor's ear. He opened his nauseating mouth, taking a feeble attempt to bite the metallic ear off of the solid helmet.

Dvanken was not ready to fight the Avenger, he was after all, barely awake. So sensing an opportunity, he cocked his head and sunk back into the shadows. Smiling all the while at his clansman's devotion, he retreated into the darkness unscathed. Unscathed, but even more eager to feast on Sabor.

Sabor pulled his left sabor back to his hip. He glanced over his shoulder, getting a clear view of the homeless man's disgusting face.

"It is time to end this, foul one. I need to get home. I'm missing my favorite television show;" Sabor mocked, snarling to let Dvanken know that his presence was not going to disrupt Sabor's life. He kept calm in his actions, controlled and precise. He pulled hard and guided the blade close to his right ear, deflecting a blow from the bone sword. The flimsy excuse for a blade shattered, showering around their heads. Instantly, the hobo released Sabor and grabbed his wound, howling in agony. Writhing on the ground, holding it, he backed himself up against the slime-covered wall, staring at Sabor like a

185

motherless child. Sabor gathered Blaine and Bryant and laid them close to his feet. He sauntered over to the cowering Otin. Straddling Otin's leg, Sabor deployed both blades and curled his lips in anger.

"I believe there is the matter of manners, old man. You don't call someone you have never met a Pig, and you damn sure do not insult someone with four-foot blades coming from their forearms. Do I make myself clear? The next time you see a Guardian, I want you to call him sir and offer to shake his hand and when he declines, you say thank you. Do you understand?" Sabor said, smiling and kneeling in front of him and placing his right arm under Otin's chin, the long blade sticking out to one side.

Otin blinked and shook his head violently from side to side, reaching up he slapped Sabor's face softly, but quickly with his shattered bone appendage. "Are, are you gonna kill me? I am so sorry. I don't even know who you are or how the hell I came to be in this damn alley. Please help me, please?" Otin said, as if his mind was released from some sort of fog. "Please sir. My name is.... " Otin looked around, searching for something. "...Oh shit; now, I don't even know my own name,"

Otin looked down into his "hands" and began to cry. The ordeal took everything out of him. He hadn't even realized that his arm was gone. Sabor stood up and laughed to himself.

"Your name is Otin, Otin Gange. I found you in this alley in some not so great company. If I were you, I would go to the police and see if anyone has reported you missing. It's a pretty safe bet that someone probably misses you. So get up. For God's sake, go clean yourself and just go to the hospital and get your arm looked at. And one more thing, if you are ever approached by a presence or a person calling himself Dvanken," Sabor paused, grabbing Otin's attention with his eyes.

"Yes, what do you want me to do?" Otin asked.

"Promise me that you will r un from him. Run from him or you are going to have to face me. And, I promise you that day will not turn out to be a good day for you. Okay?" Sabor said as he stepped back and held his arm out, allowing Otin free passage out into the light of the street.

"Thank you, oh thank you, so very much. By the by, what should I call you, that is if I ever see you again?" Otin said graciously and bowed.

"Pray you never see me again. But if you do, call me Guardian," Sabor insistently motioned the man away. After Otin slurked off into the weaving shadows, Sabor turned, shaking his head at the disgraced survivor, and snarled.

The amber glow boiled from the ends of his fingers. His eyes oozed the light.

"You!" Sabor thundered. "You are the reason your friend died. Do you think this plan of yours was worth the price you have paid? DO YOU! Your friend, your cousin, your brother in The Order, gave the ultimate, and you stand there with your face parallel to the ground, speechless. I believe that he and his entire family deserve a bit more respect than this. Don't you, Knight?" Sabor said and thrust his right sabor out. It was a woven blade with many barbs and nubs.

"Sabor, I am sorry. You must believe me. He was more than a cousin to me. He was... " Blaine started before Sabor interrupted.

"Don't give me your bullshit excuses, and don't whine to ME about how he was more than anything to you. I told you, I told him, and I told everyone that Dvanken had changed. I told every single member of The Order our ways must change, to avoid the pointless loss of the innocent, like Bryant. They have to change or we will never the Evil.

"You have to believe me. I have seen him. I have felt him, I know. I knew what his evil would be this time. He evolved. He is more evil than we could have ever imagined. He has began to premeditate. He has begun to do things we could have never anticipated. You saw how those hobo acted. He would have gladly died for Dvanken.

"Anyway, that is beside the point. You disobeyed me, and your friend died, due to your headstrong negligence. Our brother died, you must now live with that guilt. Don't turn your back on the fault, don't strive to forget it, but let it swim around in your veins and allow yourself to grow from it. The time to put down our own glories is now, brother," Sabor said with a genuine tone, then stretched his hand out to his brother. Sabor's amber glow seeped out and dissipated all around them. "Now collect your brother, and let's go back to the halls,"

"I am truly sorry. And I promise you, I will help you. I will obey you from now on. *All I want is vengeance now*," Blaine said, accepting the fact he shared blame in the death of his brother, cousin and friend.

The house of Elder Saimus Lindon was extremely quiet. The room was old, but well kept. Various busts lined the walls, with a vast sofa stretching across the width of the room. A huge television glowed softly against the opposing wall, vividly informing the two Elders what was happening in the world around them. Sitting in disbelief at the tale the anchorwoman, Serena, told with the indifference of years of the telling of a repetitive sad story, Saimus, Ellett, and I watched intently. This particular story spoke of a school bus full of high school seniors taking a field trip to the mountains to study the wildlife and vegetation of the area. The school bus had been torn in half on a snaky mountain road, apparently the entire class eaten by the growing population of timber wolves on the cliffs. There were no survivors. Other headlines of the evening hinted to the Awakening as well, not for the day to day humans, but to us, the Guardians. It was upon us again; we were at his mercy. Dvanken had risen from his Slumber.

"Can you believe this, Ellett? So soon. It doesn't seem possible," Saimus asked.

"Believe what Saim? That the Awakening has undoubtedly begun? That most definitely, we rush into an unmarked new era, one like we have never seen," Ellett responded churning in his chair.

"No, I, I can't believe it. No matter how many times it happens, I always hope that he will just stay asleep. Maybe the cycle will just end. No heroics, no gigantic battle, maybe it will just stop," the Elder said, staring off into nowhere.

"Never the less brothers, he is awake. Obviously the time to act is at hand. He kills and grows stronger, while we sit doubting that fact. We should tell Sabor, let him know what we have known, that the Awakening has happened, and we should strike while he is weak, agreed?" I added.

"Hey guys no need to sit around and talk about little old me. I'm right here. I know all about The Awakening too. Dvanken is awake and killing. He reaped one of ours tonight, Bryant Linx, almost took Blaine, his brother, as well.
"The pair went out hunting this evening. I felt something pulling away from The Order, so I followed. I got there a little too late. They didn't have a chance, by the time I arrived. He was all over them. I broke in and did what I could do to get them out. But you know it was the strangest thing. Dvanken didn't even want to start with me.   He just cowered down and left his hobo to fight me alone," Sabor said, unaware of the impact of his words.

In unison, we, quite emphatically asked, "What hobo? What are you talking about Sabor?"

"There was a hobo, didn't see him at first, but I sure felt him. The damned maniac jumped on me and started slamming my head with some sort of sword made of bone. As soon as I took care of the sword, I noticed Dvanken was gone and the hobo was on the ground nursing his wound. He couldn't remember anything that had just happened or what lead up to it. On the way back to the Halls of The Order to return Bryant's body, Blaine told me about what happened and why. They found a cold spot and this homeless guy Otin, that's the hobo's name, sitting there he started taunting them about his Master and how they couldn't do anything to him. It was weird, as if he was under some sort of spell or like he was worshiping Dvanken. I didn't think...Ellett, didn't you tell me that he didn't have any followers? After I sat thinking about the situation for a while, I decided that you all needed to know what was going on and it couldn't wait until tomorrow," Sabor concluded.

"Yes, Sabor I did say that, but... " Ellett sank back into his chair, stroking his chin, and shaking his head. "...Surely this is just some sort of weird coincidence. He couldn't be gathering followers. Could he?" Ellett's thoughts resonated all of our feelings.

"Perhaps this deranged man was on drugs. Maybe he was just some raving lunatic. Whatever he was, we cannot jump to conclusions," Saimus said ever the optimist. "Remain watchful and respectful of our situation... "

"Master, with all due respect. I know what I saw. From the looks of it, Dvanken has started some sort of brainwashed, zombie cult. I don't know about you, but I think the time for the end is here. You have put up with the death for too long. And I am sure that I have. Next week, we strike. I will need each of you to help in getting every class ready. But now, I have some goodbyes to say.
"Ellett, could you please call a meeting for me tomorro w morning at 10:00am. I will reveal everything then. Good evening to you all," with those mysterious words, Sabor left the room.

We, the other Elder' s, sat staring at one another, bewildered. Saimus quietly picked up the phone and pressed two on the speed dial, then he began speaking with a stranger on the other end of the line.

"Yes, no time for pleasantries. Send the investigators out Mason. Yes, yes now. All of them. Because Sabor made some alarming discoveries last evening. It seems as if Dvanken is recruiting the local hobos into doing his dirty work for him. The intel on this needs to be precise. And it needs to be streaming, okay? Tell the investigators to check in every three minutes, info or not. Understood?

189

Okay good then. If you need more info find Blaine, he has first hand knowledge of the site and happenings. Yes, alright then. Yes, good-bye now," Saimus ordered. The Elder hung up then sank back into his chair and his thoughts.

"What do you think..." I asked, but was cut off by a hand being raised from the prayer position the shaky pair of hands had taken. Saimus said nothing, simply sunk back into his posture and thoughts. His intensity, I had not seen this overwhelming for decades. The sight was upsetting and uplifting all at once. Sabor had turned us on our ears. We were challenging our granite ways. Maybe his plan would work, maybe. Not wanting to disturb him any further, I excused myself and felt Ellett taking the queue as well.

Outside the house, the streets were wet with the torrent rain that had now subsided to little more than a gentle mist. The elongated highlights from the street lamps criss-crossed, forming long X's the length of the road. I stepped from the cover of the massive canopy out into the mist. It was cool and it felt good. For a long moment I stood wondering what Master Saimus could be thinking about and what my own thoughts would lead to. I said my good-byes to Ellett, and we both went off to our respective homes. Surely his mind mulled the events over as feverishly as my own, pure speculation though.

The Dream

That night, The Order felt closer somehow. I felt attuned to my brothers in a way I had never experienced before. The feeling was peculiar, but intoxicating just the same. The sleep I fell into was deep and consuming, and slowly I drifted off into strange dreams.

The world. My dream world, was fuzzy, only certain details stood out strangely vivid. The color swerved in and out of focus. The skyline only a gloomy blur, but the windows glowed brilliant yellows and blues. I found myself walking down a familiar street with a familiar destination, the Lindon home. My home, my perch, the one place I feel at peace and at ease. I don't sit worrying about the horrible things I have seen during my days. Dvanken's just an unpleasant story I have heard on a whispering wind and I drift away caught in the web of chatter with the young Sabor.

I was back, back with Sabor, when he was young. I could not see him, but I knew it was him. Young, he had absolutely no clue of what he was or of what he would have to become. He only worried about his report card and if he could beat a feather down the stairs if he dropped it from the balcony. It was pleasant here, and I was at peace. I took in the dream, trying to make it last forever, holding each child-like strand tightly. I closed my eyes, sinking into the moment, grabbing it, holding on.

Before I could open my eyes, an intense heat consumed me. I sprung to my feet and threw open my eyes, searching for Sabor. An inferno had engulfed the room, but burned nothing. I couldn't see the flames, just felt the heat. There was an intense glow about the place.

I saw the pictures on the walls. The outline of a person, fuzzy at first, grew more vivid. It was Sabor, and he was reaching for me. I sprang, leaping to the coolest spot on the far wall that I could. Then, I flipped, grabbing at the chandelier. Gripping it, I spun and landed by the boy on the floor in the center of the blaze.

I grabbed him by the head, and looked down at him. He was still a blur, even as close as I was to him. The only distinct thing was his eyes. They were cold and emotionless, oozing with pain. They were so brilliant and clear on the blurry figure. The boy reached up, grabbing me by the arm and pulling. I could feel his words; he didn't need to say them. He was scared, and I was a tiny bit afraid myself.

I blinked, just for a moment and when I opened my eyes, we stood in the center of a beautiful green meadow, rolling hills, and dark clumps of trees. The sky was a perpetual sunrise fiery orange, fading to a purple rolling mass of clouds. The horizon was ablaze. In the distance, two coal black spires stretched towards the sky. I stared at them for quite some time.

Then in a sort of dance, these silhouettes of color began to dart back and forth from the horizon. I looked down at the blurry young man at my side. Sabor had vanished. I found the only thing I had in my hand was a greenish-red glob of slimy gel. A skull dangled in the substance. Not a human skull, but a head bone of my kind, a gargoyle skull with a large gash in the temple area.

"What the, who are you?" I asked in my dream. Even though I expected no reply, I was disappointed when one did not present itself.

Searching the dreamscape, I saw various deceased members of The Order. Zandalar walked by a small stream, and it was peculiar, but Noelle was sitting watching him. She slowly looked over at me and pointed. My heart raced, I was so happy to see them.

The reality of the situation then hit me. *I am in the Plane of The Order. Either I am dead, or something is terribly wrong.* I saw the other Elders that had gone before us all, and it made me feel warm and welcome. I walked toward my friends who were resting beside the trundling creek. I rehearsed everything that I wanted to say to them.

Across the plain, I saw a barrier. It was faint, in fact the only way to see that there was anything there at all, was the grass had been pressed flat. Standing on the other side of the transparent wall I saw Saimus and Simon talking. Further south, I spotted Ellett, then Sabor, and the rest of The Order, one by one. They all appeared to see the ones they loved the most. Every man struggled to reach them, desperately trying to reunite with their lost.

Feeling empowered, I started off. Suddenly, the transparent wall swirled with purple and green energy, like die into a glass of water. I had seen it many times, Dvanken was near. I flexed to prepare for battle, my claws tripling in length and glowing an intense yellow. I charged, trying to get to Zandalar, but a shock tore through my body, slamming me to the ground outside the huge box.

Getting my bearings, I looked around the vast space, but saw nothing. The sound of scratching and muffled screams echoed all around. Slowly, the wall turned solid and black. The grass was gone, only gray cracked mud remained with masses of withered black capillaries that used to be beautiful green and brown trees. Mounds of thorny bushes and spiraling razor weed stretched from the ground, covering the Plane with a maze of pain.

I could not hear the brothers on the other side, but I could feel their pain. It shredded small holes in my body. The whole landscape began to boil. I heard Zandy, his voice calling me, but I couldn't find him. Slowly, a gash formed in the wall. I rushed to see it, to see if I could save us all. Zandalar' s sabor sprung out of the hole followed by a frantic guardian.

"Take my hand, CRANDEN!" My old friend shouted.

I reached out and sank my claw through his forearm, trying to get a sure grip as not to lose him. The tear widened, and Zandalar seeped through. A smile broke his face as he felt freedom.

"Noelle is just behind me old friend. Thank you," Zandalar said. A look of agony ripped his face, and he was pulled hard back through the breach. His arm tore into two pieces, he yelled hard.

"Take care of Sabor!" Zandalar cried. I lunged, but I too late. I was moving in slow motion. My heart and head dropped as Zandalar disappeared into the pitch of the enormous box.

"NOOOOO!" I screamed at the top of my lungs, reaching through the hole desperately trying to grasp my lost friend. I found nothing.

A force of evil nudged me back to the outside of the box. Resisting, I moved ahead again, hard, determined to not lose my oldest friend again.

"You! Sole survivor. You are not welcome in the chamber. This unholy place is reserved for the enemies of Dvanken after he Relinquishes them; "A strange deep voice resonated inside the vast box.

"What? Who are you to tell me to le ave here? This is the Plane of The Order, our sanctuary. You are the one who should not be here!" I answered. Only a disgusting howl came back as a reply.

I pulled through, taking a final glance to try to see something, anything. It was a horrible sight. Chains pierced and wove themselves through each member of The Order, tying each one to their own large glowing black wood spire, stretching up ten feet from the scorched ground. The spires were identical to the enormous monoliths resting on the horizon, only one-twentieth the size. The Guardians strapped to them, were all alive, but in excruciating pain.

Everywhere, small lizard-like men, dressed in chain mail and small embroidered overthrows, chanted and danced around each spire. The tiny demonic creatures taunted and bit chunks from the flesh of each of my friends and brothers. The sickening sight instantly turned my heart black with rage.

"You get away from my friends, before something bad happens, lizard men!" I screamed. The chamber closed around me.

"Your rage is nice gargoyle, but I do not want it for now. Rest assured, your time is coming. So, you go now, and leave us to our work," the voice boomed again.

My focus drew back to my friends. Frantically, I reached for them. A large shadowy hand slammed my hand back, nearly dislocating my wrist. He/It was enormous and thin. Void of any detail, but dripping with sin and hatred. Two huge green eyes pierced the shadow and my soul.

"You are done here, Gargoyle!" It s aid gruffly. He grasped my face and shoved hard, snapping my head back. I landed in my bed in the attic of the Lindon home, awake and dripping with sweat, confused. The morning sun broke across my face. My dream was over.

"Thank God," I muttered t o myself. I mulled over my dream as I paced my floor. I stopped as I came to a conclusion.

"The Plane, something must be wrong with the Plane,"

I sat down, and meditated in my usual fashion, the same way I had done for eons when I needed to converse to the Plane of The Order. I tried and tried. Hours passed and nothing. There was a dull scratching sound and darkness, just as my dream.

It was horrible. The Plane was indeed cut off from us, and we needed help. I had to see if the others had any trouble reaching the Plane.

The love of a Father

Meanwhile, sitting silently in his prison cell, Marcus Johnson sat in his bunk rocking back and forth, holding his knees, and shaking his head the opposite way. He would scream every few seconds, sometimes-incoherent gibberish. Other times he would proclaim his innocence screaming,"no, you Bastard get away from him. You prick! I didn't do it, It, It was the monster, and he did it. PLEASE SOMEBODY, PLEASE BELIEVE ME!!!"

His pain was intense, and he had sat in it for some years now. Five to be exact, but his time was for redemption was at hand. For Dvanken had come and he was there to eat.

A slow trickle of purple miasma seeped through the window of his cell. Marcus looked out to see the moon turn from gray to a deep purple hue. He shook in fear, remembering what had come from this before. He pushed himself back frantically looking around crying.

"What else do you want, you fucker? You've taken everything! Just leave me alone and let me die,"Marcus screamed at his invisible attacker.

Dvanken sprung up, showing himself through the window.

"Now, now, Marcus. Is that anyway to talk to your friend and s avior?"

The hellish monster sarcastically smiled as he grasped the sides of the window and ripped the blocks and the window from the side of the building. The alarm sounded in the distance. The howls of the other convicts, hoping to get out, got louder. The dust settled, and Dvanken stood in the gaping hole in the side of the prison.

"I have come to collect. You once asked me,"Please"I usually collect right then, but you, I wanted your pain to stew for a while. You were to be my first meal after my greatest Slumber. So, I do apologize for being a little tardy, but I found a desperate old man just begging for my help,"Dvanken said with an evil air.

"What the hell are you talking about? I don't give a shit about who needs your help. You took little man, and no one believes me. I have been raped, tortured, spit on, and beaten in here. I never asked you for that. I never said please for that. I wanted my son. I wanted my life. You didn't care then, and you don't give a shit now!" Marcus said shooting up to his feet and slamming

195

his fist into the wall.

"I never said Please," Marcus said, pointing at Dvanken.

"My dear Marcus, you hurt my feelings. Never you say? I think your memory has began to grow a little fuzzy my dear boy. Probably too much time in this dark dreary prison cell. Ha," Dvanken said, sarcastically picking his teeth with his right index claw.

"You can say what you want about my memory, but I will never forget that day. Ever," Marcus said seriously and disturbed.

"Oh, so confident. That's good. Your embarrassment will taste nice. Well, if you don't believe my words, then won't you allow me to prove that you're losing it, human?" Dvanken proposed, motioning for Marcus to sit down on his bunk and relax. "O' do watch this, little man,"

Jutting up from the floor, a steamy reddish, purple miasma swirled up around him. The miasma began to replay the events from six years ago. In the beginning, Marcus covered his face with his two large strong hands, realizing what he was being shown. He stared down in shame, not knowing if his tired mind could handle the recollections. A tear boiled in his left eye as he heard the memoir playing in his cell.

"Dad, please don't let him take me. PLEASE, Dadd y help me!" He heard the voice of his son calling to him.

He desperately wanted to look out from the safety of his calloused hands, but his better judgment kept the appendages covering his eyes. Keeping his eyes hidden didn't help much, however. He could feel the stiffness setting into his legs. It was just like that day. The smells, the taste, even the feeling of helplessness in his stomach was the same. He was helpless, like that warm March morning so long ago, helpless to save his little boy. Helpless to save himself from the four gray walls and the daily rape/beatings. Dvanken stood towering, consumed in shadow, his arms crossed his right arm on his chin, and smiling at Marcus' pain.

"You son of a bitch! I have paid for this shit, your shit, long enough. Don't make me relive this," Marcus managed to say through the tears and the vomit in his throat.

The miasma crept through the tiny crevices in his fingers, forcing itself through his eyelids, and in streamed the events of the warm morning. The vision showed a scene of serenity and playfulness. The sun found Marcus and his son playing, wandering through the farmers' market, searching for some ripe red tomatoes and lettuce for the BBQ they had each summer to celebrate the young man's birth. This was a happy chore, and Marcus could almost smell the earth and water together with the strong scent of herbs in the air. They both were having a wonderful time, joking with the fruit and throwing oranges at one another.

"Hey bud, you wanna get some caramel apples, for after the cookout? Huh, do ya birthday boy?" Marcus asked grabbing the smiling little child. Marcus flopped the boy's legs out wide and pulled him around until he was perched with one leg on each side of Marcus's head. Tyrone loved to see the world, from this vantage. Looking down on the world, he felt like a giant. He felt so grown up and so much a part of the adult world.

"Hey, there it is, Daddy," Tyrone said, slapping his dad on the top of the head.

"Ouch bud, not so hard," Marcus said, rubbing the sore spot.

"No daddy, it's the matato store right over there," The little boy excitedly kicked his unsuspecting father.

"Hey Ty, I see it, I see it, lay off on the beatings up there, or I'll drop ya," Marcus teased as he moved his shoulder, and swung around, catching Tyrone a few inches from the ground. "See I told you. You hit the eject button, little guy,"

The two of them laughed at each other and took off, galloping, bouncing his little boy as they went. Tyrone was so vibrant and happy, as most innocent children are.

The story was totally different three hours earlier. He cowered in his bedroom scared to death, because his mother, Leah, and Marcus were having another fight. He had tried before to break them up, dodging the flying glasses and ducking between the screams. It never worked though. He felt so helpless and invisible.

Through the few short years, he had been able to take care of himself. He had learned to stay barricaded in his room and block out whatever he could. He would sit on the multi-colored woven rug in the center of his room with a flashlight and his stuffed puppy, singing the various children' s songs he had learned in daycare. This, for as long as he could remember, had worked. For a little added protection, he would shine his flashlight at the door, and his mommy and daddy's anger wouldn't turn to him. He was safe, as long as the batteries held out. The twelve-watt light acted like a force field, keeping the fighting out of his room, and it worked. The feelings of helplessness and fear made a wonderful meal for Dvanken.

The unsuspecting father and son were still busying themselves in the market, picking up the last few items they needed. As they finished, an unholy shadow focused on the feelings of the young man's past. Dvanken began to slink and stir about in the alley, sensing a good chance to prepare a much-needed meal. The busy market screeched to a halt. A purple cloud reached high up into the sky, eclipsing the mid-day sun. The only sound was a sinister snicker, and the confusion ringing inside the man and his son.

Marcus had set Tyrone down, to pay the clerk, and sensed something wrong. He turned from the mannequin standing in front of him ready to take his money, and searched for his small son.

"Ty, honey! Where are you buddy?" Marcus screamed, concerned that his son wasn't in plain sight.

"I'm right here Dad, down here," Tyrone replied, from underneath the colorful sign draped over the fruit stand in front of his father.

Marcus looked up, satisfied with his safety, and went back to ascertaining what was going on, why everyone had frozen. Dvanken reached in and grabbed the very soul of Marcus, paralyzing him with fear. He remained conscious, even barely aware that he couldn't move. Tyrone looked around with a child' s curiosity as Dvanken' s hell fog seeped in all around him.

"Daddy, hey look at this stuff!" The young man yelled, scooping a tiny handful of the smoke. But the smoke stung his hand. His tiny feet and legs began to burn as the mist slowly rose around him. "Daddy! Pick me up. Please Daddy, I'm scared," The young Tyrone tried desperately to scurry up his frozen father. Marcus simultaneously locked eyes with Dvanken and realizing that he couldn't reach his son.

"Ty, Ty, honey, I want you to run, baby. Do you understand me? Run as fast as you can. Run home; tell Mommy I love her, and I love you too little man. Damn it. For some reason, Daddy can't move babe, so just go. Okay?" Marcus frantically tried to get loose. Dvanken slithered closer, darting this way and that. Marcus looked at his son who was now frozen with fear. All the frozen father could do was gaze in terror, at the blank look falling over Tyrone's face...

"Hello there, little one. Tyrone, that is your name isn't it? Well my name is Dvanken, and I have a tiny little present for you," the monster lied.

"Really, what is it mister?" The innocent little child asked, not seeing where the voice that spoke to him was.

198

"I have the power to make the yelling stop, to make mommy and daddy love each other again. Wouldn't you like that? Wouldn't you like to play and play and never worry that their anger may drift onto you? Never worry that their hate will make them somehow not love you, make them ignore you, as they wrap themselves in their pointless little squabbles?" Dvanken said to the boy, but looking dead into the father's eyes.

"You see my little Tyrone, your mommy and daddy have forgotten that they have another responsibility. A responsibility to make you, their precious little boy feel loved. Isn't that what you want Ty, isn't it? You want your mommy to hug you and daddy to kiss you on the head goodnight, again. Of course it is. I am sure that is your most treasured dream," the despicable aberration said as he stroked the paralyzed face of Marcus, staring deeply into Tyrone's eyes. A look of distaste and malice broke over Dvanken as he prepared to feed on the child. He sensed the love swelling inside of Tyrone and it made him sick. Dvanken quickly grasped the boy by the face and lifted him to eye level, about eight feet from the pavement.

"It really doesn't matter, but do you want the fighting to stop boy?" Dvanken asked angrily.

"Why are you doing this monster? Daddy, tell him not to hurt me. Daddy, please help me, Daddy!" The terrified little boy screamed, reaching for his father. Dvanken smirked at the fear and squeezed a little harder with Tyrone's every attempt to free himself.

"Oh good Lord. Please don't do this. He's my little boy, don't hurt him. Please, take me instead, anything. Just let him go," Marcus pleaded. Dvanken stretched over and slammed Marcus's face shut with his left hand.

"There it was Marcus. Thank you. I needed that. Don't you worry; your time will come. For now though, Ssssshhhhhh," Dvanken howled, then turned, placing his full attention on the four year old boy in his right hand.

Dvanken strained his entire upper body, dropping Marcus' head. He stepped into a clear view of the horrible work he was about to do. Marcus stared in terror as a shower of crimson splashed across his face. His son's life force spilled out, covering the ground.

"You son o f a...How could you do that? He was just a kid! You mother fuc...he was my kid," Marcus tore at Dvanken's face with the one hand that Dvanken had released, while holding down the vomit in his throat.

"Poor little man, can't you see, that this is yo ur fault. Your son's pain is what drew me here, and your anger, hostility, lack of respect for his small feelings. These were the determining factors for which one of you lived, and one died. Now you must live with the pain, the pain that you yourself have caused. Rest assured, I will return to collect on your pain, I promise," Dvanken said sternly. A look of acknowledgment and regret poured over Marcus, realizing that a morsel of blame did rest on him and his wife. Along with the grief, a sense of reality that his son was gone forever, and the shame of it being his fault, overtook him.

"Please, you have to kill me now. I can't make it without him;" Marcus pleaded, grasping the hand of his lifeless son lying on the street.

"No, I couldn't do that. It would be far too easy, and I am looking forward to your taste," Dvanken said callused to the whole situation. "After your stay in jail, for killing this lovely, innocent boy, you will be a meal fit for a king, my little murderer," Dvanken had laid this trap well, and he would enjoy the agony he had painted with this death.

"Now, I must go. Rest assured however, I will see you again," Dvanken said, unfreezing reality. Almost instantly, sirens blared and the various patrons of the market place all screamed as time began to creep again.

When Dvanken unfroze the world, he left the blood of the innocent dripping from the innocent. Marcus felt the helplessness consume him, as the sirens blared, and the numbness dulled the world around him. All there was now was a void where love once lived. The love was now replaced with revenge and hatred. Even as he was taken to jail and charged with the murder of his only child, he was void of all emotion. That as I remember was a key point in the prosecutions case. "No remorse," they accused.

The trial, as I recall it, only took a single week. The sight of a blood covered man, holding his dead, limp son by the hand, cemented his guilt to the world. The jury finished deliberations in only two minutes if my memory serves. The years of abuse and the constant disbelief from everyone left him a shell of a man. His wife, who in her own right was as guilty as her husband, mailed Marcus divorce papers two days after he was imprisoned.

All of this was still nothing to Marcus. He had lost his little buddy, his Ty and he could give a damn about the rest of the world. He had sat dwelling on that day, praying that the monster would keep his promise and come back to claim him.

All of these feelings and visions came swirling back like lightning through the miasma Dvanken had spun.

"Just what do you hope to get from showing me all of this? More pain!

200

Well, if that is the case, you're failing miserably. I have all the pain that can fit in me. So, know that. You're here, just kill me, PLEASE," Marcus said, standing up and grabbing the shank he had made with his toothbrush just for when this moment came. Closing his eyes, he stretched his hands out and leaned his head back, arching and exposing his chest. Appearing completely vulnerable, Dvanken smiled, and swooped out of the shadows into the light.

"Not exactly the reaction I was going for, but it will do," With that Dvanken, stood tall and pointed at the inmate. "Your time has come. Prepare,"

Dvanken threw his arm at the center of Marcus's chest. Marcus smiled and dodged the strike, swinging his arm in a high arc and slamming his plastic knife straight through Dvanken's hand.

"Ha, ha, take that, you big son-of-a-bitch," Marcus sa id, then pulled out his weapon. Repeatedly, with surprising quickness and power, he punctured the chest of Dvanken at least forty times. The floor and the walls were covered in a thick oily, prismatic, purple gel, Dvanken's blood. Marcus smiled a maniacal grin and kept plunging the makeshift knife deeper and deeper.

"This is for all the pain and all of the bullshit loss you have put me through. I hate you! I hate you! I hate you! Die, you big piece of crap, just DIE!" Marcus screamed as he plunged his makeshift knife again, deeper and deeper, covering himself in goop. Dvanken grasped Marcus's right hand, squeezing until he lost his grip on the knife.

"You have made a mistake human. Only a Guardian's weapon can harm me, and this shard of burned plastic is far from adequate," Dvanken said, removing the shank with his index finger and thumb like something insignificant, and disgusting. Dvanken lowered his head, coming eye to eye with Marcus. He put his large finger in the center of the inmate's chest.

"Your time has come small mortal. Now you will reap your reward for your son's early death,"

Dvanken cocked his head to the side and violently gripped Marcus's neck between his powerful jaws. Reaching up in vain, Marcus grasped at the head, punching and scratching as hard as he could, tearing small hunks of flesh from Dvanken's face.

He did all of this for naught. For now, Marcus was with his son. Dvanken took his essence, his soul, and left his body lying shaking with pain and dripping with hate. Dvanken stood, straddling the fallen convict.

"You can rest now Marcus. Your struggle is over, and no thank-you is needed. You are welcome. Oh, yes, I nearly forgot. Please little human, tell your boy, Tyrone, he is welcome as well," The horrific malefactor looked up, startled, and searched the cell around him. He was suddenly and wholly afraid, and not exactly sure why.

"Who is it? Who's there ?!" Dvanken screamed, twisting and churning quickly trying to find the source of his new fear.

"Your enemy is strong!" A voice from nowhere proclaimed.

"Show yourself. I am new to this fear, and I am having trouble with it!" Dvanken confided, still very uneasy.

"No, not yet. Your enemy is stronger than you give credit. Be careful, lest ye find yourself alongside your countless fallen," the booming voice proclaimed full of bass and thickness.

"Who are you?" Dvanken asked again, but there was no reply only dead silence. "Fine! I am hungry, and I grow tired of this game," Dvanken said, flying out the hole he created moments earlier, off in search of his next victim.

A New Hope

I sat in a high balcony, eavesdropping on the pair of Keni and Sabor, continuing my duties as I had done for twenty-some years now.

"Do you ever sit and just wonder why all of this is happening to us Sabor, huh?" Keni asked, sitting on the cold dirt floor looking up at the casually propped Lindon.

"I have asked myself that exact question, since the moment that my rash first started itching. And yeah, I still ask myself that, now, every so often," Sabor said, looking down at Keni, with an expression of honesty.

"And with your questions, have there come any answers?" Keni asked picking up a hand full of brown pebbles and scattering them out in high arches across the floor.

"Not anything concrete, Ken. The only answers that I can come up with are that all of this will make things somehow better. To somehow stop the killing and give everyone the chance to just grow old together. That at least is my sappy, little romantic hope. That somehow all of this knowledge, all of this fighting can somehow bring it all into a sort of perspective, ending the suffering of our kind. I guess," Sabor added as he released his sabor, and began to pick his teeth with the katana like blade.

"I just don't know what makes me so damn special to deserve to be called a Knight, Guardian, or whatever the hell you wanna call it. I mean, shit! I never asked to be thrown into this whole situation. I wasn't raised being told about any of this, I'm sorry Sabor. I, I'm just saying I didn't ask for this. Any of this responsibility, ya know?" Keni said, not really expecting any answer, especially the one he got.

"I agree with you totally," Sabor said with a cocky smile across his face. "I don't know what makes you so damn special either. Ha," Sabor laughed and slapped Keni on the back of the head sharply. Before Keni could get too angry though Sabor began again.

"I'm just playing. I will be the first to admit I didn't believe any of the hype about this places either. What was going to make my twenty-second birthday any different from the others, ya know. But we are all special; I can see it in every set of eyes I look into around here. We will do what nature has selected us to do, don't you worry.

203

"As for your whining though, you do really need to get over it. None of us asked for any of this. None of us were raised being taught about any of it. We just adapted, moved on with our new knowledge, you see? It wasn't like I asked to be some superhero, and have these gigantic knives fly out of my arms, although, you have to admit it, they will be pretty cool when this is all over with. They should help me pick up chicks, don't you think, Master Divin?" Sabor said bowing mockingly. "Anyway, all I am trying to say is this, you are what you are Keni Divin, and nothing now is going to change it. So, if you don't want your kids to have to have this same discussion with one of their friends in a few years, then you had better come up with something pretty damn good out on that battlefield, I can't do it by myself. We're all counting on you," Sabor said stopping his joking, to be serious for a moment.

"Thanks Friend. No pressure in those words," Keni smiled his first genuine smile at Sabor ever, and it made him feel good inside.

"Sabor, speaking of my children. I don't quite know how to tell you this. I guess no better way to do it, then to just do it, so. Well here goes, you know while you were off on your Discovery, well I got married," Keni spoke, barely getting the words past the lump in his throat.

"Yes, that was the first thing you said to me when I came back. Well, it was the first thing you said when we got a chance to talk," Sabor retorted, wondering where this was going, but at the same time knowing exactly where the finish line was.

"Last week, my wife went to the doctor. She's four months pregnant! It's a boy! The coolest thing about it though, brother, is," Keni looked around, then whispered; "none of the other women are pregnant. He is going to be a solitary child like you, a chosen. Or maybe a new beginning, to a new chapter, huh? Well, I just wanted you to know first, you... "

"That's one of the greatest things that, I've ever heard. Probably in my entire life, Ken. Congratulations," Sabor said, hugging Keni around the neck and slapping his back firmly.

"...I don't know if I can fi ght, brother. My son needs a father, and I need to see my son grow up. I have longed for it my whole life. I'm sorry, I am so sorry," Keni said, as he gripped Sabor in return strongly.

"You have to do what's in your heart, Ken. This is not a choice that I or anyone else here, can make for you. Don't mistake me for heartless, I am very excited for you and I wish you luck in whatever you decide to do.... " Sabor leaned in closely and whispered,"I am behind you one hundred percent no matter what your decision, okay,"

The first round of chimes rang out, signaling Sabor's meeting had been called and was about to begin.

"Just kiss that boy for me, Guardian," As Sabor left to speak at the meeting he turns and nods to Keni. "Just remember Keni. As much as we both want to fight our destinies, yours does have a small intersection with mine, none of us asked for this, remember. We both have to wrestle these demons. We need to accept it for your son as well as for ourselves. You are a Divin," And Sabor left without letting Keni respond, leaving him standing confused and searching for an answer in the floor.

The chimes echoed deeply in the Halls of The Order. The tones signaled yet another meeting about to begin, and all members had been summoned, Greenlings, Knights, Elder's everyone. Sabor sat among Saimus, Ellett, Mason, Yorge, Symon and myself. We sat, discussing life and other meaningless dribble to keep our minds temporarily off the night we each had just experienced, and to pass the time while The Order shuffled into the meeting hall.

"So, who has anything new going on?" Symon asked half-heartedly.

"Well, this may seem strange, but I had an extremely disturbing... " I began to unravel what had happened when Symon interrupted.

"Excuse me, but I cannot hold my tongue any longer. Keni, my nephew, is going to be a father. He and his new wife, Leah, are expecting sometime in mid-summer. I am sorry Master Cranden. I most certainly did not mean to interrupt, please continue. It is just that I am just so excited. This is truly a great time. The end of the cycle of despair, and I am going to be a grandfather. Oh, what a world we live in, eh gentleman?" Symon said, smiling ear to ear.

"What a world indeed," Yorge said sarcastically. "Tell me Symon, mind you, I am just playing the devils advocate, but this world has given you nothing but loss and heartache. What makes you think that even after Dvanken is gone, the world will be some magical, happy land? Well?!" Yorge's words rang in the ears of all that could hear. After all, what kind of assurance did we have that the Cycle would end with Dvanken. After the dream I had the preceding night, it seemed possible that we would not be free in a world without Dvanken.

"Hope," Sabor said quietly from his perch behind us.

"Excuse me, what was that Sabor?" Yorge asked, not really caring what the answer was. Sabor rose to his feet and proceeded into the middle of our circle.

"I said, hope. This is what makes us think that this world can be a "Happy Land". It is hope that has kept your fathers, and your fathers' fathers, forging ahead, striving for your utopia and mine. My father gave his life to this Order, and the purpose it has served and I refuse to go down in history as one of the men who lost hope and watched Dvanken destroy our race. Do you understand?"

206

"I do understand. I have never really looked at it that way. I am sorry," Yorge said, looking down, dripping with embarrassment.

"So, I was wondering," I said, pausing just long enough to ensure there would be no more interruptions, "Last night, I had a very peculiar dream. The plane of The Order, it was taken, taken over by a strange evil, a huge black box. The guardians there were being punished and tortured. It was awful. A strange presence shoved me from inside the box, and the living Elders could be seen trying to break in. The presence told me that Dvanken sent people to him, and he was waiting for us. The dream was terribly unnerving.

"The worst part of all of this, I am not able to contact the Plane of The Order, now. I have tried for hours. All I hear is muffled screams and desperate scrapes on what sounds like a chalkboard. Have any of you been able to contact?" I asked, desperately trying to find some hint that my brothers had been able to, that maybe it was just me who had slipped out of sync.

"I...I had the same dream, brother," Saimus said, looking up in surprised and relieved.

"I had the same, as well," Ellett said, looking at his lap shaking his head.

And so on, until all had told of their dreams. All but Sabor. Sabor looked at us, as if concentrating on a different world entirely, then shook his head. Suddenly he sprang forward, taking the podium with both hands and gripped it so tightly that his knuckles where a brilliant, almost luminescent, white.

"Brothers!! The time for action is now. Dvanken is alive, and he is hungry. Already, thousands have died, and the Awakening is still fresh. The Plane of The Order has been shut off, cutting the ties to our forefathers and their wisdom. We have lost our ties to the old ways, ironically.

"I will miss the companionship of the Plane, but our task is even greater than our ancestors or our history. It is time for a new logic, a new wisdom. Our future, and the future of all, rides on that, on **our** backs, not on the backs of our history...I, for one, am happy for this. I will approach this as new loss, as a blessing in disguise; " Sabor stood staring at the countless faces blending into a colorful hodgepodge of stunned and intrigued faces.

"Each of us has been given the chance today to stand up and claim his own life," Sabor paused and looked at Keni who sat just off of the stage to the left.

"And the lives of their children. If we sit and do nothing, we throw what our fathers, and their fathers, worked so hard for. An end.

And we will be held accountable for our actions. The measure of each and every one of us, the standard to which each of us must and **will** hold ourselves

207

to, will come from the steps each of us take today. The resulting reactions will either forever haunt us, or exalt us in our own histories and the chronicles of others. My life, my story, will not end poorly. I will be proud of the chapters I have written in my own existence," The Halls of The Order echoed with the words coming from the passionate speaker.

"I have no desire to be the last of the Guardians. What I do desire, is this will be the last action the world will need from us of The Order.

"I will not be a party to the same Patriarchal beliefs, which have plagued our fathers with failure.

"You all know your assignments. Tomorrow our plan will unfold, and Dvanken will die. After eons of loss, and three clans of warriors, we will all have our vengeance for the pain he has caused...." Sabor once again looked at Keni and bowed his head in respect. Sabor could not help but feel that if Dvanken had not known his own role in The Order, then Chelle would still be alive. Maybe she would be having Sabor's own little boy. "...And keep our children from ever having to know of the losses of our generations,"

Sabor stared deeply into each focused pair of eyes, seeming to tell them that the world would be alright and the day would be theirs. Each set stared back in recognition. One by one, in succession, the gentleman began to rise. Each man stood, applauding their leader and giving their undying, unwavering support for the actions he proposed they carry out.

"Each of you are now away from the ones you love," Sabor said as Symon stood and hushed the crowd with a movement of his noble arm. "You all have duties to them, and tonight I want nothing more, than for each of you to spend as much time with them as you can. Tomorrow though, tomorrow is a different situation. Not all of you will be coming back to them, and for that I am sorry, but we all have been educated on the risk of our birthright,"

Keni looked up at Sabor, stealing the flow of the speech, and mouthed the words," thank you, friend," Then, he turned his attention to the painting of his father hanging on the wall and shook his head negatively.

Sabor began again," Brothers; I'm sorry for ra mbling on, go and enjoy tonight. Find in the faces of the ones you love why we do what we do tomorrow. Take that strength onto the fields at dawn," Sabor acknowledged the Elders, then stepped off the podium into the halls.

"Sabor!" I yelled, trying to halt the headstrong boy. "What was that in there? Why did you not stay and say good-bye to anyone?" I asked, unsure if I wanted an answer.

"Trying to lead by example, old friend. This is no time to dawdle, wasting the last chances for some of them, for most of them, to see their families," Sabor replied.

His answer being more pleasant than I had expected, I pushed the young man, hoping to coax a little more from my friend. "And who would you go see this evening? Who of your family warrants your attention on this faithful night?" I hugged him as I spoke, hoping to dull the edge of my words.

"I don't really know Cranden. All of this, it's about over. All of the pointless hurting. All of the crap is almost over, ya know? I miss them Cranden; I miss them all so much. And ya want to know the real kicker, no matter what happens tomorrow, they won't be waiting to celebrate with me. That is the hardest thing about all of this. Death is so final, and no matter what, the finality will always find us... each of us. The point of all this escapes me sometimes. Tell me something, if we kill Dvanken tomorrow? Do we have any sort of real, solid proof that he won't be back?" Sabor stopped himself, recognizing before I could say anything that he was just nervous. He looked at me, red with embarrassment, and started to say something else. I stopped him with my own comment about death.

"You don't have to apologize to me Sabor. I know why you said that, I have thought it often myself. Your nerves will go my friend. For now though, just calm your world, focus on the good times with those fallen loved ones. Remember the mornings with your Mother and Father. Remember the nights with Chelle. In those far off days, when you **knew** that I was just a stone statue on the balcony beside you. I think back to something I heard a very wise man say, when this same question of *Why?* Was posed to him. And I quote," HOPE," *I* smiled, and his embarrassment came back. "These good times will serve you well and keep you safe. I will be there tomorrow, just as I have been there for everything in your life. I will remind you little brother, of what it is you fight for,"

"Thank-you, you're right, as always Cranden. I will remember. I think tonight though, I will go home and sleep. Okay? Maybe I won't need so much reminding," He seemed so distant and so cold to me.

"Are you sure? Would you like me to come and stay with you? Just to keep you company," I asked, hoping not to intrude.

Then he looked at me so serious, but with a hint of mischief. "You never told my parents about the balcony, did you?" He smiled, laughing harder than I had heard him laugh in ages. It did me well to hear the echoes of laughter in the halls outside, opposed to the constant chatter of doubt and pessimism.

"No, your secret has remained safely inside here; "I pointed to my temple and gave him a smile. "You go, go to your home, and rest. You will need it tomorrow. Focus, gather your Vingon, and make it solid. Good night, my boy," Smiling, I walked back into the meeting chamber.

"Nesavan lenthit annominahy thins ilitn vintonganth nethrochtu nit; " the chant of the ages resonated from the alley. The words reverberating off of the buildings. Echoing and growing louder with every scream. The shadowy group could barely be seen from the street. Amongst the large clouds of steam rising from the manhole covers, the greenish tint slowly dripped from the walls.

"We are chosen among men! You and I are a part of something greater than we were, even one week ago. Master Dvanken calls us to war. The Lindon line will not yield the one, nor will The Order kill our beloved Master. The Master has foreseen this. We will all be kings among our kind. We, the watched over, the Vintonganth will be given dominion over our brothers. And in turn, we will make them pay for forcing us to live in the gutters, and cardboard towns of west Frington. Search your hearts, and decide. Where does your loyalty lye? Will you fight or will you disgrace our people?"

A surprisingly well kept and knowledgeable man, Jacobi Doralynne, spoke to the group of homeless men gathered around a burning dumpster. He was a smooth talker with hollow, dark eyes and a long face. His eyebrows jutted up like reverse mustaches. His clothing was torn and covered in filth, but his hands were spotless, his hair maintained. It was strange for a man living on the streets. The homeless men around him, however, were drenched in stink and filth head to toe. All were antiquated and brittle from the harsh nature of their lives in Cardboard Town. The alley they lived in on the West Side of the city.

A single, small hobo stood near the back of the pack, naively not caring much as to what was being said by the focal point, the man, standing on the milk crate. Instead, the tiny transient stood, glancing off here and there, intently searching the shadows. All the while, he pulled large, slimy balls from deep inside his nose, searching and, finally, wiping them on the inside of his grimy, tattered overcoat. He smacked his lips, licking them without any care in the world, just nonchalantly being in the alley. Being content in his position, the small man hummed a song from his Old World, trying to lighten his load.

"You!" Jacobi spotted the tiny man and pointed at him. "Why do you ignore the Master's words? Why do you forsake his greatness? Answer me, wretch or you will die slower than you already are," the clean-cut man said, his focus clear to the rest of the group.

"Kill him, I command you. Our Master has prompted me!" Jacobi yelled, with a hateful look about him.

The group of eighty men in unison turned, focusing on their comrade. Then closed in slowly on him, blindly obeying the man standing on the milk crate above them.

The tiny man hunkered down, begging for his life,"No, I was only trying to find Dvanken, my lords. Taking my life, it will satisfy nothing. No please! It's still me, Thaddeus,"The severity of his situation struck him, but alas, it was too late. The ravenous group of ill-kept men encircled him, gnashing their teeth, and slapping at him sharply.

"What is it you wait for? I said to KILL HIM! Do it and do it now!" The hollow eyed man screamed, still standing squarely on the milk crate, pointing.

With this gesture, the crowd moved upon the utterly helpless man. A large, African man stepped first, kicking Thaddeus like a bolt of lightning in the stomach, slamming him to the sewage soaked alley floor. The pack surged behind, tearing small chunks from Thaddeus' body, and feverishly crammed the tiny pieces into their mouths. Each hobo shook with every bite of torn flesh, celebrating the meal.

Blood soaked and full of flesh, the African man stood tall in the midst of the chaos, grabbing the necks of the two closest Vintonganth. Pulling them up to eye level, he smiled at them and let a deafening scream loose into the sky. This grasped the attention of the others, which eased back on all fours, away from the quivering carcass. His yellow teeth raced with crimson highlights, as he smiled at the pair of men.

"Go youns eet now lil' mens,"the African man said slowly, trying desperately not to mess the words up. From behind him, Jacobi applauded slowly while he descended his crate and strode to the large man's side. The African towered over the others in the alley, even the six foot, eight inch tall Jacobi.

"You have done well. You will be rewarded for sure; "Jacobi smiled while patting the large man on the chest.

"Thank you Jacobi, What is dat for?" The enormous man asked.

"You are a valuable asset, big man. I am most happy to have you in our fold. I am however, embarrassed, and at a bit of a disadvantage here, my big friend. You see, you know what my name is, but I have no clue who you are," Jacobi said, smiling as he realized, in order for the group of transients to respect him as a leader. He would need to gain favor with the one who appeared to be their present leader.

212

"Well, not too many peoples aks me fa my name, lest not round here. Bes' I can member, it's Carvin, Carvin Banks. Bes' I can member," the mountain said with an air of happiness.

"Nice to know you, Carvin Banks, very nice to know you indeed. Tell me, why are you here tonight, big fella?" Jacobi asked.

"I don' really know why. I was sittin' by me dumster, jus' thinking one day. I wasn't thinking 'bout much, jus' how happy I used a be. Wit my wife and two dauters. I wus happy, ya know, jus' happy.

"Den one day, I come home from the paper mill, 'n my wife was jus' laying der bleedin'. Couldn't find no sign of my lil' girls either. I bent down to grab my wife; maybe I coulda done somethin' to help. She was gone though, not breathing nor nuttin, jus' limp. With big ol' tears in my eyes, I looked up, and this big man wus jus' standing there, laughing at me. He was covered in blood, and he had two tiny ponytails in his hands.

"I couldn't stop once I started. I jus' kept on hittin' him. My hand went clear through to the floor through that mans' face. I jus' couldn't stop. I tore his arms off, never forget the feeling of dem tendons and bones crunchin' and poppin' loose from each other. I take dem arms an' I beats him wit' em. I hits him so much they jus' turned to jelly.

"After dat, I stood up an' went to my girls' betroom, an' I sees dat my babies been beat ta deaf. My lil' Symone, she wus danglin' by her face 'bout midway up da wall, an' Sally wus layin' on da bed wit her arms tiet behind her an' her hair jus' pulled out everywhere. I left dat night. I burnt da house with everybody in it.

"After dat, I jus' wasn't happy no more. I didn't always talk dis way ya see. It jus' seem after seein' all a dat, my brain jus' don work right. Ya know? Anyway I come here t'night cause somin' told't me dat I would find somthing here. I jus' followed my thoughts. Hell, day was da clearest thoughts I had in a while, so I jus' came,"

A sudden, intense flash of light sent the homeless men tumbling and cascading off the sticky walls of the alley. The force was deafening as it exploded upon the feasting tramps. Jacobi and Carvin stared in the direction of the power, glaring as the evil filled the alley. A malice like none of them had ever seen, swept into the alley, filling the space with feelings of shame and disgust. Dvanken had come to see his army, and he was pleased with what he saw. With a glance toward his lieutenant, Jacobi, he smiled. Then, he proceeded to the writhing, half-eaten corpse, jumping and jerking in the slime of the alley floor.

"The sweet Dance of Death. The nerves in his spine dying, bring on this breathtaking ballet. The tiny fragments of life left inside his dying brain scream and squirm, trying desperately to stay burning. Thaddeus is grasping at what is no longer his; he grasps at what has now become ours. Loathe him for his

213

selfishness and remember his arrogance.

"I am proud of your sacrifice here this night. You have given the weak to sustain the strong. In the days to come, you will need this discipline," Dvanken said, kneeling down at the side of the shuttering lump of red and yellow tissue.

"I will now reap your oblation unto me, my Vintonganth. I thank you,"

Dvanken looked into the recovering eyes of the men lying around him, then reached down, ripping the sweet spine from the body, and crunching it down.

"He tastes sweet with the fear you have placed in him, sour by his selfish love of his own pathetic life," Dvanken said, degrading the slain man. "You may reap the rest of this reject of a man. He was not worthy,"

Dvanken stood, straddling the body as the men came back in to feast on the remains like rats. He watched them, relishing the sound of human flesh ripping from bone.

"Now, my army of Vintonganth, you will be prepared. You will take your final steps in proving your allegiance to me, your final steps in insuring our dominance of the men who have passed by, noses in the air, scoffing at your varying situations, disgusted at your mere existence. You will now change into warriors for the cause, into assassins of the good. Come, follow me, and you will know what to do," Dvanken said, stepping through the sea of feasting filth to a long shadow, flickering with the light from the dumpster fire.

Reaching out his long, slender finger, he ripped the shadow into two pieces which fell to the ground like ebony ribbons. A foul gale flowed from inside the darkness, grabbing the blood soaked men's attention. Dvanken stepped inside, motioning for them to follow. The room was grand, echoing with the sound of drips in distant unseen pools. Large cauldrons filled to nearly overflowing with a bubbling green liquid, sat in two rows that stretched deeply into the hungry darkness. An intense purple flame roared under each of the cast iron pots. Lumps of decaying, black flesh lay in motionless piles scattered about all over the floor. A deep shadow hid the remainder of the room, masking the vastness it contained. Small torches hung from skeletal remains dangling from large black chains.

The men filed into the opening, then fanned out, encircling their master. Dvanken stood as the group assembled and looked around confused.

"Pain. Pain is your only true friend now. Haunting, consuming, nagging pain. Your journey, thus far in this life has been saturated with hurt. Every aspect of your pointless existence, another knife in the back from love, another

214

sick lonely night from your loss. Your very continuation has conditioned you to that one dismal certainty. You will all be in pain, until you die. This inevitability, is a pain unto itself, don't you think?

"I am your way to bliss. Conquer with me and we will rule alongside one another until we say that it is time to end it all. The very word Vintonganth means immortality. I will lead you to perfection. If you trust," Dvanken said as he slipped into the consuming shadow, leaving no trace of the beast, save his thunderous voice.

The men cautiously stepped in closer to the rows of cauldrons. With almost a sense of familiarity, each man stepped to a predestined spot. By the time each was sectioned off in his place, four men surrounded every cauldron. In unison, a chant rang from their lungs, an ancient hymn, lost over centuries of neglect. However ancient the chant, the men recited it perfectly in this place. Each one lost himself inside the melody of the song.

"You will all now, know your place. Give in to the hymn, become numb," Dvanken barked from the shadow.

The chant grew louder as they gave in collectively to the mantra. A swirl of reddish-yellow energy began to dart around the men just above their heads. The energy screamed in agony as it traveled. A sense of unrest settled over the bubbling liquid. As the Vintonganth stared directly in front of them, holding hands around the cauldrons, their eyes began to acclimated to the darkness.

As the blackness slowly melted away, an uncountable multitude of men began to emerge. Hooded in scarlet robes, their eyes glowed a subtle white. The crimson mass chanted along with the hobos, multiplying the volume and causing the light to move faster and closer. The bolt of energy slammed into the chest of one of the men chanting, knocking him loose from the others.

"Oh, that stings. What is going on aaahhh!" The man lamented in agony.

"FOCUS!" Dvanken howled as the men looked down at their co mpanion writhing on the floor.

The chant grew ever louder until each man locked into a straight posture, glaring at one another. A glassy haze seeped up from their bottom eyelid. The chant stopped suddenly. Every man dropped their head back, staring at the ceiling and raising their dominant arm high in the air.

The hymn began to roll again from the men stepping from the shadows. With a mighty yell the Vintonganth slammed their arms deeply into the cauldrons. Locking eyes with their adjacent brothers again, they began to chant, leaving their arms to sizzle in the liquid. The chant removed all sensation from the ritual; all pain was gone, only the words remained. Pulling the boiling flesh from the liquid in unison, the men revealed a horrific sight. The skin, muscle, tendons, everything melted away in long bloody strands, leaving only hardened bone protruding from just below the elbow. The men turned, facing the rows of silent onlookers. Large spinning stones sat free from the earth beside the silent warriors, turning ever faster. Each man stepped toward the waiting stones. The hooded figures chanted, reaching out grabbing the exposed pale bone and then pressed it firmly onto the rotating rock, sharpening the bone to a finely honed blade.

"These are your weapons, the blades of your rebirth, my new Vintonganth. You're next step. Your last step in the journey of your allegiance. The men standing silent, shrouded before you, are your brothers. They are the ancient Vintonganth, the loyal survivors of a lost tribe. They will help in the days to come. So shall you all,"Dvanken said as he emerged onto a large platform made out of criss-crossing thighbones.

Oddly Jacobi and Carvin were absent during the ritual. They had remained in the alley, exchanging stories of life back and forth. Jacobi's faith and devotion had warranted him the right to choose his ceremony. He wanted no part of the weapon rebirth, and his position gave him the power to pass the choice on to Carvin. Besides, Jacobi figured that the sheer size of Carvin would prove beneficial on the battlefield, and Dvanken valued and trusted Jacobi's judgment.

"Carvin, the next few days and weeks may test your faith in the master. It may test your faith in me, but you must trust the master and you must trust in me. But no matter what, please know that I have your best interest in mind," Jacobi said, feeling a twinge of guilt for drawing such a pure man into this web of death. Especially after the conversation they had just been through.

"You don' nee' ta worry 'bout me, Jacobi. I am whole mess smarter then I sound. I am here cuz it feels right in my head. Dat's it. Not 'cuz of you, not 'cuz of some Massa. Jus' me,"The brutal honesty was welcome from the large man. "Ya know, I jus' tired now. Can we goes ta sleep?" The child-like side came roaring out of the man as he spoke.

"Sure thing, big guy. Just please don't lose yourself in any of this,"Jacobi said. The two then took to the street to find a place to sleep for the night.

216

Sabor walked home to rest before the day of reckoning. He strode a little taller as he walked, so proud of what he was going to do for the unaware faces he saw walking around him; the young boys playing stickball in the street, the young girls splashing around in the open fire hydrant, the mothers of the beautiful kids watching intently from their window perches. Watching as he walked, he spied a pair of old women hanging out the windows of their apartments and marveled at the show.

"Honey you stay away from that boy. He's no good for you!" One mother yelled to her teenage daughter making out in the shadows of the front stoop.

"What the hell ya talkin' about, Janice? You sayin' that Ty isn't good enough for your precious Honey? Well, I'll tell you one thing. It ain't like the only man she hidin' in the shadows wit is my Ty!" A disturbed mother yelled to the window three stories below her.

"You gonna take that back or do you want me to come up there and shut your mouth for ya? Or you gonna be woman enough to come down here?"

The tussle made Sabor laugh, because he knew the two women and this to be an everyday occurrence in the neighborhood. The faces of the neighborhood began to blur, fading in and out of focus. The sight was disturbing, seeing the faces of the ones he knew so closely fading away, losing their identity, and losing their presence and features. Sabor looked hard at the faceless bodies running around his street and it made him wonder.

For an instant, he felt as if it would not be worth all of the pain. The joy of killing Dvanken would never replace anything he had lost. As he questioned his plan and his actions, a small face came clearly and vividly into focus. It was the face of a small girl he had often babysat, named Peyton. She was a precious little girl who had just turned four years old. She had brilliant blue eyes and a smile that would melt icebergs. She was beautiful and incredibly smart for her age. She ran to Sabor throwing her arms around him, squeezing until she nearly made him fall.

'Sabe, how are you doing? You look pretty worried 'bout somethin'. You sure you okay?" Peyton said in her angelically soft voice.

"Yes, baby I'm fine. But look at you girly, don't you look super nice today, pretty eyes," Sabor answered, tussling her hair and feeling a sense of quilt

217

for his selfish feelings moments before. Her innocent face struck Sabor with the reality of his situation, not just his own, but the reality of the entire world. There would be hundreds of thousands of people, every single day, who would not be able to see their individual versions of sweet little Peyton. But he, Sabor Lindon had the power to give every human being the chance to see their loved ones forever. Reaffirmed, he knelt down and smiled at the young girl. The world slammed back into focus every brilliant face, so alive and full of emotion.

"Ya know what sweetie? You're the reason I'm doing all of this. You and this tiny street. I love you guys," Sabor said, knowing that the little girl would have no grasp of what he was saying.

"Yeah Sabor, it is scary. Just remember to say it isn't real though, he's not something to be ascared of. Okay, buddy," Peyton said as she hugged Sabor tightly around the neck.

"Huh? Who Peytie, who's pretty scary?" Sabor asked, hoping the small girl had no knowledge of Dvanken.

"The boogie man silly. 'Member, you told me he wasn't real and I shouldn't be ascared of him," Peyton said, her attention snatched by a yellow and blue rubber ball, bouncing past them on the sidewalk.

"Bye Sabor! I'll see you tomorrow, okay!" She said over her shoulder as she tore off after the ball.

"Yeah sweetie, I'll see ya tomorrow," Sabor said, still a bit bothered about her comment. He stood up, brushed his knees, and walked to his house for a restful evening.

Sabor awoke the next morning feeling at peace and fully alive. In the street outside, he heard a blue bird singing a solitary song of happiness. Sabor felt so comfortable here, in his Mother and Fathers bed. It was going to be a great day to fight.

"Mom, Dad, today is finally the day. Chelle, I miss you so much, but today I will avenge your loss. Dad, I will get him for you, not just for you, but for everyone there. I love you all and I will come to you tonight on the Plane of The Order. We'll talk for awhile, then I will live a long happy life knowing you are all okay. I need to go now though. Remember always, I love you," Sabor said as he bounced to his feet, heading to the bathroom. He showered like he was preparing for the prom, readying himself completely. Today was an important day for him.

"I can do this. Dvanken you will pay. For I Sabor Lindon, am the Avenger," Sabor said to the mist covered mirrored, smiling.

After dressing, he proceeded to the Plains and the entrance to the Halls of The Order. When he arrived, he and the Greenlings staying in the dormitories, they were the only souls in the catacombs of the Halls. It was again a peaceful place. The ocean of calmness around Sabor felt nice; a small preview to the days to come after the task of the day was over.

"This is going to feel so good," Sabor thought to himself, as he touched every statue and painting throughout the chambers. He slowly made his way to the meeting hall. As he entered he let out a boisterous laugh and sprinted to the podium.

"LET'S DO THIS!" He s creamed into the room. Then slammed the podium and grabbed the rope dangling behind him, through the cloud of dust now billowing into the air. The rope moved, ringing the bell for the daily meeting to begin. Sabor assumed a posture at the podium that was serious as could be, but his youthful exuberance gave the stance a hint of child-like happiness.

The halls filled with Greenlings and Knights in an instant, the hustle and bustle of the men a welcome sight to Sabor. It made him feel as if the entire body of The Order was as excited as he was. The Elders, out of character, were the last to arrive. They strolled in, taking in the excited faces they saw sitting row after row, down the isles. As they passed, each row ceased its idle chitchat with reverence and respect.

"Welcome to our age Brothers!" Sabor said not allowing everyone to sit down.

"We all now know our roles. So, I will ask of each one of you only one more thing. To execute those roles...now!" With that Sabor nodded and stepped down, proceeding out to face his zenith.

'Sabor! Wait, wait you can't just spring all of that on us like this, then just walk off, with no explanation. We need time to ready ourselves, to prepare the battle plan further," Yorge Danglin screamed, ever reluctant to follow anyone' s lead blindly.

"Master Yorge, I beg to differ, I just did! Master Danglin-you are so entrenched in the old ways, we simply need to let the planning happen. We are all ready for this. Surprise will be the fiercest of all our allies," Sabor said, patting the large man on the shoulder, with his shimmering blue sabor while looking up at the towering ceilings above him.

'I have sat here in these Halls, idle. As have the rest of you, while Guardian after Guardian has died. Stumbling into the rusted traps of the old ways. Generations of beings have defended their lives, with this old way and now only traces and rantings in the History stand as testament to their societies and their losing battle. You sit waiting for some trigger, some steadfast, sure thing, to let us of The Order know when the time of the end will be. I am here to tell you, It will not come.
"As I wandered through my Discovery, I realized one powerfully true thing, there will be no outstanding event, foretelling of the conclusion of our tale. It is up to the warriors of the day, to end their own cycle of despair. It has been this way throughout all of our history. Every major overtaking of power, every uprising to save ones own life, has started with the iron will and courage of a small group of fighters, sick of the death forced upon them by their own supreme evils.
'I saw many strange and wonderful things on my Discovery, many things. But the only thing that truly moved me about this world, the only thing that made me actually want to save it again, was in my own neighborhood. A small girl, Peyton, who simply told me, to not be afraid. She forced me into being sick of the killing. I will not let that little girl know the hurt of the premature loss of someone she loves. So, I will keep that in my heart and finish this cycle, once and for all," Sabor said, turning and giving Yorge a reassuring smile and hug. The men inside the auditorium began to flood out behind and around the hairy Elder standing drenched in his own embarrassment.

Elsewhere, Dvanken watched a young cheerleader exit her school for lunch. He payed special attention to this poor young lady because of incidents he witnessed through her bedroom window. Dvanken had watched as the worst crime against a daughter befell her young, naive body, a crime perpetrated by her very own father. A crime that no little girl should be a part of, not only from her father, but from any other man. Dvanken was intent on devouring the father of the young lady, but the taste of loss wasn't in the father's world just yet. Dvanken intended to put the loss there.

The bell had rang and she was walking alone to her music class, subconsciously ashamed of what had been going on for as long as she could remember. As she reached the dark corridor on the West End of the campus, on a seldom-used path due to its extreme distance from everything; she heard a faint whisper from a deep shadow. Pausing briefly, then dismissing the noise for a breeze she continued. Dvanken smiled at the dismissal and lowered himself down slowly behind the girl.

"Are you lonely girl?" Dvanken asked.

"Who said that? Who's there?" The young lady asked spinning around and throwing her books into a small semi-circle around her feet. Seeing nothing behind her, she began to question her sanity. "Great all the bullshit has finally caught up with me. I'm insane," she said as she knelt down, quickly picking up her books.

"No my precious, you're not insane, nor are you alone. Do you want the "Special Time" to stop? Do you wish to never feel the stank, warm breath of your father on your sweet little neck ever again? One word and I will make it all stop. Ask me nicely and say please," Dvanken said as a stream of purple miasma encircled the young lady, consuming her fully in an instant.

"What is this? Tell me who you are please !?" The peppy cheerleader asked.

"I am the answer. The end to all your suffering. You can call me Dvanken; " the evil smile on his face defied explanation.

"Okay then. Why would you do this for me? I haven't done anything special to deserve anything like this," her constant abuse had destroyed her sense of self, convincing her that she was nothing and would never be anything but pretty.

"Young lady, you are so very much more than you give yourself credit for. You are indeed a special young thing," Dvanken said pausing for a moment. "Just know you do deserve this. Ask for it to end, politely and I will do so,"

221

Dvanken's smile widened as she spoke.

"Okay, would you please make my Dad stop touching me, there I said it," the young girl asked the faceless voice.

"So be it! Thank you little one," With those words, Dvanken sprung from the shadows, knocking the petite young girl to the ground. The unholy, warm slime oozed out, falling onto her tiny face.

"Relax my dear, your end is here. No more pain, ever," Dvanken said, reaching up preparing to reap her pain. But before he started, he heard in his mind.

"*Dvanken, you son-of-a-bitch. You took them. You took them all. I hate you...I hate your filthy guts,*" Sabor's voice echoed in Dvanken' s mind

Dvanken rose from the young girl, moving toward the origin of the message slowly at first. The words ensnared Dvanken, redirecting his intentions solely to the Avenger.

"*Avenger, I am ready. Today will be the day that your tale ends. And with your death so ends the tale of the Sabor Guardians,*" Dvanken thought to himself.

"Vintonganth, rally at the Halls, it is time!" Dvanken commanded Jacobi's mind, sitting and waiting in the alley, for this order.

Dvanken tore at the ground, throwing large chunks of debris on the poor little schoolgirl lying nearby. He had tasted the pain of the Avenger again and it brought back the sensations of his dream.

"I will kill you, Sabor Lindon. And after your death, The Order will fall into the entangling chaos of doubt. It will be a most beautiful day, for me. At long last, my purification of the world will have nothing to hold it down," Dvanken said as he ran, following the scent of Sabor's pain, like a hound on a fresh blood trail.

Sabor sat, consumed in the mists of the fields east of the entrance. The towering statues of my ancestors poised overseeing his plan. He carried out his brilliant plan, unraveling it to the joy of all of us, the Elders. Perching on the crest of the hollow. We would watch, insuring that the events unfolded correctly, only to intervene if the plan was failing. That was what Sabor had instructed. When in fact, I believe he actually assigned us to be here simply to hold Ellett back.

Sabor pondered the events of his adult life, focusing on the pain and turmoil given to him by the evil. He hoped to conjure the beast, with the reflective thoughts. Sitting solitaire in the dew-soaked grass, rocking back and forth, he read the letter Noelle had left to him. I saw, tracing the contour of his cheek, a single embodiment of his pain fall sweaty and cold streaming down his face. Trying not to draw attention, he slowly reached up and dried it, wiping all traces of the salty weakness away.

From our vantage, we saw hiding in the tall saw grass, the ranks of The Order. Three hundred strong, they waited, ready, poised for The Unholy to arrive. The pain he had caused Sabor would draw Dvanken, and it would be very sweet for us. Dvanken's arrival would give us all the chance to release the pain he had seeded in us all, releasing the pain upon the source.

The signal would be Sabor's actions. When he ejected his blade, holding it above his shoulder, we would rise against the beast and slaughter him. It would be a victory four thousand years in the making, and justice for the slaying of my family and my race for myself. This was a day I had waited for, for a generation of lifetimes.

"Do you think this will work?" Ellett asked us, nervously.

"It is not our place to question this. Is it?" Saimus replied, never taking his watchful eye from the lone warrior waiting to fulfill his destiny.

"I think that is exactly our place to question this. I have my doubts; on the whole, this does seem to be a well-conceived plan. But, I think we are going about it all wrong. We should, all of us, flood in at the first sign of the beast and overwhelm him with surprise," Yorge said strongly.

"That, my furry friend, would only give him a chance to retreat. This plan lures him deeply into the plain, allowing us to encircle him, and trap him with our numbers. Do you understand?" I replied, defending my friend Sabor.

"I understand, but I still don't like waiting for Dvanken to get in so close. What if we cannot get into him before he kills the young Lindon?" Yorge retorted.

"Sssssshhhhhh, all of you be quiet. The wind seems to be bringing in a fog," Saimus said, still never taking his eyes from the field. "We have our duties. Our time to carry them out appears to be now!" He finished; pointing to the grass bowing down as the miasma seeped over the grassland.

"I must take my position on the south hill, with Mason and the others. Good hunting brother's. One mission, one outcome, right?" Yorge said not letting anyone get in another word, as he stepped off to the rear of the hill, to assume his position for the eminent battle.

Swirls of magenta and deep emerald smoke danced through the long blades. The sky began to eclipse, prematurely swirling pseudo-nightfall across the battlefield. In the distance, a wall of lightning flashes, crashed, slamming the ground and cutting off any chance of a retreat for Sabor. The Avenger tensed up instinctively, without any knowledge of the evil force entering the field controlled from a long distance from the field.

"What is it that you hope to accomplish with your pain and death, Avenger?" Dvanken quietly asked Sabor's mind.

"My killing you will accomplish quite a bit, ass!" Sabor replied back to Dvanken's mind. The realization that Sabor was controlling his inner voice tore at Dvanken's thoughts.

"How in the hell did he contact my head? He is-after all, only human, right?" Dvanken asked himself; not realizing his entire chase was due to the same principal. Sabor showing Dvanken his pain, thus drawing Dvanken closer to him. Slowing down a bit, Dvanken cracked his neck and broke off down a familiar alleyway and vanished into a blast of hollow light.

Sabor smiled a coy smile, for he knew he was getting under Dvanken's skin. The plan would work and Dvanken would not live to kill again. Sabor increased the intensity on his pain as he felt the presence of Dvanken cresting the hill.

Again Sabor, broke Dvanken's mental defense saying," Come on, you weak bastard. I am here waiting, ready for you," With this; Sabor slowly released his right sabor across his lap sensing Dvankens proximity. It was a magnificent broadsword. Small inscriptions danced along the finely honed ridge, dividing the blade. The weapon glowed a brilliant blue, outlining his body, due to the early twilight. The wind swirled, throwing the evil mist across Sabor's back. A shiver of excitement and uneasiness ran up Sabor's spine.

"So it begins," Sabor thought.

Dvanken warped into existence on the plain. A ripple of heinous light broke as he materialized. With his appearance from beyond the horizon, every Greenling and every Knight flexed in anticipation. Each man replaying every battle he had waged with the evil monstrosity, drumming up all of the pain and emotion from his own personal history with the evil. Dvanken, smelling the enormous amount of fear and pain in the grassy plain, paused, then motioned to some unseen ally.

"Vintonganth! Show me your strength! Show me your undying allegiance! Destroy the Sabor Guardians. Relinquish them unto me, none shall remain alive!" Dvanken screamed, pointing to the west, pointing to Sabor.

"Arise to claim your prizes with the blood of my enemies," Dvanken added intensely.

The Evil then lunged forward, followed by a rebel yell. Inside a whirling cloud of dust, an army of men crested the hill. The army was as Sabor had reported; homeless men with strange blades of bone jutting from inside their tattered clothing. They chanted loudly as they marched mindlessly toward confrontation. The eyes of the men were soulless and hollow black.

The army added a new twist on the old ways; Dvanken had grown more complex and was prepared for the inevitable evolution of the Sabor Guardians.

"Go now minions! Kill the Avenger!" Dvanken screamed at the group charging around him like a rampaging wave of hate. The homeless men questioned nothing for they were now but soulless vessels and would carry out anything for their master, Dvanken.

Sabor sensing the foul presence, reached out his left hand and turned his palm up to the sky, motioning to his army laying prone in the swaying grass. The entire field became alive with light and three hundred sabor weapons poised, ready to fight for the good of mankind.

The two opposing forces, surging like an ocean, flooded the grassy field with violence. Both sides' intent, their eyes fixed firmly on the target charging on the opposite horizon. The surge of pure opposing energies and the screams from both sides could be felt on the ridge overlooking the battlefield. The two massive waves of men crashed into the center of the field. Each side steering clear of the young man sitting in the Lotus position in the tall grass. The soulless aberration trudged methodically toward him, leaving an eye in the hurricane of blood and aggression around them. Dvanken halted his advance slightly behind Sabor, his unholy breath charged and luminescent, oozed down Sabor's neck. The eerie mist swirled from the gaping mouth and down the young man's shoulders. Consumed in Dvanken's shadow, Sabor smiled then winked at me. I was so far away, crested high above at the egress of the hollow, I felt completely helpless. But it was my role, so I stayed, watching. Dvanken writhed with anticipation, then leaned in very close to Sabor.

"No! You get away from him!" I thundered down to the beast, but Ellett reached up, ending my attempt to help my friend.

"Understand! He must be allowed to be the Avenger. Steady The Order,

225

we have quite a fight on our hands," Ellett said, his words making tremendous sense and slamming me back into my role as overseer.

"I'm sorry gentlemen. He is just so dear to me," I replied apologetically. My words were not needed however; they all felt the exact way I did.

I watched as Sabor turned back, taking in the full width of Dvanken. He smiled sarcastically at the beast, then drove his right hand as hard as possible straight up, aiming squarely at the enormous purple eye gleaming down at him. Sabor's body followed his arm as he flowed to his feet, ready to end the sorrow of the world.

Dvanken reacted immediately, recoiling and twisting backwards. The sharp blade missed its mark; inches to the left, leaving Sabor open under his arm. Dvanken's hellish speed allowed him to spot this weakness and in turn he exploited it, grabbing the exposed Guardian by the underarm and hurling Sabor high into the air. The Avenger twisted and flipped his body, landing softly on his feet.

Sabor smirked and winked at the beast, taunting Dvanken. Then, sharply Sabor released both Sabor weapons. With a spark and a scream, the two juggernauts charged, each determined to kill the other quickly. At, the junction of the two fighters, Dvanken released two jagged, bone-like swords from his forearms, each seemingly breathing, each pulsing with sin. Small lines of purple, and deep green, red light pounding throughout the long, sharp bones.

Sabor forced his right blade strongly toward the neck of Dvanken, but, again, speed saved the evil beast. Dvanken casually deflected the blow with his own sabor-like shard, then lunged with his right weapon. The blow glanced off Sabor's shoulder, leaving a small gash ripped in his arm, exposing the red muscle. Sabor winced from the pain, but continued to fight, swirling his sabors, retracting them as their revolutions put his own body in jeopardy from the sharp blades, spinning closely.

"Is that all you've got for me, you weak piece of shit!" Sabor screamed as he smiled. The deep wound glowing a bright healing white and closed instantly.

"You gotta do better than that," Sabor said, blocking an incoming blow from Dvanken while slapping his freshly healed shoulder with the other blade.

"You will respect my power by the end of this ordeal Avenger," Dvanken howled reaching out, grabbing Sabor by the wrist digging his claws into Sabor's flesh, slinging the hope of The Order to the blood-spattered ground, then following him down, slicing straight through his chest plate, pressing hard desperately trying to shove through, to the bloody grass below.

"You see Guardian; I have been doing this to your kind and The Orders before you, for centuries. I will be here feasting on your children and your children's children, long after this day. So, I think it is you that must do better, BOY!" Dvanken screamed, smashing Sabor in the face three solid times.

The blows seemed to knock Sabor senseless. Leaving him laying still and motionless as Dvanken crawled to one knee. Prematurely holding his false victory, Dvanken opened his mouth lunging down to take a chunk of the young Avenger's flesh. In an instant Sabor's eye opened and he forced his arm straight up, sailing for Dvanken's open mouth. Locking the arm at the elbow, Sabor braced with the other arm as Dvanken came crashing down quickly. The large mouth consumed the sabor completely. Instantly, the back of the beast' s head exploded in a purple watery mass. A shiny, blue sabor shot out from the center of the shower of blood. A hellish scream blew from Dvanken, as he grasped the back of his neck with both hands and backed sharply away from the Avenger. Dvanken hunkered down and moaned as a high arcing web of flesh criss-crossed over the hole, gluing it together so the unholy beast could continue the fight.

"Young Sabor, stare into your Omega. I am eternal. I am your death, your end. For eons, I have dreamt of this. Today I will devour the hope of The Order and begin my ascension to the pinnacle of power. How sweet!" Dvanken said, shaking his head, violently throwing the remaining trickles of blood everywhere. "You will not be so lucky again, Avenger,"

Dvanken roared and charged Sabor again, each warrior not being allowed by the other to gain an advantage, deadlocked.

Sabor threw a sidearm blow, cutting a gash in the large shoulder of Dvanken and followed with a quick right cross, jabbing his blade beneath the ribcage and sticking there as the muscles contracted in pain. Dvanken grabbed the sabor and shook. A bolt of pure evil shot down the blade, like electricity through a copper rod. The emotion instantly turned Sabor's glow a deep hate red. Retracting his sabor in pain, Sabor recoiled and tried desperately to choke down the hate, overpowering it with visions of the small girl Peyton and her words of encouragement. Suddenly Sabor sprung to his feet and pointed the brilliantly glowing blade at Dvanken and spun, twisting and whirling towards the beast. With each revolution, a bolt of the red energy flew from his blade, until they were pure white.

"You have no control over me Dvanken. I am beyond your hate; it is nothing to me. But, I would like for you to taste my joy, it has been stewing for you inside me for sometime now," Sabor said, flinging an enormous bolt of white and blue swirling energy at Dvanken's head. The monstrosity ducked and the bolt severed a huge piece of the black wing-like growth on its back. And

Dvanken looked behind him in horror as it struggled to regenerate. Dvanken retaliated with a fierce charge and a simultaneous attack of the Vintonganth. The convergence of the homeless men upon the one on one battle took Sabor by surprise and he fell to their power. The gnarly teeth of the men ripped at Sabors body while Dvanken stood and yelled.

I grasped Saimus on the shoulder and pulled him a bit. He looked at me, an unspoken truth becoming evident. I needed some vengeance of my own, and Sabor needed my help. The Vintonganth had reduced The Order to a few soldiers being overcome by the initial odds of sometimes twenty to one. It was up to me to run interference for Sabor.

Surveying the scene as I made my way down to the battlefield. A strange gravity swelled behind me as I descended. I watched Sabor arch back and point both arms straight at Dvanken's head. Then the young Sabor Guardian began shaking.

Rushing as hard as I could I, dropped thirty feet to the valley floor just as it happened. Sabor stood with one quick motion, as Dvanken leapt in for the kill as the Vintonganth receded with a quick motion from their master. Sabor exploded with a shower of blue and white light power. The blast leveled everything, every Guardian, every vagabond, myself, even Dvanken tumbled onto his back. Dvanken slammed to the dirt just a few feet in front of me.

Shaking myself off and noticing Sabor was obviously drained, I charged to cut off Dvanken's direct route to him. I placed myself squarely in his field of vision. He rose up, surprised to see a Gargoyle. He sized me up. Finally, he spoke.

"I thought I had killed all of you. I can't say tha t I mind having one last taste of your kind, but I was hoping to taste the Avenger before I feasted on anything else. No matter, I simply will let your corpse rot in the sun for a moment, while I dine on your precious Sabor,"

Dvanken's words found no fear in my heart. I was prepared, I wanted him. I needed retribution for my family and for my race. I would take him with the strength of old.

"You will find me a worthy adversary, Dvanken. I will have payment for what you have put me through. I grew never knowing another like me and for this, you will give your life. Today!" I yelled, barely containing my adrenaline.

The beast charged at me, screaming, his purple eyes blazing, almost on fire. I charged in, pulling the earth with all four of my legs as hard as possible. Reaching out for one another, we collided like semi-trucks at full speed. I jerked

228

up on his arm up, slamming him over my head to the ground, then followed him down. My shoulder cracked his ribs. I heard them snap one by one. Dvanken screamed in agony.

"I had forgotten the strength of you Gargoyles. No matter, I will have to step it up to your challenge," Dvanken said grabbing at his ribs.

The mammoth evil reached up, gripping me by the bottom jaw, and yanked me to the ground with a powerful down stroke, burying my chin in the soft soil, and then he pummeled me repeatedly in the spine. I felt a warm tingle as I lost the use of my right side. Dvanken had paralyzed me with his ferocity.

Uncertain how long the paralysis would last, I knew I could not fight him with the use of only one side of my body. Pushing with all of my might and spinning up to one leg, I sent Dvanken soaring through the air. I watched him crash to the earth, sending up a cloud of dust. I stood, displaying no weakness, no pain, and just the strength of my kind. Rising to his feet, Dvanken shook the dirt from his body.

"You are becoming a hindrance to my plan, Gargoyle. It is time for you to take your leave. I have business to tend to!" Dvanken screamed.

He limped a few steps, then sprinted faster and faster toward me. I braced myself, then pulled my wings up to my side to help cushion my fall. Dvanken crashed into me. My body gave out totally. I was paralyzed, completely at his mercy.

I looked deep into the rage of Dvanken's eyes as we tumbled, and found he had no desire to end **my** existence. He was consumed, obsessed, taken completely by the death of Sabor. His entire being, even as we fought, fixed on the dazed Avenger kneeling in the grass.

As we came to rest, the unholy stared down at me, stared through me. Then Dvanken rammed a spiky fist into my chest, knocking the air from my lungs. He smiled and slapped my face. I was humiliated and terrified all at once. Dvanken towered over me, laughing. With an eerie glare he locked his eyes on Sabor, who had just regained his composure and saw what Dvanken had done to me.

"Dvanken! You want a fight? Here I am. I am the only thing in your world that matters right now, you bastard! I am the Avenger. I am your end!" Sabor said as I, paralyzed, could only watch what transpired.

"Don't confuse yourself, Avenger," Dvanken said sarcastically.

"I have other things on my mind now, many other things. My world is a web of evil that comes full circle to fill my appetite. I constantly prepare you pathetic worms to satisfy my tastes.

"For instance, even now as I plot your demise, wondering how sweet your agony will taste, in Chicago, a middle aged man is raping and killing his fifth girl this month. All because I constantly remind him of a horrible sexual experience when a young lady, resembling his victims, laughed at his genitals. And how his mother would beat him and lock him in a closet for days on end. You should see his rage. It is beautiful. His sorrow will be delicious. I will savor his regret.

"In a small, poor section of India, a group of starving men plot to assassinate their dictator, in the name of a rival fife, all for the my simple promise of food. The war caused by this action will fill my stomach for my next Slumber.

"So, you see Avenger, do not flatter yourself with delusions that you hold my unwavering interest. I, am Dvanken. I, as we speak, am planning death everywhere, understand?" Dvanken said, pointing his large finger at Sabor.

"You shouldn' t insult me Dvanken. It could be very bad for your future," Sabor said, releasing each sabor weapon.

Dvanken stood erect, preparing for Sabor's onslaught. The Avenger accommodated Dvanken's stance with a feverish barrage of slices and cuts. Nothing connected too deeply, but a few struck close to home, enough to worry Dvanken.

The field of unconscious warriors moved as the effects of the power surge faded. Every eye, good and evil, fixated on the battle ensuing in there midst. But, the infatuation with the battle subsided as the two sides remembered their tasks.

The ensuing swirls of sabor light and the splashes of blood pooling on the battlefield drew the stomachs of the three Elders with distaste for the carnage befalling their Order.

I lay bleeding on the ground, unable to move watching the rage swell on the hill. Ellett was the first to act on his rage. He stepped forward to the edge of the overlook. The massive Elder would take no more, standing idly by as his clansman were lying. And young Sabor had said they were to stay on he hill to provide cover. Sabor thought the old ways had saturated them and he wanted no pointless heroes on the battlefield.

Ellett reached deeply into his long dark brown cloak. He unsheathed an enormous broadsword, battle worn and rusted, but still visibly sharp. The handle was meant to be wielded by two normal hands, but Ellett Vettin was far from an ordinary man. He controlled the heavy blade like an artist would a paintbrush. He spun the blade in long swiping motions in front of him,

230

shredding the long blades of grass and watched as the clippings floated away caught by the wind.

I watched a smile appear on Sabor's face, as the old ways of obedience dissolved from the faces of Symon, Saimus and Ellett. The group of three threw out their weapons, glancing at one another then charging down toward the battle.

Symon was the first down the slope and instantly slammed an overhand blow, splitting a Vintonganth completely in two. He turned, looking back momentarily to his companions scurrying to join him. His armor instinctively sprung out, shrouding him as a pair of Vintonganth threw vicious straight arm thrusts at his chest. The two gnarly bone blades of the Vintonganths shattered against the hardened energy of the Elder. The pair of grimy attackers looked in awe as the massive Ellett and swift Saimus swooped down, shoving their weapons through the hobos' soft mid-sections and pulled the now dying bodies in high arcs up and over their heads.

The trio faced the raging battle, their powerful essence capturing the attention of all the warriors in the immediate vicinity. The Vintonganth slithered into a contracting semi-circle, abandoning their conflicts to attack the fresh fighters now sizing them up.

"You, Guardians of The Order! Leave us and help Sabor. We can handle these, swine," Ellett ordered, shoving the quivering man from his blade, then swiped the blood off onto the tattered rags of the hobo.

"Be gone! You heard what Master Vettin has ordered," Symon said, fortifying the command of Ellett as well as snapping the Guardians from the shock of actually seeing the Elders in combat.

The thirty Vintonganth hissed and surged head long at the triumvirate of ready Elders.

"No playing around with these maggots. Let's get them destroyed and move on. Sabor needs us. Agreed?" Ellett said, ripping the face from a Vintonganth that slinked in trying to take advantage of the lack of focus apparent in his statement.

"I do not intend on prolonging this battle. We have done that enough," Symon retorted, stepping aggressively to a group of attackers. Quickly, he beheaded one, grasped the bone shard of the second and drove it hard into the eye of the third with a grunt. The jagged bone lodged itself in the soft tissue of the brain. As the pair fell to the ground, the second one struggled to free his bone blade from the socket. Saimus stepped in; impaling the two remaining

Vintonganth with his sabor then removed the blade quickly to gut another raving lunatic charging with its hands high above its head.

"Couldn't let you two have all of the fun," Saimus added as he spotted another onslaught coming from the homeless mass. He met the blitz with a matching force, slicing through the small tangent of men unscathed.

The Vintonganth buckled under the skill and ferocity of the Elders. The threesome sliced through the obstacle course of filth and bone, wading through the dead and dying men between them and the heavy fighting of the remaining Order and Vintonganth, as well as the torrent raging on between Sabor and Dvanken.

"Hold strong men. These people are nothing. You see how the Elders are taking them apart. Mow through and converge on Dvanken. Kill as many of these maggots as possible on the first offensive," Keni Divin called out to his arm of the Guardians who had flanked the Vintonganth and were advancing toward Sabor quickly. As Keni lifted a hobo with his right blade above his head, with his left, he separated another one's head from its neck, leaving a wake of death crashing behind him. His focused and deliberate style wasted no movement and yielded great results.

Keni's armor was a beautiful sight, as intricate as that of the armor of the ancient Samurai warriors of China. The shoulder pads jutted out like wings, coming to a point just beyond his shoulders. Two hemispheres of chain mail lay across each shoulder, with a crest of etched flames burning up and out from his collarbone. His arms were heavily padded with leather and bamboo plates. The chest plate was made of a luminescent leatherish material, covered his torso in the text of The Order. From beneath the chest plate flowed a long cloth. The red cloth wrapped upwards around his head like a hood, then down through his chest and back plates almost touching the ground. The cloth was a sentimental piece made from the cloak of his father, Caden Divin.

He carried a long Samurai sword in addition to his sabor weapons. He said it had always made him feel more powerful and I must admit he was an intimidating fellow to watch with his trio of blades dancing.

His helmet, an evil sight, sported large metal horns rising from the brow, then turning in coming to a needlepoint. A golden metal piece ran through the center of the helmet, forming a point in front of his face. The golden piece was barbed the entire way back and covered in red chain mail. Keni was a indeed an imposing force, and I did enjoy watching him fight. Keni, seeing Sabor enthralled in a dusty, violent battle with Dvanken, fluidly sliced midway through the crowd of smelly transients trying to aid in the attack. Each blow from Dvanken caused Keni to wince. With each strike from Sabor he celebrated,

232

as he fought his way to the side of his comrade.

"Hey Sabor, I'm coming... alright!" Keni said, throwing a brutal blow to the side of a Vintonganth chewing on the arm of a fallen Guardian. "Try not to get killed before I can get there okay!" Keni screamed, slicing three more Vintonganth down with an impressive spinning thrust of his katana and left arm.

"Not now, Keni! I'm kinda in the middle of something, saving the world ya know," Sabor yelled as Dvanken pinned him with a swift punch to the knee, then a forearm to the throat, opening a gash that quickly healed, with a burst of white light.

"Sorry, just hold on Sabor, I'm coming!" Keni replied from the midst of a group of twelve hobos.

A strange air began to flow around Keni as he sliced through, trying to get to Sabor. A red hint began to swell in his blades and he looked a bit frazzled and frantic as he fought. But the Elder's dismissed it as the troubles in battle and continued on fighting.

Carvin Banks tore through the entangled men hovering well below his towering shoulders. Jacobi had promised him that if he would kill as many Guardians as he could and help the master to rid the world of the Avenger, then he would have dominion after the swap of power. For the better part of the raging fight he did just that.

Without a second thought he slaughtered the Guardians and left their bodies to rot. Thrashing, crushing, and brutalizing the young men on his way to Sabor Lindon, Carvin destroyed all who stepped into his path. He raged, hell bent on getting some sort of a release and a minute measure of control over his own destiny. He wanted out of the Alley and with the death of this Avenger, he was promised exactly that, so he would rid the world of Sabor without question.

The enormous aphasiatic black man fought his way to the center of the plain, then stood, silently watching. Only moving if a Guardian were to get too close to him, he would then grab the Knight by the throat and choke the life from his body, piling the bodies behind him.

Searching for the battle between his master and Sabor, the only thing standing in the way of his only true happiness. All at once, the clashing oppositions parted ways leaving a clear path to the ultimate battle raging, a few yards away.

"If dat is whose I haf ta kill, den I do it," Carvin said, cracking his flashlight-sized fingers.

Two steps into his quest, he was slammed in the stomach, by a sharp pain. Ellett had seen the happenings and had drove his sword deeply into Carvin's ribcage.

"Are you going somewhere?" Ellett asked

"I neet ta kill da hope. Da hopes of dem Guardians. Den da masta, will take us ta rule dis worlt, so den I can be happy, gin," Carvin replied, ripping the blade out of his side and tossing it to the ground.

Ellett slammed the huge man in the face with a crushing elbow, one that could, and for all accounts, would have killed a normal man. But Carvin only smiled at Ellett. The Elder, surprised by the Dvanken-like strength in this Vintonganth, unleashed a lifetime of pent up aggression onto the homeless man, breaking his nose with an overhand right, then busting his jaw with an elbow to the face, that knocked him to the ground. Ellett followed with a head butt that fractured the large man's skull. Still, Carvin only smiled at the punch-drunk Elder, who had given his all yet, the man still came strongly. Carvin swelled with anger, then fought back hard. Throwing a murderous left hook, he sent Ellett tumbling to the ground a few yards away.

"You will pay for that hobo!" Ellett screamed, wiping blood from his lip.

"Wait!!" Saimus yelled, running up behind his fallen brother. Slowly, he pointed up at Keni Divin, who appeared to be unraveling.

"Dat is da work o da masta. He not bein very kint ta dat men. Why do he make da pretty blu turn ta da red? He make all of dis hate, all of dis bad feelin. Masta don neet me and I don neet da masta, no mo," Carvin smiled at Ellett and looked apologetic as he reached down to help the Elder up. Ellett was reluctant and tried to get up on his own accord.

"Ellett. Do not be silly. It seems as if our new large friend here has seen the error in his way of thinking. You would not turn your back on a worthy ally, for your own foolish pride, would you?" Symon asked as he walked up, dripping with blood.

"No, I guess I wouldn't. Thank you, friend," Ellett said reaching up, taking the pair of hands and pulling himself up.

"Let's go see what is going on with Master Keni. And see if we co uld maybe calm him down before he does something stupid," Saimus said, pointing again at the Knight as he sprinted to join them.

Agreeing on this plan of action, the quartet headed off in that direction. The Vintonganth began to notice their leader Carvin Banks running along side of their sworn enemies, and showed their outward distaste for his switch in allegiance. They could not fathom the betrayal against Dvanken, and it angered them. They broke from their fights and perused Carvin, to punish him for his defection.

A wall of men formed between Sabor and the Elder's. Half of them faced the Guardians still-hunting the Vintonganth while the other half faced the Elders cutting off their pursuit. Symon and the others barely noticed the offensive coming at them. Their focus had shifted to the horror of Keni Divin and his fatal change.

Dvanken smiled, letting Sabor stand and heal from the latest round of blows.

"What the hell are you smiling at Dvanken?" Sabor asked sternly.

"Have you ever seen a soldier lose his mind on the battlefield? Just snap, right there in the mire from the pressure and pains of war. Then, when it all becomes entirely too much for him to bare, he kills everyone, friend or foe, sides being no longer of any concern. They call it B.S.F.S. Or Battlefield Stress and Fatigue Syndrome, I call it simply delicious. Tell me, Avenger, have you ever seen anything like this? Brothers-at-arms destroying one another, simply due to the high stresses of war," Dvanken mysteriously asked Sabor.

"No I haven't seen it, but I have heard of it. Why? No, never mind why, I don't care. Just die!" Sabor screamed, tired of the babble and ready to end the fight.

"It is actually quite a beautiful thing to behold," Dvanken said softly as he grabbed Sabor in a bear hug, then tossed him back to the ground, where the Guardian landed again squarely on his feet.

"It is me, you know. I simply explain to his tiny mind, what will happen to him if the enemy were to capture him, by some stroke of bad luck. Or, I remind him of the bully he endured in the third grade, any little memory that drudges up the pain and embarrassment of some event long ago. Your human predictabilities make me sick, at least the Gargoyles put up a fight. You make all of this entirely too easy for me. Placing so much stock in your teetering emotions and memories. That you fail to see the realization of what is going on around you. That your world can be altered by telling you a scary story. You're truly a pathetic race," Dvanken rambled.

"What does that have to do with anything, huh? Just shut up and fight me!" Sabor said delivering a stiff right jab, knocking Dvanken to the ground.

"You should pay more attention to your brothers-at-arms. That one over there, in particular. He seems a little bit fragile," Dvanken said laughing and motioning for Sabor to look behind him. We, as well as Sabor were surprised at what we saw.

Saturated in blood, Keni sliced through everything around him. The unsuspecting Guardians, the Vintonganth, he slaughtered them all with equal prejudice. Hate and fear tainted his aura. His glow morphed to a reddish-purple hue. The Guardians around him appeared as fuzzy to him as the Vintonganth. All-at this moment, were his enemy. And each side was just as vulnerable to his power.

Dvanken, sensing a chance to feast with the misdirection, smiled and moved behind a pile of carcasses to begin eating. Keni stood on a separate pile of bodies screaming, drawing all attention from Dvanken.

"You will all die today, for your allegiances with Dvanken. None of you will take me alive!" Keni yelled, streaking down the hill of fallen warriors. "You will never take me!" Keni screamed at Blaine who had been fighting side by side with him until Keni's change in attitude.

"What the hell? I'm on your side, Ken!" Blaine said, turning to stab a charging enemy in the middle of the forehead, before he suffered the same fate. A crimson shower blinded him for a split second, just enough time for Keni to step beside him. Sabor and the rest could only stare in horror as Keni moved directly behind his comrade, pulling his arm back by his side.

"You won't take me," Keni said softly as he shoved forward, piercing the back of his brother Guardian, Blaine. A thick mixture of tissue and blood exploded from his stomach and mouth. A scream of agony ripped over the field as Blaine's life drained from the wound. Blaine turned to his killer, grasping at Keni's chest and neck, desperately trying to stay in the world of the living.

"Why did you do that Ken? Aren't we on the same team, here?" Blaine asked, before the consuming weight of his own death squeezed the last traces of breath from his lungs.

Keni looked down at the man sliding from his sabor with indifference to the loss and malice for the ease in which he died. "It was either you or me. I Guess, that I chose you," he whispered, flinging the tissue from his blade, then licking the blood from the luminescent sword.

Sabor had seen enough. He could not stand by and let Keni destroy The

236

Order. It was his job, his destiny to do something. Sabor proceeded to Keni, blocking the path the crazed Guardian was cutting through the field.

"Keni! Stop this foolishness, man! You are a good guy. You aren't supposed to be slaughtering innocence, for no better reason than simply because you can. Come on, man, snap out of it before anyone else gets hurt," Sabor yelled, desperately trying to reach inside the disturbed man, to find his friend.

"What would you know of what I should and should not do? Your destiny has been laid out perfectly for you, but my story has no definite theme. For all you know Lindon, this could be my destiny. Now step away, I warn you Avenger. I won't let someone like you take me either!" Keni screamed, preparing for an attack.

Yorge had seen enough as well, and from his vantage he could clearly see the scared Avenger, and Dvanken devouring the dead on the battlefield. Seeing the Knights and Greenlings having a more difficult time than expected with the resilient Vintonganth, Yorge threw his leather cloak down in a heap on the ground, his Viking style armor enveloped him, as he turned to us.

"My place is down there. If you have everything under control here, I'll go and help. I cannot sit and watch as my boys are being slaughtered and Dvanken sits cowardly, eating the dead slain by another. I am going to help!" Yorge said, hiding his tear-filled eyes. Then he marched off as his team nodded approval and followed him down. Not that he needed their approval, he had made up his mind to fight I felt a sense of pride as I saw the massive fur covered man walking down the hill.

Yorge lumbered down onto the grassy stretch of land, axes prone, and focused on Dvanken. A small group of Guardians saw the elder descending and rushed to his side, ready to help.

Dvanken roared at the meal he had just ingested, showing his heartless bestial side. His emotion swirled about him in a purple fog as he devoured more and more pain. A soft, cold shadow interrupted Dvanken's meal, however.

Yorge stood heaving and ready for battle. His two enormous battle-axes were deployed. Glowing chains covered his armor. A Viking style helmet, with large ram horns on either side and a large mandible from a cave bear traced his beard, sat shading his face from the world. Tufts of fur covered him. Large plates of metal hung together by heavy chains. Rounded studs and sharp spikes of varying sizes covered the plates. His tremendous hands wore leather gloves with intricate writings and designs. Everything about him said he was brutal, fast, and lethal, no matter who he faced.

Yorge, with no other warning but the shadow, pulled his right hand up to the sky, muttered a prayer, and buried the axe in Dvanken's backbone. The gargantuan blade lodged deeply between the shoulder blades and would not budge from its grip. Dvanken instantly stood, releasing an ear-piercing howl. Dvanken reached back with both arms over his head grasping for the pain. Spinning and tumbling over his attacker, Dvanken desperately tried to reach the wound on his back.

Yorge hammered the neck and rear of the head as the pair tumbled along the ground, knocking over other pairs of combatants as they tangled. Yorge buried his ax into the ground trying to stop the death roll. The move succeeded, but Dvanken ended up on top of the heap, crushing the massive Guardian underneath him. Dvanken rolled off, hearing the ribs of Yorge snap like dry twigs as he moved.

'Oh, this is sweet. I will feast on an Elder on the day I destroy the Avenger and take my place as the supreme evil. We have had many battles old man, and you have always pushed this tussle of ours to the limits. And for that I thank you, but now you must die human. Go join the Plane and sleep," Dvanken said to Yorge as the fallen Guardian tried his best to rise with the liquefied bones in his chest. Yorge tried to speak, but could force nothing out save a clot of tissue and a bubble of blood.

"Then if you won't speak, I will make this quick," Dvanken said smiling.

As the abomination reached behind Yorge, his forearms began to bulge, releasing a pair of pointed bone claws, preparing to reap the pain from the Elder's core. With one swift motion, the club-like arms thundered down, knocking consciousness from the Elder. The blow left the body lifeless and bloody, a testament to Dvanken's evil power.

"I will enjoy you in a moment old friend, but now I need to see how the Avenger is dealing with my gift," Dvanken said, kicking Yorge in the head. He grabbed a passing Greenling by the scalp, removing it in one swift move. Dvanken sucked the nectar from the necklace of bones he had detached from the Greenling.

Keni lunged at Sabor, missing him by inches, then rolled to a stop, looking back where he started. Sabor faced him, shaking his head.

"You should stop this, all of this. We already have someone to kick the shit out of Keni. He's over there. And it is probably a good bet that he's the one who is messing with your head, so for goodness sake, focus man," Sabor said, barely deflecting the barrage of crushing strikes from Keni. Sabor blocked a head strike, then moved inside, stepping from the path of the counter strike and throwing Keni to his back.

Keni said nothing, only grunting as he fought. His eyes were void of emotion, his face vacant of expression. Keni continued unleashing furious blows, alternating hands, missing by only centimeters. Sabor reached out, grabbing a punch, and pulled Keni in close.

"We, have better things to do than this man. Stop!" Sabor yelled in his ear. Keni pulled back a bit and spit in Sabor's face.

"I understand and it's okay, but do not do that again," Sabor replied.

The battle continued. Keni brought his right arm up, following through and caught Sabor on the right side of his face, opening a large gash that immediately began to bleed. With this cut, Keni's blade began pulsing a deep red and purple. His eyes sank, hollowing out and started emitting a red glow as well. Sabor glanced at the wound in disbelief, and then back at Keni as a horrible expression grew over the other Guardian. Anger and shadow shrouded his face. Sabor raised his right blade aiming it squarely at Keni's nose.

"You have pushed me enough, Keni Divin. I don't want to kill you, but I will if I have to," Sabor said, crouching barely.

"You, will not take me either," Keni said very methodic and deep. Keni reached out and snared an unsuspecting Greenling by the neck and stabbed him quickly in the chest under the right pectoral.

"He was going to kill me. You must have seen it, Avenger. I did what I had to do to protect myself," Keni said again never changing tone.

"You have to stop, and if you can't do it yourself, then I think I'll have to do it!" Sabor said, intent on taking the man out quickly, and commencing his destiny.

Keni's eyes widened slightly then screamed an unholy yell. Sabor tensed and catapulted himself at his brother Guardian; he was ready for anything as he flew through the air at Keni. Keni smiled, pulling and moving a step back, giving him room to maneuver. Sabor watched Keni lock eyes with Dvanken, and then the entranced Guardian nodded approvingly to the Evil. Keni stopped dead in his tracks, releasing his weapons. Standing with arms stretched out to either side and staring Sabor straight in his eyes, smiling.

Sabor had prepared for anything, anything, but this situation. Sabor had passed the point of no return only a few inches from Keni's exposed, prone chest.

Keni stared down at his chest, pain and disbelief in his eyes. His sanity had returned. The last image he took in was his friend, his supposed savior, stealing his life with a fist through his chest.

"W, why did I?" Keni asked as Sabor pulled his fist and blade from between Keni's ribs.

"I don't know brother, I can't tell you why," Sabor said, catching his dying brother and falling to the ground.

"I am so sorry Keni, I am so sorry. I never meant to do this. It's just, you were killing everyone. You tried to kill me. I had to do something, I only wanted to knock you out, but you just stopped fighting," Sabor pleaded with Keni, his life draining out onto the ground in crimson arcs and shallow red streams.

"Sssshhhhhh. It's okay; I can see my father. I can see I am a father huh? Oh! Sabor, promise, you promise me, he will be a man. Promise me he will be a good man. Don't you let him know about evil or The Order. Tell him I loved him and I woo... " Keni choked as the words came. "...I would have made a good dad, huh, Sabor?" Keni forced out.

"The best. The best Keni. I promise you that he will know that about his father. I promise," Sabor assured the dying man, a tear stinging his cheek. Keni fought valiantly, but in vain. Swiftly, the shroud of darkness covered his world, bringing on his untimely death. With his last fragment of life he smiled at Sabor, and ran his blood soaked hand down his cheek. Then slipped off into his peace.

Dvanken smiled behind the pair, then slowly began to applaud as he surveyed what had taken place. Sabor cried violently, then, suddenly, he shoved Keni's body from his lap, searching for Dvanken.

"Don't you worry, child, I am waiting for you right here. I am anxious to see how you liked my little gift, boy;" Dvanken said provoking the man in front of him. The strain was apparent as Sabor fell to his knees, releasing his Sabor weapons out of sheer emotion. Sabor shook and crossed his arms, forming a ball in front of Dvanken.

"You should just give up. Why don't you realize that you have nothing? Your parents are dead. Your fiancé is gone. Your Order has been crushed. Your fight between good and evil, your struggle to stay alive, it is all-pointless. Pain is the only constant in this world, if I have shown you anything that is what I would like it to be. And I stand before you as that pain. I am eternal.

"Think about your quest to destroy me. Your kinds nature has caused my existence, humans respawned my evil in the dawn of history. If you kill me,

240

your nature will most certainly endure and with that my hope of life, will flicker eternal. You should all lay down your arms and accept my peace. All of your troubles solved in one swipe of my claw," Dvanken babbled on, oblivious to the power welling up in Sabor's chest.

"You don't know the nature of your prey as well as you think," Sabor retorted. Then, tired of the droning, jumped forward spun and propelled his sabor deep into Dvanken's heart. A surge of purple showered onto Sabor. Dvanken howled in retaliation, grasping Sabor by the torso with his massive hand, and squeezed hard. Sabor's armor creaked under the strain and pressure, but held strong. Sabor regained control and cut at Dvanken's massive neck, slicing half across its diameter. More purple liquid showered from the wound. Dvanken repeatedly punched Sabor's face repeatedly, flopping him around like a rag doll.

"Your father tasted beautiful. Your mother's dying words were of another man," Dvanken whispered in Sabors barely conscious ear. The brilliantly glowing weapons began to grow; they breathed with the power of joy. Then a hint of red and purple began to weave within the beautiful blue and white of the blades.

"Not now. We are so close Sabor. Please don't lose focus. The hate will weaken your blade. He will win, again. Please," I thought to myself, but could not call the words to my mouth. Helpless, I could do nothing but watch the battle.

Sabor raised his blades up to each side of Dvanken's head. The world slowed as eons of evolution and centuries of hate collided in the grassy field. Dvanken's eyes bulged, realizing Sabor's superiority and resistance to his taunts.

Sabor looked to the sky and screamed. "FOR YOU !!"

A mysterious formation of lights ascended from the ground and swayed, dancing around. The tiny sprite-like lights swarmed up and around the pair of warriors. The swarming lights echoed with the voices of the dead Orders. They spiraled up, merging with the two glowing sabor weapons pulsing beside Dvanken's face. Then, with every ounce of his strength, Sabor **pulled** the two radiant blades together. The colossal Evil wailed, releasing his natural defenses, a shield of pure hate encompassing his upper half in a bulbous shell. Sabor, still looking to the sky, continued to grind his arms, oblivious to the shield of hate.

The power of the hate surging, both outside and inside of the blades, grew ever brighter. Dvanken snarled and squeezed harder, his hands slowly tearing through the flesh on either side of Sabor. The blades stayed true to their course, severing the beast inch by inch.

Sabor smoldered a brilliant white. His blades embracing the pure blood red hate as they traveled. I watched in sheer amazement as an explosion of white light broke when the two blades penetrated the shield with a loud boom. Sabor's arms crossed with momentum, ending their journey on opposite sides of his body.

Dvanken smiled a hollow smile, not realizing his head had been detached by Sabor's pure hatred of him, the hate he had instilled in Sabor, hoping to satisfy his disgusting hunger. His smile turned to astonishment as the pain slowly crept to his neck, his grip softened, but stayed around Sabor's body and throat. Sabor saw the wound open deeper on the beast's neck, and smiled at the sky.

"I did it, Mom. I did it," Sabor said.

Sabor then looked at Dvanken turned to me, then a reverent glance to Symon, Saimus and Ellett standing holding one another in the tall grass. He stared everywhere, taking in the world, the New World he had given to us, with his sacrifice. He looked at the dead and the reviving masses on scattered on the ground, then writhed in pain as Dvanken squeezed harder with his last ounce of strength.

"Your time will expire, Avenger. I however, am evermore!" Dvanken said, quivering. Sabor watched a web of evil grow from the wound on Dvanken's neck. Determination flooded his evil face.

Feeling began to tingle slowly back into my body as I watched in absolute horror. Suddenly able to move my upper body, I desperately tried to reach for Sabor. But before I could, he looked at me, back to Dvanken
And finally at the sky, then screeched.

"I love you all!"

Sabor thundered his blades back into Dvanken just under his chest and the beast surged violently. A blue light seeped around the gashes in Dvanken's chest in small lightning-like bolts. The light radiated from the wounds on his side. The peace of the Sabor Guardians flowed through Dvanken, like a cancer, eating him from the inside. Then in a brilliant instant, another flash of pure goodness blasted from Sabor's body, covering the entire valley with the white shockwave.

When calm returned, Sabor Lindon. My friend, my confidant. Our Avenger lay on the ground severed into two pieces. There was no blood, just a white glow resting on everything, like dew on a peaceful morning. Dvanken's body lay in a heap, blown apart in several different areas. The evil lay silent and powerless now. Vengeance had come, The Avenger had seen to that. He had indeed avenged all of our losses, with the truest of sacrifices.

I picked myself up, shakily at first but ever stronger with each step. I strode to Sabor's side. Feeling destroyed inside, I stared down at his limp, lifeless body with agony in my heart. But strangely, I felt a resounding joy begin to flow up from the ground where he lay. I reached out and tugged at the lower half of his body, pulling it to its brother and I sobbed. I saw the Greenlings and Knights that were left began to writhe around, coming to their feet again.

I saw the Vintonganth stumble to their feet, looking around with new eyes. They had been taken in by the evil that was Dvanken and now they had to deal with the real world, piecing back together whatever lives they had.

The entire Order converged upon me. I could feel them all staring at young Sabor in my arms. We all wept hard at that moment, leaving little grief left inside. We all mourned the loss right then, giving the field a lump of our collective sorrow. I stared at young Master Lindon, not believing what had happened. Standing, I embraced Symon, Ellett and Saimus. They were stone-faced and serious, the only three not weeping.

"We have won brothers. Dvanken is dead; the cycle of despair is broken. Our own, Master Sabor Lindon was indeed our Avenger," Ellett said, his voice spewing an air of melancholy.

"You were always one to celebrate early, Ellett," a shattered, but familiar voice, bellowed from the back. Master Yorge, carried by two Greenlings, nursed his ribs.

"So good to see you, old man. I guess we counted you out a little early," Ellett said, sounding a bit more happy. I stayed to the rear and watched as the crowd turned its attention simultaneously to Symon Divin.

"It is indeed good to see you alive, Master Yorge. We do believe that we have won here today, with the death of Dvanken. But, we must all ask ourselves, how can we have any victory now? When so many of our souls are left grieving, even my heart now overflows with thoughts of vengeance for the loss of young Master Sabor and the others. Now, however, we have nothing to relieve our grief, nothing to exorcise the hurt upon," Symon said as he turned and walked off slowly, into the entrance to the Halls, hidden in the shadows of the Gargoyle.

THE END

Epilogue

The day was won, the cycle of despair had been broken, and The Order was still standing. Limping yes, but still standing. Master Saimus, privately leery of celebration, he felt man kinds nature, may do something to lend fuel to a trigger of Rebirth. We all followed Master Symon Divin taking the wounded and the dead, deep into the Halls of The Order, to prepare for the mass burial. Our task was a horrible necessity, on such a glorious day, but it was none the less, our duty. None of us knew evil lurked in the shadows of the field, behind us, but it did.

A shadow arose from behind the lifeless body of Dvanken. Formless at first, it quickly took the shape of an extremely tall man, The shadow man from our dreams. We believed him to be Dvanken in our sleepful imaginings, but we were wrong. The shadow ran his long, thin fingers along the corpse.

'I am Kaine. I am reborn! Thank you, old friend! With your death...I am now free. With your rebirth, we will rid the earth of non-believers forever. Giving us of the shadow the chance we deserve, our chance at true life and restoring the old ways of the Vintonganth," The shadow said, laughing hysterically. It reached down with one arm, grasping the lifeless hunk in front of him, then vanished into the shadow.

Hunters Inc.©
Bandit Films©
Executive Producer/Director

Phillip Ellett

77777777777777777777777777777777777777777777777777777777777777777777777777777777777

The Unearthly

D.O.C.©

?

The Order: the use of symbols eased the stress

✓⌐ = Space   ✱ = Period   · = Question   \ = exclamation

Vetten = 乛○

Danglin = 辻

Divin = ♉♀

Lindon = 禾ᗄ

Sabor's Symbol

The world in the day of the Vintonganth

Keepers of the promise of Hope

Ꮐᠯ ↓ ȴᠯ ↓ ⅄ ↓ ⅄Ҡ ↓ ṯᠯ ↓ ♂ ✱

nature = ⅄

Eternal = ⱸA

Avenger/Solitaire = ⅄

Death = ⱦ

Warrior = ⱦ

Evil = ⱦᵼ

Gargoyle = ⱷ

Holy = ↓⊕

Sabor = ⱦ

Faithful = ⱦb

Human = ⅄

Peace = ⱦ

Love = ✕

Battle = →✕←

Day = ⊥○⌐

Night = ⌐○⌐

mid-day = ⊢⊙⊣

Happiness ͵⁄

Good ⱦⱦ

Relinquish ⌒○

A	B	C	D	E	F	G	H	I	J	K
⊥	T	⋏	⅄	↓	⋌	Ҡ	ⱦ	ı	↑	⋌

L	M	N	O	P	Q	R	S	T	U	V
ⱦ	Ⱶ	ⱦ	ⱦ	↓	⌒	ⱦ	ⱦ	ⱦ	ıı	ⱦ

W	X	Y	Z
ℰ	8	↓	T

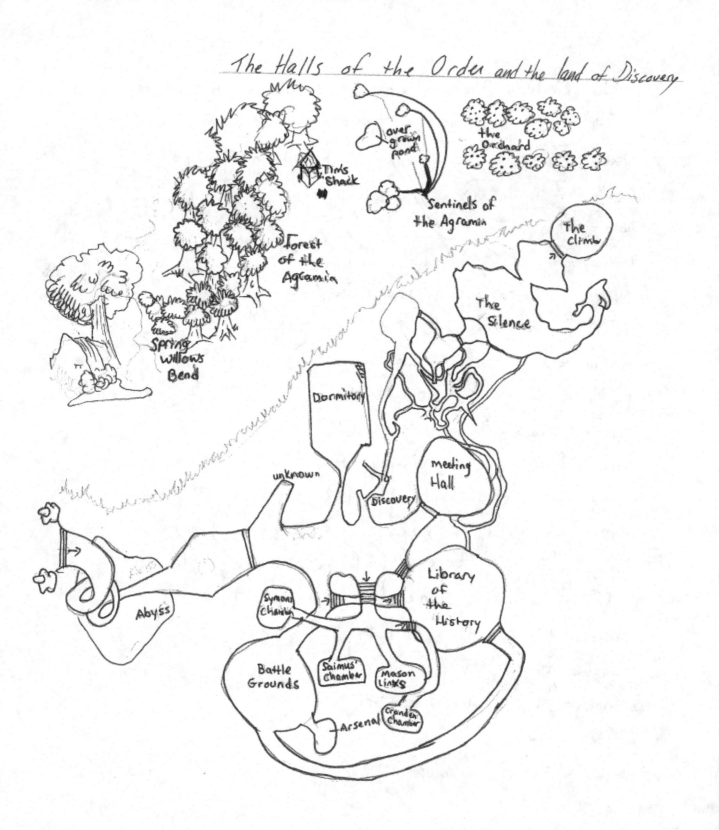

The Halls of the Order and the land of Discovery

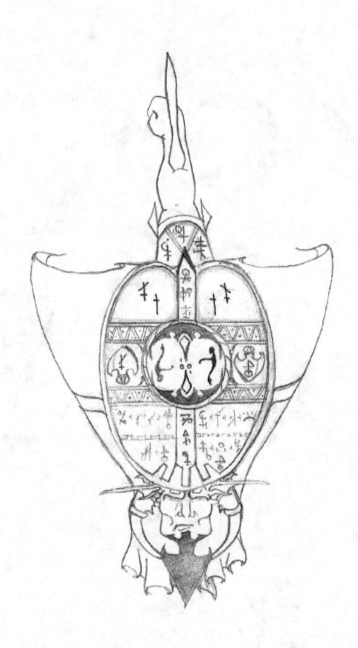

Master
Saimus Lindon

ELLETT
VETTIN

Keni
Divin

Sabor
Lindon

Printed in the United States
By Bookmasters